The Marvelous Adventures
of Serge Myrandhal
on Mars

H. Gayar

The Marvelous Adventures of Serge Myrandhal on Mars

translated, annotated and introduced by
Brian Stableford

A Black Coat Press Book

Visit our website at www.blackcoatpress.com

ISBN 978-1-61227-265-8. First Printing. Mars 2014. Published by Black Coat Press, an imprint of Hollywood Comics.com, LLC, P.O. Box 17270, Encino, CA 91416. All rights reserved.

Introduction

Aventures merveilleuses de Serge Myrandhal sur la planète Mars by H. Gayar, here translated as the first part of *The Marvelous Adventures of Serge Myrandhal on Mars*, was first published by L. Laumonier et Cie, dated 18 June 1908. A second volume followed, *Aventures merveilleuses de Serge Myrandhal: Les Robinsons de la planète Mars*, dated 15 July 1908. The catalogue of the Bibliothèque Nationale gives the date of the second volume, wrongly, as 1909, a mistake inevitably copied by numerous other secondary sources—the first of many confusions relating to this strangely problematic text.

The first volume of Serge Myrandhal's story has attracted particular critical interest because of remarkable similarities with Gustave Le Rouge's Martian fantasy published in the same year, *Le Prisonnier de la planète Mars*, in between the two volumes of the Gayar work. Le Rouge's work was also followed up by a second volume, *La Guerre des vampires* (1909)[1]. The similarities between the first item of each pair were pointed out by Pierre Versins in a 1966 essay, which was supplemented by brief comments in the articles on Gayar and Le Rouge is his *Encyclopédie de l'utopie, des voyages extraordinaires et de la science-fiction* (1972). When the essay was employed as an afterword to a 1976 paperback edition of *La Guerre des vampires*, some further comment was added by the editor of that volume, Francis Lacassin. Before discussing that issue here, however, it is worth addressing the more elementary problem of who "H. Gayar" might have been.

There is no evidence of the existence of a real person with that name, although the Versins *Encyclopédie* records a death-date of 1937, tacitly suggesting that there might have

---

[1] Both translated in *The Vampires of Mars*, Black Coat Press, ISBN 978-1-934543-30-6.

been one. Lacassin alleges, *en passant*, that the author's name was actually Gaillard, and given that one of the two Henri Gaillards who published work under that name parallel with Gayar's career did die in 1937, Versins and Lacassin might both have been assuming that he was "Gayar." However, that Henri Gaillard (1869-1937) was a scholarly Orientalist who is highly unlikely to have committed the many naiveties featured in the adventures of Serge Myrandhal, and even less likely to have been responsible for the other conspicuously downmarket works signed with variants of the Gayar pseudonym. The other Henri Gaillard (1866-1939) whose career ran parallel to Gayar's was a notable advocate for the deaf and an important pioneer of the teaching of sign-language, again highly unlikely to have been responsible for Gayar's publications.

It does, of course, seem likely that "Gayar" was derived from "gaillard," but is perhaps more likely to have been taken from the common noun—especially the familiar usage that renders it parallel to the English "good bloke" and the American "good guy"—rather than the surname. A search for the name Gayar on the Bibliothèque Nationale's website *gallica* turns up references in theater advertisements from the mid-1890s and early 1900s to a "comique" (comedian) employing that stage name, in one instance apparently featuring in a double act, Gayar et Gerdal. In isolation, that observation might be reckoned trivially coincidental, but it seems a little more significant in conjunction with the remarkable and highly distinctive literary style in which a substantial fraction of Serge Myrandhal's story is narrated. Once the introductory phase is complete, much of the consequent narrative consists almost entirely of dialogue seemingly taking place on a series of imaginary stage-sets—apparently the work of someone who thought entirely in dramatic terms, with a pronounced inclination to vaudeville humor, even in an ostensibly earnest melodrama.

Gayar's literary career, insofar as it can be mapped through periodicals currently reproduced on *gallica*, appears to have begun in 1899. Between then and 1903 he contributed numerous short stories to two periodicals available on *gallica*, the short-lived Arthème Fayard periodical *Les Romans inédits* and the weekly literary supplement of the daily newspaper *La Lanterne* (not to be confused with the Belgian satirical publication of the same name). The signature frequently appears in both periodicals simply as "Gayar," but is sometimes rendered as H. Gayar and sometimes—slightly more often—as P. Gayar. The reason for the variation is unclear, but it is possible that there were two individuals involved, who sometimes worked together and sometimes separately, in the same fashion as "J.-H. Rosny"—a signature shared at the time, with much publicity, by two brothers.

The short stories produced under the variants of the Gayar name are lightweight works often echoing, with no great distinction, the fashion for ironic "*contes cruels*" that was then at its height, routinely featuring lurid crimes, broken romances and unfortunate misunderstandings. "Les Hommes de cire" [The Wax-Men] (*Les Romans inédits* 1899, signed P. Gayar), "Le Fiacre-fantôme" [The Phantom Coach] (*Les Romans inédits* 1900, attributed, presumably mistakenly, to G. Gayar on the cover and H. Gayar at the end of the story) and "L'Homme sans tête" [The Headless Man] (*Les Romans inédits*, 1900, attributed to Gayar on the cover and H. Gayar at the end) are grotesque melodramas in which seemingly supernatural events are explained away by madness or error. The editor of *La Lanterne* was less fond of stores of that type than the editor of the Fayard publication—which used one short story per issue as a cover story to support three long-running feuilleton serials—but he did have a fondness for running illustrations of naked women on the front page of *Le Supplément*, accompanied by slightly salacious narratives such as "Mademoiselle Narcisse" (1901), signed simply Gayar.

Although the patchy representation of periodicals on *gallica* makes it difficult to be sure, this stream of short stories seems to have dried up completely in 1904, when the signature P. Gayar appeared in *La Lanterne* for the last time. *Aventures merveilleuses de Serge Myrandhal* thus appears to have been a new venture, representing a definite change in direction, perhaps in response to a marked contraction in the market for short fiction. It was not a successful venture in commercial terms, the books being somewhat fugitive; only one curt review is traceable via *gallica* and the entries for the two books in H. Le Soudier's running *Bibliographie française* were obviously written without consulting actual copies, as no date is given for the first and the date of the second is wrongly recorded as 1909—probably the source of the Bibliothèque Nationale's error.

The firm of L. Laumonier et Cie seems to have vanished after 1908, and only published a handful of titles while it existed (one of the others being an edition of Defoe's *Robinson Crusoe*). At any rate, Gayar fell silent for more than a decade thereafter, although an advertisement did appear in *Le Petit Parisien* in 1909 for a book entitled *La Fiancée du rescapé* [The Survivor's Bride] by "Henry Gayar," which never actually appeared.

The pseudonym reappeared in 1921 when *La Lanterne* ran a feuilleton novel "Cindrella" [sic], signed M. Gayar. It is unclear whether the M. simply stands for "Monsieur" or whether it is supposed to be the initial of a Christian name. The expanded version of the pseudonym, "Henri Gayar," made its first appearance in 1927 on a short novel published by Arthème Fayard, *La Fiancée veuve* [The Widowed Bride], and appeared on a number of other similar cheap publications, alongside others signed simply "H. Gayar"—there appear to be fifteen in all, although the Bibliothèque Nationale only has copies of four of them. The last, *La Remplaçante* [The Replacement], signed H. Gayar, appeared in 1937, which might have encouraged Versins in the belief that the author died in that year.

In between "Cindrella" and *La Fiancée veuve*, however, Serge Myrandhal made a curious reappearance, in an extensively rewritten version of his adventures entitled *Les Robinsons de la planète Mars* and signed with the pseudonym

"Cyrius," which initially appeared in 1925 as a feuilleton in *Le Magazine Illustré* and was reprinted in book form in 1927.

Much shorter than the two-volume original, only retaining thin slices of the 1908 text—amounting to less than a quarter of the total—those slices are reconnected by new text that makes the whole a markedly different story, about which I shall provide more detail in the afterword. The Cyrius version provides the narrative with a conventional ending—something that was conspicuously missing from the original version, perhaps having been postponed until a projected third volume that never appeared. Given the return of H. Gayar/Henri Gayar to regular publication in 1927, there seems to be no obvious reason to doubt that the author of the second version was the same person as the author of the first, although the use of a different pseudonym seems odd, and it might be as well to bear in mind that there could have been two Gayars from the start.

Most of the late Gayar works are melodramatic love stories—several bear the subtitle *roman sentimental*—with no trace of the fantastic embellishments of Serge Myrandhal's Martian exploits. One of them, however, *La Fille des Incas* [Daughter of the Incas] (1932, signed H. Gayar) is an adventure story with a "lost race" element that has some affinities with *Aventures merveilleuses de Serge Myrandhal*, and the 1908 version of the latter also has features of the *roman sentimental* in its plot and narrative method, although the 1925 version does not.

Although it was the affinities between *Aventures merveilleuses de Serge Myrandhal sur la planète Mars* and *Le Prisonnier de la planète Mars* that attracted Pierre Versins' interested attention, it is worth noting—as Versins conscientiously does—that they were not the only interplanetary novels published in Paris in 1908, and that both were preceded, albeit briefly, by Jean de La Hire's *La Roue fulgurante*,[2] which ran

---

[2] Translated as *The Fiery Wheel*, Black Coat Press, ISBN 978-1-61227-217-7.

as a feuilleton serial in *Le Matin* from 10 April to 23 May of that same year. Although the near-simultaneous publication of three pioneering planetary romances represented something of a boom, it is also worth noting that they had been preceded two years before by Arnould Galopin's *Le Docteur Omega* (1906)[3], the first French novel deliberately to adapt the inspiration of H. G. Wells' *The War of the Worlds* and *The First Men in the Moon* to a kind of action-adventure fiction similar in spirit to the kind of "space opera" that was later to become a staple of American pulp science fiction. Where all three of the 1908 novels differ from *Le Docteur Omega* and subsequent sciencefictional planetary romances, however, is that they deliberately fuse their speculative scientific elements with the "Indian mysticism" popularized by the late-19th century occult revival, in a fashion that is rare outside of the three texts in question.

In La Hire's novel, the initial transfer of the protagonists from Earth to another planet—Mercury, in this case—is achieved by alien technology; they are abducted by the eponymous object, probably originating from Saturn and deeply enigmatic in its nature and power source. Their eventual return, however, is achieved by the quasi-magical transfer of their disembodied souls, thanks to the intervention of the virtuous mystic Ahmed Bey, who is privy to the secrets of the "Brahmins," as advertised and celebrated by the Theosophists, among other occult enthusiasts. In both Gayar's and Le Rouge's novels, the thrust for the outward journey from Earth is provided by the accumulated psychic powers of a company of Hindu fakirs, organized in the former instance by the treacherous Rajah Indraghava, and, in the latter, by the enigmatically perfidious Brahmin Ardavena.

It was this distinctive mode of space travel, in shells impelled by the power of thought, that caught Versins' attention, and led him to juxtapose quotations from the two texts to

---

[3] Translated as *Doctor Omega*, Black Coat Press, ISBN 978-1-0-9740711-1-4.

demonstrate the closeness of the parallel, seemingly all the more remarkable because Le Rouge's first volume was published on 1 July, a mere fortnight after Gayar's first volume and a fortnight before the second, apparently eliminating any possibility of copying. Lacassin's 1976 postscript to Versins' essay wonders whether Le Rouge's novel might have appeared earlier as a *feuilleton* under a different name, as one of his previous novels had, but no such *feuilleton* has yet been unearthed. Lacassin also suggests that Gayar might have picked up the idea from Le Rouge's earlier work, written in collaboration with Gustave Guitton, *La Conspiration des milliardaires* (4 vols., 1899-1900)[4], but he exaggerates the extent to which the notion was foreshadowed in that earlier work.

Oddly enough, neither Versins nor Lacassin gives any consideration to the simplest hypothesis that might explain the near-simultaneous appearance of three novels with a common interest, which is that Jean de La Hire, Gustave Le Rouge and "H. Gayar" knew one another, and had discussed together the possibility of writing fiction employing psychic power for interplanetary transportation. It is not inconceivable that there was an element of competition involved in the realization of the project, resulting in a race for publication that La Hire won by a neck and a short head, also scooping a much bigger cash prize by virtue of serialization in *Le Matin*.

It is certain that La Hire and Le Rouge were old acquaintances; both had been living in the Latin Quarter in the 1890s, enthusiastically moving on the fringes of the Decadent/Symbolist Movement, to which their early poetry was affiliated, and both had followed similar career trajectories, eventually working their way out of financial hardship and

---

[4] Translated as *The Dominion of the World*, Black Coat Press, four volumes: 1. *The Plutocratic Plot* (ISBN 978-1-61227-095-1); 2. *The Transatlantic Threat* (ISBN 978-1-61227-096-8); 3. *The Psychic Spies* (ISBN 978-1-61227-097-5); 4. *The Victims Victorious* (ISBN 978-1-61227-098-2).

obscurity by becoming prolific journalists and writers of downmarket action-adventure fiction. There is no direct evidence that Gayar had been part of the same fringe literary community, but it is obvious from some of the casual references in the *Aventures merveilleuses de Serge Myrandhal* that he had some knowledge of and sympathy with the Decadent/Symbolist Movement, and it might be worth noting that *La Lanterne*'s fiction supplement became a useful refuge for several writers associated with the movement, once the end of the nineteenth century had sent it into its own spiral of decline; the authors alongside whom Gayar's work appeared there included Catulle Mendès and Gustave Kahn.

Given that the three daily newspapers with which Gayar, Le Rouge and La Hire were primarily associated—*La Lanterne*, *Le Petit Parisien* and *Le Matin* respectively—were fierce rivals, both politically and in bidding for circulation, that might add plausibility to the notion that there was an element of competition between the three novels that the authors composed on similar themes. Whether that was the case or not, it does seem implausible that the similarities between the works were due to pure coincidence, and even less plausible that there can have been any post-publication influence. Although all three novels were very obviously written in a tearing hurry, each of them probably completed in a matter of weeks, those first published as books are likely to have been in press for longer than that, and might well have been written before La Hire's serial commenced publication. Whatever the truth of the matter, however, the coincidence of subject matter helps to add interest to all three novels, in making them a highly unusual thematic nexus.

If one sets aside the specific parallels between Gayar and Le Rouge in terms of the propulsion system used to hurl the protagonists from Earth to Mars, the most obvious affinities of narrative method are those between Le Rouge and La Hire, who both became specialists in fast-paced colorful action-adventure fiction, and whose primary purpose in going to Mars was to use it as a gaudy backcloth for odysseys in exotica, of a kind that was soon to be developed in the U.S.A. with spectacular success by Edgar Rice Burroughs. Although both their stories have a conventional "love interest," it is a strictly subsidiary matter, Le Rouge's Alberte Teramond and La Hire's Lolla Mendès playing the marginal roles usually attributed to heroines in masculine adventure stories, while Gayar puts a much heavier stress of his hero's feelings for his *inamorata*. That is probably a side-effect of the general staginess of his thinking—he not only writes like an actor, but like an outrageous ham, accustomed to overplaying every aspect of his performance. It is strikingly odd that during the space journey, when the hero is alone, he spends most of his time talking to himself melodramatically, so that the account of what he experiences is almost entirely conveyed to the reader by means of soliloquy rather than objective description. That tendency has a much more general effect, in much of the first volume and almost all of the second, of slowing down the narrative pace drastically while the characters talk to one another at length or parade around the tacit stage making broad gestures. Despite its title, the first volume seems to take forever actually to arrive on Mars—La Hire or Le Rouge would have zipped through the preliminaries in a fraction of the space—and, once there, continues to embed almost all the action in retrospective accounts delivered in speech, sometimes to a seemingly perverse extent. That reflects the fact that Gayar was a less experienced writer of long fiction than La Hire or Le Rouge, but also exemplifies the way in which he was designing the action mentally as if writing a play; there is probably no other Martian fantasy in which Mars initially bears such a striking resemblance to an empty stage—although it is very noticeable that, at a certain point in the second volume, the narrative method undergoes an abrupt and extreme transfiguration, which strongly suggests that either the author underwent a very dramatic change of attitude, or that a second person took over where the original author left off.

The sum of these effects is reflected in the fact that *Aventures merveilleuses de Serge Myrandhal* was a far less widely-read work than either of its competitors, both of which were reprinted several times and remain relatively well-known, whereas Gayar's remains obscure and very had to find. The fact that Gayar's project seems to be unfinished, the second volume breaking off with a rather uncertain promise of further continuation, did not help its reader-appeal, and the fact that the extensively-rewritten version, as well as dumping much of the material preliminary to the space journey—eliminating the parallels with Le Rouge's text in the process—added an abrupt and cursory conclusion did not solve the problem of many questions that had been raised but left unanswered.

It would be inappropriate to embark on any discussion of the details of the plot in advance of the text, so I shall leave further commentary on such matters to an afterword, but it is worth observing here that the text does have some interesting and remarkable original features, and that the manner in which the author addresses the problem of designing and plotting an interplanetary adventure, although naïve and awkward, is also intriguing, and has interesting relationships with a wider range of texts and ideas than those with which it was in evident and immediate competition. As a specimen of early planetary romance, Serge Myrandhal's adventure is of considerable historical interest in its own right, and it remains very readable, amusing and—in spite of its blatant absurdity—thought-provoking

This translation has been made from photocopies of the Laumonier editions kindly made available to me by Marc Madouraud, through the intermediary of Jean-Marc Lofficier. I am extremely grateful to them for their assistance in this matter. I am also grateful to J.-P. Laigle for supplying me with a copy of the 1997 Apex Periodica reprint of the *Magazine Illustré* feuilleton version of Cyrius' *Les Robinsons de la planète Mars* for the purposes of comparison.

Brian Stableford

Book One
ON THE PLANET MARS

I. A Great Event!

"Where are you off to in such a hurry, Mr. Grok?"

"I'm doing what everyone else is doing, of course, Monsieur Durand—going to the *Athenaeum*."

"Well, that's a coincidence—I'm on my way to the famous lecture myself."

"Let's hurry, then. It's almost impossible already to find room in the fifty electric elevators going up to the great hall."

This dialogue was exchanged between two individuals who were correctly shaved, in the Yankee fashion, and wearing smoking jackets. The former was none other than the great American industrialist Joe Grok, the wealthy owner of copper mines. His interlocutor was Professor Justin Durand, a French chemist passing through New York. The two men had met the previous evening in one of the most exclusive drawing rooms on Fifth Avenue. They exchanged a cordial handshake and drew together in the midst of the dense crowd that was pouring in continuously from the staircases of the aerial railway, ferry-boats, electric cars and other public and private vehicles with which the Yankee capital is so abundantly provided.

That crowd, rumbling, whistling and roaring like a stormy sea, was about to unfurl between the walls of the vast building of the Athenaeum. It was engulfed, with formidable eddies, beneath the fifty monumental arcades, each of which terminated in the cage of an elevator able to accommodate fifty people.

Jostled, confused and bruised, Joe Grok and his new friend nevertheless succeeded in taking their place in the steel basket of one of the vast electric elevators. The operator pressed the button.

The elevator rose up to the thirtieth floor of the gigantic building with the reckless rapidity of which one can have no idea unless one has visited America.

"Do you are least have a ticket?" the professor asked his companion, who was wedged, as if in a vice, between an Englishman with a poppy-red complexion and a kind of Canadian giant with a red beard.

"Of course," said Grok, ill-temperedly. "But I couldn't get one for less than five hundred dollars."

"Damn!" said the professor, admiringly. "That's steep! I have a ticket too, but I confess that it didn't cost me anything. It was a gift from the lecturer himself. If I'd had to part with five hundred dollars, I'd have deprived myself of the pleasure of attendance, attractive and sensational as it promises to be."

"Well," said the millionaire, in a tone of conviction, "personally, I'd have paid a thousand if need be. Serge Myrandhal's lecture will be the great event of the season."

"I can understand your enthusiasm," the Frenchman replied, enthusiastically. "Just think of it! An engineer who claims to have found a means of condensing psychic fluids, storing them, and using the prodigious latent force enclosed within them—and is talking about nothing less than reaching distant planets by that means!"

"It's a dream," murmured the skeptical billionaire. "A beautiful dream, worthy of Edison, but..."

"Who knows?" the chemist interjected, excitedly. "In any case, our Edison—you'll soon have the tangible proof of the fact—has already completed half of his program. He's invented an engine capable of utilizing the imponderable forces in question, including that of will, the most powerful of the 'animic energies.' Since the day he published his first book, *Psychic Mechanics*, translated into twenty languages, he hasn't ceased working on his great project—and today, if I'm not mistaken, my friend's goal is within reach."

"So," the American scoffed, "you think we're going to see your compatriot rise up before our eyes and launch himself toward the stars like the prophet Elijah, in a chariot of fire?"

"We're not there yet. The engine—or, more precisely, the amplifier—that will function before you is only an experimental model: a laboratory model, as we say. To construct the definitive apparatus, capable of launching a projectile through sidereal space, money, and more especially the fluid agent, is necessary. Think of the colossal quantity of animic energy required to vanquish terrestrial gravity for a projectile weighing several tons. It's in order to procure that fluid that my compatriot is traveling from one continent to another and lecturing.

"Already, on his way across the world, he's recruited four remarkable producers of energy—four 'human piles' as Annabella Carpenter very aptly calls them in her article in this morning's *Herald*—who have caused a sensation, as you can see from the crowd that's pressing around us. You know that your learned female reporter, the gracious Annabella, has taken the invention under her wing."

"And the inventor too," the American added, in a tone full of implication. "So it's said, anyway. What's certain—and it's not the smallest attraction—is that she'll be in the press ranks at the lecture. Take note that it's the first time that the haughty young lady—who was worth a dowry of twenty million not so long ago—has appeared in public in the exercise of her new profession. That must flatter your compatriot, no matter how little conceit he has..."

"Serge Myrandhal is the most modest man I know," protested Justin Durand, sharply.

"Pardon me," the Canadian giant interjected, "but who is this Annabella whose name is on everyone's lips? Is she the daughter of the billionaire whose bankruptcy was in all the papers, along with his picture, the other week?"

"That's right," said the American. "Miss Annabella Carpenter. It's this evening, as I was saying, that she's ostensibly making her debut in the career of reportage—in front of the whole of New York society, which will have all eyes fixed on her. She's a proud and courageous young woman! She wrote several astronomical novels when she was rich, in an amateur way, for her own pleasure. She thought of utilizing her writing talent without wasting another day. The editor of the *Herald*, who had been one of her father's friends, didn't hesitate to hire her, at a decent salary. Everyone knows that, and as many people have come to see her as the lecturer. And don't forget that there's going to be another celebrity in the hall as well!"

"What celebrity?" asked the Canadian.

"Neither more nor less than the mysterious Ely,"[5] Joe Grok relied, proudly. "The Maharajah Indraghava and his son, the handsome Prince Djalor."

On hearing those names, the chemist had pricked up his ears. "I've heard a great deal about Prince Indraghava," he said. "He's one of those rare sovereigns of the peninsula who's been able to keep his independence intact under the English protectorate. He's famous for his fabulous wealth...and for something else: a rather strange legend.

"It's said that every time His Britannic Majesty's sepoys have tried to penetrate into his domains, they've been forced to retreat almost immediately, for reasons that have never been entirely clarified. There's been talk of inexplicable epidemics that suddenly strike all the officers, the ill will of the soldiers, and mysterious phenomena that stop the expeditionary forces at the Rajah's frontier.

"As a result, Prince Ely Indraghava is famous throughout the Orient. He's reputed to be one of those who have conserved the pure doctrine of the Buddhist religion, at the same time as the gift of operating certain prodigies that modern science is forced to admit, although it hasn't yet been able to explain them.

"Will my friend and compatriot Serge Myrandhal be more fortunate and stronger than these fakirs, whose age-old secret—the means of commanding matter—he claims to have

---

[5] The author might mean this word as a title—in the Biblical sense of "high priest," although that appellation is more usually rendered in English texts as Eli—rather than as a proper name. Either way, it eventually vanishes from the text.

usurped by purely scientific methods? I hope so, ardently. I'd even say that I'm counting on it, knowing the great intelligence of the lecturer. I don't believe that I'm going too far in telling you that we're going to see experiments that will amaze us at the Athenaeum.

"But let's not anticipate, and get back to the Rajah. As I was telling you, he's a strange individual. When he travels, he does so in the greatest luxury; his richly-costumed crews and servants give him the appearance of one of those fairy-tale princes that one only finds in India or the Arabian Nights. On the other hand, I'm told that in his own kingdom, he sometimes lives for months in the ascetic and vagabond fashion of the yogis who beg for bread on the roads and at the crossroads in cities. Many of his subjects have never seen him, and even go so far as to claim the Indraghava, Rajah of Kampour, and the Great Lama, the all-powerful Buddhist pope, are one and the same person."

"You seem very well-informed," Joe Grok put in.

"Yes, I spent some time in the vicinity of his small kingdom during my last mineralogical expedition."

"If all that's true, he's a very fantastic individual!" said the Canadian.

"There's a great deal of truth in it, at least."

"What's certain, said the billionaire, who did not want to be left out with regard to rare and precise information, "is that Rajah Indraghava is causing quite a stir in New York. Everyone is talking about his fabulous generosity, his eccentricities and the mystery that surrounds him. It appears that since yesterday, his servants have been busy preparing a private box for him in the Athenaeum, where we're going, made of cloths of unusual magnificence.

"An hour ago, his litter, carried by ten slaves—ten statues of black bronze—went through the city, heading for the Athenaeum. It goes without saying that the extraordinary individual in question doesn't take the elevator but the stairs—a staircase specially enlarged for him, for which he's had several walls knocked down! But Serge Myrandhal's impresario—

because our lecturer has an impresario, like a great tenor—doesn't recoil before any sacrifice. He knew that the presence of the mysterious Nabob would be enough to fill the hall.

"Take note that the numerous spectators who have come here solely to see the 'Mendicant Prince' won't see anything. The Rajah only goes out veiled, like a sultana! And what's more, his box will be closed on the side of the auditorium by a triple curtain of gauze, permitting him to see without being seen."

"It's a box with a lid!" joked the Canadian with the carroty beard.

"Exactly," Grok continued. "That's one of the conditions imposed by the Prince, who doesn't want his august face to be soiled by the gaze of infidels. He's said to be old and very ugly, but so far, the only person who's seen his face in Annabella Carpenter, who made her debut in the interview game with that masterstroke.

"How was Miss Carpenter able to obtain that audience, solicited in vain by so many others, including important people? In the simplest fashion—she had a very powerful intercessor with regard to the Rajah: his own son, the handsome Prince Djalor. Since the last ball hosted by the wife of the English ambassador, you see, when he danced with Miss Carpenter, the Prince has been madly in love with her. People were even anticipating a marriage, when the girl suddenly found herself ruined. I hasten to add that Djalor, who is rich enough for two, is courting her as before, but I doubt, Prince as he is, that he'll arrive at his goal, since he has a rival..."

The American was abruptly interrupted in his explanations, however. The elevator had just stopped at the thirtieth floor, and was rapidly unloading its cargo.

It is perhaps necessary at this point to offer a few details regarding the purpose of the Athenaeum.

It was one of those gigantic buildings that the Yankees proudly call "skyscrapers." Its thirty stories were built with steel beams; no wood or stone was employed.

The major part of the monstrous edifice was occupied by lecture and conference rooms, and libraries open to the public night and day. The Athenaeum, which was decorated by a stature of Minerva of colossal proportions erected on the principal facade—hence its name—was a kind of grandiose "Temple of Knowledge." Each of its ten topmost floors was devoted to a different science, but it was the last, dedicated to astronomy and equipped with an observatory, that offered the most luxurious accommodation.

Under the immense cupola with crystal panes was an amphitheater disposed in such a way as to allow more than ten thousand spectators to attend lectures on cosmography and astronomy in comfort. On the stage that occupied the back of the gigantic vessel, all the instruments designed for the study of the stars—equatorial and meridional telescopes, etc.—were deployed. Under the pressure of a simple electric lever, the immense glass dome opened, as if one were removing a quarter of the peel of an orange, allowing the vault of the heavens to be seen.

Finally, there was a powerful cinematographic apparatus, which permitted the photographic magnification and reproduction of various celestial phenomena for the benefit of the audience.

Placed at the summit of the skyscraper, that observatory was surrounded by a kind of terrace, as vast as many public squares of the Old World, which permitted the easy operation of the fifty elevators previously mentioned.

One detail worth remembering, and citing as an example to the bankers of the Old World, is that the Athenaeum had been donated by a group of powerful capitalists, each of whom had furnished one floor, in order to stimulate education in the democracy.

In that era, Annabella's father, the honorable Allan Carpenter, had been making his second billion. In order to please his daughter, rather than to obey the need for expense and ostentation that is one of the notable traits of the American character, Allan Carpenter had given the Athenaeum its topmost floor and its magnificent observatory. Needless to say, Annabella, who had always had a great enthusiasm for astronomy, had had a great deal to do with that generosity.

In the young woman's soul there was a little of the mystical poetry that sees in the stars, doubtless with reason, worlds inhabited by beings similar, and perhaps superior, to humans. She had been scarcely twenty years old when she published *The Celestial Garden*, an astronomical novel which, luxuriously published, had obtained a considerable success in the drawing rooms of Fifth Avenue. Then there had been *The Soul of the Stars*, welcomed by the world of American letters with equal success. On several occasions, Annabella had given lectures herself in the hall donated by her father, and an elite audience had come to applaud her.

Then the bad times had come. Allan Carpenter's bank had been one of the first to go bust in an American crash that claimed many victims. In forty-eight hours, Carpenter—who had reimbursed all his clients in full—had nothing left but his daughter's dowry, two hundred thousand dollars, which Mrs. Carpenter, on her death-bed, had placed on deposit in the coffers of the State, having feared—with reason—that her husband might overextend himself.

In spite of his daughter's urgent solicitations, the father had refused to touch that sum. Burning with the desire to remake his fortune, he had departed for the Far West, while his daughter, eager for the challenge and wanting to show that she was worthy of her father, had announced her intention of living solely by her pen. That resolution, and the unexpected disinterest of the young woman, no longer rich—one is not rich in American with two hundred thousand dollars—but comfortably off, had occasioned great enthusiasm in New York society.

And indubitably, that day, as the estimable Joe Grok claimed, as many people had come to the Athenaeum to see her as to hear the exciting lecture advertised by the engineer

Serge Myrandhal, the future conqueror of the "Earths of the Heavens."[6]

The impatience of the crowd, swarming under the harsh light of electric lamps, had almost reached the point of exasperation. The impetuous were shaking the grilles serving as guard-rails. Already, a few bars had come loose. Joe Grok and his two companions were beginning to feel anxious. If one of the barriers gave way, there would be a catastrophe. Hundreds of people would fall thirty stories to be crushed on the pavement.

The cries and vociferations continued to grow louder, however. At one time, a frenetic gang shoulder-charged one of the massive doors of armored steel disposed around the observatory like the vomitoria of ancient circuses, of which there were fifty, each one facing an elevator. Others attempted to smash the panes of the cupola, which still remained feebly illuminated, with revolver shots.

Cries of "Death to the Frenchman!" began to rise up.

"He's mocking us!"

A few people of good will pointed out that the advertised time of the lecture—eight o'clock—had not yet arrived, but their voices were drowned out by those of the malcontents, who were becoming increasingly excited. There is nothing as turbulent as an American crowd.

The French chemist, who had never seen such chaos, was almost repenting of having come when eight o'clock chimed on the Athenaeum's electric clock.

---

[6] *Les Terres du Ciel; voyage astronomique sur les autres mondes et description des conditions actuelles de la vie sur les diverses planètes du système solaire* [The Earths of the Heavens: An Astronomical Voyage to the Other Worlds and a Description of the Present Conditions of Life on the Various Planets of the Solar System] (1884) was one of the most sumptuous and imaginatively ambitious of Camille Flammarion's popular astronomical texts, used as a guide book by more than one *roman scientifique*.

The eighth stroke was still vibrating when the cupola lit up with the glare of a thousand Edison lamps, abruptly switched on.

At the same time, the fifty doors slid in their grooves, thanks to an automatic switch installed in case of fire or riot— and the crowd poured through the fifty entrances, uttering howls of joy, disappearing, to the very last man.

II. An Eccentric

The interior of the Athenaeum lecture room, with its elegant spans of cast bronze and its gigantic crystal-glazed dome, is one of the masterpieces of metallic art. Everything has been arranged with a view to the security and well-being of the spectators. A fire would be impossible; there is not a single cubic centimeter of combustible material to be found therein. Even the cushions garnishing the ten thousand comfortable armchairs arranged in tiers are made of fireproof fabric that is absolutely uninflammable. In addition, numerous circular corridors and the fifty doors previously mentioned ensure that the hall can be evacuated in a matter of minutes.

Above the spacious boxes of the first row, all the seats are equally good. One can see and hear what is happening on the vast stage, at the front of which stands the lecturer's podium, equally well from all of them. Everything has been anticipated to prevent disorder, jostling and encumbrance.

In spite of the architect's prudence, however, and in spite of the fifteen squads of Herculean policemen wearing leather helmets and armed with truncheons, that evening, the hall contained almost twice as many people as there were seats. They were climbing on to the entablatures and perching on the balustrades; a few had even climbed up to the ledges and were sitting astride the bronze beams of the framework.

All of that multitude, panting with curiosity and impatience, had succeeded in squeezing into the immense auditorium. The human waves were breaking against the walls and flooding the upper tiers.

Gradually, the racket decreased. From the crowd, finally heaped up, a dull murmur arrived, as confused as that of the sea when the tide is going out.

Suddenly, that rumor ceased, and two thousand pairs of opera-glasses turned almost simultaneously toward the summit of the cupola. Up there—two hundred feet above the floor!—a

25

man had suddenly appeared, tranquilly seated on one of the giant branches of the electric chandelier.

"Who's that?" demanded anguished women, seized by vertigo.

"He's mad!"

"He's going to kill himself!"

From a box decked with flags—the box of the Splendid Club—a formidable burst of laughter emerged at that moment.

"No!" cried the clubmen, who had just recognized an Englishman, a member of the club as famous for his fortune as for his practical jokes.

"It's our dear and perverse colleague, Sir Washington Pickman!"

"The Baronet."

"The Eccentric!"

"He bet ten thousand dollars that he'd be the first one in, without paying for a ticket!" said one of the group.

"He's won his bet!"

"And magnificently!"

"Except that he risked his neck scaling the dome!"

"Only one man has attempted the adventure before, and he broke his neck! And he was a professional, a roofer charged with placing a flag up there on the day the news came through of the annihilation of the Spanish fleet."[7]

"Just think that, by virtue of an inexplicable omission, he has neither a ladder, nor crampons of any sort—that in consequence, the Baronet must have made a long journey on a frightfully dangerous track, with no support, over a slippery, concave crystal ball, with no footholds..."

"A fly would have broken four of its legs doing that. Only the Englishman, the first man to climb the great glacier of Everest, could pull off that feat."

"Hurrah for the English!"

"Hip, hip, hurrah!"

---

[7] At the Battle of Santiago de Cuba (1898).

However, Pickman, who still had within reach the knotted rope that had permitted him to descend from the summit of the dome on to the chandelier, seemed to be paying little heed to the ovation of which he was the object.

The Eccentric, who, having been on his perch for hours, was doubtless feeling the spur of hunger, took a vast handkerchief in the colors of the Union Flag from one of his numerous pockets, and carefully spread it out over his bony knees.

He was having a snack!

On his improvised tablecloth he placed a paper plate containing a slice of roast beef and a slice of bread with a gilded crust. Then the original individual set down his traveling knife and fork, in order to extract from another pocket of his jacket-cum-haversack a jar of "mixed pickles," with which he seasoned his slice of beef.

Then it was the turn of a tasty chicken sausage—a "Cambridge roll"—which he devoured hungrily, while unceremoniously dropping the peelings, with utter scorn for what the cheering crowd might think.

Not a muscle in his face twitched. He appeared as much as ease on his aerial perch as if he had been sitting at a table in a restaurant. His legs, clad in knickerbockers and protected by brown leather leggings, were crossed with a casual negligence.

When no more roast beef and sausage remained, the eccentric diner opened a box of what the English call "biscuits." He seemed to have a complete food-store in his pockets. After the biscuits, which had doubtless given him a thirst, he displayed a gutta-percha cup, of the kind that can be flattened to the size of a shilling in order to be more easily transportable, and filled it with the contents of a flat bottle, doubtless full of whisky.

This time, the picnic a hundred feet from the ground was complete. The unknown man gravely shook the crumbs out of his napkin, lit a gold-banded cigar, and started smoking it with an imperturbable phlegm, which redoubled the joy and clamors of the crowd.

Justin Durand and his two companions, sitting side by side, continued to comment on the event.

"I wonder how he's going to get down?" said the French chemist.

"The same way he got up," Joe Grok replied. "That's a condition of the bet. Besides, there isn't any other. It seems that the scaffolding...."

The Frenchman interrupted abruptly. "Look—there's Miss Annabella coming into her box. She's never looked as charming. And see how fickle and easily bored the American crowd is! Already, they're no longer paying any more attention to the Eccentric, sitting up there like a parrot on a perch. They only have eyes for the brave and beautiful Annabella!"

It was indeed the young female reporter who had made her entrance in the hall.

Annabella Carpenter, clad in an elegantly-tailored costume, with suede gloves and a felt hat of severe form, offered in all her beauty a type-specimen of the Anglo-Saxon race. The careful simplicity of her clothing only made her dazzling beauty stand out more.

Very tall, with an admirable figure, she possessed a complexion of dazzling whiteness, blue eyes that were almost green, and hair with the golden glints that English painters affect in their portraits. Her high and slightly bulbous forehead, however, and the slightly willful curve of her nose, would have revealed to any observer that her beauty was combined with energy and intelligence, just as the rapid quiver that caused her perfectly-designed nostrils to vibrate from time to time indicated the keenest and most feminine sensibility.

With a courage devoid of affectation, her eyes scanned the entire hall, in which every gaze was aimed at her. In the audience, which included the most brilliant New York society, there were many of Annabella's old friends, former rivals in elegance and beauty. For some of them it was a genuine feast to see the beautiful and incomparable Annabella fallen from the rank of socialite, reduced to a salaried profession, having become a mere employee.

"She hasn't sold her big diamond yet," said one old lady, bitterly. "When one's ruined, one doesn't wear jewelry of that value."

"Especially in such a profession," said another.

"Look," added a third. "She doesn't even seem discountenanced. She's smiling."

"She's taken her ivory notebook out of her briefcase and her golden pen, and she's already started making notes."

"She definitely has a certain aplomb."

At that precise moment, a box that had remained obscure between two columns suddenly lit up.

An "ah!" of disappointment sprang from a thousand throats. A curtain of impalpable gauze—woven mist—masked the mysterious box completely.

It was there that the Rajah Indraghava, who had arrived an hour before with his son Djalor, was waiting for the session to commence.

In vain, the opera-glasses sought to explore the cloud behind which the invisible star was hiding.

A few murmurs rose up, and feet were tapping impatiently, but already, the public was offered compensation. The spectacle now passed to a box at the front of the stage, the most spacious in the entire hall. A grave individual with a pale complexion and long white hair floating over his shoulders—the head of a true prophet—and a Quaker-style coat had just entered it with a hesitant step. Behind him, at a respectful distance, came a string of women, just as soberly dressed but almost all delightfully pretty.

It was the venerable Mormon Eliezer Pellmann, the bishop of Salt Lake City, making his entrance, followed by his three wives and eighteen favorite daughters. The others had had to stay at home, for lack of room.

Thus, the Mormon patriarch, the holiest of the Latter Day Saints, had yielded to the attractions of the advertised lecture, just like a simple Fifth Avenue snob.

The American cheered the antique gentleman, the Biblical individual whose love of science had driven him to brave ridicule. The unexpected ovation made the holy man blush all the way to his ears, and no more was needed to change the disposition of the crowd, which immediately started joking at his expense.

Troubled as he was, Eliezer Pellmann did not beat a retreat. Standing up to the quips and jibes, he leaned his elbows on the front of the box and remained there, his eyes fixed on the podium decorated with the American and French flags, at which the impatiently-awaited lecturer would soon appear.

Let us leave him to his meditations and transport ourselves into the box where the Hindu princes are waiting with at least equal fever.

The Maharajah, for anyone who had seen him once, was an unforgettable individual. His brown, parchment-like epidermis, as if stuck to his bones, and his black and desiccated hands, would have caused him to be taken at first for an old man, almost a centenarian, but for the strange expression of vitality in his eyes. When one had seen those eyes, one remained indecisive, almost fearful of the strange suggestive power that emanated from them. They penetrated you—burning you, so to speak—and produced a sensation of unease comparable to that caused by vertigo.

Then too, there was a disquieting nervousness in his long stiff hands. At times, they extended with the suddenness of a spring, then to remain pendant, as if dead. Another deceptive detail was that his teeth, like his eyes, remained intact and youthful, of an ivory whiteness, in a mouth as shriveled as that of a stuffed monkey.

That bizarre individual was, moreover, sumptuously clad in a silk robe with wide sleeves and a waistcoat whose fabric disappeared beneath golden embroideries sown with precious stones. His large turban of white cashmere was surmounted by a cluster of diamonds, and his bony fingers sparkled with the rarest gems. Those on his person—about his neck, his wrists and on the hilt of the khanjar he carried in his belt—were of inestimable value; everywhere, there was a stream of stones that comprised something akin to an aureole, placing a halo of light around his spectral face.

As if to contrast with that Oriental pomp, Prince Djalor was simply dressed in the European fashion. Without his coppery complexion and a pin in his excessively gaudy cravat, he could have passed for the most correct gentleman in Paris or London. There was also a determined simplicity about the young man. Prince Djalor had been brought up in London and Oxford; he spoke English with an extreme purity, and only held European mores and ideas in high esteem. He had even made rather advanced scientific studies, devoting himself, on the advice of his father, to chemistry, physics and, most especially, electrical mechanics. We shall soon discover why...

Physically, he was a young man of aristocratic bearing, with supple and sinewy movements, symmetrical features and a slender dark moustache; his slightest gestures revealed an impeccable social and sporting education, but nevertheless combined with the secret languor, indolence and air of ennui—almost of spleen—that is the prerogative of the last descendants of ancient sovereign races.

At that moment, the father and son seemed preoccupied and worried. That was because the Rajah Indraghava had long been nurturing grandiose projects that the discovery of the French engineer, if it was real, might upset completely. The last inheritor of sciences all but lost today, which permitted fakirs to work miracles of will-power, he had broadened their scope by means of the reasoned study of modern science. No man was more up-to-date than him with the slightest discoveries made in Europe or America.

The goal of his research was to restore the all-powerful theocracy of the ancient mages, who, according to the sacred books, could resuscitate the dead, extinguish fires and calm the furious waves with a few words and gestures.

In that order of ideas, he had obtained astonishing results, but he was far from having attained, or even approached, the immense goal that he had set for himself. He too, like Serge Myrandhal, dreamed of conquering one of the worlds that twinkled so softly in the azure of the evening sky, of being the Argonaut of some planet of which his son might become the Adam of a new race, strong, happy, powerful and almost divine, leaving the old Earth prey to the struggles of gross material science, the limited and finicky science of the Occidental barbarians.

The announcement that the lecturer possessed the means of accumulating the force of the will, like vulgar electrical fluid, and of utilizing it on a large scale, had troubled and irritated the Maharajah, who had been pursing similar research for many years, to the highest degree. That, he felt more than ever, was the only means of realizing the fabulous dream of celestial migration that he had been pursuing all his life.

Had the Frenchman not announced that he had found, thanks to his machine, his "condenser-amplifier," the means of reaching the planets? So, this accursed engineer, this Occidental dog, had not only stolen his idea, the great idea of his life, the fluid motor, but also the grandiose utilization of which he had dreamed: the conquest of the Earths of the Heavens. And that thought caused the Maharajah's eyes to flare up, and his emaciated breast with its jutting ribs to swell with rage beneath the precious fabrics.

"Curse him!" he murmured. "Curse the man who has dared to get in my way, to place himself between me and the Stars! By Brahma! He shall be swept away like a snowflake torn by the wind from the icy slopes of the Himalayas!"

The fever burning the aristocratic Hindu, long accustomed to seeing everything bend to his will, is now comprehensible. He did not take his eyes off the podium at which the engineer as about to appear, and the stage where his demonstrations would take place. He frowned, as if he wanted to hasten the progress of the hands of the large electric clock by the power of his will.

Prince Djalor, for his part, was looking at the opposite side of the hall. He was invincibly attracted toward the box where Annabella, without even glancing in his direction, was continuing to make notes, under the admiring and inquisitive gaze of the multitude. He was attentive to the beautiful woman's slightest gesture, her most fugitive expression. He drank her in with his eyes!

For him, Europeanized and Anglicized, she represented the most complete ideal of feminine beauty. He wanted her for his wife, with the passionate, volcanic violence that is the foundation of the Hindu soul, simultaneously indolent and full of indomitable ardor.

The Maharajah Indraghava noticed the direction of his son's gaze, and the emotion by which he was agitated. He had known for a long time about Djalor's love and his projects, and if he had pretended to oppose them, it was solely to exasperate the passion in question, which was profitable to his future plans. From the very first day, he had had designs of his own upon the beautiful American. For other reasons—which we shall soon know—he wanted to see Miss Carpenter enter his family as ardently as his son.

Aware of the favorable impression made at first by the handsome Prince Djalor on the young female reporter, and believing, on the other hand, that he was able to incline any will before his own, he considered it as already settled, and a miscalculation in that direction on his part would have been one more disappointment to add to the others. Nevertheless, he grimaced sourly on seeing his son's dilated pupils sparkle, and extended his bony finger toward Annabella.

"You know," he said, in Pali, "that I don't want you to think of marrying that girl. She's neither of your blood nor or your rank. I've made bigger plans for your future."

"The best plan of all would be to be happy," the young Prince replied, with a melancholy smile.

"You'll be much happier if you follow my advice. I'm only asking you for a little patience."

"I doubt that. It's been a long time since you told me about your magnificent dreams. Do you think they'll ever be realized? In spite of all the respect I have for you, I confess that they seem to be to be almost impossible."

The Rajah's glare was charged with lightning. "Nothing is impossible for whoever has the will," he said, severely. "Faith moves mountains! The will creates! Haven't you seen me work authentic miracles?"

Prince Djalor could not suppress a gesture of impatience. "Those miracles, astonishing and inexplicable as they are," he said, "haven't yet permitted you to..."

The argument would doubtless have continued in that bittersweet tone, but three brief rings of a bell announced that the session was about to begin.

"Finally!" said the Maharajah, with a shiver of impatience.

A lateral door slid sideways, and eight men appeared, pushing a heavily-laden trolley covered with a sheet. The cart stopped in front of the podium and was immediately surrounded by a cordon of policemen.

When the sheet was lifted off, an enormous aluminum box in the shape of a cube became visible. Inside it, shielded from all excessively curious gazes, was the amplifier: the mysterious and prodigious machine, transported at great expense by special trains and ships from Paris to New York. All that could be seen of the apparatus were two laterally-situated handles, the purpose of which we shall soon see.

On top of the box the aides placed a light wicker bench, with insulating glass feet, on which three people could easily sit. That was what was known as "the saddle," the term having been borrowed from aviators.

Curiosity was excited to the highest degree; everyone was waiting, heart pounding with an almost painful anticipation, wondering what the result of these singular preparations would be.

Even the Eccentric finally seemed to emerge from his indolence. Clinging to his aerial observatory, he leaned over to get a better view.

III. Human Piles

It was known throughout New York that the bizarre machine that had just been brought out represented an invention of unparalleled importance. The newspapers had advertised it with an unusual luxury of attention.

The excitement of the spectators, therefore, at the sight of the singular machine that might perhaps be about to modify the conditions of human life completely, was as intense as at the most suspenseful moment of the finest of dramas.

Murmurs of astonishment rose from tier to tier, but resounding "Shhs!" were heard. Attention was over-excited, exasperated to such a degree that two men fell from a cluster that had climbed on to a ledge without anyone taking any notice.

Three men came forward through the same metallic doorway from which the trolley had emerged.

Everyone knew that these were the "human piles"—the producers of cerebral energy whose combined will-power was about to charge the machine, whose story had been widely told.

The engineer Myrandhal had chosen them from among a thousand, discovered with great difficulty in the course of his voyages, and persuaded to follow him more by virtue of the superiority of his own will than the rather high wages that he paid them.

The one marching in the lead was tall and muscular, in the full flush of youth. With curly hair and a curly moustache, he was clad in a braided sky-blue Brandenburg dolman, soft boots and knee-length deerskin trousers. He was an Italian animal-tamer named Giulio. A former street-urchin with no education and not much intelligence, he possessed an inexplicable power over all animals. An anecdote was related in his regard worthy of comparison with the legend of Androcles.

During a voyage he had made to the Italian colony of Eritrea, he had been taken by surprise in the desert by a lion. He had returned to the camp, followed by the lion, which had attached itself to his heels like a well-trained dog, and which he had immediately put in chains without he animal protesting even in the most benign fashion.

There was in that brutish brain—for outside of the gift that he possessed, Giulio was the worst of the ruffians of the Naples docks—an intense production of the will-power that Balzac called a "real substance."[8]

Behind him marched a person of the most enigmatic appearance. Barefoot in threadbare slippers, tall, thin, coifed with a pointed astrakhan cap in the Armenian style, he had a tapering nose, hollow cheeks and large, shining, almost liquid eyes, ascetic and mystical. He belonged to the sect of "whirling dervishes" and his name was Phéliny.

He realized with a surprising facility all the miracles of the Aissawa.[9] In the course of crises of ecstasy that followed his hysterical gyrations, he broke pieces of glass between his teeth and swallowed them; he lay down on beds of nails, passed a stiletto through his nose or ear-lobes, or marched over red hot coals, smiling.

He also possessed the magnetic will-power for which the engineer had sought assiduously. Without turning round, Phéliny could force passers-by to follow him, to sit down, to share their purses or their meals with him. However, he only used that prestigious power to satisfy his needs in the strictest fashion.

There was a certain analogy between the whirling dervish and the third human pile. There was the same thinness, the same frowning eyebrows, the same somber and concentrated expression, the same feverish gestures—except that,

---

[8] In *Eugénie Grandet* (1833) as well various works written in his mystical phase.

[9] Aissawa is a Sufi sect founded in the early 16th century, famous for its uses of music and dance to achieve trance states.

instead of being Persian, as Phéliny was, he was a peasant from the Cévennes, Mathieu Maugars.

Residing in a ruined hovel, a kind of cave in a desolate mountain ravine, a kind of living anachronism, he had been living like the sorcerers of the Middle Ages. A spell-caster of sorts, a bone-setter, an assembler of storms over his enemies' fields at harvest-time and a poisoner of wells, he had the reputation, first and foremost, of being a "wolf-leader"—a terrible individual who still inspires terror in certain remote rural areas, who only has to make a sign to deliver those he detests to the wild beasts whose sovereign he is.

But there was a fourth human pile.

To the increasing emotion of the spectators, four of the Athenaeum's waiters, in their spangled blue livery, appeared carrying a flat pedestal on which was propped a grotesque individual, a kind of human debris. He had neither arms nor legs: just a formless trunk in a sheath of black serge, and above that trunk an enormous, fearful head.

Of the eyes nothing remained but bloody cavities, two raw wounds, of the nose, merely a short stump; the cheeks and lips, gnawed and corroded, left teeth of dazzling enamel bare. The ensemble affected the sinister rictus of a death's-head, a specter whose vital spark had triumphed over the putrescence of the sepulcher.

A frisson of horror ran through the room, quickly repressed by a kind of respectful terror.

Thanks to the newspapers, people knew, broadly, the story of the terrorist Rywal Goledgine, whom the lecturer—at the risk of his life—had brought out of the ruins of a dynamited railway station at Weresli, near Arkhangelsk, almost a cadaver, and saved from the hands of the Russian police.

Rywal Goledgine, a knowledgeable chemist before becoming a militant revolutionary, had tried three times to kill the Tsar. With a single bomb the size of a fist, filled with a special nitrate of mercury of which he had found the formula and had contrived to manipulate without danger, he could reduced an entire block of houses, a fourteen-million-tons iron-clad or a railway viaduct to rubble, but he had fallen victim to his own discovery.

The bomb that he had been carrying to blow up Weresli railway station and facilitate the pillage of the imperial finance wagon had exploded a few minutes before the intended time, doubtless by virtue of one of those little-known molecular modifications produced in explosive materials by trepidation, heat or other ill-defined agents. It was a veritable prodigy that he had not been killed instantaneously, that he had survived frightful mutilation and burning by the explosive.

In the hospital in which Myrandhal had placed him, illustrious physicians had cared for him because his was a unique case, almost out of professional dilettantism, for the love of the art. They had succeeded in saving his life, but he had emerged a blind, disfigured amputee, reduced to muteness by the loss of his tongue, which had been resected for fear of gangrene.

Rywal Goledgine had vowed an unrestricted devotion to his rescuer. That audacious individual, who had commanded almost all Russian terrorism, had come to obey the slightest order of the engineer, in whom he had absolute faith.

The reader might be wondering how the mutilated man could communicate with his fellows in that lamentable condition. Hearing was the only sense that remained intact within him. He could hear, and he replied by means of a series of hideous contractions of his ravaged face.

Without even raising their eyes toward the hemicycle crowded with squinting eyes, the first three human piles came to take their places on three crystal armchairs symmetrically placed at each face of the mysterious cube, which the blue-clad waiters had just brought. The same waiters carefully posed the pedestal to which Rywal Goledgine as attached on the fourth of those seats, doubtless designed, in the thinking of the engineer, to insulate the producers of will from certain injurious fluids.

Almost at the same moment, the engineer—the lecturer awaited with so much impatience, the hero of the day—

appeared and sat down, slightly nervous but nevertheless calm, in the chair imitative of a Gothic pulpit that had been reserved for him.

Serge Myrandhal was about thirty years of age. Tall in stature, with broad shoulders and prominent biceps, he bore no resemblance to the professional scientists who are conventionally represented as stooped and hollow-chested, with spectacles and ridiculous mannerisms. He had a high and bulbous, slightly pensive, forehead surmounting a perfectly oval face with symmetrical lines but by no means insipid. His eyes were dark, ardent and avid, his nose and chin imperiously curved, his moustache proudly turned up at the tips. Everything about him testified to a formidable energy. His gestures were precise and sober, of masterly exactitude, and he had the clear, frank, almost harsh gaze of a technologist accustomed to maintaining his composure at all times.

Such as he was, he was a magnificent specimen of the Latin race.

A thunder of applause rose up from the crowd at the sight of the young engineer, the mere sight of whom had immediately conquered all sympathy. The women were particularly enthusiastic. Serge felt thousand of pairs of opera-glasses aimed at him with ardent curiosity.

Among the large number of billionaires' wives and daughters in the audience, many could not help thinking that, poor as he was, the young Frenchman would have made the most charming of husbands, if he had only possessed one of those titles—Duc or Marquis—of which the heirs of parvenus are so fond.

But Serge Myrandhal had already arranged the sheets of paper covered with figures that comprised his notes on the hinged table in front of him. He was about to begin, when Annabella Carpenter suddenly leaned forward in order to hear better,

Their gazes met—and then something strange happened. Serge Myrandhal, that man so chilly in appearance, felt his heart lurch. Annabella, disturbed without knowing why, lowered her eyes.

Those two souls had penetrated one another, as if in a double thunderbolt, as their gazes met.

But two other men had noticed that rapid drama and that instantaneous exchange of mysterious effluvia. They were the Rajah and his son. The latter had immediately bowed his head, his heart painfully constricted. As for the Rajah, he gripped the curtain with a nervous gesture, as if enraged.

IV. The Miracle

Making a violent effort of self-control, Serge Myrandhal overcame the emotion that had gripped him.

At a gesture from him, the applause died down. It was in the midst of a respectful silence that he began: "Ladies and gentlemen, permit me first of all to thank you—not on my own behalf, but that of science, of which I am a modest representative—for the applause with which you have just welcomed me.

"I salute, in the American nation, the youngest and most energetic people in the world. Others have qualities more refined, but America has the uncontested privilege of audacity and strength. It is the great realizer of the boldest chimeras—the chimeras that will be realities tomorrow, soon surpassed by the ascendant march of eternal progress. That is why it is not to the peoples of the Old World that I am addressing myself. It is to America that I want to submit my projects, which are called—as I hope to convince you—to change the face nor merely of our petty globe, but the entire solar universe..."

That opening had been pronounced in a warm voice, vibrant with conviction and sincerity. One sensed that the orator was not saying a single word that he did not believe. Already the audience was conquered, subjugated, persuaded in advance. Its members all recalled that the engineer Serge Myrandhal was the author of the famous treatise on *Psychic Mechanics*, already translated into twenty languages, commented on and passionately discussed by the intellectuals of all nations, which had had the shattering effect of a thunderbolt in the nebulous skies of official science.

Further applause drowned the orator's voice. There was a veritable tempest of bravos, a roar of hurrahs.

When silence was reestablished, with great difficulty, the orator got to the meat of the subject with a clarity and simplicity which demonstrated that he combined with the gifts of the scientist those of the writer and the orator.

Avoiding technical terms as much as possible, he found the means of making the theory he was presenting, as original as it was abstract, perfectly comprehensible. Above all, he separated himself from the spiritualists and occultists, etc. Without claiming that all of them were charlatans, he insinuated that a great number of them were. He, Myrandhal, had nothing in common with them; he was, primarily, a man of exact science, a mathematician who abandoned nothing to crazy hypotheses, only making use of pure logic.

"Mind acts upon matter—*mens agitat molem!*"[10] he exclaimed. "That cerebral energy, that animic fluid, which produces so many marvels, is a mechanically usable force, like all the forces of nature.

"It is this power, the most formidable of all, that has given the surface of the globe the aspect that it presently possesses, raising cities, piercing isthmuses and drying up seas. It is this force, which is truly the living and active soul of the planet, that it is a matter of applying directly, of harnessing like a horse of prodigious velocity..."

Now, he went on to affirm, that omnipotent force had been captured, channeled. The miracles of the yogis and thaumaturges of all times and all countries would be surpassed, reduced to triviality, considered as simple child's play. Humans were about to reconquer the fraction of divine sovereignty that they had lost in catastrophes obscurely designated in ancient books, in the annals of vanished peoples...

The frisson of the eternal mystery passed through the crowd like a storm wind over the sea. Grandiose perspectives opened up.

Those American materialists and skeptics widened their eyes, prey to a kind of sublime horror, so emotional that no one applauded.

---

[10] The Latin phrase is taken from Virgil's *Aeneid.*

After a few minutes of vertiginous silence, in which all hearts could be heard beating as one, Myrandhal resumed the course of his lecture. He spoke about the prodigies—very simple, according to him—that certain Indian fakirs accomplished. He emphasized one of the best-known: the "levitation" that consists of rising into the air to a certain height without any point of support, by the force of will alone.

"It is that prodigy," the lecturer said, "which science has not yet been able to explain in any satisfactory fashion, that I propose to reproduce, but not in the paltry, rudimentary fashion that consists of rising a few centimeters into our heavy atmosphere.

"Thanks to my discovery, humans will be endowed with the prodigious wings of the will, compared with which balloons and airplanes, all the machines constructed with difficulty by technologists, will no longer exist. Humans will not only move at will though the gaseous layers that surround the planet, only a few leagues in thickness, but will be able to risk themselves without peril in the gulfs of the cosmic beyond, on the imponderable waves of the interplanetary ether.

"What I propose to realize is perhaps the most sublime and most grandiose enterprise that has ever been attempted. It is a matter of nothing less than taking possession of the entirety of our solar domain, of colonizing all the planets that emerged, along with ours, from the sovereign star...

"From there, who can tell what heights humankind might reach?"

After this almost lyrical passage, Myrandhal went into more positive details. What he claimed to be able to accomplish was no hazardous hypothesis; it was an exact and definite matter. If he only had the necessary capital—for it would require money, naturally, and a great deal of it—he would immediately commence the construction of his apparatus. He would find the indispensable human piles—perhaps that was the most difficult part, but it was not impossible—and he would immediately attack the heavenly body that would reach

43

its greatest proximity to the Earth in a few weeks' time: the planet Mars.

This time, the applause resumed with increasing force, which went as far as delirium. The idea of colonizing the planets turned the Yankee brains upside-down. The enthusiasm was white hot, reaching an almost dangerous level of intensity.

The spectators uttered hoarse and guttural hurrahs, so much had they already shouted and applauded. Some threw their hats and canes into the air. The whole assembly was sweating, panting and gesticulating, quite out of breath. In spite of the ringing of the bell and the calls for "Silence, gentlemen, please!" howled by a powerful megaphone placed within arm's reach of the orator, whose vibrations were veritably thunderous, it was only after a long quarter of an hour that the lecturer was able to continue.

"As you are going to see with your own eyes, the problem has been solved—not on paper, in theory, but in a real and tangible fashion. It is true that I have only been able to realize my idea on a small scale. The condenser-amplifier—the engine, to use the more easily understandable language of the newspapers—is merely a laboratory model. As such, however, it is sufficient to convince the most incredulous."

Myrandhal then went into a few explanations of his human piles.

Those four men, of a terribly active will, were about to direct the waves of their animic fluid toward the apparatus. And it was the force in question, thus captured, but employed integrally and, in a way, multiplied tenfold, that the engineer would be able to employ at will, thanks to the secret that constituted his invention.

In addition, he made it understood that, for the full-scale construction of the ingenious machine hidden behind the sparkling walls of the vast cube, precious metals—radium, vanadium, helium and iridium—and rare sera were necessary. It is well-known that some of those newly-discovered metals are worth hundreds of thousands of francs per gram. That already

44

gives an idea of the fabulous price that the imagined machine would cost.

Furthermore, to reach the planet Mars, a projectile would be required of large enough dimension to carry, along with the indispensable food supplies and instruments, sufficient reserves of fluid to be able to accelerate the progress of the outward journey, and then effect a return journey, if necessary.

But the money—the lecturer came back to that point—was not the only thing. It would require thousands of brains of considerable will-power to charge the animic accumulator with volitional fluid and communicate to the engine the impetus necessary to reach its goal...

At that moment, an incident occurred.

In the great silence of that select auditorium, suspended, so to speak, on the orator's lips, a woman suddenly raised her hand to point at the top of the cupola, and uttered a piercing scream.

The spectators, momentarily distracted, looked in the direction of the chandelier where the Eccentric was sitting. Caught in an electrical short-circuit, the rope that the audacious individual had employed to reach the chandelier had begun to smoke and slowly to burn.

The Englishman did not appear to have attached any importance to it, however. While listening with all ears, he was occupied in peeling an orange—a refreshment doubtless necessitated by the enormous heat of the chandelier—and was negligently dropping the peel on the spectators in the hemicycle beneath him.

A murmur of stifled laughter ran through the hemicycle. The audience members wondered how the obstinate individual would get out of this predicament. They were amused in advance by the ridiculous situation in which he would find himself in consequence of the loss of his rope.

"We spoke too soon," said Joe Grok to his two companions. "The Englishman has lost his bet."

"How's that?" asked the Canadian.

45

"Remember what I said a little while ago. The Eccentric undertook to penetrate the Athenaeum by surprise and get out by the same route that he took to get in. That route—the rope—is now cut behind him, and unless someone sends him up a new rope by means of a kite, I don't see..."

"Why a kite?" asked the professor. "There must be a movable scaffold here, or something like it, which is used for cleaning the chandelier."

"There is—or rather, there was," the American replied, "but that's where the story gets complicated. A few days ago—during the last visit to the chandelier and the ventilator that surrounds it—the scaffold broke..."

"It's merely a matter of building another. Nothing simpler."

"Not as simple as that, by Jove! I'm not talking about the cost, of course—ten thousand francs at the lowest estimate; that hardly represents the Englishman's daily expenditure—but the time it would take to set up the new apparatus. It would take twenty four hours, at least. Now, during the preparations, the Eccentric might very well get hungry..."

"What an adventure!" exclaimed the Canadian. "And what an unexpected result of a crazy bet! If he's going to die of starvation up there...it would, after all, be a death worthy of a millionaire, especially an original of his sort!"

The new diversion provoked by the Englishman had not occasioned such amiable commentaries elsewhere. From a box partly occupied by scientists from Berlin, with blue-tinted spectacles, square foreheads and pale hair, brutal protests rose up, directed simultaneously at the lecturer and the Eccentric.

"That man perched on the chandelier," shouted one, "is a clown—a sidekick of the other, the engineer."

"*Tarteifle!* This is a trick!" complained another. "They're making fun of us. They're going to create an illusion with some clever conjuring. We thought we were coming to a lecture, but it's a circus performance they're putting on for us."

These objections and other similar ones, however, proffered in loud voices and demonstrating evident jealousy, whipped up a storm of protest. Cries of "Shut up!" came from all directions, punctuated with: "Throw the Germans out!" The latter hastened to beat a retreat into the depths of their box, and the crowd calmed down.

Again the entire hall became attentive. The incident was forgotten. With one word, Myrandhal had succeeded in calming things down.

The experiment awaited with an impatience that was tending to anguish was about to begin.

The moment was solemn. The engineer had got down from his pulpit. He whispered a few words into the ear of each of his producers of animic fluid.

Phéliny and Mathieu Maugars had each seized one of the movable handles that emerged from the cube, while they placed the third on the shoulder of the Russian Rywal Goledgine.

The animal-tamer Giulio, turning his back to the audience, had placed one of his large hands on the shoulder of the dervish and the other on that of the "wolf-leader." In that fashion, the psychic chain was complete.

The four men darted "volitional fluid" at the mysterious cube with dilated, seemingly radiant pupils. Under Myrandhal's gaze, animated by a somber flame, they emitted the *summum* of their will.

As handsome as an archangel in command of the thunder and lightning, the engineer stood tremulously within arm's reach of the strange machine, ready to intervene in case of catastrophe.

Now he was brandishing a kind of tuning-fork with a glass hilt and spiral prongs, which he was doubtless using to orientate the fluid at his whim. One of the prongs was formed of metal rods soldered together; the other was merely a crystal tube filled with a blue-tinted liquid.

The sight of that strange double wand could not fail to simulate the curiosity of the spectators considerably. A great silence reigned beneath the immense cupola. Several minutes went by, which seemed as long as centuries to the breathless spectators.

The four mediums, their faces contracted by a dolorous rictus, maintained an absolute immobility. Their pupils were phosphorescent. Myrandhal was pale, and his face too was contracted by the tension of his will.

Suddenly, a hum, imperceptible at first and then more distinct, was heard inside the mysterious cube. Little green sparks appeared at the corners. An indefinable odor, like that of a distant storm, spread out into the hall.

Myrandhal extended his wand.

In response to his gesture the "saddle" placed on top of the cube first began to oscillate, and then, with extreme slowness, rose into the air. One might have thought, to begin with, that there was something hesitant about its ascent, but eventually, it flew like a bird toward the summit of the cupola.

It arrived a few feet from the chandelier on which the Eccentric was perched, toward whom attention abruptly reverted.

The latter, having finished the cigar that he was smoking, made as if to drop it overboard, like everything else. Still as impassive as ever, he stretched out his arm, while protests went up from the spectators placed beneath the chandelier, who had been receiving the Eccentric's detritus since the beginning.

"No, no!" they cried. "Enough!"

"Not here."

"Get out, Englishman!"

"Get out, or we shoot…"

Two of the most excited spectators were already raising their revolvers.

Without any emotion, the Englishman gazed curiously at what was happening down below. An imperceptible smile illuminated his face.

Suddenly, as the saddle arrived within reach, he stretched out his hand and delicately deposited the litigious cigar on the seat, which seemed to have been sent expressly for that purpose.

That solution, as elegant as it was unexpected, unleashed a gale of mad laughter, which put an end to the incident. In any case, attention was now solicited elsewhere.

Serge had extended his wand. The saddle descended again with a gradual and decreasing movement. Without the slightest sound or shock, it returned to settle gently on the top of the cube, in the location it had occupied a few moments before.

This time there was a new thunder of applause. The most skeptical were convinced.

The experiment was complete and conclusive. The lecturer had provided the proof of what he had asserted. The man capable of such a miracle, operated without any possibility of deception, merited that people should listen when he spoke of conquering the empire of the terrestrial earths. Now, it was no longer merely admiration, but a veritable respect that they felt for him.

He understood that. He took account of the fact that the entire crowd was his, that it belonged to him body and soul, and that he would, so to speak, do with it as he wished. He sensed the ecstatic eyes of Annabella upon him, and felt an indescribable intoxication. At a glance, he glimpsed the realization of his grandiose projects, a glory of which no man had ever dreamed. Annabella's radiant face, which he perceived as if surrounded by an aureole in the semi-darkness of the box, became an integral part of that future happiness.

For a second, he closed his eyes, as if prey to a strange drunkenness, but he opened them again immediately. It was in a grave voice—an almost blank voice—that he resumed speaking in the midst of an imposing silence.

"Ladies and gentlemen, you have just witnessed for yourselves that the volitional fluid produced by four human piles"—he pointed to the four mediums whose faces were contracted with effort—"and stored by my apparatus is capable, at my behest, of lifting that saddle, the weight of which is thirty kilograms.

"That is merely the beginning of the experiment to which I have invited you.

"Three people from the audience may take their places on that bench, if there are any—as I do not doubt—who will consent to lend themselves to the demonstration. Those three individuals will, by virtue of the energy of the fluid alone, be raised to the summit of the cupola, and then returned to their point of departure.

"The volitional waves emitted by the human piles are sufficient in intensity to obtain that result without an accident or jolt.

"In brief, the saddle, laden with three people—which is to say, a weight of at least two hundred kilograms—will repeat the ascent and gradual descent through the air that has just been carried out before your eyes.

"It only remains, now, to select the three individuals who will lend their collaboration to the experiment."

These words provoked, beneath the sonorous cupola, a veritable storm of cries, howls and the stamping of feet. Myrandhal's proposition was so much to the Yankees' liking that they all wanted to take their places on the apparatus. They raised their arms and shouted. A few even began to insult one another and adopt fighting stances. The same exasperated cries rose from al throats.

"Me! Me!"

"No, me!"

"We'll see about that!"

Some brandished their check-books, howling numbers. "A thousand dollars! I'll buy a place for a thousand dollars!"

"Two thousand dollars!"

"Ten thousand dollars!"

"Fifteen thousand..."

There was a crazy auction, bids howled at the top of the voice by the agitated crowd, which could have been mistaken for the population of a lunatic asylum.

The honorable Joe Grok was shaking an enormous wad of banknotes like a distress flag; already, he was so hoarse that it was only in a raucous croak that he succeeded in articulating: "Twenty thousand! Cash! Twenty thousand dollars! All right!"

There was a din, a disorder, a chaos of which it is difficult to form the slightest notion. The bell and the megaphone could not make their voices heard in the midst of that pandemonium, although they were as powerful as that of a steam siren.

The four human piles remained impassive, absorbed by their task.

Myrandhal feared, however, with a legitimate terror, that the composure and volition necessary for his experiment might be corroded by that delirium. He could see the moment coming when he would no longer be able to control the fanatics. The worst catastrophes were to be feared. In their furious desire to be the first to take their places on the apparatus, they were capable of fighting, of breaking the precious machine that represented so much work and so much effort.

Already, some of them were coming to blows.

Under the pressure of necessity, Serge had a good idea, calculated to please the Yankees. He spoke rapidly into the ear of one of the waiters. A moment later, the thunderous voice of the megaphone drowned out the rumor for a few seconds, uttering the magical words: "The three places will be chosen by lot. Your seat numbers will play the role of lottery tickets..."

That proposal had a prodigious success. "Very good!" was shouted on all sides

"That's it!"

"That way, there's no privilege for anyone! Everyone will have an equal chance."

Only a few billionaires, who had hoped to win the game with banknotes, looked sullen. The majority had been won over to the lottery plan, however, and they were obliged to yield the point.

Already, with the rapidity of improvisation that is only found in America, the waiters in blue costumes were collecting the seat numbers. They deposited then, folded into four, within sight of everyone, in a large aluminum bowl placed on the edge of the stage.

In five minutes, the bowl was full. All the numbers were deposited. The audience waited, panting with a genuine fever of anguish. In the silence that had been reestablished, there were a few seconds of recollection, such that nothing could any longer be heard but the slight sound emitted by the machine, still surrounded by the four ecstatic human piles.

Slightly emotional, Myrandhal unfolded one of the squares, taken at random from the bowl.

He read: "Two thousand four hundred and nine."

A cry of joy went up from the third row of seats, and the winner, a pale and thin young man, came forward, trembling and intimidated, toward the center of the hall, under the curious gazes of all the spectators. He was the son of a rich cotton merchant, very well-known in the drawing rooms of the Five Hundred.

Already, Myrandhal was unfolding the second piece of paper. It bore the number 3,007. This time, the winner was a member of the Splendid Club with a slightly deformed shoulder.

"A hunchback," said one joker. "That's a good sign— he'll bring good luck to his traveling companions."

It only remained to draw the third number. This time, the spectators had arrived at a paroxysm of emotion. Hearts were leaping in bosoms.

Serge hastened to take a piece of paper from the bowl, and announced the number 990.

A few cries of disappointment were heard, but everyone was primarily curious to know who the last of the fortunate competitors might be.

A waiter armed with a seating list called out the name of the Reverend Eliezer Pellmann. It was the Mormon patriarch whom we saw installing himself in his box with his wives.

That discovery excited the joy of the crowd to the highest degree.

"Is he going to take his seraglio into the air with him?" someone asked.

"He won't dare!" sniggered another.

"So much the better, then," said a third. "The place can be allocated by another draw."

"Pardon me," objected a fourth, "but since he's won, the Reverend Eliezer is free to do whatever he wants with his place, even—and especially—to sell it."

"Never in this life!"

"Of course!"

During this exchange of exclamations, the venerable Eliezer Pellmann stood up. At the sight of his round face, red with surprise and—even more so—timidity, vociferations burst forth from all sides, and from the upper tiers.

"Climb on!"

"Don't do it!"

The bishop, whose anxiety and confusion were increasing by the second, took a step forward, as if making and abrupt decision, and was immediately surrounded by the women of his entourage.

Then there was a colossal wave of Homeric laughter throughout the hall.

"Hold him back!"

"He'll come to harm!"

"It's his bedtime!"

These sarcasms had a decisive effect on the Latter Day Saint. With an abrupt, violent gesture—the gesture of a man making a heroic decision—the bishop pushed away his wives and daughters and, stepping over the rim of the box, he advanced toward the engineer, who was waiting for him, smiling, encouraging him with his gaze to brave public malignity.

Myrandhal held out his hand to the Mormon, delighted and confused by such an honor, and that gesture had the sudden result of imposing silence on the mocking laughter. Scattered applause burst forth.

"Hurrah for the Frenchman!"

"Bravo for the bishop!"

"He's no longer trembling. He's a worthy fellow."

In the meantime, the waiters had rolled a mobile staircase up to the cube, which was part of the observatory's equipment.

After a few words pronounced in a low voice by the engineer, the three willing volunteers climbed the steps and installed themselves, not without a certain emotion, on the saddle.

Tall and proportionately corpulent, majestic and Biblical, the Mormon patriarch had taken his placed between the other two; he was a head taller than either of them.

"Ladies and gentlemen," said the engineer then, in an imperious tone, "the second part of the experiment is about to begin. The slightest disturbance or cry might cause an irreparable catastrophe..."

After this warning, with had its importance, Serge set the human piles in action again with a gesture of his strange wand.

There was a deathly silence in the vast dome. All hearts were oppressed, all bosoms breathless. It was no longer a matter of an experiment that might be more or less interesting to see, but of the lives of three men.

The producers of volitional fluid now had bulging eyes, clenched jaws and foreheads furrowed by the terrible effort they were making. A kind of immaterial mist lifted up their hair, making it bristle like the fur of an angry cat. Their ears and nostrils vibrated rapidly, agitated by nervous tics.

A few minutes went by, as long and tortuous for the public as for the three experimental subjects. Then the upper wall of the mysterious cube emitted a crackling sound. The crystal feet of the bench creaked.

Finally, with the same slowness as before, the saddle, laden with its three passengers, was detached from the cube. It rose up, with an ascending movement whose smooth regularity had something frightening about it.

The spectators could clearly see a phenomenon that had not been observed the first time: between the cube and the saddle there was a kind of phosphorous green-tinted fog, luminous at the base but scarcely perceptible at the summit.

Carrying all gazes and all hearts with it, the bench rose toward the terminus of its ascent.

From the height of his perch, the Eccentric watched it rise toward him, with an expression that was both amazed and attentive—and the saddle continued rising, accelerating as it went.

The fluidic mist now formed a long phosphorescent column.

The saddle was no more than a few feet from the chandelier on which the eccentric Englishman was perched.

Suddenly with a movement that no one could have foreseen, let alone prevented, Pickman grasped the branch of the chandelier that was supporting him and swung on it, like a trapeze artist about to launch himself into space.

The members of the audience shivered, holding their breath.

Then there was a scream: a single scream of horror springing from twenty thousand throats.

The Englishman, letting go, had just dropped, to sit astride the shoulders of the Mormon, dragging the overloaded bench downwards with his weight.

There was a plummeting vertical descent.

Already, the saddle was only a few yards from the floor, into which it was about to crash with its four passengers—and then the sudden miracle occurred.

With a fulgurant gesture, Serge Myrandhal had extended his magic wand, bringing the bench, from which cries of fright were emerging, to a dead stop.

The aerial chariot oscillated for a few seconds, and then began to climb again, very slowly.

The mysterious cube was suddenly sounded by a blue aureole, and a dull hum, like the rumble of distant thunder, emerged from its sides.

Finally, at a gesture from Serge, the saddle began to descend again.

Delicately, it settled on to the cube, while a sigh of deliverance, a great "Ah!" rose up all the way to the chandelier.

Suddenly, as the waiters were liberating the still-impassive Eccentric and his three companions, the latter blue with fear, a thunder of applause burst forth, in a delirious manifestation of enthusiasm.

The spectators broke the metal chairs, struck the ground with frenetic blows of their canes and fired revolvers as a sign of delight.

It was a colossal success for the engineer, surpassing all anticipation: an eruption of madness, impossible to hold back.

Too emotional to pronounce a single word, Serge made a gesture of thanks and, with one last glance toward Miss Carpenter's box, slipped away. He made his escape while the waiters took away the four human piles, the four producers of psychic energy, inert and inanimate, wrapped in blankets, their features drawn by frightful contractions and their eyes bloodshot.

If Serge had been less absorbed, less distracted and less fatigued by the terrible experiment he had just carried out, he would have seen, at the edge of the curtain of gauze masking the Maharajah's box, a black and desiccated hand, rutilant with gems, extended toward him in a gesture of menace.

A quarter of an hour later, in the vast and elegant hall that served as the Athenaeum's foyer, in the bustle of the exit, an interminable queue formed around the engineer. Hundreds of hands shook his as if to crush it. He was complimented, he was acclaimed. A few people, even more enthusiastic, talked about lifting him on to their shoulders and carrying him back to his hotel in triumph. Others embraced him.

Serge was half-stifled by these excessive manifestations. Without energetic resistance, he would have been at risk of being torn to pieces by his frenetic admirers. Already, his shirt-front was in tatters. A Yankee had carried off his gloves, which he ripped apart with his pen-knife and distributed to his friends.

Meanwhile, the crowd, rushing for the elevators, gradually dispersed.

At a given moment, he perceived Annabella a few yards away, advancing toward him, cleaving a path through the mass; he hastened to go to meet her.

The young woman's cheeks were colored by a slight blush.

"*Monsieur l'ingénieur*," she said, in French that was almost devoid of an accent, "I'd like to ask you for a favor."

"I'm entirely at your disposal."

"You've doubtless guessed what it is. I've recently been employed by the *Herald*..."

"You want to interview me—here?"

"No, sir; I don't want to tear you away from your admirers," Miss Carpenter replied, graciously. "If you'd care to indicate a more favorable time..."

"Any time that suits you," Serge Myrandhal hastened to reply, "will suit me too. I'll hold myself at your disposal all day tomorrow. I'm staying at the Atlantic Hotel, fifth floor..."

Scarcely had these words been pronounced than Serge stopped, hesitantly. Imbued with French notions regarding the education of young women, and, on the other hand, being aware of Miss Carpenter's delicate situation, he was fearful of having humiliated her by giving her his address, as he would have done to a tradesman. "No," he resumed, almost immediately. "Better than that—I'll come to the newspaper. Would you care to tell me what time I'll find you there?"

This proposal was undoubtedly not the result for which she had hoped. Annabella raised her head proudly. "No," she articulated, precisely, as if offended. "I'm the one who ought to take the trouble. After mature reflection, I've adopted a profession of which I intend to fulfill all the obligations..."

Before the young man's distraught expression, however, the haughty young woman softened rapidly. "Besides," she added, settling her frank and candid gaze on Serge, "I'm used to operating in the open. I know that you're being considerate, but you've judged me a little too much by French standards." She held out her hand to Myrandhal and continued, laughing: "No hard feelings, though..."

Myrandhal was so distraught that the reporter, self-possessed as she was, felt a similar disturbance invading her.

There was whispering around them.

Again the two young people exchanged a handshake, but their fingers were tremulous, and their palms scarcely made contact. They had understood that they loved one another, and that, as solemnly as if they had sworn an oath, they had promised, with a glance, that they would only ever belong to one another.

Serge was still under the influence of the disturbance caused by that encounter when a Hindu—whose white cashmere turban and rich silk costume made him easily recognizable as one of Indraghava's servants—handed him a letter bearing the Rajah's seal, with all the marks of the most profound respect.

In a few lines, the Mendicant Prince congratulated Myrandhal on the prodigious results he had obtained and the composure with which he had given proof of them. At the same time he asked him to come and see him at his villa, for an important communication.

After having read it at a glance, Serge slipped the missive negligently into his pocket. As is easily understandable, he had other things on his mind: the radiant image of Miss Carpenter.

He had no suspicion of the implications of that fatal letter, and would have shrugged his shoulders disdainfully had anyone told him that at that moment, it was his destiny that was close at hand.

V. Father and Son

It was at Chipside, a few kilometers from New York, with a delightful view over the banks of the Hudson, that the villa built by the Rajah Ely Indraghava was located. It was entirely constructed from cedar logs cut on the slopes of Mount Almowrat, in the sacred forest that surrounds the monastery of that name. The villa, which only one person, Annabella Carpenter, had obtained the privilege of entering, was justly deemed to be one of the curiosities of New York.

The Rajah and his son Djalor were standing in a large drawing room whose veranda, with stucco colonnettes, overlooked the Hudson. The almost dazzling magnificence of Indian taste was displayed there in all its splendor. Golden lanterns encrusted with opals and rubies hung from the vault, divided into sculpted sections, which formed as many mini-cupolas separated by pendentives. The floor was strewn with the skins of lions and royal tigers, carpets from Iran and Turkestan, and draperies of Indian brocade, cashmere and Chinese silk, ornamented with dazzling embroideries, lent the room a magical sparkle. From high-set incense-burners, benzoin, myrrh and cinnamon—perfumes cherished by Orientals—spread their fumes, creating a kind of mist of dreams.

There was material there to furnish a fine room in the richest of museums. There were idols removed from the secret crypts of some Ellora, statues of the wise Ganesh, the goddess with an elephant's trunk, Shiva the destroyer, and Kali, the protectress of the assassins known as thugs or stranglers. Further away, there was a whole collection of pipes: Persian chibouks with cherry-wood or jasmine stems; narghiles and hookahs in glass annealed with golden arabesques, with slender necks, interminable tubes; and opium pipettes like flattened mushrooms, with all the supplementary apparatus of pots, lamps, boxes and needles.

In one part of the room, a panoply that would have done honor to the royal armory of Madrid or the Louvre displayed khanjars, poisoned krises, damascened swords, rifles and pistols with jeweled butts, which put the glare of fireworks in the shade. On the ceiling, a punka—a kind of fan with vast flaps—inert for the time being, its silk cords tied up, was reminiscent of a gigantic motionless butterfly. Because of the fumes, gems and radiance, the atmosphere of the room seemed to be composed of a golden and nacreous mist.

The dominant note was struck by a gigantic gilded Buddha squatting on the symbolic lotus flower, one finger raised, with an eternally smiling expression. At its feet, sticks of perfume were burning, as in Chinese temples. A large candle of vegetable wax, graduated and divided in such a way as to measure the progress of the hours as it burned, was lit to its right.

The entire backcloth of the room gave the impression of a strange and sumptuous temple. On the side of the veranda with bright windows open over the Hudson, however, certain details modernized the appearance, displaying the commencing fusion of the calculating and practical Occident with the contemplative and mystical Orient. A bookcase full of volumes with rich bindings, and a few scientific instruments in a display case, testified to a preoccupation with the exact sciences.

Prince Djalor was dressed like a correct British gentleman, as we have already seen him at the session at the Athenaeum. Sitting in a rocking chair of American manufacture, he was sipping perfumed tea while savoring one of those delicious Indian cigars, some brands of which equal, if they do not surpass, the finest Havanas.

A "houseboy" clad in white silent and agile, had just taken away on a silver tray the remains of the oyster soup, pheasant curry and lobster cooked in champagne that had comprised the Prince's lunch. Fruit, pale ale and Stilton cheese stepped in Madeira had completed the thoroughly Anglo-Indian menu, to which the prince did not appear to have done great honor.

Djalor seemed somber, nervous and melancholy.

A few feet away from him, his father the Maharajah, squatting on a simply bark mat, wrapped up in a Tibetan goat-skin, had also finished his meal, but it had been much more modest in kind, solely composed of grains of dourah, wheat, barley and other cereals, which the old yogi seized one by one in his fingertips with simian dexterity. One might have thought that he was some strange bird in the process of peck-ing. He seemed plunged in profound meditation. From time to time his gaze went, with visible preoccupation, toward a large crystal sphere set on a bronze tripod, almost hidden in an ob-scure corner. Then he shook his head, and remained pensive, as if the presence of the iridescent globe was both something heart-breaking and consoling.

Abruptly, he got up, and with a slow, sinuous movement that revealed an infinite lassitude—an age-old lassitude—he went over to the mysterious crystal globe in which there was something paternal and heart-rending. He reached out to it with his desiccated hands, as if to warm them at some un-known flame.

A frisson of wellbeing agitated his skeletal carcass and he breathed more deeply. Truly, benevolent effluvia seemed to be emanating from the sphere, which had now become much darker, as if the Rajah's presence had drawn off a part of the light and infused it into his own molecules. The Rajah seemed reanimated and rejuvenated. He took a few strides across the luxurious room.

"Yes," he murmured, speaking to himself. "I anticipated, and partly realized, with that sphere, the idea that the accursed Frenchman has just stolen from me...I was on the track. With Djalor's help, I would have ended up finding what Serge Myrandhal has found! I was on the brink of success, and eve-rything has fallen apart. I've been overtaken, frustrated."

The father and son looked at one another.

"Do you know," murmured Djalor, in a dull voice, "that the news I mentioned to you yesterday is exact, confirmed in every point. It isn't official yet, but in a few days it will be.

The *Herald*, the great American newspaper, has assumed all the expenses of constructing the Frenchman's machine. The Metal Syndicate is putting all the necessary metals at his disposal, gratuitously, from the most common to those that are worth hundreds of thousands of francs per gram, which have only just been discovered by chemists."

"The beautiful Annabella Carpenter," interjected the Rajah sarcastically, "doubtless has much to do with that favor. She's all-powerful at the *Herald*."

"Perhaps," said Djalor, with an angry gesture, "but that's not all. The proprietor of the *Herald*, the famous Norton Bennett, wants to maintain the traditions of the newspaper, which sent Stanley to search for Livingston and organized the celebrated and tragic expedition of the *Jeanette* to the North Pole, and has devoted himself entirely to the new project.[11] At this moment he's putting him up in a cottage not far from here, on the Hudson, where he's providing the engineer with a laboratory. They're in the process of building a high protective wall around it and installing the necessary equipment, at considerable cost. The engineer left his hotel to take up residence in Norton Cottage the day after the famous lecture."

"You don't know everything," the Maharajah interjected, again.

Prince Djalor shuddered. "What else is there?"

"You'll see that I'm better informed than you are. In certain circles, an obstinate rumor is going round. It concerns a

---

[11] The proprietor of the New York *Herald* who sent Stanley to find Livingston in 1869 and sponsored George DeLong's ill-fated polar expedition of 1881 was actually named James Gordon Bennett, Jr., although he was generally known as Gordon Bennett to distinguish him from his father. The surname of the present character is rendered as Bonnell once in the first volume, and on the several occasions when the character is mentioned in the second volume, but I have unified the references by selecting the more frequently-employed name.

projected marriage between the engineer Serge Myrandhal and the very charming Annabella Carpenter."

Prince Djalor had clenched his fists angrily; his eyes had flared up, but he did not say a word.

"Well," the Maharajah went on, with a diabolical smile, "is that what you were thinking about just now?"

"Yes and no," the young prince replied, his eyebrows furrowed. "I was thinking more particularly about Serge Myrandhal, that petty penniless low-born engineer, who has put you and me to shame, wrecking our most cherished projects, forestalling us and humiliating us in everything..."

Prince Djalor hesitated.

"What were you going to say?" asked the Rajah.

"Well, Father, I confess that I don't understand why you've invited that man—our most redoubtable adversary—to come here, to your home. What do you intend to do?"

The Maharajah smile enigmatically.

"There are two things," he said, sententiously, "that the engineer Myrandhal lacked in order to succeed in his projected voyage to the planet Mars. The first is money—a great deal of money. That difficulty has been ironed out for him, thanks to the enthusiasm he was able to whip up in the Yankees. But there's still one element that he lacks, unless I become involved: what he calls 'human piles'; producers of energy sufficiently numerous and powerful to furnish the indispensable volitional fluid. All of Uncle Sam's dollars can't give him thousands of wills, both supple and powerful, overnight. I alone..."

"So, Father," Djalor interjected, "you want to associate that man with our sublime projects?" The young man's voice was tremulous with indignation.

The Maharajah's gaze was sharply ironic. The wrinkles surrounding his bright eyes deepened, and the whole of the old man's physiognomy revealed a profound and concentrated cunning. He shrugged his shoulders imperceptibly, as if pitying the naivety of his son, too honest to have guessed the treason that was already planned. "You don't understand, Djalor," he said, in a calm voice. "I don't want to associate him with my projects. I only want to make use of his discoveries to complete ours. He's an instrument that the Invisible Powers have sent me."

Prince Djalor scowled dubiously. Although he did not know the details as yet, his father's plan was repugnant to his honesty. "But later," he said, "when the Frenchman has collaborated with our work and has communicated his discoveries to us, how will you get rid of him? You can't dismiss him after having...robbed him like that."

The Maharajah uttered a little sarcastic ripple of laughter. "Once in my realm," he murmured, "in the Monastery of Almowrat, where I'm the absolute master, he'll be at my discretion. Willingly or not, he'll have to submit to my will. I want him to become similar to one of the slaves who answer to me, bowing down to the ground when I give them an order."

Prince Djalor remained silent for a few moments. Then, abruptly dropping his cigar into a jade ashtray, he said: "I take back what I said to you just now. Even if everything happens as you anticipate, though, there's one thing for which I can't console myself—this marriage, about which people are already talking."

The Maharajah straightened up slowly. "The marriage between Annabella Carpenter and the Frenchman, about which people are talking, will not take place," he declared, in a dry voice that was almost a hiss. "I promise you that."

"Who will prevent it?"

"Me."

"You, Father!" exclaimed the Prince. "I thought that, on the contrary..."

"I'll prevent the marriage—but on one condition, which is that you do *everything I wish*, that you obey me without question, and, if necessary, without seeking to understand."

The young man was violently disturbed. "Father," he said, eventually, "I accept. I'll obey you."

The Maharajah had a triumphant gleam in his brought eyes. He sat down again on the mat, from which he had got up in order to go and obtain a little vital warmth from the sphere charged with effluvia, and in a vibrant voice, he began to speak: "Today, Djalor, I want you to know a little more about my vast hopes. I've already told you, more than once, the doctrine that I've been able to extract from our sacred books.

"Man is a child of the Sun and of the Earth, but he is not born on the Earth. He arrives there from a nearby planet, probably Mars. And it is that voyage which it is a matter of remaking, in the reverse direction.

"For us, Mars is the most accessible and the most habitable planet. It is a miniature Earth, we are assured by the scientists of the Occident, all of whose treatises I have read. There is, however, for the conquerors who have the audacity to land there, a marvelous realm there, an entire treasure of sentiments, thoughts and unknown sciences! Other plants, other animals, new minerals and unknown metals await the bold explorers of the celestial earths.

"On Mars, a human race, doubtless once superior to us but now decadent and moribund, is calling to us and extending its arms to us across the infinite ocean of the ether. It's there that I want to transplant our religion and our civilization, to create a new, regenerated, immortal race, liberated from disease, vice and hatred.

"And do you know who will be the Adam—as the Christians put it—of that new race? It will be you, Djalor! It is you, my son, who are called to become the ancestor, perhaps the god, or at least one of the gods, of Martian generations!"

Djalor looked at his father. The young man was stupefied, as if trembling with sacred horror.

"I knew a large part of your plans for astral colonization," he murmured, lowering his head, "but I didn't know that you had designated me for the august role of the ancestor of peoples."

"In my mind, I've always seen you as the root-stock of new posterities—but I have another surprise in store for you.

Do you know who your companion will be—the Eve with fecund loins who will collaborate with you in the great work?"

Djalor had gone pale. "I...don't know," he stammered.

"It will be the woman you love, Annabella Carpenter, that perfect, robust, almost unique exemplar of a strong race. Yes, it will be Miss Annabella herself."

"Then you consent...?" stammered Djalor, stunned by joy.

"Not only do I consent, but I wish it! Annabella is the woman selected by me from among all the daughters of the earth. It was a long time ago that I cast my eyes upon her."

"But only yesterday, that marriage displeased you."

"Child! It has never displeased me. My resistance was merely feigned. I wanted to be certain of your love for her. Now, my paternal dissimulation has become unnecessary. I have studied Annabella in accordance with the principles of the seven sacred sciences. She unites the nineteen perfections. I have interrogated by the future by means of sand, water and the stars. It is Annabella who must be the mother of the supreme race."

Djalor listened to these words as if he were hearing celestial music. He was enraptured, ecstatic. Of all that the Maharajah had just said to him, he only retained one thing: his father was permitting him to love Annabella Carpenter; that had been granted to him. The rest did not matter, so far as he was concerned. To depart for the planet Mars in Annabella's company seemed to him to be perfectly simple.

Let us admit that beneath his grave Anglo-Indian indolence, Prince Djalor concealed an enthusiastic and ardent soul. For many years, his father had trained him only to be moved by the most extraordinary things.

Why should he have had any doubt?

He saw his father, whose power and immense knowledge he respected, whom he had seen performing, in his own fashion, the celebrated miracles of the yogis, adding a blind faith to the audacious project. He knew what a profound affection the old man had for him, the last scion of an illustrious, privileged race...

Besides which, the opinion of a man of high scientific worth like the engineer Serge Myrandhal had made a deep impression on him. It must be possible to reach Mars, since the two men he held in the highest esteem—his father and the engineer—had arrived at the same conclusion, having departed from opposite poles. The yogi and the mathematician came together at that point.

Djalor was at that point in his reflections when the note of a gong resounded and a white-clad houseboy came in.

"The engineer Serge Myrandhal," he announced.

"Show him in!" exclaimed the Rajah, his pale eyes sparkling.

VI. The Association

Having come from New York to Chipside on one of the gigantic multistory ferry-boats that travel up the Hudson, the engineer Serge Myrandhal had no difficulty finding the way to the villa inhabited by the Rajah Ely Indraghava. The first idler on the quay had immediately pointed out an elegant and sumptuous construction on the edge of town, whose gilded turrets emerged from a wood of cedars and plane-trees. It was surrounded by a high wall, fitted with sharp spikes that would make climbing over impossible.

At the end of the deserted road that wound around the princely property the engineer found himself confronted by a massive door made of thick oak planks joined together by strips of wrought iron. He rang a bell, was examined through the grille of a judas-hole, and was eventually admitted by two white-clad sepoys armed with curved swords.

He went through the grounds behind them, climbed the marble stepped to the front door and went into a waiting room furnished with the luxury that was displayed everywhere in that sumptuous dwelling. Serge Myrandhal only stayed in that room for a few minutes. Almost immediately, the Rajah's houseboy came to fetch him in order to show him in.

On hearing his rival's name, Prince Djalor had risen to his feet with an abrupt surge of anger. The two men met on the threshold and the Prince, after a glacially correct bow, stood aside to let the engineer pass. Their eyes had met, however, and Djalor, whose impetuous temperament was incapable of dissimulation, had revealed a somber gleam of hatred.

The engineer, still under the influence of other preoccupations, had not noticed.

Already, the Rajah was advancing to meet him, his hand extended in a princely gesture of courtesy and nobility. He invited the engineer to sit in one of the vast Chinese armchairs made of porcelain that are so comfortable in hot countries.

"Be welcome, *Monsieur l'ingénieur*," he said, in perfectly correct French. "I'm happy and proud to receive your visit. You amazed me the other night, at the Athenaeum." And he added, with an amicability that was truly seductive on the part of such an individual: "Even though I'm blasé with regard to miracles."

And as Serge Myrandhal excused himself modestly, attributing the merit of his discovery to the hazard that sometimes favors seekers and gives them more than they had hoped to find, the Rajah went on, with the same princely affability: "No, Monsieur Myrandhal, don't talk about hazard…there is no such thing. Refer instead to your tireless labor, your marvelous qualities of calculation and intuition, and the patience of your research."

In that atmosphere of apparent cordiality, the visitor quickly felt at ease, almost at home, in spite of the fantastic décor that surrounded him. The conversation immediately took on a familiar, almost confidential tone.

"What if I told you," the old man said, having squatted down on his mat again, "that I too have dreamed many a time of utilizing the prodigious energy of human brains to reach the neighboring planets?" As Serge Myrandhal made a gesture of astonishment he continued: "Yes, many a time, in the golden mourning-dress of our beautiful Indian nights, motionless on the high terraces of the Monastery of Almowrat, it has occurred to me, while contemplating the infinite swarm of stars, to think about means of reaching them. I've always thought that the animic fluid was the only possible means."

"I'm glad," said the engineer, inclining his head, "to have been anticipated in my work by Your Highness."

The Rajah smiled with feigned bonhomie. "Let's not exaggerate," he said. "I wouldn't want to claim the role of precursor of your admirable discoveries. My idea remained in the state of a dead letter. I never sought to realize it. It was merely a vague dream hatched in the mystical mind of a contemplative old man, who does not know the first thing about modern science."

The old man had spoken in that fashion in order to reassure the scientist completely, and convince him that he was not dealing with a rival. At that moment, however, his sparkling pupils had strayed involuntarily toward the crystal sphere, and a grimace of hatred had curled the corners of his parchment-like lips.

Entirely overwhelmed by the charm of the welcome he had received, the engineer had not noticed that fugitive expression. He was a thousand leagues away from supposing that the ostentatious Maharajah could be harboring any evil intention toward him.

"At any rate," the old man said, "thanks to you, the chimera has become a reality. You would not believe how interested I am in your grandiose project. I intend to give you proof of my esteem for you and my admiration for your work. When I asked you to come to see me, it was not to satisfy a vain curiosity. I wanted to help you in the measure that is possible, and I believe that I can do so better than anyone else. That said, I shall get straight to the point. This is what I propose: that you come and carry out your experiment in my realm, at the monastery of which I am the high priest."

"But what difference would that displacement make to the prospect of success?" the engineer could not help objecting.

"Patience—I'll tell you, and I'm certain that you'll share my opinion. You possess the engine, but you don't possess a sufficient quantity of the fluid required to activate it."

"That's true," the engineer admitted. "It will certainly be very difficult to find the enormous number of human piles that I need. I've known from the outset that that would be the greatest difficulty. I was sure of finding the money sooner or later, but the fluid..."

"Well, I'm in a position to remove that obstacle and solve the problem at a stroke."

"How?"

"The monastery of Almowrat, in the Himalayas, is a veritable city, and it contains no less than ten thousand fakirs, or penitents, all trained to the most difficult exercises of the will, and who are all obedient to me, as their spiritual leader as well as their temporal sovereign."

"They would be the ideal human piles," the engineer put in.

"That's what I thought—but that's not all. You know that all the monasteries, all the bonzeries, and all the cells of the contemplative yogis perched in the inaccessible caverns of the Himalayas or the Shivalik mountains are in constant psychic communication. Without messengers or telegraphy, we can transmit news or instructions to one another with the speed of thought.

"In brief, I can organize matters in such a way that thousands of the faithful of mystic and contemplative India will pray simultaneously, and transmit the effluvia of their will, refined by meditation and privation, to your receiver. The volitional fluid will radiate from those purified brains in powerful waves, like those of a majestic river, with such intensity and abundance that it will triumph over space and time. All that depends on me, and me alone.

"Well, that formidable power, I will put at your full and entire disposal. In exchange, perhaps I shall ask you one day to take advantage of your marvelous discovery."

The Rajah had pronounced these words with an impressive nobility and simplicity. He had spoken like a true sovereign. His thin figure had straightened; his physiognomy reflected a majestic affability.

Serge Myrandhal was profoundly moved; his heart was overflowing with gratitude and joy. Thanks to the unexpected collaboration of the Maharajah, the problem was now completely solved. The energy source had been found; success as assured.

"You're doing me a service of inestimable value," he stammered.

"You accept, then?"

"With enthusiasm. But how can I repay you?"

71

"Firstly, by succeeding. You and I are working for science and for humankind." A glint of savage joy had appeared in the old man's fickle pupils. He went on, very calmly: "So, Monsieur Myrandhal, you and I are now collaborators. My opinion is that we should set to work as soon as possible."

"That's necessary," the engineer relied, becoming pensive. "It's in three months—which is to say, in the second fortnight of August—that the planet Mars will be in the proximity most favorable to our attempt.[12] Unless we put off the realization to an indeterminate and distant epoch, we need to be ready in three months."

Rapidly, Serge Myrandhal brought his new protector up to date with the situation. He told him about the generous decision made by the directors of the Metal Syndicate and the commission furnished by the *Herald*, whose proprietor had put an entire laboratory at his disposal.

The Maharajah listened with extreme attention, and refrained from saying that he already knew most of the details in question.

Without surrendering his secret, the engineer added a few technical explanations regarding his engine-amplifier and the vehicle in which he intended to travel.

"But that's not all you need to succeed," said the Rajah, not without a perfidious hidden agenda. "It's necessary that your discovery isn't stolen from you at the last moment; it would be as well to take minute precautions, and to be extremely suspicious."

"Don't worry—all imaginable precautions have been taken, or will be when the time comes. The model you saw at the Athenaeum is guarded night and day by a squad of policemen, watched themselves by two incorruptible detectives. The Norton villa is surrounded by good walls that are in the process of being further reinforced, and the workshop in

---

[12] Mars and Earth were in conjunction on 22 August 1908, and would not be again until 27 September 1910.

which I shall manufacture certain components personally is a basement inaccessible to indiscreet gazes.

"The components of the apparatus for which I shall be forced to have recourse to industry will each be cast by a different company—one piece, for example, by Krupp, another by Creusot, a third in England, at Maxim's, a fourth at Carnegie's, and so on. I alone, which one carefully-chosen assistant, will carry out the final assembly. To complete the precaution, components that do not respond to any need, items of pure fantasy will also be ordered here and there, to deflect curiosity and espionage. I've thought of everything, you see."

The Rajah remained silent for a few seconds. If he had thought momentarily that the engineer might reveal his secret at the outset, he had been mistaken, but he did not let anything show. His manner conserved the same affability and sovereign cordiality.

"How long will the construction of the apparatus take?" he asked

"About a month. As for the voyage from here to the monastery of Almowrat, I don't have a very exact idea of that."

"That's the first thing we'll have to examine together," murmured the Rajah, counting on his meager fingers. "A week to get from New York to San Francisco. That's not too much, with the bulky material that will be accompanying us, and over which we'll have to stand guard ourselves."

"Let's say a week, then. From San Francisco to Calcutta, even by chartering a special steamer, will require a fortnight."

"Even more, as we have every interest in navigating with extreme prudence. A shipwreck or serious damage to your apparatus would annihilate all your hopes. From Calcutta to the city of Karputhala, the capital of my realm, is four full days by rail. This is perhaps the first time I've rejoiced about having allowed the English to link my capital to the railway network of the Indian peninsula.

"It's from Karputhala to the monastery of Almowrat that the transportation will be most difficult and awkward. No more railway, and hardly any roads. Fortunately, we have elephants, the most practical means of locomotion in that region. I estimate that it will take at last a week to cross those fifty leagues in mountainous country, still covered in large part by virgin forests of cedar, fir, Aleppo pine and ilex."

"That's a total of thirty-six days. That's a long time, for the final assembly, preparation and calibration, and the trials, will require a month, if not more, and we're running the risk of being caught short. It's at the last moment, most of all, that we need to have plenty of time, not to be rushed, if we want to succeed in our difficult enterprise. So, the slightest negligence, the slightest omission, might have terrible consequences..."

"I agree, Monsieur Myrandhal," the Rajah interjected. "So let's try to gain a week or ten days on the approximate figures we've just established. Don't forget that in Karputhala you'll be my guests—which is to say, the Maharajah's guests—and that I possess absolute sovereignty over all my subjects there. You'll see what I'll be able to do to accelerate the transportation. But while I think about it, I forgot to ask you what the weight of the apparatus will be."

"About a hundred tons, but it can all be dismantled, and hence easily transportable."

"It's not as much weight as I'd anticipated. In that case, we'll doubtless gain some time. I'll occupy myself immediately with the organization of all that. I'll leave today—tomorrow at the latest."

"Already!" murmured the engineer, a little surprised.

"Yes," said the old prince, smiling. "In a week's time I ought to have reached my realm. I confess to you, in all sincerity, that it's solely because of you and your experiments that I've prolonged my stay in New York. In your own interest, however, in order to prepare the way, I need to leave as quickly as possible."

Myrandhal thanked his protector warmly, knowing him to be as interested in science as only princes can be, when they wish to dabble in it.

It was agreed that the engineer would embark for India and reach Karputhala with the shortest possible delay.

The young man had already stood up to take his leave when the Rajah, taking his hand in his own mummy-like hands, placed a ring ornamented with a beautiful diamond on one of his fingers. "You know, *Monsieur l'ingénieur*," he said, with his most gracious smile, "that India is the land of precious stones par excellence. I possess in my treasury a collection of these brilliant pebbles that is said to be incomparable. You will permit me, I hope, to give you this ring in memory of your visit and the pleasure I have had in conversing with you."

Once again, Serge Myrandhal thanked the man he regarded as the most loyal of friends and the most magnificent of monarchs, and bade him farewell. He was guided from room to room by the servants who had introduced him, with all the minutiae of Oriental ceremony.

His heart was afloat in joy. In accordance with a very apt popular saying, he felt as light as a bird, almost drunk on the unexpected good fortune that seemed to be attached to his enterprise.

The door-curtain had scarcely closed behind him when Prince Djalor came in through the other door. He was immediately struck by the expression of diabolical satisfaction radiating from the old prince's features.

Personally, he was dejected and consternated. "I chanced to hear the last few words of your conversation," he said. "We're leaving, then?"

"You misheard," the old man replied, cheerfully.

"What do you mean?"

"I said that I was leaving—me, which is quite different. I didn't mention you. I can see that you're already in despair at the thought of quitting the beautiful Miss Carpenter, but you can be reassured on that point. I'm not taking you with me. You can stay here, to watch over your interests and mine. You'll come to join me at the same time as the engineer, with whom my plans are proceeding admirably. Until then, and while making yourself useful, you'll have the leisure to pay court."

"Father!" stammered the Prince, dazed with gratitude—and he kissed the old man's hand, in the Indian manner.

At the moment, Djalor was giving no thought to the perfidious and criminal aspects of his father's plans. He only saw the pleasure of remaining near his dear Annabella. In order to win her, he was ready to accept tasks entirely contrary to his honest and gentlemanly character, and his Asiatic princely indolence. Carried away by passion, he did not reflect. He did not even perceive that he had just involved himself in a complicated scheme from which he might not be able to disengage himself subsequently.

For the moment, he was entirely given over to his dreams of happiness and the magical vision of Annabella Carpenter.

VII. In the American Style

On emerging from the Rajah's villa Serge Myrandhal headed toward the center of the town, where he had noticed an electric car station. He had almost got there when he heard an unusual rumor of voices behind him. The explanation did not take long to become clear.

"It's him!" cried one.

"Who?"

"The famous Frenchman, of course, who's going to travel to the planets."

"Serge Myrandhal!"

"Where is he?"

"Are you sure?"

"I was at the Athenaeum."

"Hurrah for Serge Myrandhal!"

"Myrandhal forever!"

Myrandhal knew from experience how rough Yankee enthusiasm could be, so he hastened to leap into a passing electric cab.

Half an hour later he got out in front of the door of Norton Cottage, the property placed at his disposal by the proprietor of the *Herald*.

The engineer was radiant. He could not remember a day as happy in his entire life. Everything was going as he desired. He had found the psychic energy that he had so far lacked; at the same time he had won the amity of a Prince, an Asiatic autocrat, who was putting his sovereign power at his service. Furthermore, he had a rendezvous with Annabella that very evening.

Before going through the gate, the engineer could not help casting a glance over the works with which an entire army of laborers was occupied, and which were advancing with prodigious velocity.

A mere day earlier one entire side of the property had only been enclosed by an acacia hedge, and in its place a wall was emerging from the ground that was already a foot high. Stimulated by the exorbitant wage of ten dollars a day, the workmen were laying bricks with fantastic rapidity. As soon as a section of wall was finished, another crew, with the aid of huge trowels, coated it externally with bituminous cement that dried almost as soon as it was in place.

In addition, on the top of the existing walls, a third crew—this time composed of metal-workers armed with a powerful acetylene torch were setting in place a metal grid whose stout bars, barbed at the bottom and the top, ought to defy any attempt to climb them.

Serge Myrandhal was wonderstruck. He could see that improvised construction rising up visibly, under the pressure of dollars. He had never had such a clear and exact idea of the power of American activity. Evidently, the Yankees, spurred by the spirit of competition, had resolved to dazzle the man who had astonished them first.

All round the cottage a host of idlers, whose patience was inexhaustible, were watching the also emerge from the ground with profound attention. They were held back by a cordon of policemen who would not let anyone approach. The precaution was not superfluous. In the crowd, a hundred reporters, notebooks in hand and pencils behind the ear, were stirring, jotting down everything they saw or heard. Others were brandishing their kodaks and taking snap after snap. The ensemble exhibited the animation of a Babelesque hive.

As the engineer cut through the crowd with the aid of two policemen, he thought he recognized therein two of the Germans who had raised such coarse and maladroit opposition to him at the Athenaeum. Evidently, the prodigious discovery was being watched, attracting the espionage of all the great industrialists of the Old and New Worlds.

The engineer smiled. His invention was one that was almost impossible to happen upon by chance.

He went through the gate and into the narrow grounds that surrounded the cottage, where detectives were patrolling gravely, accompanied by mastiffs with terrible jaws, which made the ideal guard dogs.

The engineer headed directly for the laboratory situated in the basement of the cottage. There too an almost ferocious activity reigned—the kind of activity that only the divine dollar can stimulate to the point of exasperation.

In the vast room, entirely lined with porcelain tiles, a squad of highly-skilled metal-workers was hastily connecting up the stout copper cables that terminated in a powerful electric furnace. A forge and various machines—tools adequate for the manufacture of metallic components of medium dimensions—were already in place, with crucibles, hammers, cupolas and all the indispensable equipment. Employees of Steever & Co., suppliers of chemical products, were noisily unpacking crates and arranging bottles and jars on the shelves of glass-fronted cupboards.

It was a rapid, almost instantaneous visible change of décor.

Dusk was falling.

Delighted by what he saw, and having given his instructions and darted an expert eye over everything, Myrandhal climbed the stairs going up to his bedroom.

When he got there he was blinded by a dazzling glare. Fifty electric bulbs had just been switched on in the grounds, illuminating the various worksites, where the labor would continue until dawn. New crews were arriving to replace those who had finished their shift.

Serge noticed, among others, a whole squad of gardeners and nurserymen, graduates of the New Jersey College of Horticulture, carrying flowers and green plants in pots, including saplings, already considerable in size, with which they set about feverishly establishing patterns, beds and lawns.

Captivating as the spectacle was, the young man, who had not stopped thinking about the anticipated visit for a moment, soon moved away from the window and took out his watch.

"Just time to change into something appropriate," he murmured. "Annabella will be here in a quarter of an hour."

He went into the dressing-room, to which a bathroom was adjacent, equipped with the latest improvements in hydrotherapy. He emerged again shortly afterwards, showered and shaved, clad in an elegant smoking jacket.

To moderate his impatience he spent a minute running though the voluminous correspondence piled up on his desk.

The bell at the main gate rang. A minute later, the well-trained servant that Norton Bennett had placed at his disposal brought in a visiting card inscribed: *Annabella Carpenter. Reporter, New York* Herald.

VIII. *"To be Continued on Mars..."*

It was the first time the American woman had come to the young man's home.

The interview arranged at the Athenaeum—which, our readers will remember, was supposed to take place at the Atlantic Hotel—had not happened.

In fact, the day after the famous lecture, the proprietor of the *Herald*, adroitly stimulated by Annabella, whose article attracted a great deal of attention, had precipitated himself into Serge Myrandhal's room while the latter was only half-awake and taken him away in his automobile, with all his luggage, and had installed him half an hour later at Norton Cottage, immediately setting in train its transformation in view of its new destination.

The journalist and the engineer had met before, either at the *Herald* or at the home of their common patron Norton Bennett, but this would be the first time that they young couple had found themselves alone with one another, and the thought of that *tête-à-tête* filled the Frenchman's heart with a tender emotion.

"Send her in," he ordered—then changed his mind. "No! One moment. I'll go to her."

He ran out. He arrived at the door in time to greet Miss Carpenter, who had just got out of a forty-horsepower vehicle with copper trim.

"Monsieur Myrandhal," she began, in a teasing tone, "you thought that I wouldn't dare to face the lion in his lair, but here I am. I've even chosen dusk—a particularly dangerous time, if we can believe French novels. But duty before all, and I need more information from you regarding the great invention. I used up the last lot in yesterday's article, and our readers, ever more avid and insatiable, expect their daily fodder. For that reason, I had to take the risk..." She paraded an amused glance around, and concluded: "Fortunately, I see that there are considerable police forces here. That's reassuring."

At these words, a shadow of melancholy had passed over Serge Myrandhal's face; he had been hoping for something else.

Miss Carpenter noticed that, and held out her hand to him in a spontaneous gesture. "Come on," she said. "You're not going to sulk over a ridiculous joke. It's easy to see, Monsieur Inventor, that you've never flirted—and I congratulate you for it. Personally, I'm the least flirtatious of American women, but I'm a tease—a terrible tease. Life will doubtless punish me for it, but what do you expect? I've been so spoiled until recently, that my faults have only increased and run wild. You must think, with good reason, that I'm a detestable woman?"

"Oh!" exclaimed the Frenchman, awkwardly. "You know that's not so, Miss Anna...you're an exquisite adorable woman!"

While conversing, the young couple had moved toward the house that served as Serge Myrandhal's lodgings, but as they were about to cross the threshold the young woman paused involuntarily. For the first time, in spite of her self-confidence and in spite of her ironic opening, perhaps uniquely designed to conceal her anxiety, the American hesitated. She had been brought up in the liberal Yankee fashion, accustomed to pay little heed to obsolete prejudices and conventions, but she suddenly experienced an insurmountable embarrassment at the idea of going inside the dwelling in the engineer's company.

With the divine instinct of love, she had understood that Serge Myrandhal was in love with her, and she had sworn to herself that she would never have any other husband. That no doubt, was the source of the strange emotion by which she was agitated.

At that moment, however, one of the detectives patrolling the grounds approached the engineer and Annabella, not without having taken the precaution of typing the redoubtable mastiff he had been holding on a leash to a plane-tree.

"What is it?" Myrandhal asked, impatiently.

"I believe, sir," the detective replied, in the calm tone particular to Yankee policemen, "that it's my duty to warn you. You can do as you please, but the locality is swarming with spies of all nationalities. They want to have your secret at any price. Be sure of your guards. I wouldn't be surprised if an attempt is made tonight to get into the cottage."

"Thank you," Myrandhal murmured. "I'll be doubly vigilant."

He was about to go on when another interruption arrived. This time it was a policeman, one of those charged with guarding the gate. His arm was in a sling, and a trickle of blood was running from his hand, which was wrapped in a handkerchief.

"What's that?" exclaimed Myrandhal. "You've been wounded?"

"Yes sir, but it's not much—a thrust from a stiletto in the flesh of the hand. It was in trying to arrest a malefactor, an urchin not much taller than my boot. Can you imagine that the scoundrel was in the process of sawing through one of your beautiful new bars? I'd grabbed him in the act, and didn't think I had anything to fear from the runt, but the kid suddenly shook himself free and scarpered, not without sticking me first. Oh, the little rogue! The most annoying thing is that we haven't caught him. He had accomplices who helped him get away."

"It doesn't matter," said Myrandhal. "You've done your best, and I thank you." At the same time, he slipped a bank-note into the policeman's good hand; the latter caused it to disappear adroitly.

"And now," said Miss Carpenter, smiling, "the most urgent thing is to bandage your wound. I'll do that. Have you a first aid kit, Monsieur Myrandhal?"

"Yes—in my study."

"Well, lead the way."

Ten minutes later, the detective and his subordinate, whose hand Annabella had bandaged with professional dexterity, withdrew, proffering lavish thanks.

Serge and Annabella scarcely perceived that they were now alone in the study. The incident, in giving them a diversion from other thoughts, had had the advantage of putting them perfectly at ease with one another. Now they were talking with the utmost cordiality, with the camaraderie full of frankness and gaiety that is so easily established, in America, between young men and women.

Annabella had taken out her propelling pencil.

"Now, Monsieur Serge Myrandhal," she said, "I have to acquit the duties of my profession. I'm going to interrogate you..."

"At your orders...and you've arrived at just the right moment. I have some big news to give you..."

And in a single rush he told her about his meeting with the Rajah and the extraordinary proposal the latter had put to him.

"Needless to say," he concluded, "I accepted. You can imagine with what joy and what enthusiastic gratitude. But there's one person to whom I owe an even greater gratitude—that's you, Miss Annabella."

"You're exaggerating my small role," the young woman murmured, smiling.

"No!" Myrandhal exclaimed, forcefully. "No, it's you to whom I owe all my good fortune. Your smile, your grace—that's the charm, the magic spell that has opened all doors to me. Without you, without your notoriety, without your sensational articles, which have stirred up the public, raised Yankee enthusiasm to white heat and forced your editor's hand, so to speak, I would never have obtained the precious collaboration I now have.

"And since, for the first time since these definitive events, we find ourselves alone, let me lay at your feet the tribute of my infinite gratitude. You have been more than a help to me, more than a collaborator: a veritable associate.

You have been—and, I hope, will continue to be—my Lucky Star!

"Henceforth, thanks to you, I'm sure of success, sure that, in a matter of weeks—mere days—I'll reach the mysterious planet that we're about to see lighting up in the Orient."

"What a prodigious dream!" exclaimed the young woman, adroitly deflecting the conversation. "And to think that the dream will soon be a reality—in a matter of days, as you say. You have no doubts, then? You're entirely confident?"

"Totally, absolutely confident," Serge Myrandhal replied. "A confidence such that if I had beside me a dear individual, a sister or a brother..."

"You'd offer to take them with you?" said Miss Carpenter sharply, her beautiful face illuminating suddenly.

"No, Miss Anna," Serge replied, calmly. "Great as my chances are, that would be too grave a matter for me to take the initiative. But if that person, dearer to me that my own life, were, by virtue of her anterior studies, to decide for herself in full knowledge of the circumstances...if, after mature reflection, she asked to accompany me, I would accept without any hesitation, any remorse..."

Before the sentence was finished, the reporter had turned her head away, her soul full of a delightful anguish. She had immediately understood that the "dear individual" in question, able to decide in a full knowledge of the circumstances, to whom the inventor was referring, was her. And that indirect invitation, the idea of accompanying the man she loved on that prodigious voyage, made her amorous heart, fond of adventures, beat in the most delightful fashion.

At that moment, she was studying her companion between half-closed eyelids; and Serge Myrandhal, with his handsome face to which genius added its flame, appeared to her to be more handsome than any of the heroes of history or legend: more handsome, in spite of his unromantic costume, than Christopher Columbus standing on the deck of his caravel, or Lohengrin towed by his swan...more handsome than Prometheus, the vanquisher of gods!

She collected herself momentarily, and then, with a slightly mocking accent of coquetry, belied by her gaze, she said: "*Monsieur l'ingénieur*, it seems to me that we're straying from our subject. Let's not forget that I'm a reporter on a mission. As I told you when I came in, the *Herald*'s readers, ever more numerous since your lecture doubled our print run, are expecting their daily pittance.

"It's a matter, if not for you, who have nothing more to desire, but for me, who might never have such an opportunity again, to maintain the vogue on which my future as an independent woman depends. This evening, I propose to announce your association with Indraghava—which, unfortunately, is taking you away, stealing you from young America!" The young woman pouted adorably, in a coquettish fashion, and continued: "As an American, I'm jealous, and I warn you that my dear compatriots are going to murmur. They had hoped that it would be from New York that you would launch yourself toward the stars. To appease them, to create a diversion, I'll talk to them about our preparations for your imminent departure. It would be useful if I could fix an approximate date. That's why I'm asking you: when do you expect to get under way?"

"For India?" asked Serge, smiling, "or for Mars?"

"For India, to begin with."

"In a month, or thereabouts—which is to say, in mid-June. If things continue to progress as they've begun, in the American fashion, all the apparatus ordered from various factories, on which people are working feverishly, will be ready three weeks from now. A week should suffice for me to assemble and adjust them, and carry out a preliminary trial.

"For my part, I'll employ that time in producing certain components that constitute the delicate and secret part of the invention—components that only I can manufacture. So, announce boldly that in a month's time, everything will be ready, and that on the fifteenth of June at the latest, we shall take the train to San Francisco."

"Good!" the young woman replied. "The Transcontinental Railway—in which I still have a few shares, left over from the crash—will bank colossal receipts, thanks to you. Similarly the Trans-Pacific Company, which operates the service between San Francisco and Calcutta. I'm sure that thousands of tourists will invade India in your wake."

"What's the point, since they won't see anything? Apart from two or three privileged friends, the list of whom I shall have to submit to the Maharajah in advance, no one will be admitted into the monastery. The experiment must remain secret. That's one of the conditions imposed by my all-powerful collaborator, and I didn't put up any argument. So, if you think it appropriate warn your compatriots..."

"God forbid!" the young woman cried. "It's obvious, Monsieur Scientist, that you've never been a journalist or a novelist, like your humble servant and admirer. Otherwise, you wouldn't suppress so unceremoniously the principal, if not the only, interesting link retaining our readers.

"But now let's talk about the other departure—the great departure for the stars! Just now you mentioned a few weeks. I didn't think things would move so fast. You must be in a great hurry to leave us!" Miss Carpenter raised her eyes to look at her interlocutor tenderly as she concluded.

"It's necessary!" Myrandhal replied, in a profound voice. "As you know, you who read the heavens like an open book, in a few weeks the planet Mars will be in an eminently propitious situation, which won't recur very soon. That will last until the fifteenth of August, the twentieth at the most. It's necessary that I bid adieu to the Earth before that deadline.

"Then again, I have another reason, just as pressing, which incites me to make haste. You know the Rajah, since you've interviewed him. You've doubtless been struck by his truly alarming state of decrepitude. Remember that the old man in question, the moribund, might die at any moment, and everything would be compromised."

"I don't think there's any danger of that," Miss Carpenter replied, slowly, as if weighing her words carefully. "Either

I'm much mistaken, or there's a vitality in that shriveled body that will surprise us all. What struck me most of all is the extraordinary vivacity in his eyes—that sharp, troubling gaze. Were it not for the fear of declining in your esteem, of passing for a nervous girl, I'd almost say that the old man frightened me..."

The Frenchman smiled indulgently. "That's the first impression I had, too, but it dissipated quickly before my host's amiable manner. As for the precariousness of his health, it's Indraghava who mentioned it first and gave me that further reason for hastening our departure for India—so insistently that we divided up the remaining time without further ado: one month for the construction of the machine, as I said at the beginning; one month for the journey from here to Karputhala; one month for the ascent to the monastery and the final preparations. That brings us to the beginning of August, which is the crucial time.

"That's when Mars passes the meridian at midnight: the fatal hour, the signal for the great *forward ho!* My heart shivers at the thought…and it seems now that time is passing very quickly…too quickly..." Serge hesitated, as if fearful of saying too much, and then went on, almost immediately: "My dear collaborator, I dare to hope that until that fateful day you'll continue to lend me your precious concourse…that you'll come with us to the monastery."

"That's a promise!" said the American, impetuously. Then, taking hold of herself, she continued: "Do you imagine that I'd leave the glory of such sensational reportage to anyone else?"

She rose to her feet then. "Now, Monsieur Myrandhal, you're going to accompany me to my carriage. It's getting late and I have a long article to write."

"You're going already?" the engineer murmured.

"I must."

"So be it. But before you go, at least let me show you how the various enterprises are progressing. That's part of your job—isn't it necessary for you to inform the public and your employer as to the fashion in which his orders are being executed?"

"Well, all right," the young woman said, taking the Frenchman's arm. "Let's make the proprietor's tour."

The two young people went out.

Night was falling gradually in the garden, drowned by a violet mist. The first stars were lighting up in the firmament. Here and there, enormous electric globes were sizzling, illuminating the work-sites, where the labor was still continuing. Workmen were coming and going, attentive and mute, but neither Myrandhal nor Miss Carpenter, absorbed by other thoughts, seemed to be paying any heed to that hive of activity.

Instinctively, they had steered away from the light and the noise, toward a small clump of parasol pines planted at the back of the garden. They moved forward, invaded by a strange anguish, a delightful disturbance, which they did not have the courage to break through. They were silent, fearful of disturbing the divine silence in which their entire souls were in communication with words.

Suddenly, Annabella, feeling Serge's arm trembling under hers, pulled away gently and let herself fall on to a stone bench nearby. "I'm a little tired," she murmured, very softly.

As Serge, very pale, sat down beside her, she suddenly extended her arm toward the Orient. "Oh!" she exclaimed, delightedly, almost ecstatically. "There's Mars, there's the star…the star that is showing you the way!"

Serge had raised his head immediately, and both of them, their faces radiant and transfigured, contemplated the golden planet, which seemed to be giving them a sign, summoning them across the sidereal immensity.

There was a long silence, during which the lovers could hear their two hearts beating in unison. Then, suddenly, Serge's pale forehead slumped, while a hoarse and profound sigh, almost a sob, was exhaled from his bosom.

Immediately, Annabella put her white hand on the young man's tremulous shoulder. "What's wrong, Monsieur Myrandhal," she stammered. "What are you thinking about?"

"I'm thinking," the engineer murmured, in a lugubrious voice, "that in a few weeks, I'll be far away from you, lost in the heavens...that I might not see you again...ever...*nevermore!* I was so happy yesterday...why have you come?"

That dolorous voice, the secret that had suddenly escaped, in a few halting words, from that heart swollen with love, moved Annabella to the deepest fibers of her being. Her heart raced, and a vivid incarnadine colored her cheeks.

"Calm down, my friend," she began, in a hesitant voice.

"No," Serge replied, somberly, almost grimly. "No, Miss Anna, it's necessary that I speak." in a supplicant tone he continued: "Listen to me, Mademoiselle, I beg you. Don't interrupt, or I'll never, never have the courage to confess the secret that's crushing me! Listen to me...and help me...otherwise, I'll never dare to tell you that I love you...that I love you madly."

"My friend..." Annabella tried to begin.

"No, don't interrupt" Myrandhal repeated. "Don't disturb me...or I'll no longer have the strength to finish. You can reply afterwards, and I accept in advance your sentence of life or death. Remember that I'm not a sociable man. Apart from the time devoted to indispensable sports, I've lived my life buried in laboratories. I don't know how to talk to women, and this is the first time I've talked to a young woman, a real young woman...hence my religious, sacred disturbance on the threshold of mystery, before the great Isis...

"Oh, poor scientist that I am, I thought I knew nature and life. For years, I've studied the celestial infinity, and I was ignorant of the other, the one contained in each of your glances, in the blink of your luminous eyelashes. But I feel now that I would no longer be able to live without you...that it's necessary, here or on that distant earth shining in the Orient, that I have you by my side—or else I'll die.

"Miss Anna, will you be my wife?"

After that last sentence, uttered in a breathless voice, Myrandhal straightened up. Now that he had spoken, and unburdened his heart, overflowing with love, he dared to look his destiny in the face. Suddenly, his convulsed features relaxed, and an expression of ineffable bliss illuminated his face.

Annabella, her eyes moist, smiled, and extended her arms to him in an adorable gesture. "My friend," she said, "this is my response..."

Serge had seized the American woman's trembling fingers, and was covering them with kisses.

"Finally," he murmured, "I can breathe! How small a thing is a man, and what magic there is in love! I was dying just now, and one word from you has sufficed to bring me back to life. Once again, I've recovered my zest for life and my work...the work that will no longer separate us, since..." The Frenchman hesitated.

"Since I'm going with you!" cried the young woman, with juvenile enthusiasm.

"I daren't ask it of you..."

"But yes! It's entirely understood! Are you unaware, my husband, that a wife ought to accompany her husband everywhere? Or is it, perchance that you're thinking of abandoning me...already! So it's decided, irrevocably. As soon as our marriage is consecrated, I go with you. A honeymoon trip to Mars! That won't be banal!"

And as, at that explosion of child-like joy, a shadow passed over Myrandhal's face, Miss Carpenter rose to her feet. "Come on, Monsieur Scientist," she said, gaily. "Don't be jealous. The adventure enchants me—certainly, the prodigious voyage is well designed to tempt an American, but what pleases me even more is my traveling companion. That's a declaration, it seems to me! And on that note, I must run..."

The American woman was already moving away toward the gate, laughing tremulously.

Two minutes later, Myrandhal helped her into her car, and how his lips lingered over his fiancée's hand!

"Come on," said the young woman, wagging her finger at him. "Finish, Monsieur Scientist. To be continued in the next issue, as the feuilletonists say. Or, rather, no...to be continued on Mars...!"

IX. Pickman

Scarcely had Miss Carpenter gone than the detective responsible for the security of Noton Cottage, whom we have already seen at work, appeared before Serge Myrandhal.

"Monsieur Engineer," he said, pointing toward the study window overlooking the garden, "you have a visitor."

The Frenchman, still under the spell of his conversation with his fiancée, was dreaming, with his elbows on the desk. He could not suppress a gesture of annoyance.

"A visitor?" he said. "But I'm not expecting anyone. I don't understand why you let him in. The orders don't permit any exceptions..."

"Pardon me," stammered the agent, who, to boost his audacity, was fingering in his pocket the large tip that had just been surreptitiously offered to him. "Pardon me, Monsieur Myrandhal, but the gentleman who asked to be let in is a very rich man...I mean, very influential, an important person. That's why I didn't think I should turn him away. Besides which, it would have been a waste of time. When one thrown him out of the door, that one, he comes in by the window, or else the chimney. You can guess who I mean—the Eccentric...the Eccentric, in the flesh."

"The Eccentric..." said Serge distractedly, his thoughts elsewhere. "What's that you're saying, Mr. Stick? Who's he?"

"The Englishman—you know! The one who was perched on the chandelier at the Athenaeum. The millionaire fantasist, the Baronet, Sir Washington Pickman." And the detective, wanting to prove that he was a polyglot capable of making a pun in French, added with a sly smile. "Pickman...the *pique* man...as you can see from here."

Serge looked in the direction indicated, and saw a man, a tall long-legged fellow marching placidly back and forth along a path. It was the Eccentric, wearing his invariable Alpinist's costume: leather leggings, knee-length trousers, a reefer-jacket with countless pockets and an alpenstock.

"You see," the detective continued, ironically, "that our Eccentric has gone to some trouble for you. He's renounced his helmet and put on a bowler hat, which doesn't suit him. As for the alpenstock—the *pique*, as I said—don't be surprised to see it in his hand. The Englishman is never apart from it. Every day, that mania gets him stopped at the doors of theaters, churches, even some restaurants, and there are indescribable scenes over that pikestaff. It's a fetish, according to rumor.

"In the course of numerous perilous ascents, that bit of wood has saved its master's life on several occasions, it's said—but he'll tell you that himself. I'll go fetch him, shall I, sir?"

Myrandhal had gradually relaxed. He smiled, interested by these details and by the memory of the scene at the Athenaeum—a scene that had certainly caused him a terrible emotion, but which, by way of compensation, had multiplied his triumph tenfold.

On the other hand, distracted as he was, his natural intelligence had immediately divined the secret motive for the agent's zeal.

"Well, go on," he ended up saying, "if you must."

Less than two minutes later, Pickman made his entrance, alpenstock in hand. He nodded his head curtly by way of a salute, stretched himself out unceremoniously in the rocking chair that Serge indicated to him, set his long staff horizontally upon his lap, and then, in a voice devoid of inflection—a nasal voice like that of phonograph, which lent itself to facile mockery—he started speaking in French with a strong English accent..

"I beg you to excuse me, sir, not for forcing my way in— I had no alternative—but for approaching you without having been formally introduced. Alas, I couldn't find anyone to do that for me. My friend Prince Djalor, on whom I was counting, told me to go to the Devil, as you say in France—but he'll pay for that. I'm related to the Viceroy of India, and I'll get my

94

own back once out there. I can assure you, believe me, that the saffron-faced little fop will pay. I swear by John Bull!"

The Eccentric twirled his staff nervously. "And Miss Carpenter!" he said, suddenly. "Another one who let me down! She promised to bring us together, and then changed her mind at the last minute. She laughed in my face—and the worst of it is that I can't hold it against her. I'd forgive the little minx anything...she's like my protégée, or my ward, at least...I knew her father well, and I was to have been her god-father, but God damn it, I was on the other side of the world at the time, lost on the Antarctic ice-sheet. I'd wagered that I could climb Erebus, the famous polar volcano. Won the bet, of course—that's my game, climbing, and what I say, I do, al-ways! Doesn't affect the fact that I broke my promise—so, you understand, one has obligations...

"Let's understand one another; it's the other way around, the opposite that happened. One isn't used to contradiction, and it makes me angry. So, when the crash happened, I tried save her father, and he flew into a temper. A self made man, he doesn't accept help. Then I fell back on my god-daughter, I learned that she was working for the *Herald*, and I was humil-iated, heart-broken. Can you imagine? A beautiful young girl, well-educated, one of the queens of Fifth Avenue, the ward of Washington Pickman—an old madman, but who has a heart—doing a pauper's job! I hastened to write to her immediately, to put myself at her service. I offered her a dowry, so she could marry anyone she wished...her Prince, young Djalor, or anyone else..."

At that name, Serge had pricked up his ears. "Is she in love with him?" he asked, his expression troubled. "I mean...*was* she in love with him?"

The Eccentric shrugged his shoulders. "No," he said. "You're insane...pardon me, you're in error...that's it. Her, love that fop with painted fingernails! You don't know her. She's an American, a virile person. Too effeminate for her, the Hindu. Oh, she was flattered by his suit, obviously. She might be an American, and money doesn't turn her head, but she's a woman…but as for what you suggest, no, don't make me laugh!

"Where was I? It's your ludicrous question that made me lose my thread. I was explaining to you that I'd sent a letter to Miss Anna, in which, as a last resort, I offered to marry her. I'm a good catch, you know! A hundred thousand pounds a year. And that was a sacrifice—for me, I mean. I love my ward, but not in that way, you understand? And then, a globe-trotter, always on the road, doesn't marry…or, to put it better, I'm already married. Look, here's my wife!"

The Englishman, gradually becoming excited, held up his alpenstock.

"This cane, you see—that's my wife. Perfect! I put her under my arm, and she goes with me everywhere, as a good wife should. She sustains me in the difficult passages. If an unsafe glacier presents itself, or a shaky rock, or a suspect snow-bridge, I put out my cane to sound it. I interrogate her, and she replies—all right! Apart from that, she never says a word. She's a model wife.

"Because, you see, I'm like Socrates, myself. The babble of women—Anna excepted, of course—their henhouse cluck-ing, gets on my nerves. Add that my cane, the one you see here, has saved my life. So, we're never apart. We've slept together in the snows of the pole, and the torrid sands of the Sudan. We'll sleep together under the grass of Kentucky—that's my parish in Essex. All that's to explain to you that I've come with…" Abruptly, the Englishman passed his hand over his brow. "Damn!" he said. "There I go, losing track again. Excuse me, sir, I'm not in the habit of getting confused in my speech…

"Oh yes! So, I was saying that I'd offered to rescue my ward in that fashion, but she received me even more poorly. Papa had been content to look at me with his American eye, but with the little one, it was another song entirely. You'll never guess, sir, what she said to me in reply."

"What did she say to you in reply?" asked Serge, who as decidedly intrigued by the conversation.

"Nothing at all! She didn't reply at all. She simply sent me her seconds—two friends from the Ladies' Club! The little scatterbrain claimed that I'd insulted her gravely and wanted to kill me without further ado. And she would have done it, I can assure you...

"You're laughing. There's no reason for that. You don't seem to be aware that Annabella can handle a foil and a pistol like a master. So much so that I made my apologies. I'm sixty years old, so you ought to understand...and since then, I, who've always loved and adored my god-daughter—who have no one but her in the world—have been literally mad! I'm talking about her to you, as I talk to everyone, like an old fool.

"Oh, sir, what a brave and honest girl! What a noble heart and soul! She really is her father's daughter. She only lacks one thing, and that's being English!"

Serge Myrandhal drank in these words.

The Eccentric, who was nothing less than an "old fool," and who, beneath a somewhat rebarbative exterior, hid a great finesse, had immediately, and at the first stroke, been able to find the way to Serge Myrandhal's heart.

"Of course," Pickman continued, "my beautiful ward is a trifle stubborn, and quick to take offense...and in that regard, a piece of advice: you're paying court to her...yes, it's futile to deny it, you're paying court to the beautiful Annabella; the whole of New York is talking about it...well, be circumspect. Whoever rubs her up the wrong way gets stung, as you've seen. So, be prudent—if not, do you know what will happen one fine morning?"

"I can guess," said Serge, smiling. "Two envoys from the Ladies' Club."

"Exactly. Two seconds! And as you aren't her uncle, and aren't sixty years old, you'll have to go to the dueling-ground, if only out of gallantry. Three bullets in the chamber—those are the conditions of our chivalry. And once on the meadow— I mean, in the field—do you know what will happen?"

"No, but I have my suspicions."

"Not at all!" cried the Eccentric. "You're going to say that you'll apologize, or refuse…or that you'll fire into the air. You won't have time, Monsieur Frenchman. As soon as the *go* is pronounced, your pistol will be shot out of your hand! Then, disarmed as you are, you'll still have to face two more shots from your adversary, and it's the conclusion you can't guess.

"Coldly and calmly, at thirty paces, my terrible god-daughter will trim your moustache with bullets. One to the right, *zim!* One to the left, *vifft!* You'll hear them whistle. After which, Monsieur Conqueror of the Stars, dishonored and shaven, there'll be nothing left for you to do but take the first steamer back to France!"

Having said that, Pickman uttered a shrill laugh, like the cry of a corncrake, with which the Frenchman joined in with the best will in the world.

"Thank you for warning me," Serge said, almost immediately, "but I don't suppose that it's purely for that reason that you're here. It still remains for me to discover to what I owe the honor of your visit."

"The thing is," the Eccentric replied, having resumed his customary impassivity, "that my god-daughter, who has been interested in astronomy since early childhood, is enthusiastic about your project, and even, a little, about you…yes! One can say that. She's no longer merely dreaming, under the pretext of reportage, of accompanying you to old Indraghava's monastery…but further still, perhaps…all the way to Mars!"

"Did she tell you that?" asked Serge, sharply.

"Well, no!" exclaimed the Englishman. "But I guessed it, by Jove! I'm an old fool, and I've never had a child, but all the same, I can read the heart of a girl I love. Oh, believe me, she's burning, *dying*, with the desire to go with you. It's obviously not her father who'll stop her—another eccentric, old Allan, a cold hothead immune to astonishment, who doesn't suspect a thing, and has as much idea about his daughter as a trout about an orange. You'll have some idea when I tell you that, compared to him, I'm practically a sage. Don't laugh—it's the truth.

98

"Look, I can hear the dialogue between the daughter and the father as if they were here.

"'I need to leave you, Papa.'

"'All right, dear. Where are you going?'

"'Mars.'

"'All right then. Are you coming back'

"'I hope so.'

"'Good. Bring me back a stone for my collection. I don't have one.'

"Anna has doubtless told you that her father collects aeroliths—'moonstones,' as they were once called."

The baronet made a grand gesture, and, with comical explosiveness, said: "There's a screw loose in that family, I tell you! So what's clear is that it's not the father—an old madman, in truth—who'll put up any opposition. Provided that decency is saved, that before you nestle down in our chariot, your celestial sleeping-car—where you'll be alone in somewhat close company, I expect—you've appeared before the minister of the parish, and provided that you also promise him a pebble for his display-case, Anna's father will give you *carte blanche*...

"There remains her guardian..."

"Ah!" murmured Serge, thus far delighted with what he had learned, but seeing the first obstacle rear up. "Miss Carpenter has a guardian, then?"

"Yes, sir."

"Who is...?"

"Me!" said the Englishman, touching his breast in an important manner. "Oh, I'm a guardian in much the same way as I'm a godfather, unofficially...nothing in writing. When Mrs. Carpenter died, and it was necessary to choose the family counselor whose functions were rightly mine..."

"I can guess," Serge interjected, smiling. "You'd gone to the Devil...lost on the Antarctic ice sheet."

"No," said the Englishman, "not exactly. I was at the other end of the world, at the North Pole. I'd wagered that I could cross a glacier that no human foot had tried before me.

If you ever pass that way, you'll find my name engraved on a stray block of stone, with the date. That's what I always do—you'll find my signature in the four corners of the globe...

"But to get back to my ward...as chance would have it, I was in New York when the crash happened, and before he left for the Far West, my friend Carpenter confided his daughter to me. He asked me to look after her."

"Which means," said Myrandhal, looking his interlocutor full in the face, "that you're presuming a duty, albeit rather vague, to thwart your pseudo-ward's plans."

"Me!" the Baronet protested. "Never! Agree, however, that I don't have the right to disinterest myself in her completely. Oh, I don't want to tyrannize her—I'd come unstuck. She's an *enfant terrible*, an indomitable young woman who can only be guided on condition that she doesn't feel the bridle...so, don't worry, and don't look at me sideways like that. My god-daughter is free, as free as air! She can go to the Himalayas, to Mars, and then to Saturn, further if you want. I only put one condition on that."

"Which is?" Serge asked, impetuously.

"That I go with you..."

Serge Myrandhal made no reply. He was thinking.

Here we are, he said to himself. *Here we are, at the goal of that long conversation. Pickman's telling the truth in representing himself as Anna's friend and protector. I remember now that she mentioned him to me, and their statements are concordant. So it's necessary for me to treat him carefully, to gain time. Later, we'll see...*

"Well?" said the Baronet, brusquely. "You're not saying anything? Is that a refusal?"

"I'm neither refusing nor consenting...yet. It depends on too many things. Your proposal has taken me somewhat by surprise. You have a way of gripping people by the throat. I need time to think."

"Take your time," said the Englishman, phlegmatically. We're not leaving for another month."

The engineer darted a sideways glance at his interlocutor, wondering whether he was bluffing or speaking seriously, but Pickman's physiognomy was impenetrable. Before going any further, Serge wanted to discuss the matter with his fiancée, and sought a means of getting rid of the Eccentric without offending him.

I believe I have it, he thought. Aloud, he said: "Assuming that Miss Carpenter does go with me, from the moment that she sets foot on the *Velox*—that's the name of our craft—Miss Anna will be the captain of my ship; she'll be in command. It's therefore up to her to decide whether..."

"I'm doomed!" cried the Englishman, getting to his feet abruptly. "Not daring to refuse me yourself, you're sending me to my god-daughter. You know my weakness for the child, who abuses it. You also know that, just as I can't do anything to oppose her, she won't do anything without consulting you. Well played, Monsieur Frenchman! But I'm tenacious, you know—as tenacious as an Englishman, like Wellington at Waterloo, and I won't resign the game as easily as that. I have another proposition to put to you, and this time, I'll put my cards on the table.

"Before going on, I ought to tell you that I'm...I'm reputed to be an eccentric, but I'm not; I'm simply obstinate, a stubborn man who always finds the way to get what I want in the end. What I say, I do, always! Understand that—it's important.

"Thus, I said that I would get into the Athenaeum before anyone else, and gratis...and I got in through the roof..."

"You very nearly stayed there," murmured Serge Myrandhal, amused by the memory.

"No," said the Englishman, imperturbably, "The difficult part, believe me, is climbing up. As for coming down, that always happens. Thanks to you, I even made a very graceful descent...agreeable, I must say. It was the first time I'd sat on the wind. It's very good—no jolts, soft as a feather. I'd have liked it to last longer, if it hadn't been for that old fool

Pellmann, gnashing his teeth and biting me in the calf. In fact, that's perhaps what you have against me?"

"Me?" exclaimed Serge, with an explosion of cordial hilarity. "Believe me, no! Oh, I'd have consigned you to the Devil for a second or two. You nearly compromised my experiment, and you gave me a terrible fright."

"There was no reason. Personally, I'm never afraid."

"You were risking your neck, though."

"Risk calls to me, attracts me. Then again, I had confidence."

"Confidence in what? In me, or the apparatus? You didn't know one or the other?"

"No, not in the apparatus, in you. At the first glance I could see that you were a man, Monsieur Engineer, and that one could count on you...rely on you...so I sat on your bench, that that's that!" The Englishman was becoming excited as he jabbered on. "And then again, there was something that couldn't be said—that people had traveled on the fluid but that I, Pickman, hadn't!

"It isn't your reputation that's at stake here, but mine, that of my exploits, permit me to say. I know you, and I render you justice—you, on the contrary, don't know what you ought to make of me, not at all. I'm a fanatical globetrotter. At twenty, I'd been around the world three times, and since then, I've found the world too small, and I'm looking for something else. Do you understand?

"In the meantime, to occupy my legs, I started climbing; there are a few fine ascents to my credit. I was the first to climb Gaurisankar, the highest peak in the world, 8,840 meters, between India and Tibet. It's been done since, but I hold the record. My celebrity dates from then.

"I was also the first to climb Aconcagua in the Andes, 6834 meters. If you ever go there you'll see my name, with the date that confirms it. I won't mention other mountains, which are molehills. In truth, I think that the Earth is a ridiculous ball, with its mountains. Talk to me about the moon, with its fifteen-thousand meter volcanoes. That's a nice height, by

Jove! Since I read that in my almanac, I've only had one dream: to take a trip up there. And I count on succeeding, now that I know you. We'll go together..."

"I've never said anything about that," Serge objected, swiftly. "The moon doesn't interest me—for the moment, at least."

"Yes," said the Englishman, "you'll go. You'll go with me—to please me!"

"You're admirable!" exclaimed the engineer, laughing in spite of himself at that formidable aplomb. "You have no doubt about anything..."

"A man who has doubts is doomed. It's written in the Bible, if you recall: 'No man, having put his hand to the plough, and looking back...'[13] I forget the rest—not important! Now, a good Englishman never doubts. He goes straight ahead—all right!

"That posited, I arrive at the proposition that I put to you just now. You don't want me as a traveling companion, as a passenger—very well, that's you're right. Take me as an associate, then, let's make a contract. Wait—you'll understand!

"You already have two associates: one for the money, Norton Bennett; the other for the fluid—the animic force, as you put it—the Rajah. Well, you're going to break with them and take me in their place. Yes, I alone can supply ten times more force and money than them. I have in England a company formed as a Trust; the government is involved. We'll have as much money as necessary. As for the fluid, its better still, as soon as we—the English—take a hand in it.

"The English are the masters of India, masters of the fakirs—can you imagine how many? Indraghava has ten thousand yogis in his convent; we, in the whole of India, Tibet and Ceylon, have more than a hundred thousand, and it's that ten-fold force that I'm offering you. We'll gather all the wretches

---

[13] "...is fit for the kingdom of God." Jesus, quoted in *Luke* 9:62.

together on the banks of the Ganges, the sacred river, and make them pray by means of force."

At that, Myrandhal burst out laughing, frankly. "Not a bad idea, in fact!"

"Then you accept?" said the Englishman, impetuously.

"No, I can't. You've come too late. But for that, perhaps…but there's no point in examining your proposal. I've made commitments."

"To whom?" cried Pickman. "To the Hindu? He doesn't count, and will do what we want. He's an English subject. As for the proprietor of the *Herald*, we'll compensate him, that's all."

"You think he'll agree?"

"He'll have to! If he makes difficulties, we'll force him by buying his newspaper. I've already acquired a hundred shares. You haven't signed anything, I know. So, you see, there's no objection."

"There is for me," the Frenchman replied, forcefully. "Those gentleman have my word. So…"

"So you're refusing!" cried the Baronet, furiously. "You're refusing to let me set foot on Mars with you. However, in addition to Anna, there's one other that you've accepted."

"Who told you that?"

"I guessed. I know that you've ordered two shells, two *Velox*es—a small one first and then a larger one, capable of carrying two people. It's *Velox* number two of which my little madcap ward is dreaming. I conclude, therefore, that there will be two voyages."

"It's possible," Myrandhal agreed, "but nothing is certain yet. The truth is that, in view of certain circumstances and the Rajah's assurance that we'll have all the fluid necessary at our disposal, I ordered a second *Velox* of less restricted dimensions, with more room inside. As for the first, the smaller model, I had intended to leave it here, until Prince Djalor's father asked me via his son to take it with us."

"He's the one who intends to make use of it?"

"Yes—or, rather, his son. Nevertheless, it's only a very vague and very distant project. It will be necessary, for either of them to risk it, that the news I send back from up there—for we have a means of maintaining correspondence—should be particularly favorable."

"And that second voyage doesn't offend you?"

"Not at all. It's one of the clauses of our association with Indraghava, and I couldn't refuse anything to a man who is bringing to the common enterprise the most important element after the invention, properly speaking. I'm the one who will depart first; mine will be the honor of being the first to set foot on the unknown planet. That's the limit of my ambition for the time being."

"Well," said Pickman, who had listened to these details with a marked attention, "too bad—and since you're intractable, I'll try to reach an understanding with the Rajah. But I hope to do better…much better...

"As it's necessary to anticipate everything, though, one more question. Once up there, to whom will the planet belong, you or the Rajah?"

"My word," said Serge, smiling. "We haven't thought about that yet. Anyway, Mars certainly being inhabited, the question doesn't arise."

"Yes it does!" cried the Baronet, furiously. "It does, damn it! Oh, that's the French all over…always the same. Whether Mars is inhabited our not, it's a colony for the taking, and we'll be there, we English."

"A colony! You want to colonize Mars?"

"Why not? You were the first to mention it, at the Athenaeum."

"That's true, but I was talking about the future—a future that I don't see, as yet. The time is a long way off when there'll be pleasure trains circulating between the planets."

"Who's talking about trains? One man's sufficient…one man with a flag. He plants it, and that's that: the claim's made. So, I have another proposal to make to you—the last. I assume that you'll arrive on Mars first. Whether the planet is deserted or not, you have the rights of the first occupant. What are you going to do? Are you going to take possession of it in the name of France?"

"In truth, I don't know. Perhaps, perhaps not. I've told you that in the circumstances—given the impossibility of exploiting the heavenly body in question, except for the good of science—such a formality seems to me to be futile, and, to tell the truth, rather ridiculous. I'll be content to give French names to the lands and seas I discover. Thereafter we'll see; it's not probable that I'll have any competitor up there, any rival with whom I have to reckon."

"Who knows?" the Eccentric murmured. "At any rate, you're hesitant. Well, I have an idea—a bizarre idea, but practical. Mars will belong to you, and you don't know what to do with it. Sell it! I'll buy it. How much?"

Again Serge Myrandhal burst out into child-like laughter. "You really are unbelievable!" he said. "Sell a planet—that's very English."

"Are you refusing?" the Englishman interjected, bitterly.

"No."

"Finally!"

"I believe that on that terrain we can make a deal. You've opened my mind, and since the realizations of which you're dreaming are possible, in sum, and since we're under the regime of the *entente cordiale*, I can't see any objection to giving you a share in my future domain!"

"That's the ticket!" cried Pickman, a vague smile illuminating his bony face. "That's straight talking. We'll draw up a contract and, as soon as possible, we'll go to the embassy to get it signed."

"That's moving a little rapidly. How the devil are you going to divide up a planet as little known as Mars? How can the frontiers be drawn? We really ought to wait until we possess a map more precise than those of the astronomers—a map made on the spot..."

"No," groaned the Baronet. "No need for a map! I have another means, much simpler, which will suppress any objections. Would you like to hear it?"

"Go on."

"Here goes—listen carefully, with all your ears. On Mars, in contrast to our globe, there's much more land than sea. Those lands, those continents, will be the property of France, the terrestrial power; the seas will remain communal and undivided, as is only fair. For us, the English, we'll be content with a parcel to be determined, slightly larger than the present United Kingdom. In exchange, the canals—the famous canals of Mars, where they be natural or artificial, will be England's with a strip of land to either side."

"Damn!" said Serge, who could see the imperialist ears of John Bull looming up. "But, according to the configuration of Mars, it's the empire of the seas that you're attributing to yourselves, nothing less. The means of opening and closing the gates to them at will. It's Gibraltar and Suez all over again…"

"You don't want it?" cried the Eccentric, breathlessly.

"Perhaps," Myrandhal went on, a gleam of malice having just appeared in his eyes. "All things considered, I accept. It only remains to agree on the price."

"Hurrah! That's settled, then. As for the price, it's not a trivial thing like that which will set us at odds. If you want billions, you'll have them. Speak bluntly. Name your figure, I'll accept. Old England is rich."

"So am I," Serge replied, proudly. "Richer than you…a thousand times richer. Up there, on Mars, I own gold mines, diamond mines, unprecedented, fabulous wealth! So it's not money I'll ask of you, but something else."

"What, then?" asked the Englishman, slightly anxious.

"Very little. Simply return to us one or two of the colonies you've taken from us—Egypt, for example, or India."

This time, Myrandhal had found the means to drive his visitor away. At the mere mention of India, the Englishman, his face scarlet, had taken a step toward the door.

"Monsieur," he grumbled, in a restrained tone. "You're joking. Know this: the English take, but they never give back. That said, I'll retire; I sense that I'm about to do violence, and tomorrow, the little one—I mean that little pest Anna—would force me to apologize to you. But you were wrong to make fun of me. I have a great deal of sympathy for you, myself."

The Eccentric was already moving toward the exit, followed by Serge; he went through the garden with long strides. When he reached the gate he turned round suddenly, and in a voice still trembling with anger, he said: "Sir, one last word, to recapitulate. So it's clear, is it not, that you're refusing to take me with you?"

"Address yourself to Miss Carpenter..."

"No point; I know her response. Similarly, you don't want me as an associate?"

"I'm committed elsewhere...."

"Good; let's pass on. Finally, you're refusing to sell me Mars?"

"For money, yes."

"Well, I know what I have to do. I came to you honestly, my hand extended. You want competition, war—you shall have it! And you'll lose everything. Oh, you great French fool, you presumptuous young man! You think you're sure of your success—well, hear this: the last thing I shall say to you..."

The Englishman had struck an earnest, solemn pose, and his little colorless eyes had a strange gleam, a flash of steel blue.

"Hear this," he repeated. "This is what I, who never lie, am telling you: *There is a man who will reach Mars before you!*"

"Who?" asked Serge, incredulously.

"Me."

"You?"

"Yes."

"How?"

"I don't know—but I know that I shall go. I've said so, and what I say, I do. *Au revoir*, sir!"

X. Velox no. 2

A fortnight had gone by. Serge Myrandhal's success was assuming enormous proportions.

It had required heroic courage and an entire squadron of servants and detectives to resist the frantic enthusiasm of his admirers, not to be submerged by the heaps of letters and telegrams that arrived by every post from all over the world and not to be stifled by the embraces of the "fans" who lay in wait for him every time he stepped outside the grounds of Norton Cottage.

Every morning, the *Herald* published a front page article on what was already being called "the great enterprise," curiously documented and illustrated with photographs. In a matter of days, the newspaper had multiplied its circulation tenfold, and three European editions were being sold in Paris, London and Berlin with the same success as the American edition.

The signatory of those articles, which were producing such a great sensation in public opinion, was always Annabella Carpenter, and that circumstance was appreciated all the more by the public because the engagement of Annabella and the young man was already almost official. For the readers, the sentimental charm of a love story was added to the powerful attraction of the audacious interastral flight.

The work, driven by the kind of furious ardor that we have already witnessed, was approaching its conclusion. Already, in the middle of the enclosure, the metallic vehicle that was to traverse space, the *Velox no. 2*, was completely assembled and fitted out, hoisted on to the truck that would transport it to San Francisco, from which it would be embarked for India. The day fixed for that first departure was a veritable scientific solemnity.

At two o'clock in the afternoon, several electric coupés came to a halt one after another outside the gate of the cottage.

They were bringing the few privileged individuals admitted by the engineer to visit the *Velox* before is embarkation.

Among them were President Rosenfeld, the most popular politician in the United States;[14] Norton Bennett, the proprietor of the *Herald*, accompanied by Annabella and a few of the newspaper's major shareholders; three directors of the Metals Trust; and a small number of scientists and artists.

Finally, it would be unjust to forget, among the individuals we have already encountered at the beginning of the story: Prince Djalor, always impeccable, although a trifle melancholy since the news that Annabella's engagement had become semi-official; and the honest Canadian Ned Friedlander, beside whom advanced, alpenstock in hand, our friend Pickman, who, although annoyed with Myrandhal, had not been able to resist the attraction of the sensational ceremony.

Let us add that the Frenchman, full of disdain for the man who had dared to pose as his rival to his face, had put the coquetry of a good sportsman into the insistence that the Eccentric should accompany his ward to Norton Cottage. He wanted to show him that he had nothing to fear, and nothing to hide.

Also among the small number of the elect were His Excellency the Plenipotentiary Minister of the French Republic, who was escorted by the chemist Justin Durand, a friend of the inventor, and his inseparable companion Joe Grok, the industrialist.

No other guests had been admitted, in spite of the most urgent solicitations. The discontented were, therefore, numerous. In the street, a turbulent crowd was being held back, with great difficulty, by fifty vigorous policemen.

The spies, reporters, curiosity-seekers and everyone else who had hoped to penetrate into the mysterious cottage, were profoundly disappointed. Without the energetic attitude of the

---

[14] The actual president of the U.S.A. in June 1908 was Theodore Roosevelt.

policemen, they would certainly have attempted an invasion by force.

Meanwhile, Serge Myrandhal had come to met his guests and conduct them personally to the *Velox no. 2*.

They found themselves in the presence of a cigar-shaped metal hull, blue-gray in color, which was somewhat reminiscent of an enormous torpedo or a small submarine. Let us say immediately that, like a submarine, the *Velox* was designed to maneuver in the seas or the famous canals of Mars.

About forty-five feet long, the *Velox* measured exactly eleven feet three inches from its base to the hatch on top. Apart from the conning-tower on top—a tower partly retractable for movement while submerged—the only other swellings in the hull were enormous portholes with lenses of rock crystal.

"Gentlemen," the engineer began, I'll show you in detail all the interior components and fitments of the *Velox*. As you can see, the apparatus resembles a miniature submersible. I have particular reasons for giving it that form. My intention is to fall directly into one of the seas or one of the vast canals that furrow the planet Mars. The *Velox* is, therefore floatable and submersible.

"After having served me as an aerial vehicle, as an 'aeronaut,' this *psychoscaph*—which is to say, a container moved by psychic force, if you will permit the slightly barbaric neologism—will serve me as an aquatic vehicle. It is not without reason that I've adopted this amphibious system, imitative, in a way, of flying fish.

"We know nothing about the nature or the character of the inhabitants of Mars. They might be barbaric, bellicose and formidably armed. Enclosed in my *Velox*, I can, in any case, hold them off and, thanks to the canals, transport myself rapidly, in total security, from one part of the planet to another. With that objective I am taking a propeller and a rudder that are easy to fit, and even an automobile, for excursions on the continents..."

"But what will you do," asked President Rosenfeld, very interested, "if you ever take it into your head to come back?"

"I'm counting on doing that, Mr. President. I wouldn't go if there were no hope of returning. I believe I've resolved the difficulty; I shall take with me a sufficient reserve of animic fluid to regain our old planet whenever I wish."

"Marvelous! You'll be awaited here with impatience, and welcomed with the enthusiasm merited by an argonaut of the earths of the heavens, a Christopher Columbus of the planets."

At this compliment, punctuated by an approving murmur from the audience, the engineer bowed, blushing slightly. Then, after a slight pause, in the midst of a religious silence, he continued.

"The hull, formed of an alloy of chromium, steel and vanadium, is capable of resisting the most formidable pressures. It is doubled, in any case, and there is a gap between the two hulls filled with an appropriate insulating substance. I won't say much about the conning-tower, which scarcely protrudes and is hermetically sealed. The hatch will only be unscrewed after my arrival on the planet.

"Now you're going to be able to take account of the interior fitments. We'll go inside the *Velox* and visit the five compartments composing it, in succession."

That announcement caused a considerable stir of interest and curiosity. At a signal from the engineer, one of his assistants attached a ladder to the narrow walkway situated at the rear of the psychoscaph. Then he operated the manual control of the seal of the hatchway. The hatch opened and a narrow opening appeared, a kind of miniature cylindrical bay, just sufficient to allow a single person to pass.

"This way, gentlemen," said the engineer, cheerfully. "Follow me, without fear. I'll go first to lead the way."

While speaking he had climbed the iron ladder and inserted himself into the narrow passage. One by one, with the President in the lead, the guests followed in Indian file.

"As you can see," the engineer said, "this first, rather narrow compartment serves as both a kitchen and food store and as a store-room for instruments, tools and weapons. Here, in a very small volume, are enough concentrated food supplies for several weeks. This is an electric cooker with saucepans, equipped with a graduated semi-circular dial and a needle..."

"But why is the cooker electric?" asked the President, and added, not without a touch of humor: "Couldn't it be animic, or fluidic, like the rest?"

"Undoubtedly," said the engineer, undisconcerted. "Cerebral energy, once captured, can be subjected to any application, just like any other force, but as I have just explained, I need to be extremely miserly with the fluidic reserves that will permit me to make the return journey. That's why I'm not only taking accumulators and an electric motor, but a steam engine and an internal combustion engine. All of them will prove useful on Mars, where combustibles and electricity ought to exist in as great abundance as on Earth."

Now the engineer indicated a host of objects stowed in thick leather sheaths along the walls, all the way up to the rounded ceiling of the compartment. "I won't list all of this paraphernalia," he murmured. "You can see that not an inch of space is wasted. There are indispensable precision instruments, tools of primary necessity, weapons of every sort and caliber, including two mountain machine-guns, which will make our automobile, if the need arises, into a formidable war-machine."

Serge had opened a metallic door fitted with a rubber rim that ensured a perfect seal. By the soft light of a small electric ceiling light, a cabin appeared. It was fitted out with comfort of luxurious simplicity: furniture of light lemonwood, a thick carpet, furs, a few bronzes, two or three precious trinkets and a low bed with lacy pillows made it into a retreat that was entirely feminine in its elegance. A bathroom with a minuscule tub and shower-head was hidden behind a vast curtain of the same mauve blue as the rest of the hangings. The cabin was evidently designed for a woman.

While the engineer gave a few hasty explanations, all gazes instinctively went toward Annabella, who, apparently very calm, and slightly hidden behind the group of guests, seemed to be absorbed in making notes. A slight blush, however, and an imperceptible tremor of the lips showed that her indifference was not as complete as she wanted everyone to believe.

Prince Djalor had looked successively at Serge Myrandhal and the young woman, and had gone pale.

Already, though, the engineer, opening another door, was introducing his guests into the next compartment.

"This room," he explained, "occupies the exact center of the vessel and is situated immediately beneath the conning-tower, to which the spiral stairway on the left gives access. It's there that the passengers of the *Velox* will spend most of their time. It will be the dining room, the study and the living room.

"I forgot one important detail. You see that platform at the top of the stairway: it's the station of the captain and helmsman, when the Velox is navigating on the surface of the water. From there, thanks to the electric panel fixed within arm's reach, I can control the entire machinery of the submersible: the various accumulators, dynamos, propeller, rudder, etc. I can open a porthole, release the lead counterweight in the form of a sheath that protects our external keel, fill or empty the ballast-tanks. Even so, it's only case of extreme danger that I'll have recourse to those maneuvers, always hazardous even on the best-equilibrated submarines.

"The other apparatus—valves to evacuate detritus and vitiated air, liquid air inhalers, diving-suits, etc.—isn't much different from the apparatus in use in all submarines. One point to note, however: my compass, thanks to a process of magnetization that I'll keep to myself, doesn't obey terrestrial magnetism, too weak and uncertain over the distances we're traveling, but solar magnetism, much more powerful. That way, I'm sure of not losing north."

The guests marveled as they examined all the equipment, so complete and soberly comprised, and so ingeniously packed into such a small space. They looked at all the objects and utensils, simultaneously light, solid and comfortable, which represented, in terms of square feet, the last word in progress and perfection.

Among the visitors, however, there was one who was studying everything with avid, almost hypnotic attention. That was Sir Washington Pickman, the Eccentric. From time to time he dropped back slyly behind the group of guests, took a pencil from his pocket, and rapidly noted a few figures or a diagram on his impeccably bleached shirt-cuffs. Annabella's notes were certainly not as complete as his. He did not miss a single word of the engineer's explanations.

Serge Myrandhal had already passed into the fourth compartment. It was a very simple cabin. A narrow bunk, a bathroom equipped with the strict necessities, a bookcase full of books, and a few strangely-formed instruments, formed its entire furniture.

"I infer that this is your cabin, Monsieur Engineer," murmured the President.

"It's not very sumptuous, as you see, but nothing essential is lacking."

"Would it be indiscreet to ask," the President said, "what that bizarre machine is, with the multitude of small levers, and that globe in which gold leaves radiate from a crystal coil in a spiral, seemingly agitated by a continual tremor?"

"There's no indiscretion. That apparatus, which I call, perhaps a trifle presumptuously, a *telepath*, is a kind of telegraph moved by animic energy and based on the same principles that led me to construct my condenser of volitional fluid. Thanks to the telepath, I expect to remain in communication with my friends throughout my voyage from the Earth to Mars and my sojourn on the planet..."

"And able to keep the readers of the *Herald* informed!" proclaimed the honorable Norton Bennett, in a thunderous voice.

"Of course," said the engineer, smiling, not without exchanging a furtive glance with Annabella, "the *Herald* will continue to be the best-informed newspaper, not only on Earth but in the solar system. It's a record that it will hold for a long time, if it only depends on me!"

Then he continued his explanations.

"As you've noticed, the *Velox*'s compartments are equipped with electric radiators. It's thanks to those and the double hull that we can resist the absolute cold of interplanetary space, 270 degrees below zero..."

"Pardon me," Washington Pickman interjected, striking the floor with his alpenstock in a mulish automatic gesture that amused the audience, "But you've forgotten to tell us what's underneath this."

"Simply our provisions of water, liquid air and electricity..."

By way of thanks the Eccentric uttered a kind of approving grunt, and hastily scrawled a note on his sleeve.

Serge Myrandhal had already opened the final door. "It's this compartment, the equivalent of the first you visited, that contains the animic condensers and the steering mechanisms. This is where the pilot is stationed who will guide the *Velox* through the sidereal ether."

The engineer closed the door of the redoubt almost immediately, cutting off the questions that the Eccentric was doubtless already preparing to ask.

The tour of the *Velox* was concluded.

The guests, marveling at what they had seen, emerged one by one from the hull of the psychoscaph, where they had seemed to be living in a dream for a few minutes.

A surprise was awaiting them.

While they were inside the aerial ship, the décor of the grounds had been modified, as if in response to a stage-manager's whistle in some great theatrical extravaganza.

The *Velox*, decked from one end of its hull to the other with French and American flags and gigantic bouquets of magnolias, roses, orchids and camellias, had been hitched to a powerful traction engine.

A few paces away, a table was waiting, laden with all the elements of a light lunch.

"Gentlemen," said the engineer, not without a certain restrained emotion, "the *Velox* will depart for San Francisco in a few moments. It's the first stage of the journey that will end on Mars! I thought that it would be nice to baptize her in your presence—all of you who have supported, helped and encouraged me, permitting me to realize my dream, who have been my friends and collaborators, of unwavering devotion."

An energetic hurrah from the entire audience punctuated those final words.

"The godparents are both here," the engineer continued, when silence was reestablished. "They will be, if they will do me the honor, President Rosenfeld and Miss Annabella Carpenter."

"I'm very flattered," the President relied, gravely, "personally and on behalf of the people of America, by the great honor you're doing me. I accept with great pleasure."

Shortly afterwards, the President led Miss Carpenter to a small podium set up in front of the *Velox*. There, Annabella took a bottle of champagne from a servant and broke the gold-sheathed neck against the pointed prow of the psychoscaph. A flood of blonde foam inundated the metal of the hull. The *Velox* was baptized!

A triple salvo of hurrahs welcomed the young woman's gesture.

At the same moment, after a signal from the engineer, the *Velox* moved off.

A strong picket of guards was waiting at the gate. The escort surged forward, opening a way through the frantically clamoring crowd, and then disappeared in a cloud of dust.

In the meantime, in the grounds, the toasts commenced. President Rosenfeld stood up, glass in hand.

"Gentlemen," he said, with a delicate smile, first I propose we raise our glasses to the heroine of the day, the first and most gracious collaborator of our hero Serge Myrandhal, the godmother of the *Velox no. 2*. Miss Carpenter, I drink to your honor and your happiness!"

A concert of applause welcomed this allusion, and the rest of the toast was downed by the acclamations.

Early the next morning, at the Palace Hotel, Justin Durand was taking his bath when Joe Grok hurtled into the bathroom. He was brandishing an issue of the Herald striped with enormous headlines:

PLOT FOILED
THE HERALD ON THE ALERT
etc.

"You haven't read the news that has all of New York in uproar?" he exclaimed. "Yesterday evening, almost immediately after the presidential visit, the inventor and Miss Anna secretly took the train for San Francisco.

"An earlier train had left an hour before carrying all the equipment—so we've been robbed! The great projected ceremony, the triumphal procession that ought to have accompanied Myrandhal, is off. And I'd paid a thousand dollars to hire a simple balcony! Well, what do you think? You don't seem surprised at all."

"I knew all that," said the chemist, smiling.

"What! You knew?"

"Yes. You're forgetting that Myrandhal is my friend, and that, thanks to one of his marvelous telepaths, I'm in communication with him."

"In that case," cried the billionaire, hotly, "you'd do well to inform him as soon as possible of what's happening at Norton Cottage."

"What is happening, then?"

"Something terrible and unexpected, which demonstrates the determination of certain people to steal your compatriot's secret. At midnight, three hundred masked men descended on the villa. They overwhelmed the police, broke down the gate and invaded the basement. Fortunately, they didn't find what they were looking for. The laboratory was empty, dismantled.

118

That doesn't affect the fact that there's still a battle raging around Norton Cottage. The villa is on fire!" The American concluded, triumphantly: "That's something you certainly didn't know!"

"But we knew perfectly well that our enemies, after having failed in their attacks several times, were about to attempt a violent blow—hence the clandestine departure arranged a week ago."

"A week! And you never said anything to me! You let me hire a balcony! You even accepted a place on it."

"I'd given my word."

"Yes, I understand. By way of compensation, I hope you'll be less secretive in future and make me party to the news you receive, thanks to the famous telepath."

"I would, but there again my hands are tied. My compatriot has a formal contract with the *Herald*."

"That's true," said the American. "Business is business."

Nevertheless, doubtless in the hope of learning some unpublished detail that would win him glory in the drawing rooms of Fifth Avenue, Joe came to his friend's residence almost every morning to read the *Herald*.

Every day, the dispatches became more interesting, and the public literally snatched the newspaper's four editions out of the vendors' hands. At certain hours there were veritable mobs outside the *Herald*'s offices.

One of those dispatches, covering several columns, excited honest Joe's admiration especially. It was the description of Karputhala, the city of pink marble, the Maharajah's capital, and its palace.

"To cap it all," he exclaimed, "there's the nocturnal festival held by the nabob in his gardens prior to his departure for the convent of Almowrat. Oh, if only I'd been able to leave New York!

"Frankly, I'd have given half my fortune to see such a magical spectacle: the Rajah scintillating with precious stones like an idol; the bayaderes, the marvelous park where tigers with velvet and silk coats, more diamond-laden than the grey-

119

hounds of our elegant strollers, wander at liberty among the rose-bushes and jasmine!

"Then, the complete change of scene at the departure: a stroke of a gong, and everything's extinguished. In the immense courtyard paved with cedar-wood, the caravans—two hundred elephants and as many camels—are lined up, waiting for the master…people are already anxious…

"Suddenly, a man appears, barefoot, clad in sackcloth, with a pilgrim's staff in his hand. It's the Mendicant Prince! He takes the bridle of the first camel, and the entire column moves off in the midst of a religious silence.

"What do you say, eh? Another eccentric, that one!"

The chemist smiled. "By the way, do you have any news of Pickman?"

"No—he's disappeared, but no one doubts that he's on his way to the convent of Almowrat. Your friend and his associates, who avoided him the first time, might have brought off that coup, and taken the strictest measures, but they won't stop him. No one's ever stopped the Eccentric, anywhere. There'll be one man there to witness the departure of the *Velox* for the stars, and that's the Baronet!"

"I doubt it."

"You're free to do so. Pickman hasn't taken me into his confidence, but I know him well enough to guess that he hasn't said his last word. According to rumor, the Steel Company—the Trust's rival—has constructed a second *Velox* in great secrecy, which can only have been commissioned by him. What would you say if he arrived on Mars before your friend?"

"I defy him to do that! It's impossible!"

"Impossible for us, but for him…who can tell? If you knew him as I do, you'd know that it's necessary to expect anything from the old devil."

XI. At the Monastery of Almowrat

When she woke up that morning, Annabella took some time to get her bearings.

Having arrived at the monastery of Almowrat the previous evening, in pitch darkness, she had immediately been taken to the apartment specially fitted out for her. Falling asleep, she had gone to bed immediately, and her new abode was now appearing to her for the first time.

The sun, already high, was shining through the arched windows.

Before her, there was a horizon of somber forests and ruddy, jagged mountain, which surrounded the plateau on which the monastery, as vast as a city, had been constructed.

In the background, the snowy caps of the last peaks of the Himalayas were sparkling with an immaculate whiteness.

Annabella felt enormously distant from the world she knew. The civilized world seemed as remote as a mist of dreams; she thought that she had been transported centuries back in time.

Her room, however, without offering the luxury of the palace of Karputhala, presented all the necessary comfort and elegance.

After a rapid lunch, the young woman went into the room that served as a drawing room, and from there on to the balcony, protected by a cloister of colonnettes, that extended externally.

She found Serge Myrandhal there; he had already been up for two hours, and was in the process of bringing his travel journal up to date.

The two young people greeted one another effusively, and Serge Myrandhal deposited a respectful kiss on the hand that his fiancée held out to him. Then they both spent a few silent moments contemplating the heavy black stone cupolas of the monastery-city, perched like an eagle's nest on a plateau half way up a giant mountain.

Suddenly, Annabella smiled.

"I mustn't forget my professional duties, though," she said. "The *Herald* must be waiting impatiently for my dispatch. The last time I telegraphed was from Karputhala, where the line stops. Since then..."

"Don't worry, my dear Annabella," the engineer interjected, hastily. "I've thought about you. Your telepathic apparatus was the first I unpacked and set up. It's in the antechamber, from which you only have to transport it to your bedside, so as to be always ready to respond to the first appeal. That's what I've done with mine, and I've already given my news to my friend Justin Durand."

The American woman frowned.

"Oh! Are you, by chance, going into competition with me, Monsieur Engineer? You must remember that the *Herald* ought to be the first..."

"Don't worry!" Myrandhal hastened to protest. "I know and respect the rights of our all-powerful collaborator. My old comrade is a discreet man, aware of the agreements that bind me, and incapable of abusing a confidence. I'll add that my dispatch, were it to become known, would only serve to inflame the curiosity of your subscribers, given its concise and incomplete form. The proof is that it read: *Monastery of Almowrat. Arrived safely.* That's all! I agree, nevertheless, that, strictly speaking, I ought to have submitted my telegram to your inspection. I hope you'll forgive me."

"I forgive you," the young woman replied, smiling. "But only on one condition..."

"Which is?"

"That you don't do it again."

"That's a promise."

"And that you help me telegraph the newspaper. I'll talk, and you can operate the controls."

"At your orders."

Serge Myrandhal preceded the young woman into the room where the telepath was. He switched it on, and the gold leaves began vibrating.

An hour later, the writer specially delegated by the *Herald* to keep track of the audacious enterprise knew all the details of the latest stage of the journey and was able to give its countless readers a first description of the famous monastery of Almowrat.

Once that was done, the two fiancés returned to the balcony. A shadow had suddenly troubled the young woman's bright eyes.

"Serge," she murmured, in a low voice, "I want to tell you something that's been bothering me, rightly or wrongly. I've wanted to raise the question for some while, and the time has come.

"I might be mistaken, but my woman's instinct makes me dread that your Hindu associates, who have never inspired much confidence in me, might attempt to take possession of your secret, supplant you and depart before you. I might be wrong, but I sense around you an atmosphere of espionage and treason. In particular, I'm worried about the first apparatus you constructed, the *Velox no. 1*."

"My dear Annabella," the engineer replied, swiftly, "you know that the first model was commissioned for me alone, when I was unaware of the happiness that awaited me. After that, it was necessary to make one that was larger and more comfortable..."

Annabella blushed imperceptibly.

"I intended to leave the *Velox no. 1* in New York," the engineer went on. "It was on the insistence of Prince Djalor, who asked me on his father's behalf, that I was obliged to bring it here. They thought, as is their right, of coming to join us up there later—much later—but I doubt that they'll ever attempt the adventure. The Rajah is too old and his son too effeminate for such an enterprise. Nevertheless, they talked to me about it again yesterday evening, and I promised—it was an implicit clause of our contract—to furnish them with the means. Note that I couldn't do otherwise. I need them..."

Miss Carpenter shook her head. "I understand," she said, "but I mistrust your generosity and your frankness, which prevent you from seeing treacheries of which you're incapable. Would it not be possible, without annoying our associates, to proceed in another fashion? Thus, all the components that you've manufactured in duplicate, the engine that is now, and will remain after our departure, in the Rajah's possession...once again, have you no anxiety?"

"I can assure you that I have nothing to fear. You can see for yourself. I had the duplicate components of which you speak made in my own—our own—interest. It's necessary to anticipate everything. What if, in this inaccessible place, far from cities and factories, one of the complicated and delicate mechanisms were to fail, for some unknown reason, or sustain some damage...?"

"There'd only be a delay."

"Yes, but as our days are counted, the delay would take on catastrophic proportions. It would be a fatal and definitive check. With my duplicate components, it's a risk I avoid.

"Besides which, it's necessary not to forget that the Rajah and his son have rights over my invention, which they've so fortunately completed. I'm bound to them by a contract, which is no less imperative for not being written down. I won't be the first to break my word, and you've been impressed yourself, in the course of our journey, by the urgency and zeal with which our friends have supported me."

"That's true," said the young woman, still unconvinced. "But it's precisely that excessive zeal that sometimes worries me. These people are too polite..."

"Listen," said the young man. "Would you like me to reveal my secret to you in its entirety, as I've already offered to do many times?"

"No," Annabella replied, forcefully. "You mustn't. It would be a further imprudence, perhaps the gravest..."

"A further imprudence!" exclaimed the engineer. "What do you mean? Explain yourself, please."

"It's rather difficult. For some time, my nights have been troubled by strange nightmares. I sense confusedly that I'm the object of a kind of suggestion, that a will as strange as it is foreign is trying, in some way, to violate my thoughts, my mind...to introduce itself into my mind as if breaking into a house...and I think about the burglars that were swarming around Norton Cottage..."

"We're no longer in America."

"How do you that those who want to frustrate you haven't followed you? But let's leave that and get back to the nightmares I was talking about. Astonished by the bizarre phenomena—absolutely new to me, who have always slept like a baby—I've searched for the cause, and this is the reasoning I followed, going from deduction to deduction.

"Let's not name anyone, but you have envious, jealous, determined enemies—bandits who won't stop at any crime to obtain possession of your invention. These enemies suppose that I, your fiancée, know the secret of the engine-amplifier, and, not being able to attack you, whose powerful brain is proof against such maneuvers, they thought of getting it from me.

"They hope, by means of the mysterious key known as suggestion, to open the most secret compartments of my mind. Perhaps they've succeeded, but they haven't found what they were looking for. The drawer was empty. And that's why I don't want to put anything in it, why I refuse to know your secret."

"As you wish," the engineer murmured, impressed in spite of his optimism by the justice of her reasoning. "Nevertheless, while accepting your thesis and not giving you anything that might be stolen from you, I intend to reassure you. Although I'm as unsuspicious as you judge me to be, I've also taken my precautions, and a theft—even operated in the subtle manner that you dread—is almost impossible."

The engineer took his wallet out of the inside pocket of his jacket. "You'll understand..." He opened the wallet and took out a pinch of minuscule filaments, gold-green in color. "The entire secret," he said, "the entire mystery, resides in these fibers of an alloy whose preparation requires an exceedingly delicate dosage and a twist that only I know. It's this filament that I introduce into the apparatus every time, which is then ready—loaded. Without that, nothing functions, and after every experiment, the filament, melted and volatilized by the enormous power of the animic fluid, has disappeared without leaving any analyzable trace. Do you understand now?"

"I feel reassured," said the young woman, smiling again, "but hush—here's Prince Djalor coming toward us, at the far end of the gallery."

The fiancés advanced to meet the Prince, who greeted them with his habitual correctness, always imprinted with a kind of melancholy, which was accentuated as soon as he found himself in Annabella's presence. He asked the two young people if they were satisfied with the first night they had spent at the monastery of Almowrat, and almost immediately offered them a tour of the old monastery.

"My father," he said, "sends his excuses for not serving as your cicerone himself, but he's particularly absorbed at the moment, as you'll understand. I'll try to stand in for him, although his explanations would doubtless be more interesting than mine."

"I suspect," the engineer murmured, "that we'll be able to see marvels equaling those we were able to contemplate in Karputhala, which my memory retains in dazzling fashion."

"They won't be marvels of the same sort," Prince Djalor replied. "I'll show you—it's necessary for you to see—what prodigies the will can accomplish. It will give you an idea of the prodigious psychic power stored here." He turned to the young American. "I don't know, Miss, whether I ought to ask you to come with us. You'll see some horrible spectacles." Pensively, he added: "Except that there'll be the elements of a sensational article for the *Herald*. No one has ever seen at close range what I'm about to show you."

"If there's an article for the *Herald* in it," Annabella replied, bravely, "I won't hesitate. Professional duty before all! I'll try to be courageous."

Following the Prince, the fiancés went down a staircase with heavy banisters sculpted with interlaced snakes, and steps worn down by the centuries. They went through several courtyards with dilapidated colonnades. There was not a soul to be seen.

The sculpted façades displayed upright hieratical figures of mystical rigidity, like certain palaces of ancient Egypt. Their features, scarcely sketched in the black rock, had expressions of pitiless ferocity.

"Those," the prince explained, "are statues of some of our primitive gods, whose all-powerful will extracted the world from chaos." He put a finger to his lips. "In the place we're about to enter, I recommend the most profound silence and firmness. Do your best not to seem affected by what you see."

He opened a bronze door. A majestic courtyard appeared, surrounded by a forest of pillars. In the center was the sacred pool that is invariably found in all Hindu temples.

Annabella and Serge went pale, scarcely able to suppress an exclamation of horror.

On the edge of the muddy water, where the Brahmins made their ablutions and washed the statues of the gods in a ritual manner, a hundred men were heaped up or laid out in contorted and grimacing poses.

Annabella was gripped by anguish. She thought for a moment that she had been transported into one of the circles of the Chinese hell, the most complicated and most ingeniously barbaric of all.

"Where am I?" she asked Prince Djalor, who remained impassive, like a man long accustomed to such spectacles.

"This is the place where the fakirs reside, the yogis who—of their own free will, don't forget—submit themselves to tortures and ordeals with the objective of making themselves agreeable to the divinity and being admitted more rapidly to the ineffable nirvana.

"Look! Here's one who, in order to remain faithful to a vow of silence, has sewn up his lips with silver thread, leaving nothing but a minuscule opening. He can't eat anything except a little thin rice broth, which he sucks through a straw.

"This one has nailed his ears to the trunk of a tree. He's been there for years. Slowly, the trunk has grown and has stretched the lobes, which now resemble the wings of a bat.

"This one has kept his hands joined together and bound with cords for so long that the fingernails have driven through the flesh, at the almost inevitable risk of perishing of gangrene. He has doubtless only escaped death because of his frightful thinness. The putrescence can find nothing to devour in that mass of bones. At present, though, he's obliged to crawl like an animal to his bowl and lap up his rice like a dog.

"What do you think of such stoicism?"

Annabella made no reply. She thought she was the victim of the most abominable of nightmares.

Meanwhile, Prince Djalor continued to move forward cautiously through the squatting or sprawling bodies, as if he were walking through a battlefield strewn with the dead and wounded.

A little further on he pointed out a fakir so perfectly motionless at the summit of a column that his body, naked and skeletal, the color of old ivory, seemed to be carved of stone itself. One might have thought him devoid of life. His white beard hung down to his navel and little birds had built nests in his bushy hair, without being disturbed. Little golden lizards ran over his thighs, scarcely as wide as an ordinary man's wrist, and darted between his mummified toes.

Further on, other fantastic individuals agonized beneath piles of stone slabs or were buried in the mud, where insects were devouring them, without a muscle in their face quivering or any contortion betraying their suffering.

A few were writhing on beds of hot coals, which they had to extinguish with the blood oozing hideously from the burns with which they were covered.

There were several who were lying on sharp spikes, which penetrated profoundly into their flesh.

Annabella turned away in horror at the sight of a huge bamboo wheel that was turning with extreme rapidity, bearing the bloody bodies of three old men, whose hips and shoulders were traversed by iron hooks. Wherever she directed her gaze, however, there were similar spectacles of horror, similar scenes of horrifying torture.

"Let's get out," Serge Myrandhal murmured in Prince Djalor's ear. "I think that Annabella is feeling sick."

"You're right. I've been used to these spectacles for such a long time that I didn't calculate the effect that they might have on an impressionable feminine nature."

"Yes, I beg you," the young woman murmured, "let's go. I'm running out of strength."

The Prince hastened to satisfy Annabella's desire, stammering vague apologies. In his urgency, however, he tripped over one of the bodies lying on the ground.

One might have thought it a mutilated cadaver rather than a living human being. His blinded eyes were no more than two bloody holes, two frightful gaping wounds. He had cut off his nose, his ears and, more frightful still, his lips and part of the musculature of his mouth. His teeth were bare. He was reminiscent of some character in the *danse macabre* or one of the most terrible tales of Edgar Poe.

It was more than Annabella could bear.

She fled, closing her eyes, chilled by horror, all the way to the bronze door that had given the access to that terrible place.

The prince and the engineer hurried to catch up with Annabella, who, leaning against a pillar in the neighboring gallery, gradually recovered, breathing in one of the revulsives most effective in such instances from a bottle of "lavender salts."

"I never imagined that such frightful things existed beneath the face of Heaven!" she exclaimed, after a brief interval. "How can your father, the Maharajah, tolerate such horrors, Prince?"

"He doesn't tolerate them," the Prince replied, a trifle embarrassed. "He doesn't have the power to prevent them. He would lose a great part of his authority over his subjects if he tried to stop these fanatics torturing themselves so cruelly. You'll see in due course, in any case, that the Rajah has done a great deal to restrain and moderate these futile martyrdoms..."

"I can't help feeling sickened and indignant," said the engineer in his turn.

"Do you want to know what I think?" said the Prince. "To be sure, I disapprove of the excesses, the abuses of that exaggerated exercise of the energetic faculty, but you'll agree with me that it's thanks to that power, that methodical training of the controlled will, continued over the centuries, that certain marvelous results have been obtained. Isn't it thanks to the psychic contention of thousands of poor yogis that you're going to be able to realize your marvelous project? It would certainly be impossible to do it with the brutalized wills of Occidental individuals, disseminated in a thousand futile preoccupations."

"That's an argument *ad hominem*," said the engineer, smiling. "I have no reply to such an argument, since I shall be one of the first to profit from the meditations of these fanatics."

"In any case," the prince continued, "We don't only have hideous spectacles to offer you. There are less frightful ones." Pushing a cedar-wood door ornamented with pentagrams that was facing the bronze door, he went on: "Come into this room with me and you'll see something that, although it's not terrible, is just as marvelous."

"Let's go in," said the engineer.

"Let's go in," repeated Annabella, after a slight hesitation.

The room into which they went had a high ceiling, and was absolutely bare, with paving-slabs of black porphyry covered with ancient Sanskrit inscriptions.

At first, Annabella did not perceive anything extraordinary, but, having raised her eyes, she uttered a cry of astonishment.

Grouped slightly below the center of the ceiling, slightly hollowed out in a vault, three human beings were suspended in mid-air with no kind of support.

"You see here," Prince Djalor explained, "a manifestation of a phenomenon well known to scientists under the name of levitation. It's by the power of their will alone that these three monks have risen from the ground and can maintain themselves in the air for as long as they wish."

"I've read accounts of the feat related by a large number of trustworthy travelers, but I've never witnessed it," said Annabella. "I don't deny that I much prefer this strange miracle to those I've just seen in your torture garden..."[15]

At that moment, the solemn sound of a gong rang out.

The prince made a gesture. "My father's summoning us," he said, in a respectful tone. "Come with me—I believe he needs to talk seriously to Monsieur Myrandhal."

---

[15] Although this phrase is *jardin des tortures* in the original, it nevertheless re-emphasizes an echo in the previous scene of the descriptions contained *Le Jardin des supplices* (1899; tr. as *Torture Garden*) by Octave Mirbeau, one of the classics of Decadent prose.

XII. In Which Events Move Rapidly

A fortnight had gone by. It was the thirtieth of July.

That morning, Serge Myrandhal and Annabella had just come down from their apartments. They were in the first courtyard of the monastery when the entrance door, opened by the old bonze who was in charge of it, gave passage to a Hindu whose meager torso was only protected by a scrap of cloth covering his loins. Over his shoulder was slung a brown leather bag. In his left hand he was waving, with an incessant and automatic movement, a sheaf of metallic rods whose sound was supposed to drive away rattlesnakes. His body was streaming with sweat.

"The mailman!" said Annabella, joyfully. "There ought to be a letter from my father."

The young woman was not mistaken. The Hindu took a large envelope from his bag covered with multicolored stamps and handed it to its addressee in exchange for a silver rupee.

The young woman scanned the missive at a glance; her cheeks colored with a blush of pleasure.

"Good news!" she exclaimed. "Father tells me that the Reverend Jonathan Burrett, who is to bless our union, is on his way. As long as he arrives soon!"

"He'll arrive," the engineer replied. "I'm confident— your father understands the situation. Remember that in one of my previous letters—the one in which I asked him to accept me as a son-in-law—I explained to Mr. Carpenter that the most favorable interval for our departure was between the first and the fifteenth of August. Remember, too, his enthusiastic response. He hoped to be able to come, and he was already talking about chartering a special ship."

"Yes," the young woman murmured. "And the Reverend Burrett is just as resolute, it seems. He's a missionary, a man hardened to all fatigue, as my father says. He'll travel night and day. Read it for yourself."

132

"All's well, then," said the young man, after having perused the letter. "I see, too, that your father has succeeded in beginning to rebuild his fortune."

"And my guardian," the American woman went on, laughing in a child-like fashion, "the eccentric Pickman—do you think he'll arrive in time? He's promised to be my first witness, but since his last dispatch, not a word…might he be annoyed with us?"

Serge laughed too, at the memory of the famous conversation. "I'm not worried about that," he said. "As a good Englishman, Pickman is a slave to his word and his rendezvous. Time is money…

"He's an excellent fellow, fundamentally, in spite of his manias and his slightly…brusque manners. Besides, I'll wager that, like all eccentrics, he's mathematically exact in his punctuality.

"Then again, he loves you too much not to be present on such a solemn occasion. Come on, everything's going well, and it's up to us to make haste now. For the first time, work will continue all night if necessary."

"As it did back at Norton Cottage…"

"Yes. It's necessary that the track from which the *Velox* will be launched is finished before tomorrow. Now, if you wish, let's go see our workmen; our presence stimulates them."

A few hours later, shortly before midnight, the old monastery presented an unaccustomed activity, which would have made the old monks shiver in their tombs.

A long line of Jablochkoff candles departing from the breached ramparts scaled the steep slope of the mountain to a culminating point four kilometers away. By the electric light that patched the darkness with long bright beams, twenty elephants specially trained for the work, like those owned by all the Anglo-Indian railway companies, were finishing placing cross-ties and rails of the track.

Everyone knows the promptitude and precision with which the intelligent pachyderms lift up rails or cross-ties with their trunks and set them down gently in the correct location, without missing it by a centimeter. Behind the mahouts who were encouraging them with their cries and caresses, a crew of coolies were rapidly tightening the wedges and bolts.

Already, the steel ribbons raised toward the sky—toward Mars—at a forty-five degree angle, were cutting through the darkness like twin lightning-bolts.

Departing from the summit, the line went down to the monastery situated below, and terminated inside a profound high-ceilinged crypt whose walls and vault had been partially demolished to accommodate the track. That was where the *Velox no. 2* was, installed on the launch-truck that would roll all the way to the top of the mountain, from which it would take off for the Empyrean.

Behind the long metal vehicle was situated the engine-amplifier, similar to the first experimental apparatus that we saw in the hall of the Athenaeum, but much larger in its dimensions.

The strange wand of which the engineer had made use during the memorable ascent of the three spectators was there again, considerable enlarged and fitted by a knee-joint to the upper wall of the cube instead of the "saddle." It was extended vertically, but it sufficed to fold back the "trolley" to put the *Velox* in contact with the propellant machine that was to project it toward the stars.

Finally, half way along the side of the motor, a large metallic wheel could be seen, fitted with controls somewhat reminiscent of steering-wheels, moving in front a graduated circle. This was the "activation wheel"—the device that, when the moment came, would open up a fluidic current of formidable power.

Another important detail: all the walls of the vast subterranean chamber were lined with long silky threads of all colors, which gave the crypt the appearance of a marine cave with walls covered in extremely fine algae. Strangely, these threads seemed to have a life of their own.

Some of them, gray in color and initially dull, suddenly took on a bright coloration, of orange, red or blue. They began vibrating, slowly bristling until they were perpendicular to the wall, standing up like the hair of a terrified man. From their tips flowed a soft yellow and blue phosphorescence, which filled the entire crypt with gleams that had something magical and immaterial about them. These gleams converged, attracted by a superior force, on the cube, which seemed to be absorbing them avidly, penetrated by them.

The reader has doubtless guessed that these threads, several thousand in number, all planted in miniature ampoules, were nothing other than receivers of the animic fluid emitted by the innumerable penitents and fakirs under the Rajah's orders and directed by them toward the crypt. The differences in brightness and rigidity were due to the various degrees of material displacement or intensity of the human piles.

There was something grandiose and terrible about that crypt, with its sculpted arcades of grimacing gods, where the energy of thousands of human brains was being stored.

Meanwhile, the intensity of the light was increasing by the minute, until it became fulgurant; at the same time, the temperature was rising. The cube now seemed to be aureoled by a kind of luminous mist, like the smoky vapor emitted by retorts of phosphorus.

At that moment, the only door of the *Velox*, the automatic valve situated at the rear, opened with a dry click.

The engineer Serge Myrandhal appeared in the narrow passage that served as a threshold of his strange dwelling. With one hand on the brass rail, he started climbing down the metal ladder hooked on to the guard-rail,

Half way, he turned round.

"Well," he said, "are you coming, my dear Annabella?"

"I'm following you," said a voice that came from inside the psychoscaph, "but whatever you say, I'm sure I'm not mistaken. Something abnormal is going on here. There are objects that seems to me to be out of place. Something's amiss."

Annabella, entirely devoted to her investigation, continued to remain out of sight.

"My dear friend," replied the ever-confident Serge, "I can't see what you're worried about. Everything seems to me to be in its place."

Suddenly, however, the young woman uttered an exclamation of surprise, and in a tone of annoyance she said: "This time, it's too much. I'm not the victim of a hallucination. I came smell a pipe. Some insolent individual has been smoking in my bedroom. *Shocking*, as my old governess would say."

The young woman had just appeared on the walkway. She tapped her foot, pointing an accusing finger at the Frenchman, in a manner that was supposed to be menacing. "Do you, perchance, smoke a pipe, my dear fiancé?"

Myrandhal smiled. "I'm not afflicted by that vice," he protested. "I only have the occasional cigar—but I'm quite ready to give it up, to please you. In any case, I very much doubt that the plant Mars is provided with tobacconists."

Again Miss Carpenter tapped her foot. "That's the French!" she exclaimed. "Laughing at everything. I persist in my affirmation. It reeks of pipe-smoke, horribly."

"Pure imagination, I swear. No one here, so far as I know, enjoys that odious instrument. It's probably the emanations of the accumulators, which..."

"You can say what you like!" cried Anna, impetuously. "And getting back to it, I insist that there are objects in the cabins that are no longer in the same place. Someone's been in here..."

"There's nothing extraordinary about that, my dear Annabella. It's Prince Djalor or his father. They come here every day, as is their right."

"Exactly. It's to them that I'm alluding. I think they prowl around too much, observe too much. I sniff some treason on the part of that old Maharajah, some sly scheme..."

"My dear, I assure you that your suspicions are unfounded, and exceedingly unjust. The Rajah has rendered me the most eminent services."

Pointing at the walls of the crypt, streaming with light, he said: "It's thanks to him that this river of energy is flowing in here, like the water of a thousand streaming feeding a lake. Haven't I explained that, even if the Maharajah had evil intentions, he couldn't discover my secret. You've seen the filaments without which the rest of the apparatus is useless."

Annabella took hold of her fiancé's arms, gently. "I'd really like to believe you," she said, submissively. "Does a woman have the right to an opinion? In France—I'll be French soon—a wife only has the right to shut up. You're the stronger, and you've abused that to martyrize me already. What will be, will be, great Lord! But be careful, Monsieur Frenchman, be careful. I'm American, myself, and the fatal *yes* hasn't yet been pronounced."

She burst into joyous laughter, with which Myrandhal joined in chorus.

Then, abruptly passing on to another idea, she menaced him with her gloved fingertip again. "I have a complaint to make," she said. "I want to know what's in the little box that you received so mysteriously from New York the other day. Why haven't you shown me?" Pulling a face she added: "Perhaps I'm being indiscreet?"

"No," Serge replied, embarrassed. "I swear to you…"

"Don't swear!" said the American, petulantly. "I can see by your confused expression that you don't have a clear conscience. After all, it's none of my business. You doubtless have your reasons, and I can only bow down to them for the moment. I'll see later what there remains for me to do." Annabella had suddenly struck the offended pose of a jealous woman.

Myrandhal did not know what to think. "I wouldn't want, for all the world, that you should think me capable of finding something from you," he declared. "I'll tell you everything, but it will spoil the surprise I wanted to give you on your birthday..."

"Which is the day after tomorrow, August the first..."

"I haven't forgotten. Do you still want to know my secret?"

"More than ever!" exclaimed the fiancée, whose lovely face lit up with a smile.

Myrandhal took a morocco-leather jewel-case out of his pocket and opened it.

"A watch!" the young woman exclaimed, not without a hint of astonishment.

"Yes," said Myrandhal, smiling. "A watch—but not an ordinary watch."

"What's different about it?"

"My dear Annabella, it's a Martian watch. The hours are regulated as on the planet to which we're going, where the day is thirty-seven minutes longer than ours. Look, it's a small masterpiece of scientific jewelry; the movement of the two moons of Mars, Phobos and Deimos, is reproduced here in these little lateral dials..."

Annabella was profoundly moved; her large blue eyes had suddenly misted over. "I beg your pardon," she murmured, enveloping her friend with a tender gaze. "I wanted to tease you a little..."

"You're completely forgiven."

The young woman had taken the Martian watch in her hands. She examined the elegant trinket curiously, whose case, artistically carved, represented the *Velox* afloat in a sky constellated with diamonds and rubies.

"It's adorable!" she murmured. "The winder has the form of a sun, and the whole circle is sown with little stars." With the gesture of a curious child she put it to her ear, and pouted prettily. "But it's not going."

"Big baby! It won't go until we're up there. Its first tick will coincide with our first step on the planet."

Annabella was still listening. "Yes!" she suddenly exclaimed. "It is going! I can hear a tick-tock..." She lowered her head, and with a tender coquetry, she whispered: "No, it's our hearts beating…quite loudly, in fact…" Piously, she kissed the watch and slipped it into her bosom. "I'll keep it there forever!" she said, gravely.

Serge, too emotional to speak, thanked her with a squeeze of his hand.

"How, in the midst of all this turmoil," Miss Carpenter added, "did you remember my birthday? I'd almost forgotten it myself, and the surprise is all the more agreeable for it."

"I hope that it would be even more complete. I dreamed of landing on Mars on your birthday—and that's the day on which I would have given you the watch. From that moment on, given the annual rotation of Mars around the sun, which is 669 days, you'd only have had a birthday every two years…"

"That's exquisite!" cried the American. And how lovely it would have been to get there in time! I would have been so happy to begin my twentieth year up there, with you! Is it impossible, then?"

"It's very difficult."

"Even if we leave right away? What if we try? Don't you want to?"

"I want whatever you want, but I repeat, it's almost impossible. You can see for yourself—only I'd be obliged to give you the figures, and I'm afraid…"

"Don't be afraid. Figures don't frighten me now, and besides, I'm so interested…"

"In that case, I obey. Anyway, I'll simplify. We'll leave out the fractions and the quarter-seconds with which some astronomers abuse us. Thus posed, these are the givens of the problem: at this moment, the most favorable, and until August fifteenth, Mars it at its minimal distance, fourteen million leagues. Light, at the formidable rate of eighty thousand leagues per second, takes three minutes to cross that distance, but the *Velox* is far from possessing that velocity—which isn't one, properly speaking; it's a long vibration, without real displacement.

"Add that, with regard to us, it's difficult to evaluate the exact potential of the mysterious agent that will project us toward the Empyrean, and difficult to estimate the depreciation to which that force will necessarily be subject on the highways of the Ether.

"At a rate of two hundred and fifty kilometers per second—a frightful, mortal speed—the *Velox* would take four days and fifteen hours to reach Mars. If we could go fast as five hundred, it would take two days seven and a half hours.

"As you see, even by doubling..."

"Well," cried Annabella, enthusiastically, "let's triple it, and arrive in time to celebrate my birthday on Mars! Note that you'll need flowers, and as I only like roses and orchids—doubtless unknown species up there—you'll have to bring a bouquet from here. Now, if you want to give me pleasure—the greatest in my life—and not to give me flowers that aren't very fresh, you'll have to resign yourself to going seven hundred and fifty kilometers a second...or a thousand, if necessary."

"That's the velocity of a comet..."

"Then we'll play the comet. You know that I'm being serious, and that what I want, I want! So, tell me frankly: is it impossible—absolutely impossible—to arrive on Mars the day after tomorrow?"

Miss Carpenter was speaking with such fire, such enthusiasm, that Serge felt shaken, infected by the intoxication of speed for which so many automobilists pay with their lives.

"No," he replied, "not absolutely. But in all probability, the fluid of our terrestrial factory wouldn't be sufficient, and we'd have to have recourse to our accumulators, to squander precious reserves..."

"Well, squander away," said the young woman. "Burn out the machine—what does it matter, provided that we get there? It's a matter, as my worthy guardian would say, of setting a record that won't soon be beaten. Doesn't that tempt you?"

"Yes, but I'm hesitant. To dip into our fluidic reserves…we need them in order to remain masters of the *Velox* in case of an accident. Most of all, we need them to get back."

"We won't come back, that's all."

"And if Mars is uninhabitable…"

"Impossible! As long as we're together…you see, I have an answer for everything. In consequence, enough discussion. We're wasting time, when we could be *en route*. In a word…and just say yes or no, nothing more…is it possible?"

"It's possible."

Increasingly carried away, the American clapped her hands. "In that case, Monsieur Frenchman, I'm taking you away…abducting you…we're going right now"

She had grabbed her fiancé by the shoulders and was dragging him. Bewildered, bowled over by the young woman hanging on to him—entwined with him, as it were—Serge Myrandhal allowed himself to be dragged. He followed her lead, without knowing, and without even asking, whether his fiancée meant what she was saying or not. It was one of those moments when the most earnest of men can commit the worst imprudence.

As for Miss Carpenter, simultaneously impetuous and reflective by nature, her enthusiasm, real and spontaneous as it was, lacked foundation. The time it took her to traverse the crypt was sufficient for her to get a grip on herself and envisage the incredible folly of her first impulse.

She hesitated, and sought a subterfuge—an escape route—which her alert mind rapidly discovered.

Having reached the foot of the ladder, she released Myrandhal's arm, and changed direction yet again. He expression suddenly severe, she pointed at the *Velox*, and in the coquettishly quarrelsome tone that had already enjoyed so much success, while she frowned and a gleam of malice appeared in her eyes, she said: "Tell me, Monsieur Frenchman, do you imagine that I can go in there and leave, just like that, alone with you? But we're not married, and you'd compromise me horribly! Now, I don't like that. My dear guardian must have

141

told you that I know how to make a man respect me! Tomorrow, you'll receive a visit from my seconds. Here's my card!"

She held out her hand to Myrandhal—who, utterly nonplussed at first, soon smiled, delighted to see the incident resolved in such a fortunate manner.

"What a pity!" cried the American, who could not let it go so easily. "What a beautiful dream destroyed! Oh, if that honest Jonathan Burrett had only had the good idea of arriving today. If he were here, the situation would be saved! But we can't think about it anymore, and will have to content ourselves with leaving in time, before the fifteenth of August. Just as long as the venerable clergyman gets here before then!"

"As to that," Serge replied, "I'm not worried. The pastor will be at the monastery in a week, perhaps sooner if, as your father hoped, his friend was able to take the first ship leaving for India."

At that moment, a man in a turban appeared at the entrance to the breach, illuminated by the phosphorescence of sorts that the fluid-saturated crypt was projecting. Recognizing the foreman of his Hindu workmen, Serge advanced to meet him, followed by Annabella.

"Sir," said the man, in English, "Allah has sustained our efforts. The track is complete." And he pointed along the central pathway at the elephants, who were coming back, carrying the tools, piles, cross-ties, wheelbarrows etc. that were no longer necessary on their backs.

Myrandhal congratulated his overseer and bade him farewell, after giving him a golden rupee.

In the meantime, Annabella contemplated the sky, as she frequently did, with a wondering, almost ecstatic gaze. The stars were shining with an incomparable gleam through the pure air of the mountainous region.

A little below Mars, ready to cross the meridian in its turn, Jupiter, the monarch of the heavens, was advancing at the head of a cortege of stars, which it eclipsed with its white fire, and in the distance, toward the Orient, the pale light of distant Saturn could be distinguished.

As soon as they were alone, the young woman lowered her gaze, and in a voice charged and vibrant with the ream she had just had, she said: "Do you know what I'm thinking about, my friend?"

"At a guess, you're thinking about Mars."

"No, my dream took me much further—all the way to Saturn and beyond, to the extreme limits of the solar system; and I hope that dream will be a reality one day, that the *Velox* won't stop half way."

"I'd like nothing better."

"In that case," the young woman continued, studying the shining words—the giant Jupiter; Saturn wearing its beautiful rings like a Moor's head-dress; old, cold Neptune, lost so far from the sun, condemned to eternal polar night—"I was thinking that those planets, so dissimilar to ours, are certainly inhabited, but by beings very different from us."

"No doubt about it. Creation—life—is everywhere."

"Yes—but what life? What are the beings that are stirring, who might perhaps be looking at us at this moment and asking themselves the same question? Are they beings composed of an ephemeral body and an immortal soul, who are, like us, only passing? Do they live, and die...do they love...up there?"

"Certainly," the young man replied, impetuously. "Love, the attraction of souls—like gravity, the amour of matter—is a universal law. It's even the one and only law, the one that has populated infinity, that has caused those billons of stars, of suns, to spring from the burning bosom of God, every one of which, like ours, illuminates an entire world, an entire universe...

"Now, what are the beings that gravitate up there? That something impossible to know, and which it would be madness to imagine in accordance with the few data that we possess. That would be wanting to match our feeble imagination against the resources of Nature, which are infinite in every respect.

143

"Perhaps, one day, it will be given to a human, a privileged being, to see those distant relatives..."

"Oh!" declared Miss Carpenter, in an ardent invocation. "If only it could be us!"

"Until then, we can't know anything about them—I mean, nothing about their bodies, perishable things condemned in order to live, to perpetuate themselves, to submit to the humiliating functions of animality, to model themselves according to their environment, their climate...

"It's quite different for the soul, the pure essence, freed from matter and death, and one can assume that the soul of a Jupiterian, for example, only differs from ours in the degree of its perfection, by virtue of a more or less complete knowledge of the god, the true and he beautiful.

"Personally—although I wouldn't want to seem too mystical—like the Rajah, I'd willingly admit the theory of spiritual reincarnation, already glimpsed by Pythagoras, our old master in mathematics. I firmly believe that our sun is not only a planetary center, but a psychic nucleus, around which our immortal but perfectible souls rise by degrees, transmigrating from planet to planet, getting closer at every step to the superior beauty that is nothing other, according to Plato, than the splendor of the truth."

Serge raised his inspired face toward the firmament, and continued: "No, those sparkling heavenly bodies—Jupiter, even Neptune—are not empty. The heavens are not empty! No, those planets are not the desert worlds that some people imagine, from the little that we know. There are superior races up there, which once came to the Earth. It's the abode of the fortunate, and that's where we shall rediscover those we have loved!"

At these last words, pronounced in a warm. Vibrant voice, the young woman sensed her yes moistening with tears.

"Oh, my sweet friend," she murmured, "now much good you do me! You've never spoken better in accordance with my heart. It seems to me that it's my late mother, so tender, who's expressing herself through your mouth, and like you, I firmly believe in the migration of souls. Our relatives, our friends, are up there in the heavens. They're waiting for us! And look, my dear fiancé—it's necessary that I tell you an idea that I've had many times since we've been here, far from the world, confined in this somber monastery with that enigmatic and all-powerful old man.

"You've soothed all my anxieties, but our happiness is so great, that it seems to me impossible, and I sometimes have the sensation of living a dream whose awakening will be terrible! A woman's imagination, no doubt, the fear of a woman in love trembling for her happiness; but there's one thing that consoles me, and that's my belief in the immortality of the soul. I say to myself, my dear friend, that nothing can separate those who love truly; that if ever you succumb to some ambush, I shall fight to save you to begin with, and then to avenge you—after which, my work done, I shall be able to join you. I shall find you up there, on one of those bright planets, where those that we have loved live!"

Serge Myrandhal took his fiancée's hands and pressed them to his lips. "My dear Anna," he stammered, "my sweet and tender love!"

Already, however, Miss Carpenter, fearing that she had softened too much, was gently pulling away. Becoming mischievous again, she exclaimed: "Oh look! A shooting star!"

"Make a wish."

"It's made."

"What is it?"

"I'll tell you. My first wish, to land on Mars the day after tomorrow, my birthday, is no longer realizable. But if, at least, we could be married by then..."

At that precise moment, one of the monastery's servants, clad in one of the buttonless black robes, maintained only by a belt, that Buddhist priests wear, came into the crypt, seemingly a little frightened by the strange phosphorescence.

He handed the engineer a black-framed visiting card: that of the individual awaited so impatiently, Jonathan Burrett.

Serge showed it to his companion. "Victory!" he exclaimed. "The star has granted your wish."

And with a spontaneous, irresistible impulse, the fiancés fell into one another's arms.

"Victory!" exulted the American. "We'll marry tomorrow—and on the day after, *en route* for the stars!"

"And now," Serge concluded, "let's go and greet the worthy gentleman. He must be getting impatient..."

The young people had scarcely drawn away when, behind them, in the *Velox*, a head appeared, slipping prudently out of the partly-open door.

The eyes of the unknown man, all that were visible in a bushy black beard that rose all the way to the eyelashes, reflected a malign joy. Bent double, one might have thought him a hunchback afflicted with an enormous belly, swaying like a bladder inflated with air. He emerged silently from his hiding place and started coming down the psychoscaph's iron ladder.

Having reached the bottom and looked around carefully, the false hunchback straightened up. "By the horns of Beelzebub!" he groaned. "I need to stretch my bones. It's really not comfortable in that storage-locker. On the other hand, I've learned some interesting things. I'll be glad to be able to sleep in a bed like everyone else—but I'd better keep my eyes open, al the same. It's necessary to expect anything from a lunatic like that little Carpenter girl, the Eccentric's ward. Oh, the little minx—what a tease!

"There was a moment just now when our love-birds nearly flew the coop without saying goodbye to anyone. Fortunately, I was there, as I shall be the day after tomorrow...and with that, let's get some sleep! I'm sure now of not missing the bus!"

146

XIII. "Forward Ho!"

In the meantime, the Mendicant Prince's narrow cell was the theater of another, no less important, scene.

Djalor, who had been living in mortal apprehension since being informed of the arrival of Jonathan Burrett, had just come into his father's room. He sat down in the Oriental fashion on the fiber mat comprising the only furniture of that monastic interior, and waited.

Squatting at the other extremity, his back to the wall, his knees under his chin and his eyes tightly closed, the Maharajah seemed to be asleep, but he had seen the other come in, for almost immediately, and without deigning to raise his withered eyelids, he said, in a shrill tone as distant as a dream: "You again! Why are you disturbing my nirvana?"

"Father," murmured Prince Djalor, "you know I'm suffering..."

A shiver of impatience agitated the old man's skeletal body. "I was decidedly mistaken," he interjected, in a sarcastic tone, "to send you to the home of the English who dare to call themselves our masters. I hoped to infuse you with some of their virtues, but you've only picked up their vices."

"You're cruel, Father. You love me, I know; you can see my anguish. You're the only one who can lighten it, but you remain silent. You shut yourself away in tragic silence. Why won't you..."

"Why do you doubt?" cried he Mendicant Prince, coming fully awake this time. He had folded his arms over his meager chest, and a flame of life colored his prominent cheekbones. Angrily, he repeated: "Why do you doubt? I've promise you that Miss Carpenter will never be the Frenchman's wife. Have you ever known me break my word?"

"No, Father, but something might happen at the last moment, some unexpected intervention, that can disrupt the best-laid plans. As long as we were alone here, where you're the

147

absolute master, I've had confidence in you, and obeyed you in every detail. I've put a brake on my passion and a seal on my lips. I've smiled at my rival and condemned my eyes no longer to see the one of whom my soul is full.

"But it's no longer the same today!

"An Englishman, an unknown—and doubly dangerous, in consequence—has introduced himself into this abode under a name and a pretext that are both undoubtedly false, and for a week, he's been hiding from everyone...

"The monk who received him at the secret door, who only perceived a fraction of a beard beneath the pulled-down hood of his robe, and you are the only ones who have seen this strange individual's face. All I know about him is what you've deigned to tell me: that his name is Archibald Denvalor and that he was sent here by the district governor—who wants, he claims, to be represented at the marvelous experiment we're preparing.

"All that is extraordinary, to say the least. The delegates of the English government usually behave in a far more cavalier fashion. Ordinarily, it's in broad daylight, with a large cortege, that they come among us. This one, by contrast, has slipped in like a thief...

"But what surprises me most of all is that you, so jealous of your slightest prerogatives, have welcomed this intruder without a murmur; that, far from forcing him to explain himself, you're helping him to hide. I know that a man who has reached the level of sanctity where you exist receives enlightenment from on high refused to mortals still retained by the bonds of the flesh, but I have my lover's instinct, which warns me...

"Believe me, Father, this man is dangerous!

"Is he a friend, a relative of our guests, who is attempting to watch over them, to protect them in secret? Might he not be one of these innumerable detectives hired by the *Herald*, who pullulated back there, around Norton Cottage, who has caught wind of our plans and has come here incognito in order to defend the invention of which we intend to take possession?"

The Rajah shrugged his shoulders imperceptibly. "My child," he jeered, "I'm glad that your love has not put your vigilance completely to sleep or obscured your understanding. Your mistrust, although misguided, is legitimate; in sum, I congratulate you on it.

"As for the Englishman, banish all anxiety on that subject. Denvalor isn't dangerous. He knows nothing of our plans, but I've known his since the first day. He had scarcely crossed the threshold of this cell than I read his face and his heart like an open book.

"For now, I'll only tell you one thing: Archibald Denvalor is neither a friend nor an enemy. We could make him an associate, but that would do him too much honor..."

That superb indifference reassured Prince Djalor. He was about to reply when the sound of a gong suddenly rang out in the nearby corridor.

Djalor shivered and leapt to his feet with the agility of a young jaguar.

"That's for me," he said, in an anguished voice. "There must be some important news. Excuse me, Father."

He launched himself toward the door...

When he came back, a few minutes later, his face was distraught, his eyes hollow, burning with fever. "Father!" he said. "All is lost! The minister, Jonathan Burrett—may Hell confound him!—has just arrived, with the authorization of Annabella's father. The Frenchman and his friend are mad with joy. They've announced that they'll marry tomorrow, and launch themselves into the heavens the day after!

"The Frenchman's already giving orders, as if he were at home. He's just instructed that the crypt and the *Velox* should be decorated with flowers. It's there, in front of the apparatus, that the nuptial service will take place..."

Despairingly, Djalor wrung his long, slender hands, whose bones clicked. In clipped sentences he gave a few more details, and then, with his throat tight and his mouth convulsive, he groaned: "No, it can't be! I love her too much..."

A cloud passed over the decrepit face of the Mendicant Prince. The man, in whom almost nothing human remained, had felt a string vibrate in his shriveled heart.

"Djalor," he said, in a grave, almost gentle, voice, "Djalor, my child, the hope and pride of my race, calm down and listen. Nothing is lost, and the pastor's arrival will have no other result than to hasten our triumph. We are the masters here. The inventor, his invention and his fiancée belong to us. I've promised to give you the woman you love, to throw her into your arms a virgin, and I will keep my word. You know on what condition..."

The Prince lowered his eyes in shame. "Yes," he said. "You want me to help you rob my rival. I shall obey! For you, for her...I shall go as far as dishonor, as far as crime..."

"Pusillanimous soul!" murmured the Rajah, scornfully. "Heart of a jackal! There is neither dishonor nor crime for men such as us, acting in the name of a superior principle. It is Brahma who commands, and delivers our adversaries to us, bound hand and foot. It is necessary to act..."

"Command," said the young man, convinced. "I'm ready. But how can we prevent what is in preparation? Tomorrow, or the day after, at the latest, the Frenchman will depart, taking his fiancée...his wife...and his secret with him..."

"No! declared the father, curtly. "The secret—the secret that will give us a world—will remain here, in our hands. I have discovered it; I now possess it in its entirety. As I no longer have any need of the inventor, I shall kill him...or, even better, get rid of him by sending him far away, to a place from which he will only return with our permission...which is to say, never.

"As for Miss Carpenter, who is your destiny, she too will remain in our hands."

"How?" asked the Prince, feverishly. "How will you do that?"

"What does it matter?" said the Rajah, with a sudden abruptness. "I can only tell you one thing Tomorrow, when the moment comes to embark, the Frenchman will have changed his mind. He will depart alone, leaving us his invention as the price of our aid, and his wife as a hostage.

"It will be thus because I wish it, because it is right that it should be thus. We are hesitating because everything is in our favor. Another few hours, one more move, and the game is won, all along the line. I am taking possession of what I consider to be my property, and getting rid of an inconvenience: an inconvenience that I am making into a collaborator—a test subject, as you say in your laboratories—who will inform us as to the habitability of the planet."

"Are you sure?" asked Djalor, already half-convinced by his father's unshakable assurance. "Myrandhal might suspect our ruse, our treason, and refuse to communicate..."

"He will suspect nothing," the father replied, his lips pursed, "and it doesn't matter; I've anticipated the possibility and I have the means to constrain him."

"What means?"

"There are several. The simplest is that the lovers, as soon as they are separated, will certainly communicate via the telepath, of which I too know the secret. What is simpler than eavesdropping on their communication? If necessary, we shall only have to suggest certain questions to Miss Carpenter, who will become our unwitting and benevolent secretary..." The Mendicant Prince concluded, with a ferocious snigger that showed his sharp teeth: "Everything is already planned and weighed, you see. In making your rival depart alone, I shall strike a double, a triple blow! I shall conquer a woman for you, and a world for me, of which you will be the first couple...and I shall be avenged!

"I shall be avenged for that which was stolen from me by the victor of the Athenaeum, who will become once again what he should never have ceased to be, an instrument of our service, a lowly creature on which we shall carry out our experiments *in anima vili* as you say."

"What about the other one?" objected Djalor. "This mysterious Denvalor? What will you do with him? You have no fear of him, you say—I have no difficulty believing you, but

151

still... Judging by his letters of accreditation, this Englishman, whoever he is, has connections, and authority with which we have to reckon. If he's there are the moment of departure, he'll discover our trick; he might become inconvenient. Suppose he sides with Miss Carpenter..."

"The Englishman will not be any hindrance," Indraghava declared, in a peremptory tone. "If he takes it into his head to see too clearly, he can be eliminated, sent far away like the other. In any case, the hypothesis is gratuitous. Far from getting in our way, Denvalor will assist us, if he is asked. It will be sufficient to associate him with our work—to make him believe that he is an associate—and he will do whatever we wish.

"Do you doubt that? Well, you can judge for yourself. You shall see"—an enigmatic smile creased the terrible Rajah's parchment-like lips—"that, like that ridiculous Eccentric, *what I say, I do*...always!

"For nearly a week, Denvalor has been asking for a second meeting, always refused. Go out and give the order that he should be fetched as quickly as possible. Then, hide behind that curtain"—the mage pointed at a door-curtain of coarse fabric masking the entrance to a second cell—"and from there you shall listen, and you shall see...

"I want to give you that further proof of my power over the other Aryans, those ingrate and degenerate sons who, because they have made a few improvements of the science we discovered thousands of years ago, think themselves our equals, our masters. How ridiculous! I hope that, after that, you will no longer doubt me, and will obey me blindly."

"Yes, Father."

Less than ten minutes later, the man we have just seen sliding out of the *Velox* made his entrance, followed by a silent monk carrying a poorly-wrought stool, which he placed in front of the Master's mat.

Archibald Denvalor, interpreting to his advantage the long-desired meeting that had suddenly been accepted, seemed very proud, inflated by his sudden importance. He paraded his arrogant, provocative gaze over the bare walls, and the sordid old man, still ensconced, his eyelids lowered, who had not deigned to greet him even by means of a gesture.

When the mute servant had withdrawn, the Mendicant Prince pointed to the seat and, in excellent French—the Rajah never spoke the language of the abhorrent conqueror—said in an indolent tone: "Sit down, Mr. Pickman."

His visitor started and blushed. That simple sentence had sufficed to deflate the presumptuous individual, who let himself fall on to the proffered stool rather than sitting down.

"What's that?" he stammered, passing his strong hands over his moist brow. "What, that, sir? You say…by Jove! If you weren't an old man... You're joking, I think..."

"It's you who are joking," the mage replied, curtly and harshly. Then, abruptly changing his attitude and in his most amiable manner, he continued: "Come, come, my dear Baronet. You've lost. Be a good sportsman. You've lost, but your honor is safe. Your disguise was superb. Even my son, your fellow for more than a year in the Splendid Club, was taken in, like the rest. With the father, it's not so easy, and I'm astonished that you haven't approached me, at least, without your face uncovered, without that beard and your fake paunch.

"Come on, my dear Pickman, you're an Englishman, and a man of intellect in consequence; you know India and its yogis; you've witnessed incontestable instances of 'second sight'—and it's in the presence of one of those thaumaturges, and not the least, that you attempt a childish, comical trick?"

The Eccentric was on the spot. Angrily, he twirled his absent alpenstock on his knees.

"As for me," his mocking interlocutor continued, "I haven't even taken the trouble to see you, remember. You hadn't even crossed the outer wall when I was aware of your coming and your plans, Mr. Pickman."

"My plans!" stammered the Englishman, increasingly bewildered. "You know what I've come to do here? No!

That's impossible. Everyone thinks I'm in San Francisco. I telegraphed..."

"Another trick that stuck out a mile, that dispatch. It would have been sufficient to give you away to Serge Myrandhal if he were not distracted—doubly distracted, as a scientist and a lover. Otherwise, given the overtures you made to him—for you've spoken to him, that's obvious—he would have seen the trap right away."

"That's true, murmured the Eccentric, red with confusion. "I'm an old fool, yes—a lumbering brute, that's what I am. So you know my plan."

"For a long time."

"And you're going to stop me?" Pickman said, anxiously.

"I didn't say that."

"Oh!" The Eccentric's eyes lit up with hope.

"I didn't say that," the mage repeated, still smiling. "I'm not a jealous man, myself—not ferociously jealous, like my associate—and I haven't taken sides in your personal competition. Until now, I've remained neutral, and I'll continue to do so—always provided that you don't harm the common enterprise."

"I've no intention of doing that!" the Englishman protested, striking his breast with demonstrative violence. "I'm a gentleman, a pure soul, by Jove! All I ask, personally, is a place on the *Velox*...that's all."

"Then we might...yes, we might, perhaps, come to an understanding," the Mendicant Prince insinuated. "I like you..."

"You too...I like you!" exclaimed the Eccentric, impetuously. "You're a good chap, a fine fellow...I mean, a worthy man...a generous heart, that's it. Apologies...I've lost the thread. I must seem stupid to you..."

"Not at all," the Rajah replied, with a thin smile. "I'm not suspected of affection for your people, but your enthusiasm appeals to me. I like your juvenile valor, your style, your 'forward ho!' attitude, as you say, and I might even help you..."

"You'd do that!"

"Perhaps…if your intentions are pure. Before anything else, let me tell you that your means—the idea of leaving hidden in the *Velox*'s hold—is no good. For several days you've been slipping in there every night, at the risk of being asphyxiated by the emanations of the accumulators. You haven't been caught so far, but that couldn't be long delayed. A man of your size doesn't hide easily, and although our scientist is distracted, Miss Carpenter has an American eye. Beware...

"Why, since that inconsiderate fellow Myrandhal was so intractable in your regard—which is hardly gallant toward your god-daughter—didn't you address yourself to me boldly and frankly? You know that my son and I are also planning to make the great voyage..."

"Yes, I know—the *Velox no. 1*. I know about that. Serge—that inconsiderate fellow, as you put it—told me about it. But can you launch it? That's the objective...I mean, the objection..."

"What a question! You're forgetting, my dear Pickman, that it's me who supplies the fluid..."

"No, only the motive force—but the amplifier, as he calls it: do you know its secret?"

"I know enough to be able to make use of it whenever I please, if that's sufficient for you. It was one of the clauses of our association, and if your intentions are honest, I'm ready to let you take advantage of it."

"All right!" cried the Eccentric, leaping off the stool—but he sat down again almost immediately. "Except," he went on, "that there's a catch…I mean a hitch...

"According to what he told me, Myrandhal is going to leave first and arrive on Mars first. Isn't that so? If it is, then I'll lose the record. That's the question, you understand?"

"I understand perfectly. Myrandhal does, indeed, have to depart before anyone else; that's specified in our agreement, which I intend to honor strictly, to the letter—nothing more and nothing less.

"As for landing on Mars first, that's a different matter. There, the field is free, open to competition. With the means at our disposal, provided that we don't leave it too long, we might well be able, not merely to catch up with him, but—who can tell?—perhaps even overtake him."

At that idea, the Eccentric leapt up again, mad with you, his eyes wide. He applauded with his strong hands, as large as shoulders of mutton.

"Bravo!" he cried. "Hip, hip, hurrah for Old England! A steeplechase to the planet! That's magnificent...fantastic! No such thing has ever been seen. A handicap through the stars, and it's the outsider, the Englishman, who'll win! Rule Britannia! It's prodigious! Well done! Oh, if they knew about this at the Splendid Club, what colossal bets they'd be laying! Look at the odds! I'll take ten to one, and I'll bet..."

The Eccentric continued in this burlesque manner for another full minute. Then he calmed down slightly. "You're sure of success, then?"

"As much as one can be. I've told you that we have immeasurable reserves of force here. Take note, too, that the *Velox no. 2*, even far away, outside our sphere of gravity, will still remain subject to my psychic influence, and that very probably, in spite of the fully-charged accumulators he's carrying, I can still, if not stop him, at least slow him down..."

"No! Shocking!" cried the Englishman, hotly. "It's necessary, sir, not to do anything felonious. We must win the great battle by playing straight. And we *shall* win—hip, hip hurrah for England!"

On receiving that admonition, the Rajah had frowned momentarily, but now he was smiling. *That's right*, he thought. *Enthusiastic and honest, in the English fashion—that's the man we need.* "So, my dear Pickman," he said, "you agree to join forces with us against Myrandhal. You're with us?"

"Yes I am," declared the Eccentric. "I'd risk my life for that. That Frenchman offended me gravely; I'm going to…what do I have to do?"

"Very little. As with you, Myrandhal has offended me, with his pride, and his mistrust. While respecting our contract to the letter, I want to teach him a lesson in modesty. To do that, I need someone, an associate..."

"And you thought of me! Thank you!"

"Exactly. I'll even say, although you'll accuse me of bluffing, that it was me who suggested to you, at a distance, the idea of coming here..."

"No! That's true!" the Eccentric affirmed, becoming a flatterer for the first time in his life. "That's true, by Jove! I remember now...you're a prodigious man. Well done!"

"As for what you have to do," the mage continues, "very little. Continue hiding, playing dead, and wait. The *Velox no. 1*, ours, is ready and provisioned. An hour after the Frenchman's departure, it will be hoisted on to the rails…and on its way!"

"All right!" howled the Englishman, applauding loudly again.

Shortly afterwards, he withdrew, enveloped by the Rajah's indefinable gaze.

XIV. Married!

In accordance with Annabella's wishes, the marriage was celebrated the following day at midnight, twenty-four hours before the departure for the stars. The young woman had wanted those two events, the crucial turning-points in her life, to take place at the same hour: the moment when Mars passed the meridian.

The ceremony, a very simple one, had just concluded. Annabella and Serge were alone with Jonathan Burrett in the *Velox*'s crypt, decorated with flowers—roses and jasmine.

The Rajah, still impenetrable, and Prince Djalor—the latter livid beneath the make-up with which he had coated his cheeks—had retired discreetly as soon as their royal signatures had been added to the document drawn up by the pastor.

The Reverend J. Burrett, a stout man with a jovial face, but endowed with an exquisite tact and delicacy, closed his Bible and led the newlyweds to a bench situated a few yards away, at the entrance to the garden. He invited them to sit down beside him, and then, in a paternal tone, he said: "My friends, I have only a few more things to say to you, and one desire to express, and then I too shall leave you to your happiness, blessed by God.

"It's no longer the pastor who is speaking, but the friend, the man who represents, for the moment, your whole family, Indeed, I'm not only replacing your guardian but your father, who is struggling out there in the Far West. He's already received the telegram sent this morning, and he's thinking about you at this solemn moment. He'll be thinking about you even more tomorrow, at the moment of the great Exodus...the moment when all eyes in America—what am I saying? in the entire civilized world—will be upon you.

"But it's not your glory, which will be great for centuries to come, but your happiness with which I'm concerned, and I want that happiness, my dear children, to be as complete as your valor, as vast as your enterprise, deserves...

"You are a privileged couple, elected among thousands to realize the most prodigious conquest in human history. The Eternal has chosen you both; he has given you beauty and strength. He has marked your young foreheads with the sign of heroes and prophets, in order that you might go on high to carry the good word.

"Tomorrow, beautiful with youth and faith, radiant with love, you will quit this Earth, you will fly like the angels through the constellations, realizing the most marvelous endeavor, living the most sublime dream that the human mind has ever conceived.

"At the mere thought of that marvelous adventure, my mind is troubled and my heart fills with a patriotic pride. I am proud, as a humble associate, an old priest brought from afar to bless you, that it is my country, America, that has given a hero like you a companion worthy of him. And I think, with a thrill of enthusiasm, of that unknown planet to which you are going, a new Adam and a new Eve, to be fruitful and multiply, in accordance with Jehovah's command.

"But I'm talking too much, talking about glory to you who have happiness, and in the meantime, the minutes are going by, the golden sand of Time is flowing. This is the august moment: on high, angels are passing, bearing in their arms the souls of generations to come. This is the moment celebrated in the Song of Songs, at which the shadows bow down and the husband goes to the wife...

"It seems to me that a few moments ago, I perceived behind you a grave and tender face: that of the angel of holy love, who will conduct you to the nuptial chamber. It's to him that I confide you, after having blessed you one last time!"

Jonathan Burrett placed his hands on the heads of two spouses, and withdrew.

Left alone, the young people remained silent, listening to their hearts beating precipitately. Serge had taken Anna's tremulous hand and was squeezing it gently.

Around them, in the age-old gardens, an indefinable odor was floating, and the foliage, bathed in moonlight, was stirring. From the overheated crypt, the scent of jasmine and roses drifted on the breeze. Under the bench, a cricket sang, seemingly counting the seconds...such brief seconds, and yet so full, enclosing an eternity...

Suddenly, the young woman rose to her feet.

Serge leaned toward her, his face ecstatic. "I won't say adieu," he murmured, in a breath.

She turned away, her face pink with modesty, and fled, leaving a kind of wake behind her.

Her dress gleamed one last time, then disappeared in a moonbeam.

Myrandhal, his heart overflowing with an ineffable joy, lingered for a few moments more. Then he got up in his turn and headed through the garden to the wing of the convent that had been prepared for them. In a few strides he had negotiated the pathways and had climbed the stairs leading to his wife's apartment.

Once there, his pace slowed. He wanted to anticipate his happiness...

His soul rhapsodized, he went along the corridor at a supple, elastic pace, barely skimming the floor.

The décor, which was not unfamiliar to him—the old walls illuminated by lamps burning in front of statues or covered with pious, even sinister, inscriptions; the bas-reliefs in which yogis writhed in torment; the thicket pillars whose heavy shadows were projected by the moonlight coming through the narrow windows on to the flagstones worn away by the bare feet of monks; the whole severe and disquieting ensemble of a Buddhist cloister—had the effect on him of an enchanted palace.

Like Victor Hugo's lover, he marched, "fully alive, through his starry dream."[16]

---

[16] The original quotation "*Donc je marche vivant dans mon rêve étoilé*" is from Hugo's *Ruy Blas* (1838), but the addition

Once or twice however, he thought he heard the noise of sandals, and stopped, gripped by an obscure presentiment.

There's someone here, he thought. *Someone's following me...might it be Prince Djalor?*

Serge turned round, clenching his fists, ready to defend his happiness. At that moment, between the pedestals of two gigantic Buddhas, a man emerged from the shadows and threw himself upon the Frenchman, gripping him with his thin arms.

It was the Rajah.

"My friend," stammered the old man, distressed. "Where have you been? I've been looking for you for an hour!"

"What's happening?" exclaimed Serge, distressed in his turn. "Has Anna...?"

"No! Madame Myrandhal is in her room. It's not to do with her but you, your invention, ours..." While speaking, the Mendicant Prince had seized Myrandhal's arm and as dragging him through a labyrinth of corridors and staircases toward the pitch dark gardens. "Come quickly," he sent on, breathlessly. "There's someone...a malefactor...down there in the crypt, in the *Velox*...someone's trying to rob us! What can I do? I'm an old man, and my son—you can guess why—left the convent an hour ago..."

Myrandhal had drawn a revolver from his pocket and was running, followed close behind by the mage, who was wheezing ominously.

The crypt, into which he soon hurtled, was in exactly the same state as he had left it a few minutes earlier. Two torches were on the point of going out. The flowers and green plants, strewn on the ground all the way to the ladder of the *Velox*, had not been disturbed.

"I don't see anything..." Serge began.

"Yes! The trolley!"

The arm connecting the motor to the *Velox* had been lowered, as if someone were about to depart...

---

of *tout* before *vivant* was supplied in a secondary rendition of the quote by the composer Hector Berlioz.

One twist of the wheel, and the projectile would be shot into the sky like a bullet.

Myrandhal raised his hand to push back the lever connecting the current, but the Mendicant Prince stopped him with an abrupt gesture,

"Look!" he said, his teeth chattering. "Look at the door"—he pointed to the valve at the rear of the *Velox*, which was open. "There's someone in there—our thief! I can hear footsteps..."

Already, Myrandhal had climbed the iron ladder and gone into the psychoscaph.

Indraghava followed him at an unsteady pace, and stopped on the top rung. "Well?" he asked, in a choked voice, quavering with alarm.

"I can't see anything," Serge said, having already gone through the first two compartments.

"Look out!" recommended the mage, increasingly anguished. "Be careful!"

Because of his excitement and the precipitate run, the old man was tottering on his emaciated legs. In order not to fall, he had to grab hold on the lever controlling the seal of the valve.

There was a dry click. The door had just closed behind the inattentive Myrandhal, and Indraghava's face had suddenly become terrible. As nimble as a monkey, with an agility that made his old skeleton creak, he bounded to the activation wheel, which he began to turn...

What followed—a drama that unfolded in less than a second—is indescribable.

A convulsive face appeared at one of the portholes of the *Velox*, and then flew away at a vertiginous acceleration. A horrible scream, a superhuman scream, caused its sides to quiver.

Almost at the same moment, the *Velox*, reaching its full speed, appeared to extend, to stretch, covering the entire course of the track, all the way to the summit...

Then the rails reappeared, shiny and empty.

High above, in the sky, there was a strident whistle, the cry of a steel bird cleaving through the air at the speed of a bolide—and that was all.

As for the Rajah, he was still turning the control-wheel

As the needle on the dial completed its rotation, providing the full intensity of the current, the entire crypt became incandescent. Wires melted, and were volatilized; tongues of fire licked the walls, while a steel bar left on the edge of the track, weighing a hundred kilos, began to twist, coiling like a snake around a centenarian oak tree.

At the same time, fiery sparks sprang from the Rajah's hair, beard and eyelashes, so that he seemed momentarily to be enveloped by flames. Terrified, and burned all over, he was obliged to let go of the wheel.

Staggering, half-killed by the frightful discharge, he slumped against the back wall. He remained there for a long moment, his throat and lungs contacted, his body shaken by titanic convulsions.

Soon, however, life reappeared; his diaphragm dilated like a bellows filled with air. As his respiration returned, a ferocious smile creased the terrible old man's desiccated lips. His bright and terrible eyes were flamboyant with pride.

"That went well!" he murmured. "I promised the Frenchman a wedding night without parallel, and I kept my word. If my son hadn't left, like an idiot, like a coward, he would be delighted! We'll finish the job without him. To the other now—Miss Anna!"

He was still speaking when he perceived the American woman, fully illuminated by the glare of the of the phosphorescent crypt.

Clad in a simple peignoir, her beautiful hair braided for the night, her brow furrowed, she had just emerged from the breach in the wall through which the machine had taken flight.

Standing at her window, gazing at the stars, she had heard and seen—insofar as it was visible—the steel bird plunge into the darkness.

Sensing treason, she had run through the gardens. The disappearance of the *Velox* confirmed her fears, but she was far from suspecting the truth, of glimpsing the full horror of the situation she was in.

She looked around, her eyes full of menace, and said, I an imperious voice: "What are you doing here? And where's Serge my husband?"

A sadistic joy was sparkling in the Mendicant Prince's cruel eye. "Your husband," he said, gesturing toward the gardens, "has gone."

"Gone!" murmured the wife, struck full in the heart, but not yet understanding.

"Yes," the sinister old man continued, sarcastically. "It was an accident. He came with me to cast one last glance at it. Someone—a bandit—had primed the apparatus. Then..."

A hoarse sob cut off his speech. Annabella had understood, and put both hands to her breaking heart. Her eyes turned back, biting her lips, digging her fingernails into her flesh in order not to scream in front of her enemy, she tottered, as pale as candle-wax.

Then, making a prodigious effort of will, of pride, she succeeded in overcoming her horrible anguish. Her eyes blazing, full of lightning, menacing and terrible, like a wrathful archangel, she took two steps toward her torturer, who beat a retreat.

Before that superb creature, magnificent in anger and in love, the mage, in spite of all his psychic power, was momentarily overwhelmed.

"You're lying!" she said, in a vibrant voice.

"Well, yes," the Rajah replied, suddenly assuming a soft, compassionate voice, toying with his prey. "I wanted to spare a newlywed a painful truth, but you're forcing me to speak. There was no accident. Your husband left because he wanted to, and because he had to, because it was the only means of breaking an engagement made too lightly."

The Rajah's accent was so sincere, and Annabella's distress so great that she did not protest immediately.

She lowered her head, and was thoughtful, her mind and heart crushed. With a mechanical gesture, she had undone the cord securing her peignoir, and was swinging it in front of her like a sling.

"You understand," the Hindu continued, his tone gradually becoming ironic, "that my friend Myrandhal never seriously intended to take you with him. What childishness! It would have been contrary to our agreement. However, he needed you; you've been very useful at the *Herald* and elsewhere, so he promised you everything you wished—marriage and the rest—but it was only a lure, a pretence, one of those promises one makes to little girls.

"Your marriage isn't even valid, and I assure you, Miss Carpenter, that you'll never call yourself Madame Myr..."

He could not finish the insulting assertion. Brandishing the cord like a whip, the American had just truck him across the face.

"Wretch!" she howled. "Don't insult the man I love! You're lying, and I know everything. I guessed it all, suspected it for a long time. I even warned my husband! Poor and loyal friend, who didn't listen! Nevertheless, don't be too hasty to gloat. You haven't won yet. Serge is up there—I'll go to join him if he doesn't come back; but nothing—*nothing*, you hear—will prevent us from seeing one another again, from loving one another.

"As for you, your crime, your abominable treason, you won't profit from it. You think you know our secret, but you're mistaken. Our precautions have been taken, and well taken. You won't have Myrandhal's invention, or his wife! And it's his wife who will punish you, who will avenge him, you hear! I'll denounce you to the English authorities."

Indraghava, who was calmly wiping his swollen eyelids, from which a trickle of blood as running, laughed shrilly and hoarsely.

"I pity you, Miss Carpenter," he sniggered. "You're forgetting that I'm the master here, and the only master! You've entered this convent, and you'll only leave dead or submissive, accepting all my conditions. You're my prisoner, my hostage, and I'm keeping you."

At that threat, Annabella made a superb gesture of defiance. Her only response was to hurl a gaze of crushing scorn at her enemy. Then, disdainful, as haughty as an offended queen, still brandishing the whip with which she had just chastised her insulter, she went back to her apartment.

For his part, the mage had run into the corridor adjacent to the crypt. He struck a gong suspended from the top of a column. Almost immediately, the monk who always followed him in more or less considerable proximity, emerged from the shadows, and the two men embarked on a feverish conversation.

For her part, Madame Myrandhal, who knew that she must be ready for anything, went into her apartment, all the doors of which she bolted carefully. At the sight of her empty bedroom—the bedroom of a virgin wife and widow!—all the courage and pride she had sustained thus far suddenly collapsed. She fell on to her bed, in tears, and writhed there, biting the pillows in order to stifle her sobs.

Two brief, imperious raps on the door of the antechamber, recalled her to herself. Then there were furious, muffled blows. Action was following close behind the threat, and her domicile was about to be violated!

Frightened, she looked around, and saw the telepath that Serge had given her a few days before—and a gleam of joy, of love, lit up her ravaged face.

"Let me warn him, at least!" she sighed, running to the apparatus. "Let me talk to him one last time!"

Close at hand, however, the blows redoubled on the door to the corridor, which would soon be broken down.

Panic-stricken, the American had seized the signal-key, which she was manipulating with a feverish finger.

My dear husband, she began...and at that word, so sweet, her tears sprang forth again...

XV. The Great Dark

Meanwhile, the *Velox*, launched at prodigious speed, had traversed the terrestrial atmosphere.

With one bound, it had cleaved through the illusory blue vault that we call the firmament, which is nothing but an optical effect produced by the form of our eyes and the color of the gas in which we bathe.

After a few seconds, the horrible whistling and the suffocating heat caused by the friction of air on the hull had ceased completely.

Now, the psychoscaph, having arrived in the absolute void—the interastral void—was flying soundlessly, without a shudder. To the person inside it, it seemed to be motionless, just as the Earth does not reveal its enormous speed of thirty kilometers a second. And yet, a human eye capable of perceiving it at that moment would have seen something frightful: a black dot, a long dark streak, traversing the sky from end to end in less than a second and flying on and on, madly!

Leaning against the wall of the central compartment, against which he had been thrown at the moment of the fatal launch, Serge Myrandhal had not uttered a word or made a movement. He seemed thunderstruck, flabbergasted, like the upright cadaver discovered among the still-smoking ruins of Martinique, who fell into dust at the first touch...

His stunned brain, as if paralyzed, as devoid of thought or definite sentiment; but before his wide eyes—the vitreous, atonal eyes of a madman—there were two terrible, tortuous images.

There was a man, a stranger, whose name he did not know—a little, diabolical old man—maneuvering some kind of wheel.

Then, beyond that, on the far side of the tall trees swaying gently in the embalmed nocturnal breeze, a lighted bedroom...the bedroom of a young woman, glimpsed from afar,

167

like a paradise—and in the middle, all alone, seemingly wait-ing, a woman, weeping...

His wife!

"Anna!" he moaned.

Suddenly, emerging from his stupor, he uttered a terrible roar, the cry of a wild beast whose nourishment has been snatched away.

She's calling to me, he thought.

And the desire to save the woman he loved, to race to her aid, vanquished the crushing torpor by which he had been overwhelmed. His face, distraught, almost cadaverous a few seconds earlier, was now fulgurant. The hero, the man who had vanquished nature, had just got a grip on himself, drawn him upright, ready for the fray...

With long strides he headed for the forward compart-ment. It was there, it will be remembered, in the "engine room" of sorts, that the recording apparatus was, the accumu-lators and, above all, a priceless resource, the reserves of psy-chic fluid stored for the return to Earth, and which could—which had to—permit him and his wife to come home...

By the light of the radiant walls, the young man consult-ed a dial indicating the velocity of his invention, and could not suppress a shudder of horror.

"Thirty-three kilometers a second!" he murmured. "And as it's a matter of a supraphysical force, which doesn't de-crease, or only decreases very slightly, with distance, I'll be on Mars in a matter of hours—and that's not what I want!"

While reflecting, Serge had rotated a commutator with an anxious finger. Again he consulted the dial, and went pale. The needle indicating velocity was leaping madly.

"Seventy-two!" he stammered, fearfully. "Ninety-six...a hundred and twenty...a hundred and thirty-two. We've quad-rupled our speed in a matter of seconds. The contest is impos-sible—I'm beaten!"

Gripped by rage, he seized another lever with both hands. He clung on to it, accumulating all his will-power, ex-tending all the energy of which he was capable in the opposite direction to the force that was driving him on with lightning speed.

Almost immediately, however, after a final glance at the counter, he let go of the commutator and, from the depths of his bosom, from the depths of his entrails, twisted by a nameless anguish, a hoarse plaint emerged.

"It's all over!" he croaked. "I'll never be able to oppose the psychic current that's driving me. I'm no longer master of my ship. My terrestrial force-factory is overwhelming me, and will do so until the end. I should have anticipated that danger and forestalled it, but it's too late.

"Only one man—the mage—might perhaps be able to bring me back, and even then, who can tell? My momentum is such that, by the time it relaxes slightly, I'll have fallen into another sphere of attraction—that of Mars. I ought to have foreseen this, and not trusted the sinister old man!"

At the name of Mars, great as the distress of the lover was, the curiosity of the scientist awoke again.

He searched for the planet through the little porthole to the right, but only saw a black wall, nothing but a black wall. The star, placed on the axis of the *Velox*, which was heading directly toward it, was invisible from that position.

Then, with the scarcely-conscious desire to find another observation-post, he went back to the central compartment. He went at a mechanical, quasi-somnambulistic pace. His brain, woken up momentarily, was gradually falling back into is initial stupor. The instrument of thought, so powerful in our hero, was no more than an organic mechanism, so to speak, an automatic recorder of sensations and numbers, something like one of the multiple counters that could be seen hanging on the walls of the *Velox* on all sides.

As he went into the compartment, Serge uttered an exclamation of surprise. The large portholes were veiled with a fine lacework of frost, which, at that moment, had something lugubrious about it. One might have thought that they were dead eyes, petrified by horror.

"It's the cold," he said, drawing nearer. "We're traveling at this moment through absolute cold, 270 degrees below zero!

"A few minutes have sufficed to refrigerate the *Velox*, which was red hot a little while ago. In another few seconds if I don't open the radiators, the thermometer will fall to fifty below, then a hundred, and I'll die. The numbness is starting already, cerebral anesthesia...and it's doubtless thanks to that that I'm still alive. My paralyzed brain is hardly thinking, and I'm suffering less."

While speaking, he wiped away the layer of ice blurring the crystal with his sleeve. He leaned forward to look through and recoiled, shivering, at the terrible appearance of the sky that he had just glimpsed.

A funereally black sky...a cataclysmic sky!

Toward the pole, the Great Bear shone menacingly. Here and there, a few stars, and everywhere, darkness, opaque darkness, the Great Dark of which the Bible speaks.[17]

All around him, the firmament extended like a mortuary drape studded with gold. Serge Myrandhal had reached the regions "mute of light," according to Dante's expression, the terrible sky that "knows neither dusk nor dawn."

Another phenomenon: the luminous beams spring from the portholes, which, a little while before, in the terrestrial atmosphere, had given the *Velox* something akin to wings of flame, had also disappeared. The luminous current, invisible

---

[17] The phrase employed in the original text, *Grande Ténèbre* [sic] does not appear in any French version of the Bible that I can identify, in which darkness tends to be signified, as is usual in French, by the plural *ténèbres*. It does crop up in the singular form, however, in some Christian mystical writings in French, where it refers specifically to the "superior obscurity" of the "inaccessible light"—i.e., to God in essence, beyond all names and forms, stripped of His attributes. I have translated the phrase as Great Dark rather than Great Darkness to stress that a particular meaning, albeit not a Biblical one, is probably intended.

because it did not encounter any reflective matter, was lost; or rather—since nothing is lost—went a long way, to the end of the world, to be reflected by who knew what distant planet!

For a long minute, Serge contemplated the tragic scene.

The universe is terrible, he thought, *and the firmament is not what poets and lovers imagine. Scientists know that truth, but they scarcely suspect the horror of it!*

What is the World, in fact—our world? A bubble of gas, a grain of dust, lost in the ether...

What is daylight—our daylight? What is the dawn, the light with its thousand fires? What is the rainbow? An optical affect.

Oh, how formidable Creation is, looked in the face, outside the frame, the milieu of illusion in which we were situated by an unknown law!

For hours, perhaps days, I shall travel without encountering a ray of light, one of the sunbeams that rejoice the human heart! And yet everywhere around me, near me, there are stars: the moon, the planets, which are shining but without illuminating!

There is, above all, the sun, which no longer sets for me, which will never set again until my arrival on another world. At this moment it is shining out there, silvering my hull, but between us, all around us, there is night...implacable and opaque night!

I knew that, personally. I knew, in theory, that nocturnal, sinister aspect of the universe. Whence, then, comes this tremor, these cold droplets trickling over my temples? I knew the spectacle that awaited me, and yet my mind is troubled. My blood is chilled and my hair is bristling. It's the frisson: the great frisson of the abyss! The one that gripped the wicked angels precipitated by the archangel Michael, who fell for seven times seven days through the void.

Decidedly, the space, not only space but interplanetary space, that I declared to be our domain, is forbidden to humankind. I thought in my pride that man was the glorious son of the sun, the master of all the worlds that gavotte around the sovereign star. I was mistaken! Man is only the child of the Earth, the humble product off vile clay, condemned to crawl eternally through the primordial mud.

I wanted to break the divine order, to brave God, and that terrible and jealous God has punished me as he punished Lucifer!

In Serge's mind, those thoughts and impressions, which we have taken a long time to describe, presented themselves almost simultaneously, in a rapid and confused fashion.

Suddenly, his face convulsed.

"Insensate that I am!" he groaned. "I was about to associate a woman with my folly. She would curse me if she were here…but no, I'm blaspheming, and I want to believe in God, in love…I don't want to doubt either her or myself. The two of us would have succeeded, vanquished Nature, or we would have died together!"

The window had misted over again. Serge stifled a sigh and shook himself, as if to tear himself away from the tortuous thoughts that were invading him.

I need to see! he said to himself. *I need to embrace my distress in all its sinister splendor. I'm going out, climbing up on to the walkway…*

He took two steps and stopped, abruptly.

"My diving suit!" he exclaimed. "I forgot that, outside the hull, there's no longer any air, that there's an absolute void. This is the moment to test my machine."

Immediately—driven as much by a confused curiosity, which, in spite of everything, survived in the scientist, as by an obscure need to create a diversion from other anguishes—he went into his cabin in quest of one of the items of apparatus with which he had equipped himself in case the atmosphere of Mars was not breathable.

It was a simple diving-suit helmet, but improved by Myrandhal, equipped with an ingenious reservoir of liquid air sufficient to maintain respiration for more than twenty-four hours.

Serge screwed the enormous copper ball over his shoulders. As usual, it was fitted with three powerful lenses like the eyes of some marine monster. Then he wrapped himself, from the nape of his neck to his heels, in an ample fur with long silky hair, designed to protect him from the terrible intersidereal cold. It was one of those cloak-bags divided in the bottom half of which people make use in Alaska, and which is secured at the wrists and ankles by means of drawstrings.

Thus equipped he headed for the door—so tragically closed a little while ago!—opened it resolutely, and advanced on to the narrow landing from which the *Velox*'s ladder, dispatched with him, still hung.

He had scarcely grasped the frail guard-rail than his garments, saturated with interior moisture, bristled with icy needles, but Myrandhal took no notice of that. He leaned over avidly, his mouth twisted by a cry of amazement: "The sun!"

It was, indeed, the sun—but a terrible, tragic sun! A bald star, devoid of radiance, devoid of a halo! A dead sun, invincibly giving rise to the idea of an immense putrefied and phosphorescent cadaver.

It appeared in the distance, at the limit of the horizon, like a large incandescent millstone,[18] with an unsustainable glare that did not illuminate. That glare, like that of the *Velox*, that vibratory movement, for lack of a substance, any reflective matter capable of vibrating in unison, was lost in the void.

And it really was a frightful, sinister thing, that white sun, devoid of radiance and glory...

"One might think it were the end of the world," Serge murmured. "The wan 'great Star' that will see the death of the Earth."[19]

---

[18] I have translated *meule* as "millstone" because that seems a likelier intention than the word's other meanings, which refer to hayricks or round cheeses.

[19] The reference is to *Revelation* 8:10.

Sometimes, all around the disk, brief pink or crimson flames rose up vertically, giving the impression of some formidable explosion.

"Solar eruptions," murmured Myrandhal, moved in spite of himself by the prodigious spectacle of those fiery tempests.

Abruptly, he had to bow his head, his eyes being dazzled, burned by the ardent nucleus. He turned his back on the star, and for the second time, uttered a cry of surprise.

In front of him, the *Velox*, bombarded by the obscure effluvia emitted by the sun, was shining like the moon on its fourteenth day, and that contrast between the ambient night and the long, rutilant copper spindle had something fantastic about it.

One might have thought it a golden olive magically ripened by the black wall of night.

Serge had bowed his head, and was thinking.

"What a silence!" he murmured, pensively. "What calm! No sound, no breath, not a quiver. We seem to be motionless, and yet...

"It really is nothingness, the void, death.

"What is the Ether in which I'm floating? What is that mysterious, imponderable, invisible fluid that fills the whole universe—not only space, but substances themselves?

"What is the nature, the essence of that fluid, which is nothing and perhaps everything...which, awakened, condensed, vibrating in a certain way, becomes of Force and Matter, which creates the Universe entire?"

While raking over these philosophical theories, already envisaged many times over while he was working on his great endeavor, Serge Myrandhal raised his head.

For the second time, the terrifying, pitiless aspect of the abyss through which he was flying aimlessly terrified him. With a strange gesture of sudden dementia, he shook his fist at the stars.

"No!" he cried. "God doesn't exist, and the heavens lie! What calls to us thus is nothing but a frightful desert! Nature is accursed and the universe empty. Everywhere, there is nothingness, death. Death, the final refuge..."

He fell silent; then, with an abrupt, reactive, angry movement he turned round again. With one hand over his eyes, to avoid sunburn, he inspected the sky, trying to get his bearings.

"What's that?" he suddenly exclaimed "The moon! It's not in its place!"

Far away, beneath his feet, he had just perceived a long, broad and bright strip, with a cold steely glare: a gigantic scythe slicing the horizon, the scythe of Time floating in the void.

"The Earth!" murmured the engineer, going pale. "It's the Earth. Earthlight! I can only see a crescent, a spindle, but that's exactly what I wanted."

At the sight of that world, from which he was banished, exiled forever, he started trembling in every limb; his teeth chattered.

"Earth!" he repeated, in an agonized voice. "And that continent there is Asia. It's the Himalayas! The convent is there, there, in the center of that dark patch. That where *She* is waiting for me, where *She* is weeping!

"I want to go there...I want to get her back...and I can! We're still under the influence of the planet; it's attracting me. I only have to let myself go, to fall! I'll never see her again, but what does it matter? At least I'll sleep my final sleep close to her, in the same region of the heavens! We'll be buried in the same soil, and perhaps, one day, the wind—the wind that marries the flowers and transports the pollen—perhaps the wind will mingle our ashes..."

Serge interrupted himself mentally to devote himself to one of the calculations of which he had the habit.

"It's really true," he resumed, almost immediately. "We're still in the grip of terrestrial gravity. No other star in the vicinity to deflect me from my terrible trajectory. Like Lucifer cast down, I can fall, travel through the nothingness, the night, for days, and toward the middle of the fifth, or thereabouts, already pulverized and reduced to the state of vapor, I'll arrive. What a fall, and what a prodigious, unique death!" At that thought, his tormented heart swelled up with a noble joy. "Finally," he concluded, in an explosion of pride that terminated in sobs, I've found an end worthy of me! A death equal to my dream and my superhuman love!"

Immediately, with a wild frenzy, he overstepped the fragile barrier that separated him from the abyss, launching his head forward, but he could not tear his body free, weighed down—solidified, so to speak—as it was by frost. His limbs, his joints, the entirety of his human machine, stopped by the sidereal cold, refused to obey.

He could only succeed, with difficulty, in liberating his fingers, hooked around the protective rail.

As the same time, a sharp, intolerable burning sensation ran through his whole body. His skin, his cheeks, sunburned and frozen at the same time, split and burst beneath his mask; his eyes were bleeding, blurring his vision.

Simultaneously, his breath failed. The air in the reservoir of his diving helmet must have solidified.

Half-asphyxiated, incapable of thinking, he went back inside precipitately, closed the door, and took off his helmet. It took him several seconds to recover consciousness fully.

He was coming round, crushed, exhausted and shivering, when, close at hand, in the central compartment, a bell rang.

The young man shivered, as if in response to an electric shock, and like a madman, he leapt up and ran.

"A dispatch!" he howled. "A dispatch from Earth! It's her, it's Anna! Thank God! I knew that she was thinking about me, as I was about her. Except that the dispatch, launched in my pursuit, has taken a certain time to reach me."

The strip of paper in the Morse apparatus was already unrolling, and Serge read it, desperately.

My dear husband,

I know everything. I have just caught the mage in the crypt, and he has confessed, with horrible threat.

Don't worry, my beloved, I'm not afraid, and it's not for myself that I'm weeping...

But time's pressing...already they're breaking down my door. I'll only tell you one more thing: the bandits won't take me alive.

I'll die before...remember what we said yesterday about the migration of souls...I'll go to join you.

Soon, on Mars! I give you my lips.

My door's giving way...au...

There was a nervous tremor, a few disordered clicks, and the apparatus became still.

What did that tragically interrupted *au* signify? *Au revoir? Au secours?* A maddening mystery.

Meanwhile, Serge Myrandhal, his face convulsed, was still listening, his ears pricked, his eyes fixed on the telepath, as if to hypnotize it, to command the miracle that he wanted from it...

It seemed to him, in that minute saturated with anguish, that the apparatus, which he knew to be extremely delicate, almost alive in its sensitivity, was about to obey, like a telephone...

A few seconds went by; then, with a haggard expression, in a demented voice, he croaked: "Ah! They've killed her. She's dead! My turn!"

Head down, he rushed at the wall, and fell back, his scalp cut open, bleeding.

In the meantime, deprived of its captain, the *Velox* continued its implacable course, moved by a superphysical and vertiginous force.

It flew like a lightning bolt from one sky to another, carrying toward infinity and eternity the man who had created it, already moribund, in his rigid shroud of hardened steel, writhing in a pool of blood.

177

XVI. The Dove of the Ark!

How many hours that unconsciousness lasted, Serge was never able to calculate exactly...

He stirred momentarily, doubtless awakened by an incomprehensible noise coming from outside, which was communicating strange trepidations to the *Velox*.

Everything aboard the psychoscaph, which shortly before had been floating mutely in the silence of the interplanetary void, was now vibrating.

The hum, however, muted at first, was gradually rising up the sonic scale, sometimes rising to shrill notes.

Soon, there was a resounding howl, plaintive and disturbing, like the noise of the winter wind in the trees. Serge half sat up and passed his hand over his head, which was no longer bleeding.

"Anna!" he moaned.

A piercing clamor, an authentic whistle-blast, strident and sinister this time, drilled into his ears. Almost immediately, three more blasts resounded, brief and urgent...genuine cries of alarm!

One might have thought that the *Velox*, that marvelous machine animated by a mysterious force, "thinking," in a sense, was warning its master, signaling a danger, an obstacle into which it was about to crash, with a formidable impact.

That was Serge's impression. He leapt to his feet immediately. He moved back and forth across the compartment, parading his gaze from right to left.

"It's stifling in here," he murmured. "Where are we?"

Suddenly, above a porthole, russet smoke rose up; long red tongues sprang forth and flowed, licking the ceiling.

"Fire!" he stammered. "The *Velox* is burning!"

He seized a vaporizer of liquid air, and directed the glacial jet at the fire, with immediate effect. There was a crackle, a rain of ash and sparks, and through the half-consumed curtain the incandescent wall appeared.

"The hull!" Serge exclaimed. "It's the hull that's red hot! We're traveling through a gaseous mass, but what kind? If it the vivifying air of a planet, or the asphyxiating tail of some vagabond comet? What is this unknown world precipitating itself upon us with lightning speed?"

At the thought of the prodigious encounter, the frightful collision, Serge felt his hair stand on end around his white forehead.

For a second time, before the inevitable, certain catastrophe, he thought about death, about Anna, whom he was about to rejoin...

A further brief, imperative whistle-blast stopped him on that fatal slope. All his energy had suddenly reawakened. The instinct of survival, the love of danger, the desire to fight, to vanquish Nature—the dream of his entire life—was suddenly resuscitated, abolishing all other sensations.

He closed his eyes, as if no longer to see the sweet phantom, and swore that he would not think about her again until he was out of danger. Then, stimulated by that virile resolution, gathering all his physical and mental strength for the supreme struggle, he headed at a firm pace toward the "compass" suspended nearby, in its crystal case.

"That's bizarre!" he said. "The direction needle isn't even oscillating, and we haven't deviated from a straight line. The world on which we're arriving must be semi-fluid, extra-light, devoid of sensible attraction. Is it a matter of some gaseous comet or one of those minuscule planets that circulate around the sun, fragments of some shattered globe, too weak to capture us as we pass by?

"In that case, the most favorable, a fall might be avoided, thanks to our formidable speed, and our fluidic reservoir, which I'll unleash in its entirety in order to struggle against the new attraction. We'll pass by then, shaving the obstacle."

Almost immediately, however, he shivered, a cold sweat on his temples.

"Unless," he stammered, "that planet, that gigantic bo-lide, is directly ahead of us, in a straight line. In that case, our direction can't vary, but with the aid of its attraction, our speed will increase in frightful proportions!"

Fearfully, Serge consulted his counter—and stood there stupefied.

Far from increasing, the frightful velocity of the begin-ning of the voyage had suddenly fallen to fifty meters a se-cond, the speed of a swallow on the wing.

The needle of the speed gauge, whose mad leaps had frightened the traveler during the departure from Earth, was now trudging over its dial. One might have thought that the *Velox*, having reached some crowded intersection of the uni-verse, was moderating its pace of its own accord, like a well-trained horse.

Nevertheless, under the influence of the star in view, an acceleration was becoming manifest, albeit scarcely sensible as yet.

Serge started counting. "Fifty-one...fifty-two...fifty-five meters... We've taken more than ten minutes to gain a few meters per second. I was right; the strange world we're ap-proaching unexpectedly is very light, or very distant. We're not falling yet, and there's still hope...

"In spite of that, the situation is grave; the peril, although less immediate, persists in its entirety, and I only just have time to do everything possible to avoid it. Above all, I need to know where I am, and what the gas is through which we're presently flying."

Immediately, without pausing for a second over the mul-tiple dangers of the maneuver, Serge, with hasty, feverish ges-tures, put on his diving suit and headed for the rear compart-ment.

As he was about to release the valve, he hesitated. He had just remembered the terrible, dark scene that had fright-ened him so much a little while ago: that glacial, funereal sky, that star of terror contemplating the disaster with its pale eye.

But curiosity and the thought of the approaching, imminent peril quickly got the upper hand.

Serge opened the door and launched himself out on to the walkway—and, for the first time, his contracted face relaxed, animated by a furtive joy.

"The star has disappeared!" he exclaimed, suddenly relieved of an enormous weight. "The Great Star that seemed to be illuminating the end of the world! And the sky is immediately softened, humanized, after a fashion. There's no longer that opaque night, that sinister, implacable aspect that caused me to blaspheme."

In fact, the atmosphere in which the *Velox* was bathing, doubtless little different from terrestrial air, was producing the same optical effects. The stars were twinkling gently in the dark blue of the Empyrean.

"Finally," Myrandhal murmured, his soul dilating and his heart beating more rapidly. "Finally, I've found the heavens again, the deceptive azure vault, as tender as a woman's gaze…the dear, gentle firmament of poets and lovers—and they had the right of it, against science…

"Here I am, back in the world of 'illusions,' the only habitable one. I was wrong to revolt just now. God is good and the universe isn't empty. Creation is beautiful, except, like the Egyptian deity Isis, she doesn't like to be looked in the face. Woe to whoever dares lift the redoubtable veil of the goddess!"

While his thoughts agitated, Myrandhal, his mind freer, his brain more lucid, observed and compared.

Evidently, he thought, *all my sensations prove—the azure vault, the air that's caressing my hands—that I've arrived in proximity to a planet, but which one?*

Mars is still millions of leagues away. What if it were Earth, toward which some miracle had brought me back while I was asleep? A prodigy of love, Anna's appeal, more powerful than all the volitional power of the Mendicant Prince?

Serge was about to soften, forgetful of the still-imminent peril, but he started.

"No," he said. "I've sworn not to think about that." And he launched himself back inside the *Velox*.

At that precise moment, the psychoscaph, as if it wanted to recall its master to duty, began to produce the murmurous sound, like the buzzing of an irritated bee, that was its alarm signal of sorts.

Serge ran to the recording apparatus.

"Still the same direction," he murmured, "but the speed is increasing slowly, proof that the star is getting closer. The situation isn't critical yet, but it's getting worse by the minute. It's necessary to act. Let's take care of myself first, my wound. I'll need all my physical means, and more; we're arriving at a perilous moment…perhaps the last!"

He took off his helmet, and observed that it was full of blood. His wound had reopened, doubtless under the weight of the apparatus, and was causing him pain.

Rapidly, Serge washed the wound, and wrapped an antiseptic and anesthetic bandage around his head. Then he drank a large glass of a kola remedy that he had prepared personally for such extreme cases. Immediately, a gentle warmth spread through his arteries.

His injured brain, animated by blood loss, and his entire physical and mental state, exhausted by his unparalleled traumas, were about to acquire an artificial vigor that might save his life. Already, Serge could feel that wellbeing, that fever of life, similar to a slight intoxication, which infuses the veins with a new ardor and shows everything in the most propitious light. He was not far from seeing the wound he had received as one of those mysterious aids of Destiny.

"Who knows?" he said to himself. "But for that bleeding I'd be dead, struck down by congestion. Now for the *Velox*! First of all, I have to identify the nature of the gas through which we're flying, which will be the first datum regarding the mysterious world that has thrown itself into my path. It's obviously a matter of a considerable gaseous mass, afflicted by violent currents—veritable storm-winds. Just now, when the Velox whistled so obligingly, we must have been passing through one of those cyclones. Now, is this, gas—this atmosphere—breathable?"

Serge was thinking about making a quick analysis of the ambient air when a cooing coming from a storage locker caused him to change his mind. He ran to it, and came back carrying one of four turtle-doves, which, in imitation of Noah, he had planned to send out when the moment came.

From his watch-chain he detached a minuscule seal that his fiancée had given to him, bearing an interlaced A and S, moistened the indelible ink, and stamped both of the bird's wings.

Having done that, he carefully opened one of the small portholes in the central compartment and deposited the messenger—which he scarcely hoped to see again—on the narrow sill. Dazzled by the light projected through the lenses, but glad to be free, the bird flapped its wings joyfully and flew off. It let itself fall along the luminous beam, at the end of which it disappeared.

The proof was there!

Incapable of waiting any longer, Serge opened the window wide and stuck out his head, his neck and the whole of his upper body.

His cheeks whipped by the wind of the course, with blood infusing his skin, he plunged himself with delight into the beneficent gaseous shower and bathed in it.

"It's air! Pure air!" he murmured, filling his lungs with an indescribable voluptuousness. "It's terrestrial air—but a trifle cold."

Indeed, snowflakes were floating around him.

Serge hastened to close the porthole, and then suddenly froze, his feet nailed to the floor, his eyes haggard, as if fascinated by horror. In front of him, five meters from the window, a terrible face had just appeared: a monstrous face, part-human and part-owl, with a mouth equipped with sharp teeth, a stiff moustache like a hog's bristles and large staring eyes like the large bright golden eyes of nyctalopes...[20]

Serge was put in mind of a giant bat, of some prodigious vampire—but the horrible vision had already disappeared.

He passed his hand over his forehead, moistened by fear.

"It's an illusion," he said, "A creation of my overworked brain. Indeed, I remember that when I was asleep jut now, I dreamed about similar beings. Besides, how could such a monster be sustained at such a height? We'll go take a look, though. I'll go out and look for the monster in the sky—but I know it doesn't exist. It's pure and simple auto-suggestion."

His disturbance had almost dissipated, and yet, in spite of himself, he thought about the flying demons that, according to one tradition, inhabit certain accursed planets. He thought, in particular, about the authentic monstrous flying creatures that had populated in Earth in the early ages of the world, such as the pterodactyl.

He thought it prudent, in consequence, to arm himself. At hazard, he picked up a Colt revolver and a solid dagger with a short triangular blade, put his marine telescope under

---

[20] By "nyctalopes" the author presumably means nocturnal animals. Given that the next sentence refers to an impression of a giant vampiric bat, however, it is not inconceivable that there might be something more to the peculiar coincidence of imagery, given that Gustave Le Rouge's similar Martian fantasy features giant vampiric bats and that Jean de la Hire made mention in the second feuilleton he published in *Le Matin*, in 1908 of a human "nyctalope"—meaning someone capable of seeing in the dark—a new version of whom was later to feature in a long series of *feuilletons*. Given that this episode is entirely gratuitous, serving no function within the story, one is tempted to wonder whether Gayar might have known something about the contents of works by Le Rouge and La Hire that had not yet appeared in print but were soon to do so, and was deliberately dropping a hint to that effect.

his arm, and went out, leaving his helmet—unnecessary henceforth—in the wardrobe.

He opened the valve and paused, as before, shivering, his heart inundated by a joy that almost caused him to faint.

To the right, as if at the wave of a magic wand, the sky had just brightened abruptly. Day was breaking, still pale, but more beautiful than ever.

Immediately, everything was transformed, everything was smiling: the air, the heavens...

The Orient, in the distance, was decked in crimson and gold; glorious rainbows rose up, sparkling with all the colors of the prism, and along that triumphant road the light advanced, strewing rises beneath its feet...

Backed up against the metal hull, Serge contemplated the ineffable spectacle, which would have caused the knees of the most insensitive person to buckle.

"It's Aurora!" he stammered. "The divine Aurora, the daughter of God, that I thought I'd never see again. I'm saved! Thank you, almighty God!

He had completely forgotten the still-impending catastrophe, the errant star into which he was perhaps about to crash...

Soon, coming from the depths of the horizon, a streak of fire, a fluid golden arrow traversed the sky, and a star appeared: a glorious fulgurant disk, from which torrents of multicolored flames flowed.

It was the sun, rising over the unknown planet!

Myrandhal had fallen to his knees, and the most ardent prayer that had ever sprung from a human breast was exhaled by his heart.

He remained collapsed in that fashion, prostrate before the sovereign star, for some time, stammering the bewildered hymn that "cavemen" murmured every time the sun returned, which they had believed to be lost forever.[21]

---

[21] The idea that primitive cave-dwellers were amazed by every sunrise, having become convinced during the night that the

Finally recalled to reality, returning his attention from the heavens to the "earth" that he sensed getting nearer and nearer, suddenly monopolized by an intense curiosity, he leaned over the frail guard-rail and contemplated the unknown panorama emerging from the darkness...

Beneath his feet, less than a mile away, and immense white, moving extent, a sea of clouds, was agitating, pierced by the sunlight and tormented by a rising wind. Here and there, immense vortices were hollowed out, immense funnels animated by a king of gyratory movement. Serge aimed his telescope at one of these vertiginous gulfs with crumbling walls of vapor and gazed into it avidly, his eyes bulging, injected with blood like those of a man threatened by apoplexy.

His temples were buzzing, his arteries throbbing as if to burst, and yet he could not make anything out as yet—nothing but a flat chestnut-brown plain, still drowned in shadow.

Gradually, however, the interior layers of the atmosphere brightened in their turn, the last mists disappearing.

Now, Serge perceived a boundless desert, a kind of red-tinted Sahara furrowed by long rectilinear valleys, trenches of a sort extending geometrically from north to south.

Then the landscape was suddenly illuminated, the trenches sparkled, and Serge, his face transfigured, uttered a cry of triumph.

"The canals!" he shouted. "The famous canals of Mars! I've arrived!"

As before when he had rediscovered the radiant star, Serge Myrandhal took some time to recover from the immense joy that overwhelmed him.

So, he had succeeded; he had reached his goal without knowing it.

---

sun would never reappear, makes little sense, but it is memorably featured in a strikingly bizarre short story by the Symbolist writer Bernard Lazare, contained in the collection *Le Miroir des Légendes* (1892).

The unknown, redoubtable world that had frightened him a little while ago was the one that he had been inclined toward for months. He had succeeded in his prodigious adventure, and had reached the planet about which he was no longer thinking, after so much anguish!

Leaning over the rail, his hair whipped by the wind of the abyss, his body lifted up by a delightful vertigo, he contemplated his conquest

Through his joy, that world, which his telescope had just shown him to be arid and desolate, now appeared to him as a magical land, like the terrestrial paradise to which the venerable Jonathan Burrett had made allusion a few hours earlier in his Biblical homily.

Suddenly, his heart lurched. He thought about his companion, the promised Eve, his wife, who was moaning out there in the depths of the sky, perhaps lying dead, having the horrible weight of the monastery, her tomb, above her young head"

Instantly, he shook his head.

"No," he murmured, "she's alive! The Hindus wouldn't dare. She's too precious a hostage, and they need her, especially now that they know—they must know—that my secret has escaped them...

"As for Anna, I know her virile intelligence, her courage, her cleverness, her prudence! Why didn't I listen to her sooner! So long as a glimmer of hope remains to her, she'll defer her fatal resolution to put an end to her days...

"So she's alive! Besides which, if it were otherwise, I'd know. Liberated from terrestrial chains, her soul would have come through space and time to find me. I would have felt her passing around me.

"She's alive...and I'll find her again. Launching myself from Mars as I did from Earth, I'll go to find her, to rejoin her!"

He started; a rush of blood colored his cheeks.

"What if I were to go, to try right away?"

187

Immediately, though, the folly and futility of that attempt became apparent to him, and his eyes, momentarily dazzled as if by the sight of the sun, closed again.

"No," he said, "I don't have sufficient means. If I want to get my wife back, to avenge myself on the mage, I need to go about it another way—and I shall. I want my revenge!

"I'm arriving on a habitable world, older than ours and hence more advanced in its civilization, in its science. I shall find, among our Martian cousins, all the help and assistance I need to attempt the return journey with every chance of success. It's a new game that's beginning between the Hindus and me. They've won the first round, but I'll have my turn, and it will be terrible!

"And I have confidence; I'm hopeful! The mysterious forces that have seconded me thus far won't suddenly withdraw. If I've survived, avoided the frightful catastrophe, it's because God in on my side...

"I shall return. I shall see the sweet Earth, the abode of my human brothers, again. And that's what it's necessary to tell my dear wife as soon as possible. I'll tell her that I to have been saved...that I'm thinking about her, that I love her more than ever...forever!"

He hastened to the central compartment, but by the time he had reached the telepath, ready to activate it, he had already changed his mind.

"What's the point?" he murmured, with a grimace of discouragement. "If Anna hasn't telegraphed me again, it's because, as her dispatch anticipated, she's a prisoner, at least kept out of sight. What good will it do, then, to send another dispatch, intercepted in advance, that can only end up informing my enemies, warning them of my intentions. The first and most important precaution is to mistrust the mage, whose psychic superiority and supremacy probably remains redoubtable in spite of the distance, even on another world. Patience! My time will come..."

Comforted by this prospect, his soul caressed by a first ray of hope, a ray sweeter than "the first fires of Aurora,"

Myrandhal envisaged, incontinently the means of realizing his second voyage, the return to Earth—the more difficult of the two.

Before thinking about that, he ought to set foot on Mars, and he could not attempt anything on that sort as long as he had not reacquired mastery of the *Velox*. It was necessary, first of all, to make sure that the apparatus had finally escaped the potential superiority of its terrestrial powerhouse, and take advantage of it to redirect the psychoscaph—which, influenced by gravity, was tilting forward—and moderate its velocity, which was increasing in a worrying fashion.

Swiftly, the young man went into the helmsman's chamber, moved a few controls, consulted various indicators and came back radiant.

"That's it!" he sang. "The sinister Rajah has forgotten me, or is no longer able to do anything, and the *Velox* will henceforth be obedient only to me. Finally, I can take the tiller again!

"On the other hand, I still have sufficient fluid to fly for some time yet, and to 'make a parachute' when I go down. I can land whenever and wherever I wish, in the most propitious place. In order to decide that judiciously, the first thing to do is to determine which region of Mars I'm in—to take a bearing, as mariners say. It's high time, after all these shocks, to get a grip on myself, to *situate* myself in time and space.

"First of all, what time is it? How long did it take me to accomplish my formidable journey?"

Myrandhal took out his watch. It had stopped. He consulted the two precision chronometers installed nearby in a suspended frame.

"Also stopped," he said, disappointed. "That's strange. What can have caused that accident? It only required a slight push of the pendulum to start them going again, proof that nothing is broken. Perhaps the interruption was only due to some magnetic phenomenon, which I don't have time to investigate. Whatever the reason, I'm deprived of an important notion, and in consequence, I can't tell how long it took me to get here. Twenty or thirty hours, undoubtedly. That represents a formidable velocity: the velocity of one of those 'moonstones,' which are instantaneously melted and vaporized on impact with an atmosphere. The smallest bolide, one of those grains of sand drifting in space, would have sufficed to pulverize me, but an unknown power is watching over me..."

During this monologue, Myrandhal had picked up his marine telescope again. He opened one of the large portholes in the central compartment and set about examining the Martian landscape over which he was flying.

The dome of vapor that had intercepted his view a little while ago had completely disappeared, dissipated by the sun that was rising rapidly over the horizon.

At that moment, according to the indications of the measuring device, the *Velox* was flying at an altitude of about twenty-two thousand meters. In two hours of flight he had only descended three thousand meters, and the reserves of fluid measured by the psychometer had only decreased by a negligible quantity. Thus, Serge observed mentally once again, given the relatively weak intensity of weight on Mars, about a third of Earth's, the descent was taking place in the best conditions for which one could wish.

From the considerable altitude at which he was flying, and thanks to the greater curvature of Mars, Serge could see a considerable fraction of the planet, a "cap" almost as large as Europe. With his telescope he could make out the contours of seas and continents, the lines of gulfs and straits, and the pattern of the canals, perfectly. As he knew the map of Mars by heart, he quickly got his bearings.

"There's no doubt about it," he soon cried, joyfully. "We're floating over the Mädler Sea in the northern hemisphere—and, in consequence, at the very spot I anticipated and chose. While I was agonizing, the marvelous machine that the *Velox* is flew to its destination without any deviation.

"That heart-shaped land is Laplace Land.[22] We're in the polar circle, but even though it's claimed hat Mars is an old, frozen world, I can't see the slightest trace of snow or ice. It's true that I've arrived in summer.

"Everything seems empty and uninhabited—the land, the sky and the water. No trace of any city or civilization. A desert—I'm sure of not being greeted by arrows!

"It's now a matter of landing, of launching the psychoscaph into the open sea, for I must certainly stick to my plan of diving. It's the surest means of deadening the fall, of protecting my precious and delicate vehicle, on which I'm counting more than ever, by means of that liquid mattress. The slightest shock or rip made by those sharp rocks I can see down there would suffer to compromise me return for a long time, if not forever."

Increasingly reassured by what he could see and what he hoped, Serge Myrandhal closed the porthole again and occupied himself with the descent. He consulted the sun with a slightly artificial gaiety.

"It must be about nine o'clock," he said. "I'll try to land of Mars on the dot of mid-day…lunch time!"

He went into the engine room and set about diminishing the resistance of the psychic accumulators considerably. Immediately, the *Velox*, subjected to the preponderant influence of weight, accelerated its fall.

Two hours later, he was flying eight hundred meters above the Mädler Sea, a few miles from Laplace Land.

---

[22] There is a *Mer de Mädler* [Mädler Sea] and a *Terre de Laplace* [Laplace Land] in the far north of Camille Flammarion's map of Mars, as reproduced in *Terres du Ciel* and elsewhere, but the author seems to have made an error of transcription, as the "heart-shaped" body of land adjacent to the "sea" in question on Flammarion's map is *Terre de Lalande* [Lalande Land], while *Terre de Laplace* is a peninsula attached to *Continent Copernic* [Copernicus].

Serge slowed his descent then and, armed with his telescope, began to examine the Martian sea with all the attention of which he was capable. In fact, one hast question remained, on which the issue of the descent depended. Was that liquid splashing less than a kilometer away water—water such as it exists on Earth, with the same density, and hence capable of supporting the *Velox*, whose floatability had been regulated in accordance with the weight of terrestrial water?

Everything seemed to indicate as much: the gradually increasing humidity of the atmosphere, as revealed by the hygrometer; the whiteness of the surf, the movement of the waves and the play of the light on their crests, sometimes iridescent with all the colors of the prism.

"Let's go," our hero ended up concluding. "The proof is there. I could investigate further, but there's no need. Besides, my *Velox* is also a submarine, of the most advanced sort. I have the means to refloat it almost instantaneously, if it changes to plummet beneath the waves. It only remains, therefore, for me to transform my aerial vehicle into an aquatic vehicle. My preparations are made and it won't take long."

The engineer went into the rear compartment, where, along with food supplies and weapons, the tools and other equipment necessary for the landing were stored. He soon emerged, carrying over his shoulder a light rudder made of a sheet of steel and an electric control mechanism. He opened the valve and attached the precious apparatus to the brackets set up in advance for that purpose at the rear of the *Velox*, just above the walkway.

Setting up the propeller below the walkway presented a few more difficulties, but the inventor's foresight had reduced them to a minimum. First he set about freeing the axle installed in the hold under the floor of the psychoscaph. When the steel rod was extended to the required length, Serge fitted the helix to it. It was difficult for one man working alone—constrained to operate with one hand, in order to be able to hold on with the other—to put that relatively heavy piece of equipment in place, but the circumstance had been anticipated and the propeller could be dismantled. The engineer only had to screw on the hub and then the three blades, one after another, and the operation was concluded in ten minutes.

That done, Serge climbed the narrow ladder permitted access to the central dome and installed himself on the little platform fitted here, just below the conning-tower. It was the control-station for the electric motors installed in the forward compartment.

Myrandhal moved the levers on the control panel in front of him and made sure that the propeller and the rudder were working perfectly. In the same way, after having established the necessary contacts, he tested the various mechanisms that would permit him to control all the complicated machinery of the *Velox*: the psychic and other accumulators; the back-up dynamos installed in the hold, the automatic latches of the portholes and the hatch, and the release-mechanism of the counterweight—in case of an unexpected plunge.

After that he went back inside and carried out a minute inspection of the *Velox*, now mutated into a submersible, checking the seals on the portholes and the ballast tanks.

During these preparations, the psychoscaph, which had not cased its slow descent, arrived within a few feet of the Mädler Sea, whose waves occasionally lapped its hull sonorously.

Myrandhal put on a lifebelt, went back up the stairway to the captain's bridge, and took up his station at the electric control-panel.

The solemn moment had arrived.

It only required a momentary distraction, one false move or an error of calculation—some trivial forgotten detail—to bring about a catastrophe. Serge knew that, but he was confident. Even so, he was a trifle pale; his eyes were anxious and his throat was dry.

As he reached for one of the levers, he heard a flutter of wings immediately overhead. He looked up through one of the narrow crystal slits arranged around the perimeter of the conning-tower, and perceived, flying only a few meters away, the pigeon that he had launched as a scout a little while before.

"The dove of the Ark!" he cried. "It's a good sign."

He gave one last thought to his wife, and then pulled the lever.

"Adieu!"

The *Velox* dropped vertically and disappeared into the waves.

Two hundred meters away it resurfaced, white with foam, and, with its top opened, proceeded with its first trials of navigation.

The submersible steered marvelously. He increased its speed, stopped, swerved to port and starboard. One might have thought it an enormous strangely-formed Martian fish, or some amphibious monster emerged from its grotto and frolicking in the sunlight.

Then the *Velox* set a course southwards, toward Laplace Land, and set off at top speed. It moved as smoothly, as nimbly and as joyfully as a young shark beginning its first voyage around the world...

XVII. Wedding Night

Less than forty minutes later, Serge Myrandhal saw land surge forth a quarter of a mile away: a desolate, arid land, always the uniform color of brick. Only a few scattered red tufts represented the Martian flora.

Serge would have liked his first steps in his new domain to be in a more engaging landscape. In any case, there was no urgency about going ashore; it was better, taking advantage of the marvelous means of locomotion that the *Velox* provided, to explore the planet a little more first.

He searched for one of the canals he had glimpsed during the descent, and soon found one. It was an arm of the sea about a hundred kilometers wide, so far as he could tell, and it headed southwards as far as the eye could see. Serge moved along it, searching for a more inviting location: a bay or a port worthy of the beautiful name of Anna, which he gave it in advance.

The *Velox* progressed at a good speed for two hours and the country did not vary. The right bank, which was about a cable away, unfolded flat and bleak, the color of rust, suggestive of an immense sheet of lava frozen by a gust of the wind of chaos.

Standing on the walkway, with his upper body protruding from the conning-tower, Myrandhal, more disappointed the further they advanced, contemplated the panorama, which seemed to him to be desperately monotonous.

"What solitude," he thought aloud, "and what silence! It seems that Mars really is a dead world. Not a tree, not a bird, not a spring, not a valley, not a hill, not even a cloud…nothing to animate the landscape. The rivers have dried up, the mountains have been leveled, the valleys filled in. Time has passed this way, polishing the planet, making the ruddy surface into an immense bleak expanse of desert. It will be the same for the Earth one day.

"Even the sun—the sun that seemed so beautiful this morning—produces les light. It's only been three hours, but one might think that the light has diminished already. It's true that I'm twice as far from the star, whose diameter, if I could look directly at it, would seem to be reduced by half. It's also true that we're in the shorter days of the Martian summer in this hemisphere of the planet.

"Decidedly, Mars is a world, if not dead, at least uninhabited. I was congratulating myself a little while ago, but I'm almost grateful now. There's something anguishing about this funereal silence. I'd have preferred, at the risk of my life, to have to confront, if not other humans, then animals—something alive.

"I would have liked, at least, to have to contend with mysterious forces, with one of those phenomena with which writers of fantastic fiction populate unknown planets: sky-piercing volcanoes, cataracts of fire…but there's nothing! Nothing but placid deserted canals, which inevitably make one think of some sandy town in Holland or Bruges-la-Morte."[23]

Then, suddenly, he said: "Hold on! One might think that life is reawakening. The current, imperceptible a little while ago, is increasing rapidly, and the sky is changing too. Is there going to be a storm, a cyclone? So much the better! The *Velox* has nothing to fear, and it will break the monotony."

Swiftly, Serge grabbed the telescope that was suspended from his belt and directed it southwards. In the distance, cutting into the implacable blue of the sky, a small white patch had just appeared, with coppery glints.

"It's not a cloud," Serge soon observed. "It's too low…it's more reminiscent of mist rising from the ground. What can it be?"

---

[23] *Bruges-la-Morte* (1892) is a novel by the Belgian writer Georges Rodenbach, nowadays hailed as one of the archetypal products of the Symbolist movement, the protagonist of which a grief-stricken widower, with whom Myrandhal might well have found some reason to identify.

To content his thirst for marvels, at least in imagination, he set about building the most extraordinary conjectures, which he eliminated successively.

Soon, he slapped his forehead. "Of course! It's a city. It's smoke—I should have thought of that sooner. All great cities—Paris, London—have that roof of mist, and to judge by the dimensions of that one, the city it marks must be colossal in size!

"Who knows, perhaps I'm arriving at the Martian capital, in some gigantic agglomeration where Martians from all over the world, having abandoned the sterile countryside, have taken refuge, and where they live in some strange fashion. That dome of vapor in the respiration of an entire humankind, the breath exhaled by billions of engines that are whirring and pouring out there. It seems to me that I can hear the hum of a great factory."

In fact, for several minutes, a dull rumor had been audible in the south. At the same time, while Myrandhal gazed into the distance, the rapidity of the current as increasing in a disquieting fashion. Too absorbed, however, Serge paid no heed to it. Meanwhile, waves were beginning to rise. The water was boiling, steaming. Although the sun was already low on the horizon, the heat was becoming oppressive.

Very surprised, Serge got down from the bridge and, through one of the upper portholes, plunged his hand into the water; he snatched it back immediately.

"It's hot water," he murmured. "I've just encountered a 'gulf-stream'...or rather—and the volcanic appearance of the landscape is another indication—a hot spring with a considerable flow..."

Serge stopped the engine and, increasingly intrigued, recommenced examining the cloud, which he could now make out more clearly.

"That's bizarre," he thought. "The cloud's floating on the water. So it's not a city. It might be an island, it's true, or a volcano...but no; at this distance, I'd be able to see its sides. And now the speed of the flow is beginning to take on menacing proportions. The noise is getting louder too. What a racket! I think it might be as well to stop."

Rather anxious, Myrandhal restarted the propeller and put the engine in reverse. Carried on by its momentum, the *Velox* covered a further two hundred meters and then stopped, paralyzed, incapable of going upstream. It pitched and creaked impotently, threshing the water with its hectic propeller, tossed by the waves, still increasing in force, surging upon it from all directions.

Soaked by the spray and whipped by splashing water. Serge felt a frisson run through his flesh. Immediately, he released all the available current, harnessing at a stroke all the electrical force stored in the hold.

This time, the submersible succeeded in extracting itself from the liquid grip. Panting like a wrestler, its four dynamos roaring, it had begun to describe the arc of a circle with a large radius when a big wave hit it directly in the side. The frail vessel heeled over, and was dragged a hundred fathoms further the middle of the stream—and all was lost! It was a flight toward catastrophe, toward the unknown, a race to the abyss!

Serge only just had time to close the conning-tower. His face on fire, his eyes glued to the visor, he looked out, convinced that he was the plaything of one of those mysterious forces that he had provoked a little while before, against which human beings can do nothing.

"No," he said to himself, "there's nothing to be done. The Nature that I challenged is taking her revenge. I have an anchor, but the cable would break like a thread. As for diving, why? The current is obviously faster down below than on the surface, and, if it's a choice of deaths, it's better to finish in daylight. That way, at least I'll know the name and see the face of the phenomenon that is dragging me away and is going to swallow me! The cloud's still growing...it's coming closer, racing, flying toward me like a cyclone...!"

The sun had set when, after a vertiginous course, Serge Myrandhal arrived within a quarter of a mile of the prodigy, still invisible, hidden behind its cloud like thunderous Jupiter.

The din, which had not stopped increasing, had now become something extraordinary, without any possible comparison to terrestrial sounds. Ten simultaneous thunderclaps would only give a feeble idea of it. At every crash the ground trembled and the *Velox* vibrated like a gong. Serge felt that his temples were shattering, and his eyes were bloody, as if a ten-ton cannon were being fired next to his ear.

Dazed and stupefied, invaded by such strong curiosity that he almost forgot the imminent peril, with his eye to the visor, Serge contemplated the monstrous and inexplicable phenomenon.

"No," he repeated, for the hundredth time, "it's not a volcano. It's almost dark now; I'd be able to see the flames." He interrupted himself abruptly. "A cataract!" he cried, going pale. "It's a waterfall! A Martian Niagara! Why didn't I think of that?"

He shivered. Up above, at the top of the cloud, there was a stir. Soon, a prodigious spray of water appeared, inclining graciously, describing a spiral. One might have thought it the crumbling arch of some gigantic viaduct. The fall lasted for several seconds, and then the mass fell into the sea, raising a formidable wave.

Launched like a bullet, creaking in every joint, the *Velox* ran over the crest of the wave.

"It really is a cataract," Serge stammered, "but instead of falling down it rises up. It's the world upside-down!"

At that precise moment, a final explosion, more powerful than all the rest, swept the sky clear, and the Prodigy appeared.

"A maelstrom!" Serge howled, his hair rigid with horror. In front of him, beneath his feet, a precipice half a league wide, a liquid gulf with spinning walls, had just opened up. From the depths of that abyss, forming the axis of the whirl-pool, a prodigious column of water—a monstrous, spitting, fuming jet—launched into the sky!

It was a geyser and a volcano at the same time. A Geyser-Volcano!

Now, night having fallen completely, tongues of fire could be seen furrowing the geyser at its base. Jets of lava were melting; enormous blocks were soaring like bomb to explode in mid-air. One of them passed, whistling, within a matter of inches from Serge—who, clinging to his porthole, fascinated, paralyzed by the horrible spectacle, was still watching.

Meanwhile, the *Velox* had climbed the cushioning rim surrounding the whirlpool and had begun to descend the fatal slope. Again it was gripped, hurled like a roulette ball, spinning around. The violence of the maelstrom was so great that, swept by the centrifugal force, the solid bed of the gulf appeared at times: a rubble of volcanic rocks from which flames were spurting

One might have thought it the fuming gateway to Tartarus.

Sometimes, one of those rocks, torn away, seized by the geyser, shot up vertically. Serge saw one block of several tons fly toward the zenith.

Suddenly, the *Velox* was seized in its turn and projected to the summit of the geyser, in mid-air. For a second, it danced up aloft like an egg-shell in a fairground shooting range. Then everything collapsed, and everything seethed before Serge's eyes, blinded by the blood of his reopened wound.

When he was able to get a grip on himself again, the *Velox* was floating in calm water, a cable from the shore.

A further prodigy: the geyser-volcano had disappeared, and once again, there was silence—a funereal silence.

In the sky, there was a huge cloud, and on the water, enormous high waves—indications of continuing submarine explosions—were the sole indication of the place, a mile away, where the Prodigy had been.

Darkness had fallen, and millions of stars were dotting the azure mantle of the firmament.

Serge did not even ask himself what had happened, and how he came to be still alive. He no longer had the energy to be astonished. Snatched from his post, he was lying at the bottom of the staircase, half-unconscious.

Around him, wings were fluttering. It was one of the turtle-doves, escaped from the broken cage, which was fling about madly, bumping into the walls.

Almost at the same moment, something warm and flaccid slapped Serge in the face.

"Water!" he croaked, raising himself up.

It was, indeed, water. Split by the shock and already three-quarters full, the *Velox* was sinking.

A few seconds more and its captain, buried alive, screwed into the steel helmet, disappeared under the waves.

Serge only just had time to climb up, open the hatch atop the conning tower, take two steps along the hull and dive.

Danger gave him a supreme burst of energy. In any case, the shore was nearby, and the current was running toward the land. A few swimming strokes sufficed for him to reach the shore, where he let himself fall down, exhausted, in a faint.

He shivered, gripped by the nocturnal cold after his long immersion in the hot water of the canal.

At the same time, an anguish, dull at first, but becoming sharp and painful rose up within him, climbing from his loins to his empty, buzzing head.

Soon, a plaint sprang from his tortured entrails: the moan of a defeated man.

"I'm hungry," he murmured, in a faint, child-like voice, while two large tears ran down his emaciated cheeks.

Throughout his long voyage—which is to say, for thirty hours, perhaps more—Serge had only consumed a cordial, the glass of kola, whose comfort, although artificial, had lasted a long time.

"I'm hungry," he repeated.

And from then on, everything was wiped out, abolished. Serge was no longer anything but an unconscious creature, a famished animal in search of fodder. His head empty, he dragged himself along on all fours, turning over stones, digging in the sand, in search of one of those mollusks that abound on the shores of terrestrial seas.

There was nothing—not even a sprig of weed—to put into his mouth. Mars really was a dead world, decidedly an accursed planet.

After a time, he perceived one of the ruddy tufts he had glimpsed before, and dragged himself toward it, at the cost of enormous effort. His hands and knees were bloody, and a pink sweat was oozing from the pores of his distended skin.

Finally, he reached the plant, the object of his ardent covetousness.

It was a bouquet of rigid stems bristling with coarse hairs, devoid of flowers, leaves and fruits, a harsh, sterile herb, a true plant of the dunes.

Serge grabbed it in both hands. Devoid of roots, the plant came away in its entirety, and he perceived a brown bulb with a layered rind, reminiscent of an onion, which he stuffed into his mouth.

Sand grated between his teeth, but he paid no heed to it, any more than to the slightly bitter taste. Afterwards he attacked the stems, from which a milky sap oozed, similar to that of a poppy.

Either because of the effect of the sap—perhaps narcotic—or because he no longer had the strength to suffer, Serge sudden felt an immense relief. His numbed intelligence revived, throwing off gleams like a dying lamp. He sensed that his end was near, and his tormented face lit up with a smile of joy, of deliverance.

"I've found the remedy for all my ills," he stammered. "I've been poisoned. Thank you, kind plant, relief of castaways! I have nothing more to do than dig my grave."

In the course of this monologue he set about digging in the sand with his trembling hands. In a matter of seconds he had opened a cavity a few inches deep, into which he started feverishly putting his papers and his jewelry.

This way, he said to himself, *those who land here in years to come—when nothing remains of my bones, absorbed by the soil—will know where I died. Anna, if she ever comes, will know where to kneel.*

He filled in the hole, and rolled a few blocks of lava on top of it to build one of the cairns with which explorers lost at the pole strew their funereal route.

After which, holding a photograph of Anna in his hands—the only thing that he had kept—he lay down on the strand, waiting to die.

Above him, the sky scintillated; a calm, an august serenity, fell from the stars, filling the heart of the dying man with an infinite bliss. His emaciated face was radiant with tenderness and joy. He thought that he had accomplished his duty and was about to rejoin the woman he loved.

He lowered his gaze from the ethereal vault to the photograph of Anna, which he pressed against his lips.

"My work is done!" he murmured. "The task has been hard, but I've toiled well. I've toiled for Science and for Humankind. I've shown the way to the stars!"

He raised his gaze to the stars again. "The heavens haven't budged," he went on, "or rather, it's me who hasn't budged. What is the distance between the Earth and here?—a single step in infinity! Our firmament—that of the sun—hasn't changed much. The moon has disappeared, replaced by two other satellites, Deimos and Phobos. One other change. Jupiter, which we were contemplating yesterday evening at the convent, is closer…it really is the monarch of the heavens, and perhaps Anna is contemplating it at this very minute.

"As for the Earth, it hasn't yet risen, but it's coming…it's coming to bid me adieu...

"And now, everything is finished...

"I'm going to rejoin my beloved..."

Serge shivered suddenly, and raised his head, lifted up by a titanic convulsion.

"Who's calling me?" he croaked. "Anna! Is that you?"

His eyes wide, his mouth agape, as if in ecstasy, he went on: "Yes…yes, I recognize you…your voice…your sweet face! I knew you'd come...I was expecting you!"

Suddenly, though, his voice was extinguished.

He fell back, breathless, his face a frozen mask.

Was it a mirage, or one of those miracles engendered by love, which can also move mountains?

Was it the living spouse, or her spirit, her soul, which came through space for the eternal marriage, to fuse with the disincarnate spouse?

Perhaps, one day, some telepathic message launched from on high will permit us to inform our readers, and unveil for them, by the same token, other secrets of the planet Mars.[24]

---

[24] The volume concludes at this point, but the author adds a footnote subverting the seemingly-conclusive ending: "Coming soon: *Les Robinsons de la Planète Mars*, a sequel to the adventures of the principal characters introduced in this volume."

BOOK TWO
THE CASTAWAYS OF MARS

I. A Martian

When, after quite a long time, Serge Myrandhal recovered consciousness, and perceived the person who was lavishing cares upon him, he uttered a hoarse shout:

"Anna!"

And again he fainted, not having the strength to support such happiness.

The American woman took advantage of it to pour another mouthful of cordial between his teeth. Then she made him breathe from a bottle of lavender salts.

The injured man shuddered; his eyes opened again, but closed again almost immediately, full for fear.

"It's a shade," he muttered, "a phantom. She's dead. But me, am I alive? Am I dreaming? Anything's possible. I don't know any more; I can't see any more. Everything's dancing, whirling around me.

"I'm in a whirlpool. The maelstrom! Do you hear it? You can hear the monster roaring. It's claiming its prey...

"How cold it is! And that odor of sulfur! It's the very breath of Hell, the wind from the abyss. And yet, it was so beautiful a little while ago in the garden. The birds were singing in the foliage, and I was sitting with my bride..."

He fell silent.

Anguished, Anna leaned over him.

"Mercy!" she murmured, in a faint voice. "Has he gone mad? It's doubtless that wound on his head. Oh my God, has he been returned to me only for me to lose him immediately?"

She stood up suddenly and turned round, as if to ask for help.

A hundred paces away, a man, who was doubtless watching, immediately emerged from behind a heap of sand. He took two long strides and stopped.

"No!" shouted the American woman, abruptly changing her mind. "He's better. Go away. It's best he doesn't see you."

In fact, Myrandhal's face was transformed, illuminated, as it had been a little while before, when he had uttered Anna's name.

He had gripped the young woman's skirt, and was feeling it, rubbing it with trembling, feverish fingers.

"It's you," he stammered. "It's really you I'm touching! Am I still dreaming?"

Madame Myrandhal leaned over the young man and her lips brushed his burning forehead. "Yes, it's me, my friend Wake up."

Serge began trembling in his every limb.

"Her voice!" he stammered. "It's her voice!" Suddenly, with a single bound, he was on his feet. He had embraced his wife and he was covering her with bewildered kisses.

"Anna…it's you...my bride…my wife! It's you!"

"Yes, Serge, it's me…my love…my dear husband! Finally, you're awake…you're awake. Oh, how fearful I was!"

They hugged one another ardently, madly; then, mutely, their faces bathed with delicious tears, they stood there, intertwined, for a long time, living one of those moments that cannot be described.

Finally, Anna disengaged herself gently. "Come on," she said, in a soft voice. "Let's not stay here any longer."

She tried to draw him away, but Myrandhal's feet were nailed to the ground.

"Just a moment," he murmured. And, placing his hands on his wife's shoulders, he said: "Let me look at you, fill my eyes with you. How beautiful you are! I've never seen you like this. So it's you—it's really you!

"Is it possible? Yesterday, we were talking in the garden, and now, here we are on Mars, together, as we were back there. Is my dream continuing? But no…all this is real. When

I doubt, I have only to look up at the sky. The stars are there to bear witness! There are the two moons, Deimos and Phobos. That golden globe rising slowly toward the zenith is Earth...

"What silence! What joyful peace!"

Myrandhal stopped, as if seized by a sudden idea, and looked at the sea.

"Nothing there any longer," he went on. "The thunder is silent. How strange it is! The prodigy was there just now, the maelstrom. It was roaring..."

"What are you talking about?" he young woman exclaimed, prompt to take alarm. "That's twice that..."

"Don't worry," said Serge, smiling. "I'm in my right mind. I'll explain it to you later. Besides which, you'll doubtless have the opportunity to see the terrifying phenomenon for yourself before long. It's obviously one of those intermittent geysers, like the ones on Earth—but what violence! What a mighty jet! I'm still wondering how I was able to escape it. I'm utterly bewildered, as if I were emerging from some frightful nightmare...

"Except for you, who have always been present, I don't remember anything—or almost nothing—of what preceded the catastrophe, and I'm trying to remember...

"How do you come to be here? It's a mystery, a miracle! But I'm no longer astonished by anything. For twenty-four hours I've been living in the midst of the fantastic, the plaything of prodigious forces. I have you: that's sufficient for me..."

"So you don't remember anything?" Anna said.

"Yes, but it's distant, vague. As soon as I try to fix an idea, everything trembles, spins, like the maelstrom just now. I can't distinguish the true from the false, the real from the imaginary."

"Try. I'd like to know so much myself—to know what happened to you, what harm you've sustained, in order to care for you better. How were you wounded?"

207

Serge put his hand to his head. "Yes," he said. "Why, you've bandaged me! Fortunate wound! Without that, I'd probably have gone mad."

"How did you do it? Was it the geyser?"

"No, it was in the *Velox*, after the departure from the convent. I'd just read your dispatch…"

"You received it?"

"Yes. Then, I thought you were dead, murdered by the bandits, and I felt on to a sharp panel."

Anna shuddered, and enveloped Serge with a loving gaze. "And afterwards?" she said.

"Afterwards, it's more confused. I remember that it was black, ever more black…a funereal, horrible black. A terrible sky! And in it, a pale, wan sun…"

"Oh yes," the American murmured, shivering again. "It's frightful. I was there, and I saw it myself."

"Hours passed," Serge continued, "and then the star disappeared. What a relief, what a sigh! It wasn't as black. The stars were shining, as they did back there is the garden, and I thought of you."

"Dear soul!"

"Meanwhile, the sky gradually changed. The tender blue vault reappeared. Then I saw the dawn, the rising sun, and I prayed."

"Me too!" Annabella murmured.

"Mars was before me," her husband continued. "I was almost happy. Something told me that we'd see one another again. And I came down in the sea. The *Velox* swam like a fish. And suddenly, the catastrophe…a kind of submarine volcano, a waterspout, threw me up into the clouds. How is it that I wasn't crushed, pulverized a hundred times over? I don't know.

"Shortly thereafter, the *Velox* sank…poor *Velox!* I was able to escape, to reach the shore…and there I collapsed, out of strength."

"And afterwards?" asked the American, breathlessly.

"Afterwards it's even more confused. I dragged myself over the sand. I was dying of hunger...atrocious hunger. Finally, agonized and defeated, I lay down to die. I called to you, and suddenly I saw you, as if in a mist, but I didn't recognize you. I was delirious."

"Yes," said Anna. "Oh, how I trembled."

"And when I came to, I thought the delirium was continuing. I thought I was mad—proof that I wasn't, but my reason was jibbing before the miracle. I wondered whether it wasn't in the other world that we had found one another. I was convinced that I was dead."

As he pronounced that word, Serge turned round and pointed at the cairn. "Look," he went on. "I was so convinced that I was dead that I'd built my tomb in advance, after a fashion...that heap of stones you see there. It's under there that I buried my papers, my jewelry. I wanted to make sure that, once my body had disappeared, if you ever came—for something old me that you would me—I wanted you to know where to pray, for you to have a souvenir. I'd only kept one thing: your dear image. I looked at it while I was dying!"

While speaking, Serge had drawn his wife toward the cairn. He knelt down, moved away the blocks of lava and started feverishly digging in the sand, from which he soon pulled out the various objects he had buried half an hour before.

"Look," he said, "here's my notebook, my watch, and the seal you gave me. Here are your letters...all my life, my heart, my soul! I was there, in my entirety. What does the rest matter, the perishable flesh, fodder for grave-worms?

"Oh, how happy I am! How good it is to live, to stir this soil into which I felt myself descending forever, dissolving, as it were. How good it is to believe, to love!

"I was dead! An angel came, touched me, and I'm alive! I'm alive! What intoxication!

"A man buried alive, who gnaws his fists, and suddenly sees the tomb open, and the light shine...the sweet light...must experience what I'm experiencing."

Serge Myrandhal seemed completely recovered now. The cordial, wine and concentrated meat extract he had absorbed a little while before had done him a great deal of good. He was talking and acting like a healthy man.

Nevertheless, his weakness persisted, and the effort he had just made had exhausted him. He was out of breath, and drops of sweat were trickling down his thin cheeks.

His wife became anxious. "Leave it at that," she said. She took a tablet from a box. "Here, chew this—it's concentrated peptone."

Serge pulled a face, like a capricious invalid. "No," he said, with a sort of puerile stubbornness. "Why do you want to make me think that I'm ill? I don't like taking medicine."

"It's not medicine," said the American. "It's food. I take one every day; that's what keeps me going. You ought to have done the same—but there's still time." She suddenly changed her tone, becoming coquettish, as in the garden at Almowrat. "Go on, to please me, take the tablet."

"Since I tell you that I don't need anything, I don't want..."

"But I do want," Anna interjected, stamping her foot. "And then, Monsieur Myrandhal, you promised to obey me, in everything and always. Do you remember?"

Serge's gaze softened immediately. "So be it," he said. "But after you. Taste it first..."

The young woman understood. She broke the tablet, keeping one piece and holding out the other to him, on which her teeth had left a damp trench. "You now."

Avidly, Serge seized the tablet, which he chewed joyfully. "There!" he said. "You're a sister of charity, an angel, an enchantress! That tablet was nothing but a piece of dried gelatin, but you touched it with your lips and made it a balm, a marvelous elixir. I can feel it gliding through my veins like a subtle fire. I was still weak, although cured, but all my strength has suddenly returned. My blood is pulsing more rapidly. I feel rejuvenated, ready to brave anything!"

And to prove that he was telling the truth, he took his wife in his arms and, setting off at the double, ran to deposit her ten meters away.

"Well?" he asked. "Are you convinced now?"

Serge was bathed in perspiration, and his eyes were shining; the American was slightly anxious about that excitement. "Yes," she said, "and the proof is that I'm taking your arm to support myself. I'm the one who's weary. I've been searching for you all day; we've been wandering along the shore for an hour. It's late, and we ought to go back."

"Go back where?" Serge asked, distractedly. "And why? It's so nice here. If you're tired, let's sit down and talk."

Madame Myrandhal uttered a brief mutinous laugh. "Are you making fun of me, Monsieur my husband? Do you take me for a little savage, who sleeps in the sand? I told you that we're expected. We have to go back."

"Go back?" said Serge, scanning the nocturnal landscape with a circular glance. "Where to?"

"Home."

"Home…this is getting stranger and stranger. You have a domicile here, in this desert?"

"Yes…the *Velox*."

"The *Velox?* I thought it was at the bottom of the sea. Have you recovered it, then?"

"Yes, but not yours—the other one, the *no. 1*."

"The *no. 1?*"

"Yes—the one that the Mendicant Prince was to use."

"Ah!" Serge exclaimed, his face clearing. "That's the means that brought you here, then? He was afraid…he's repented…"

"Not exactly. There was a fight, but we won. It's a long story, which I'll tell you shortly, at table. I didn't want to tire you out."

"Always that idea. But I'm not ill, my dear Anna, I swear. I've never been ill. A nervous disturbance, the effect of emotion, and weakness too. I was wrong not to take anything. As for this wound, it's nothing. There'll be no sign of it to-

211

morrow." Another idea suddenly made him start. "Then the other ship's here!" he exclaimed, his face radiant. "The *Velox no. 1*. We're no longer castaways deprived of everything. We can navigate, come and go, explore the planet, search for more hospitable terrain! We can leave if necessary. Quickly, tell me: is the other *Velox* intact?"

"Entirely intact. Not a plate out of place."

"That's marvelous. Take me to it right away. I'm in haste to see it, to touch it. Why can't I see it? Where is it? Is it far away?"

"No—about a mile."

Serge stood on tiptoe. "I can't see anything."

"The sand's hiding it. There's nothing as deceptive as shifting dunes. Just now, while looking for you, I almost got lost once or twice. Fortunately, we have an excellent reference-point. You see that rock over there, that sort of obelisk overlooking the beach?"

"Perfectly. One might think that it was a bell-tower..."

"That's the word—I'll keep that. It will be our bell-tower. Well, it's there. The *Velox*—or, rather, the *Annabella*, since that's the name it's been given..."

"A beautiful name!" Serge murmured.

"...is beached a little further on, about three hundred meters..."

"Let's go, then. It must be late—what time do you think it is?"

"My watch has stopped."

"Like mine. I suspected as much."

"And not only mine, but all the clocks on board."

"When did they stop? On arrival...?"

"I don't know. I'd lost all notion of time, and I didn't think about consulting the chronometer once. Our journey might have lasted twenty or thirty hours; is it the first or the second of August? I can't tell. And what does the terrestrial time matter? We're on another world, on Mars."

"We're on Mars," Serge repeated, like an echo. "I need to repeat that in order to believe it. You said just now that you'd been searching for me all day; in consequence, we must have arrived, together, almost at the same time, at dawn."

"That's right. And what a dawn!" the young woman exclaimed. "I'll never forget it. What a shiver, when I recognized the famous canals. So, the *Annabella*, left to her own devices, as it were—for I had nothing, or almost nothing, to do with her direction—had continued on its route without deviation an inch. She steered like a living being who knows where she's going—unless she was drawn, attracted to Mars by some unknown force, by some occult power that will reveal itself later. Several times, during the journey, I had the sensation that a mysterious will was watching over us."

"Me too."

"It's like our arrival at the same point, almost at the same time. Doesn't that make you believe in that intervention, in some mysterious protector who was bringing me to you? God was evidently on our side."

"Yes," the engineer murmured. "Take note, though, that the thing might have a simpler explanation. Launched from the same point, in the same direction, by an identical force, the two psychoscaphs were bound, like two bullets, to end up at the same place. We had the same itinerary; in a word, we followed one another. Notice too that I'd often mentioned the Mädler Sea to you, where I counted on coming down. You might have remembered that, and unconsciously, without being aware of it, steered the apparatus in that direction."

"It's possible. In any case, from that moment on, I started steering in an effective fashion. I was familiar with the various items of apparatus."

"You didn't have any difficulty?"

"Not once. You had explained those in the *Velox* to me so often, and they were the same. Of course, from then on your itinerary escaped me. First I searched for you in the air with the telescope. The *Annabella* flew at a considerable height for some time, in order to see further.

"Then, not having discovered anything, I concluded that the *Velox* had come down right away, and that it was already

213

heading for the shore, so I came closer to the sea and started to described concentric circles of increasing radius. But I couldn't see any more trace of the *Velox* on the water than in the air. It's true that so little of the vessel protrudes that the slightest wave might hide it.

"That's why I'm so late. Finally, as the sun was setting, I set forth along the canal. Something told me that you must have gone in that direction...

"It was getting dark rapidly, and I was beginning to despair. Briefly, I heard a horrible noise..."

"The maelstrom," Serge murmured.

"Yes I understand now. Darkness had fallen, though, and my anguish was increasing. One hope remained, though. A presentiment—one of those mysterious warnings in which you and I believe, told me that you were there, nearby, struggling against some incomprehensible phenomenon. I wanted to call out to you, to shout: 'Be brave! Someone's coming to your rescue...' And once again, I looked for the telepath, and I found it behind a divan, where it must have slipped when we took off. I called to you, but you didn't reply..."

"That's explicable," Serge replied. "At that moment I was in the middle of an atmosphere saturated with electricity, in the middle of a storm. The feeble waves of the apparatus must have gone astray..."

"That's what I thought, too. In fact, the racket suddenly became frightful. One might have thought it an artillery battle between two fleets. Suddenly, everything went silent...a deathly silence...and I let go of the steering wheel. *It's all over*, I said to myself. He's doomed... "

"I'd just saved myself."

"I was sobbing. Suddenly, my companion uttered a cry that I can still hear: 'A wreck, there, near the bank!'

"It was the *Velox*, coming back up to the surface. It sank again almost immediately, but the hatch of its conning-tower was open, and I realized that you must have escaped that way and swum to the shore.

"Close by, there were shifting dunes. I sailed straight for them and our ship ran aground gently on the sand. A few moments later, we were beside you, and you opened your eyes."

Serge hugged his wife impetuously. "What you have done is marvelous—marvelous, for a woman..."

"I wasn't alone."

"That's true...I saw someone a little while ago. I remember now...a man. Where is he, so that I can thank him? Why has he gone away?"

"For the sake of discretion. And then, I feared that his presence here might displease you. I remember that you were determined to be the first man on Mars, and I feared that you'd see him as a competitor, a rival for glory."

"Glory," Serge murmured. "What a vain word, after such ordeals." Again he embraced his wife. "This is my glory, and I want no other. The man who has brought you to me will never be a rival. I feel that I love him already. So you can name him without fear. Who is he?"

"Guess," said Anna, who was reassured.

"How do you expect me to guess? Is it someone I know?"

"Yes."

"And who was at the convent with us?"

"Obviously."

"It's not at all easy, you know...we were alone, with no friends. I can only think of the reverend. That's it. You already mentioned abducting him..."

"No, it's not him."

"Then I give up. And what does it matter? I have no need to know him to love him. Take me to him so that I can take him in my arms. Where has he gone? He was here just now, behind that heap of sand. Where do you think he is?"

"Back at the ship, no doubt. I expect we'll find him setting the table. Perhaps he's scold us a little for being so slow. We've been wandering in the moonlight for more than an hour. We've taken the lovers' route...

"Our friend is a hearty eater—one of those imperturbable Anglo-Saxons whom nothing troubles. At the battle of Tsushima[25] he was aboard the Japanese flagship, and at the height of the battle, when hundred-ton cannons were blazing, do you know what he was doing?"

"No."

"Eating lunch sitting astride a yard-arm."

"I've got it!" cried Serge, laughing. "This time, I've got it. It's Pickman."

"The very same."

"What a man!" Myrandhal continued. "And what a good companion, what a jolly fellow! He swore to make the voyage and he's kept his word, to our great good fortune."

Again he burst out laughing. His wife did likewise.

"I can breathe easy," she said, then. "Just as long my dear guardian is as agreeable. I can't help feeling a certain anxiety, I confess. You know his mania for setting records. This morning, when we spotted you, he didn't want me to hurry the landing, so that he could mark the record and the time. Fortunately, our watches weren't working.

"Until then, he'd convinced himself that the *Annabella*, being lighter than the *Velox*, would arrive first—and now we don't know what time it is, and have no way of checking the time. Imagine his disappointment! He's heart-broken, and I'm wondering how he'll greet us. It's necessary to expect anything from an eccentric of his stripe. He's capable of not wanting to recognize you."

"Don't worry," said Serge. "I'll soon soften him up. I'll make concessions..."

"No!" cried the American. "That's exactly what I don't want. Let me handle it. My guardian is a good man, in spite of his manias. If you'd seen his emotion just now, when we found you lying on the sand. He loves you, deep down..."

---

[25] The major naval battle of the Russo-Japanese War, fought in May 1905. The Japanese won.

"And I adore him! But where is he? Where's the *Annabella?* We're only a short distance from the 'bell-tower' and I can't see anything."

"Come on," said Madame Myrandhal. "We're nearly there."

After having gone around one last mound of sand, the two young people stopped in amazement.

In front of them, at the foot of the obelisk, the Eccentric, holding his alpenstock in one hand, on the end of which a lantern was swinging, and a brush in the other, was in the process of applying red paint on the base of the monolith. Already, an inscription was displayed in letters a foot high:

SIR WASHINGTON PICKMAN
1 August 19**

On hearing the sand creak, he darted a glance sideways, and calmly continued his task.

Discontented with this welcome and losing patience, the American ran toward him.

"My dear guardian," she said, "may I introduce my husband, Monsieur Serge Myrandhal..."

"Your husband?" said the Englishman, without turning his head. "What's this nonsense? God damn it! Have you lost your mind, Miss Anna?"

The final digit had been filled in. Unhurriedly, Pickman wiped his hands, turned round, and at the sight of Myrandhal, muttered: "Why, who's this gentleman?" Then, addressing the young woman, he said. "Well, Miss Anna, be polite. What are you waiting for? Introduce me to this young Martian."

II. Peace is Made

The bluff was so colossal, and so unexpected, and the Eccentric had said it so seriously, that the American, who had been on the point of getting annoyed, was gripped by irresistible laughter.

Her husband was also making superhuman efforts not to burst out laughing.

The Englishman was still waiting, impassively. "Shocking!" he ended up saying. "Miss Anna, you're a silly girl, and unseemly. I forgive you because the voyage has troubled your mind slightly. It's stupid to laugh like that."

Myrandhal feared that the Baronet might really be offended, so he took a step forward.

"Monsieur," he said, courteously. "Believe that..."

"Prodigious!" cried the eccentric. "They speak French on Mars! It's bizarre, but everything is upside-down here." Becoming amiable, he went on: "In any case, sir, I'm delighted to make your acquaintance. You can serve as our interpreter. Furthermore, I'm delighted that your wound is better. You were wounded in combat, I suppose? You must tell us all about it at table, for I'm inviting you to dinner. I'm keeping you. You're our guest, our hostage. Oh, don't worry—you'll be well treated...

"As soon as possible, we'll exchange you. There would be a preferable arrangement, and we'll make it with great pleasure—I and my ward, Miss Anna Carpenter, whom you see here. That would be, if it's agreeable to you, for you to stay with us..."

"But I'd like nothing better," said Myrandhal, with the utmost seriousness.

"All right! I can see that we'll get along. You understand that we're a little like castaways here, like Robinson Crusoe, the great English hero. We need someone who knows the

218

country, the indigenous customs—a Friday, in sum. Would it please you to accept that role?"

"Gladly."

"All right!" the Eccentric repeated. "And now, my friends, to table. I'm as hungry as a shark."

Madame Myrandhal observed this scene without saying a word. She was thinking, wondering what her guardian was playing at, and not knowing whether to laugh or get annoyed.

Myrandhal, for his part, was avidly contemplating the psychoscaph lying about a quarter of a mile away.

The Englishman took a step. "Forward march!" he commanded, dryly. And, in a lower voice, as if he feared being overheard by his ward, he added: "My dear Friday, I have something delicate to discuss with you."

"Speak, my dear Robinson."

"This is it. You seem like a gallant man. In fact, perhaps you're not as Martian as you'd like to have us believe. Well, you see that young woman—the one who bandaged you and brought you here. She appears to be quite rational..."

"Indeed."

"Wrong! My ward's mind is severely deranged. I'd already perceived it during the voyage, but it has suddenly taken on greater, yes, unexpected proportions. Reasoning is futile. Best, I think, to explain the matter to you.

"So, my ward is a lunatic, as I said. She's seeing double, and mistakes you for her boy-friend, a certain Myrandhal, who's a long way away. So, you understand, it's necessary to do as I do, to lend yourself to the game, otherwise she might easily..."

The American was not listening. Her brows furrowed, she was looking at the rear of the *Annabella*, where something was floating that puzzled her: a square piece of muslin with orange stripes, which was difficult to make out in the gloom.

She suddenly stopped. "That's too much!" she exclaimed. "An English flag!" And she turned to her guardian, her eyes blazing. "Mr. Baronet, you're going to take down that rag right now. I stopped you a little while ago, and you've

219

taken advantage of my absence. It's naughty! It's a crime, an infamy!"

"An infamy," muttered the Eccentric, disconcerted by the abrupt attack. "What do you mean? What's biting you, Miss Anna?"

The American stamped her foot. "First of all, I forbid you to call me Miss Anna."

"Forgive me, Madame Myrandhal. I forgot..."

"And then, I told you that I don't want that flag. There's only one man who has the right to plant his flag on Mars, and that's my husband, here present."

The Englishman nudged Serge with his elbow. "You see, sir? That's what I was saying. I'll try to reason with her. Help me...

"By Jove, my dear Anna, you're making a mistake. You've forbidden me to raise my flag on Mars, and I respected the order. I'll respect it as long as it isn't proven that I set foot here first. But on the *Annabella*, it's a different matter. God damn it. I have the right. The ship belongs to me..."

"Oh!" said Anna, calming down. "It belongs to you..."

"Yes. I conquered it in battle. You were there and can bear witness to that. I'm entitled to say: the *Annabella* belongs to me; it's English territory, on which I have the right to plant my flag. Don't you agree, sir?"

"Entirely. In your place, I wouldn't have been so pernickety. I'd have hoisted my flag on the land itself, boldly. I can assure you that no one would have protested."

Pickman had pricked up his ears, wondering if he had heard correctly. "Not even you? And yet you might, perhaps...you're the first occupant...as a Martian, I mean..."

"Oh, I'm a very recent Martian," Serge replied, smiling, "and perhaps I won't be one for long. I have a revenge to take on Earth, and am only waiting for an opportunity to quit this excessively inhospitable world. Don't worry, sir, it's not possession of this desert, these few square feet of sand, that will cause us to quarrel."

"A few square feet of sand!" murmured the Eccentric, delighted by what he heard. "That's the way they talk…always the same, these crazy Frenchmen. Good for pulling chestnuts from the fire. So, I only have to wait…he goes, I stay, and once alone, I annex! All right!" In a louder voice, indifferently, he added: "So you're going to leave Mars?"

"As soon as possible."

"And if others take it?"

"What would they do with it? I once said to someone, who looked a lot like you, that the time is a long way off when pleasure trains will be circulating between the planets."

"Yes," said the Englishman, feigning a detachment that he was far from feeling, "You're absolutely right. There's no point envisaging such a fugitive prospect. I agree with you, my dear Friday."

The American shrugged her shoulders at that word. "What a ridiculous joke," she murmured. "I warn you, my dear guardian, that I'm going to get annoyed if this goes on."

"But I'm not joking, I'm being serious..."

"Thank you very much! Then it's seriously that you're claiming that I'm mad?"

"No!" protested the Englishman, swiftly. "I was wrong to say…yes, I was joking then. You're not mad, Miss Anna…Madame Myrandhal, I mean."

"It's you who's an old madman."

"No, me neither. However, we don't see things the same way. So, there's a mystery..." The Englishman slapped his forehead. "I've got it!" he cried. "I've found it!"

"What have you found?"

"The key to the mystery. We're both in our right minds. It's not us who's seeing double—no, it's this gentleman, quite simply."

"You're being ridiculous," said Anna.

"Wait," said the Eccentric. "Let me speak—I'll prove it. You'll be forced to agree, since I'm reasoning in accordance with your own ideas. A hundred times, Anna, you've said to

221

me that each of us has a double somewhere, another self, on another planet, who calls to us...

"So, everything is explicable! You're right, and I'm not wrong. Or, to put it better, we're both right, since Monsieur Myrandhal, as you call him, and Friday, as I call him, are one and the same...why are you laughing? Does that seem ludicrous to you?"

"Indeed."

"No. It's true—perhaps, at least...let's suppose that it is, that it's the only way of reaching an agreement. You can see that I'm making concessions..."

Madame Myrandhal shrugged her shoulders without making any reply.

"You're sulking!" said, the Englishman, crestfallen. "And yet, I'm doing what I can! I take our guest as my witness that I'm doing what I can—aren't I, sir?"

"Absolutely."

"Ah! You see, Miss Anna...I only want to reach an understanding with the two of you—with you, sir, even though I have reasons for holding a grudge against you. Let's leave that aside, though, and make peace. I'd like that. But it's still necessary that I know your intentions. The first point that might have set us at odds, the possession of Mars, is settled—or rather, set aside. The question doesn't arise for the moment—but there's something else that bothers me."

"What's that?"

"This: whether you're Myrandhal or his double, the matter concerns you intimately, and you're certainly aware of it. You've heard mention of the great enterprise, the great race organized by an American newspaper: the race from New York to Mars."

"Indeed."

"You know that Myrandhal—the one in New York, I mean—and I were competing to win the cup..."

"I know."

"Well, now that everything can be explained...Anna's holding it against me that I'm not stepping aside in favor of

222

her 'dear heart.' More than that, she's accused me of having lacked honesty, and yet, I swear to you that I've never done anything incorrect. I'm a gentleman..."

"I never doubted it," Myrandhal protested.

"Thank you," said the Englishman, immediately. "Oh, the battle has been rude, and if we've achieved a dead heat...you'll permit me to suppose that until the negative is proved..."

"I permit everything."

"Thank you! So, I was saying that, if we'd arrived neck and neck, I'd have merit. You ought to understand that if the struggle was unequal between me, an old globe-trotter, and that young man, who is a famous scientist...you can see that I'm rendering the same justice..."

"Thank you," Serge murmured, in his turn.

"So, I repeat, I've done nothing improper; I've only taken advantage of opportunities. A Rajah I know had a psychoscaph, another *Velox* that he could launch second. He ceded his right to me, one way or another—that's between us—and I got aboard with my ward. The *Annabella* departed, according to the agreement, a long time after the *Velox*— almost two hours—it remains to be determined which of the two machines won the race. One, the *Velox*, was giving weight, but receiving time; the other was doing it the other way around, to equalize the chances—a handicap, what! Launched with the same force, but lighter and faster, the *Annabella* ought to have overtaken her competitor. Did she succeed? That's the question. Which arrived first? That's what it's necessary to establish, to prove..."

"It's proven," Serge replied. "It's the *Annabella*. Her name has brought her luck."

Pickman's face lit up. "Do you have proof?"

"No, but it's probable, as you say—so probable that I'm ready to concede it..."

"God damn it!" exclaimed Pickman, raising his arms in the air with a furious expression. "That's not the point at all! It's a matter of sport, this issue, and it's necessary to proceed properly. War and business are one thing, but sport is another. Here, honesty is required. I'd be delighted, and I'd give my fortune and my head together, to be able to put on my card: *First man on Mars*—but I need it to be the truth. I don't want a title accorded by kindness, by gallantry.

"You can understand now why I'm in a hurry to discover who the record belongs to, and I think you can help us. So, I'm asking you a question that's been burning my lips for a long time: what time was it—I mean, the terrestrial time—when you arrived on Mars?"

"I don't know. All the chronometers on board had stopped.

"God damn it! Just like ours. Tell me, then, what time was it on Mars, according to the sun? You must have measured its height."

"In truth, no," Serge replied, insouciantly. All that I can say is that the sun had risen. As for measuring its height above the horizon, I didn't think of it..."

"I thought of it!" cried the Eccentric. "It was all I thought of, throughout the voyage. So, as soon as we recognized Mars, I measured the height of the sun—exactly two and a half degrees—and ours as well. Those two measurements combined permit the specification of the time—the Martian time, if course. If you'd done the same, the problem would be resolved. We'd only have to compare them...

"What a pity, sir! You've done us considerable harm. You don't think you can repair that omission?"

"It would be difficult. If I had my ship, my apparatus, perhaps it would be possible, by a sequence of deductions...unfortunately, they're at the bottom of the canal. I'll try, though. I'll do everything I can to give you satisfaction. Rely on me, my dear Robinson."

"Thank you, my dear Friday!"

They were only a few meters from the psychoscaph now.

Suddenly, Serge, leaving his companions, ran toward a nearby sandy mound. He had just perceived a sprig of the "castaways' herb" to which he might have owed his life. At the top of the ruddy stems a few pale flower-heads were sway-ing, reminiscent of lilies of the valley.

"Flowers," Serge murmured. "I want to be able to cele-brate my wife's birthday."

He picked the most beautiful stems, tied them up with a twig, and hid the bouquet in his bosom.

As he completed that operation, he heard an altercation flare up between his companions.

When he came back, the Eccentric was alone. Head bowed, his expression crestfallen, he was scratching the sand with the tip of his alpenstock.

"Where's Anna?" the engineer asked.

The Englishman pointed to the young woman, who was on the walkway of the psychoscaph. "She's gone," he said, piteously, "and I think she's really angry."

"Angry with whom? Me?"

"No, not you—quite the contrary. Me. She's just been quarreling with me again."

"About what?"

"You. She wants me to apologize to you…or at least give you an explanation."

"But I won't allow…you don't owe me any explana-tions."

"Yes, let me do it. There's no inconvenience, now we're in accord about everything. Obviously, I was a little ill-tempered at first. You hadn't been friendly toward me—but since then, you've made amends. Above all, you've promised me to establish the true record. I was annoyed with you just now—hence that ridiculous bluff."

"Not at all. On the contrary, your idea was very amus-ing…"

"Bah, you understand the joke—but she doesn't want to. She's just told me. So, it's necessary to put an end to it. There's no more reason for it, anyway.

Leaning on the rail of the walkway, the American was waiting. Her guardian shot her a sideways glance.

225

"You see," he murmured. "She doesn't trust me. She wants to make sure that I'm making amends. She's a tyrant! Just as long as she stops sulking once the ceremony's over and done with..."

Abruptly, like a man submitting at his cost, the Eccentric held out his hand to the engineer. "With that, let's end the joke. Monsieur Myrandhal, I offer you my apologies; let's make peace."

"I'd like nothing better."

"Me too. I hold you in high esteem. We should have been friends for a long time It's you who..."

The Eccentric could not complete his sentence. From the walkway, making a bound of thirty feet, a dog had just leapt upon Pickman's shoulders. He nearly fell over.

The animal—a Saint Bernard of considerable size— continued its hectic bounds, raising clouds of dust every time.

"It's Stop," grumbled the Eccentric. "Peace, Stop! What a crazy devil! He doesn't understand that on Mars, his weight of hundred and thirty pounds becomes barely thirty. It's the second time that the satanic fellow has knocked me over. Anna knows it, and I'll wager that the little pest has unleashed him deliberately."

In fact, on the walkway, Madame Myrandhal was laughing uproariously. She clapped her hands.

"Let's eat!" she cried, joyfully. "The table's laid. Let's not wait any longer. I'm as hungry as a wolf, God damn it!"

The Eccentric had raised is head. "Good," he said, joyfully. "That's much better. She's making fun of me. Peace is made! To table, sir!"

III. The Drama of Almowrat

The *Annabella*, into which we are introducing the reader for the first time, had the same dispositions as the *Velox*, except that it was smaller by a third and did not have separate cabins. From the store-room one passed directly into the central compartment beneath the conning-tower, and from there into the engine room.

"Sir," said the Eccentric, "Before anything else, I'll do you the honors of our dwelling. I'll show you, not the vessel itself, which you know as well as I do, but its equipment. You'll be astonished by the cargo that I've succeeded in lodging in this egg-shell. It's a masterpiece of stowage, without boasting. I was a midshipman once, and it's served me well. So, before sitting down at table, I'll give you the proprietor's tour, if you wish."

"I was about to ask you," Serge replied. "I'd be interested to see how this machine, which appeared to me to be a trifle fragile, stood up to the journey."

"Marvelously," replied the Englishman, triumphantly. "It's true that we had a master pilot: my ward, here present. She manned the helm, and by Jove, she astonished me—and I'm not easily astonished. I wish you could have seen her, especially during the landing. She executed a descent and a swerve at top speed that were a veritable marvel."

Myrandhal squeezed his wife's hands. "My dear Anna," he murmured. "Where would I be without you?"

Meanwhile, the Eccentric had started walking the young couple from one end of the submarine to the other. They lent themselves to that whim with a good grace, but were scarcely listening to the former midshipman's expert explanations, spiced with marine terminology. Entirely devoted to their happiness, they were whispering in one another's ears.

Nevertheless, as they went on, one thing that surprised Myrandhal was the enormous quantity of food supplies and machinery of every sort heaped up in the three compartments. They were everywhere.

"That's surprising" he murmured in the American's ear. "For the worthy Pickman to have accumulated so many provisions, he must have been certain of making the voyage."

"He says so," the American replied, smiling, "but he's boasting. He merely hoped so, and had, entirely at hazard, packed his bags. It appears that, the day after his entry to the monastery, an entire caravan arrived for him, more than fifty camels..."

"Fifty camels," murmured Serge. "In that case, we can only see part of the cargo here. What could there have been in all those crates? All that is strange, as is the presence of the Eccentric in the convent. What was he doing there and why was he hiding? Obviously, he was preparing a coup—as was his right. I should have suspected it, and my word, I agree that he employed his time marvelously. Perhaps he intended to leave before us—before me. In fact, the *Annabella*, you said, left the monastery an hour after the *Velox*?"

"An hour and a few minutes."

"It's necessary, then, that the *Annabella* must have been fitted out without our knowing it, fully loaded—ready to depart, in sum. That's a mystery."

"Yes," said the American, not without a certain hesitation. "That's a mystery. During our journey, I tried to make my guardian confess, but he seemed so embarrassed, and ashamed, that I thought I ought not to insist...

"To tell the truth, and to deal with the delicate subject in one go, my feeling—which, I divine, is also yours—is that an association had been formed, a conspiracy against you, between my guardian and the mage, that horrid monk who had inspired such a revulsion in me from the very first day..."

"How right you were," Serge murmured.

"Except," Anna went on, "that as soon as the Baronet—a gallant man with a great heart, in spite of his passion, which sometimes blinds him—saw his accomplice's infamy, he pulled himself together and made an about-turn, in such a way as to redeem the situation entirely.

"What his exact intentions were, it's probably best not to inquire too closely, and only to see one thing—his subsequent conduct. He's fully repaired the wrongs that he might have done. After all, it's Pickman alone who has saved us—you and me. Without him, we'd be separated forever."

"That's true," Serge murmured, raising his wife's hands to his lips.

Shortly afterwards, the tour concluded, the voyagers returned to the central compartment, where the table was laid.

"That's enough for this evening," said the Eccentric. "I'm hungry. Tomorrow, we'll make a more detailed tour, for I have many interesting things to show you. I've thought of everything—there's everything, all the way to radish seeds and special thread to make fishing lines."

While talking, the Englishman had opened various tins of food. As they were taking their places at the table, Serge leaned toward his wife and took out the bouquet he had picked and hidden.

"My dear Anna," he said, "permit me to wish you happy birthday. It might be a little late, and these flowers are very modest, but they're the only ones I could find on this arid world..."

Tenderly moved, the American had thrown herself into her husband's arms.

As for the Eccentric, seized by a sudden enthusiasm, he applauded with his huge hands and became excited. "Hip, hip, hurrah!" he cried. "Well said! Bravo, sir! I'm entirely of your opinion. Perhaps it's not as late as you think, and there's always time to do the right thing. Imagine that I didn't think of it! I'm an ass!"

In his turn, Pickman threw himself upon his ward and hugged her wholeheartedly. He was so emotional that he nearly hugged Serge too. Then he ran to the store-room and came back carrying a bottle of champagne, which he immediately uncorked.

"To the health of Madame Myrandhal!" he declared. "To our all-round success! Today is a great day, and it's necessary that the celebration should be complete. Wait!"

Again, the Englishman ran to the store-room. He soon emerged again, brandishing a large flat tin, which he set about opening.

"A plum pudding!" the Eccentric howled, having arrived at the peak of his enthusiasm. "I was keeping it for a special occasion; what better one could there be? And it will be excellent, by Jove, although tinned…besides, I have a means of making it new…fresh, I mean."

The Baronet poured half a liter of rum over the pudding, and set fire to it.

The young couple looked on, amused and bewildered.

"But where the devil did all that come from?" asked the engineer. "This ship is a veritable treasure-trove—a Mère Gigogne's cupboard!"[26]

Meanwhile, the Englishman had stuck a knife into the national pudding.

"This is some party!" he murmured. "I'd give a great deal for the members of the Splendid Club to be able to see me now."

"And the *Herald*, which we're forgetting!" cried the American, suddenly remembering her duty as a reporter. She was already sitting at the telepath's signal-key and spelling out the dispatch that she was sending: "*Mars, Mädler Sea. Arrived safely. Desert world. Details tomorrow*…and that's enough for now. Will the dispatch arrive, though?"

"I hope so," Myrandhal replied, "but I can't be certain."

"My dispatch reached you, though."

---

[26] Mère Gigogne [Mother Ginger] is a stock character in French puppet shows, who has a large number of children and works wonders in order to feed them. She might be a version of the character in the English nursery rhyme "There was an old woman who lived in a shoe…."

"Yes, but that was a much shorter distance. Until now, the newspaper telegraphed us every day, but it's been at least twenty-four hours since we received anything. That gives me doubts. I wonder whether the apparatus really has as much power as I hoped. In any case, the paper's reply, or its silence, will settle the matter. We have only to wait."

"That's right," the reporter replied. "If the apparatus is defective, we'll have to improve it. Is that possible?"

"I'll try, if you insist."

"I do insist. Don't forget, my dear husband, that you've made a formal promise not to impede my career."

Once their initial hunger had been appeased, Madame Myrandhal began to relate what she called "the Drama of Almowrat."

"I'll resume, she said, at the moment my dispatch left off: '*my door's giving way. Au revoir.*'

"It was *au revoir* that you were trying to say?" asked Serge, swiftly.

"Yes, but I didn't have time to finish. The horrible Rajah had just grabbed my hand, and a dozen monks with ugly faces were surrounding me, dragging me toward the antechamber."

"The wretches!" murmured the young man. "Where were they taking you?"

"I was wondering that when a formidable growling resounded and I saw a beast, which seemed at first to be frightful and monstrous, bounding into my room..."

The Englishman laughed. "It was Stop," he explained. "The old fellow, coming on the scene."

"At the same time," the young woman continued, I saw the men who were holding me leap into the air, their faces crushed, gnashing their teeth..."

The Eccentric extended his bony fist like a boxer.

"That was me," he said, simply. "Three punches, and they were sorted..."

Myrandhal seized the Englishman's hand, and pressed it in his own. A little more and he would have raised that fist,

231

bristling with russet hair, to his lips. "My dear Robinson," he said, "I owe you more than life. You risked being killed..."

"Pfft!" said the Eccentric, disdainfully. "It was nothing, really—the monklings knew nothing about boxing. My only merit was arriving in the nick of time, like Blücher at Waterloo. I'd heard the screech, you see—the whistle of the *Velox*—and immediately thought of some trickery, some dirty deed on the Rajah's part. I'd seen him prowling around too much, that night. I called my dog—he always sleeps with me—and forward ho! There were monks running ahead of us and I only had to follow them to find the right place.

"God damn it! When I saw what was happening...those dozen apes attacking my ward...my heart leapt in my breast like a football. If Anna hadn't held me back I'd have massacred the lot..."

"I was just in time," Madame Myrandhal resumed, unable to help smiling. "My guardian already had the Mendicant Prince under his knee. The monk was choking, sticking his tongue out."

"The vile beast!" muttered the Baronet. "One second more, and I'd have strangled him like an owl..."

"Fortunately," the American continued, "I'd recovered my composure. I threw myself on my uncle like a fury..."

"A fury, in truth," the Eccentric approved. "I'd never seen anything like it in my life..."

"'Let him go!'" I howled. "'Let him go—I need him!'

"'Why?' my guardian asked, amazed. 'Pull yourself together, Miss Anna. Explain yourself. What do you want to do?'

"'What do I want? I want to go in search of my husband. First, get everyone out.'

"The Baronet distributed a few punches, which cleared the place completely. Left alone with my guardian, and the mage, to whom he was still holding on, I went into the dressing-room to change. Less than ten minutes later, I came out full dressed, my suitcase in my hand, ready to depart.

"'Where are you going?' Pickman asked. 'I don't understand. Explain, by Jove.'

"'I've told you—I'm going to Mars. There's another psychoscaph—the *Velox no. 1*. The Rajah has to give the order to get it ready. We're going, and I'm taking you with me.'

"At that announcement, the Baronet uttered a cry of joy, a veritable roar. At the same time, he picked up the mage, tucked him under his arm, and held him there effortlessly. 'All right!' he shouted. 'It's settled. I'm with you—all the better, then, that the *Velox* is all fitted out, ready for take-off. Indraghava was going to leave tomorrow, and even proposed to take me with him. Oh, the wretch—I understand now. It was just a pretext to make use of me...'

"At that moment, there was a racket in the corridor. It was Jonathan Burrett, arriving in his turn, knocking everything over as he came. He came to place himself at my right hand, taking an enormous revolver out of his Quaker overcoat, a pocket machine-gun...

"My two defenders looked so terrible that no one in the convent, that city of more than ten thousand monks, dared to raise a hand against us..."

"Pardon me," the Eccentric interrupted, pouring himself a glass of old whisky. "It's necessary to get things right. In truth, you're making us look too good, my dear ward. Probably, the Rajah only had to raise a hand to launch all those thin apes against us, and there would have been a massacre, but he was too sick. He sensed, too, that at the first gesture, I'd crush him like a viper. So he preferred to negotiate. That was better for him and for us, who had need of him, after all."

"It's possible," Madame Myrandhal went on, "but reflection only came later. It was you, my dear guardian, and the worthy Burrett, who won the game by your attitude. It was only in the crypt, where we'd just arrived, and you'd relaxed your grip slightly, that Indraghava thought about negotiating.

"My guardian had put the revolver to his head, with that concise persuasiveness of which he has the secret. 'Now,' he said, 'You have the coolies, the rails, the elephants. Set it up.

233

Have them bring the *Velox* out, put it in place. If it isn't done in thirty minutes, I fire!'

"The mage reflected for a moment, and then asked: 'Is the pastor going with you?'

"'No,' the Reverend replied, divining the Rajah's thinking. 'I'm going back to America. As soon as my friends have gone, I'm leaving the monastery. And don't try to get rid of me. My whereabouts are known, and there's an American consul in Karputhala. On the other hand, if you accept our conditions, and fulfill them to the letter, I promise, on my word of honor, not to breathe a word about the drama. No one will know about your crime but God, who will punish you in His own time.'"

"That's right!" exclaimed Serge. "That's what it was necessary to do. The mage belongs to me, and I'm the one who'll punish him."

"The Rajah hadn't said a word," the American continued, "nor sketched a gesture...except that he must have done something, for one of the monks, who was trembling with fear, suddenly made off. A few minutes went by, and then the coolies suddenly appeared, dragging rails and cross-ties.

"The Rajah had accepted!

"Entrusting the mage to the pastor, Pickman took command of the crew, and they set to work feverishly. It was a matter of placing twenty meters of rail to the cellar next to the one where the *Velox* was stored. An hour later, the track was in place, the needle was brought into play, and the *Velox*, sliding on its truck, came to take its place in front of the engine-amplifier.

"Pickman came to me. 'All aboard for Mars!' he joked. And, seeing tears in my eyes: 'Pardon me, Miss Anna, but you mustn't cry. You mustn't, by Jove! It's not the time. We need you. I believe you know how the machine works better than I do. My part's done—it's up to you now. You're our captain. Be strong, a true American, by the living God—or we're doomed. Is everything ready?'

"Those forceful words recalled me to my duty. At the same time, I shivered, gripped by a sudden anxiety. 'No,' I replied, 'Something's missing.'

"'What?' asked Pickman, suddenly anxious.

"'Come on—I'll explain on the way,'

"You'll have guessed, my dear Serge, where we were going—to your room, to search for one of the filaments needed to arm the engine. I'd suddenly thought of that, and shuddered. If, by chance, the wallet in which you kept the precious filaments was on your person at the moment of your departure, ours would be impossible.

"'By Jove,' groaned the Eccentric. 'We'll see about that. We only have to ask the mage. He's bound to have what you're looking for.'"

"No," said Myrandhal. "I'd taken my precautions too, and the filament was only to be given to the Rajah later. The wretch wanted to play false, and fell into his own trap..."

"The scoundrel!" murmured the Englishman, between his teeth. "He'd told me that the possessed the secret in its entirety. He was lying, the blackguard!"

"It's the biter bit," Madame Myrandhal went on. "I knew that myself, and you can imagine my anxiety as we went up to our apartment. Fortunately, the wallet was there, on the night-stand! It was the first thing I saw when I went in. God was with us! That idea restored all my courage, all my presence of mind. Less than five minutes later, the engine was armed and I went into the psychoscaph.

"I had no trouble finding my way around. All the apparatus I saw there, I knew. I'd seen it already on the *Velox no. 2*; you'd shown me how it worked, and I remembered every last detail. Your voice had engraved a course in mechanics in my memory, in my heart, and I found it when the moment came.

"An immense confidence had invaded me. I was in haste to launch myself on your track, and yet I remained calm and lucid. The consciousness of my responsibility had made another woman of me."

"Yes, Anna," the Eccentric said, approvingly. "You've been marvelous from that moment on. A captain, a true captain, that's what you've been, and there aren't many captains of your caliber in His Majesty's fleet. I know that, by Jove! I'm proud of you, my dear Anna—you're worthy of being an Englishwoman."

"However," the young woman continued, "I went up on to the walkway in order to give the indispensable instructions to Pastor Burrett. He was the one who had to open the formidable current, when the time came, that would project us into space.

"He listened to me attentively and went to his post beside the engine. Pickman, who was there, whispered a few words into his ear and then came to join me. My worthy guardian was seething with impatience and rambling: 'Well, are we going? I've found a name for our machine that will bring her luck: the *Annabella*. Only, get on with it—it's a matter of catching up with that damned Frenchman. Fortunately, I've had a word with the Reverend, He's going to stoke up the power...'

"That statement didn't strike me at the time, any more than the signs the Baronet was exchanging with Burrett. I was too absorbed—so absorbed that it was only then that I noticed that the mage was with us on the platform. Pickman was still holding him by the throat. 'What are you doing?' I said, nonplussed. 'Let that man go.'

"'No,' he said. 'I need him.'

"'Why? What are you going to do?'

"'Make sure he keeps his word. Who can tell? Perhaps the thin ape could stop everything with a sign at the last moment? So, you understand...once we're off, the current on full, I'll throw him overboard. Too bad if he breaks.'

"'But he'll be killed! I don't want that. Let him go,'

"'No,' said the stubborn old fool. 'Don't worry—I'll let go of the old man in time. Go on. Forward ho!'

"I didn't have time to reply, gripped by a shudder of horror...can you imagine that our worthy Burrett, at that 'For-

ward ho!' which was doubtless a signal between the two conspirators..."

"Oh!" the Eccentric protested. "Conspirators! You're
harsh, Miss Anna…Madame Myrandhal, I mean."

"I stand by the word, my dear Pickman. Your impatience
nearly cost us dear. You'd thought it a good idea to give the
pastor instructions contrary to mine, and catastrophe was
hanging by a thread. One second more and the *Annabella*,
instead of launching slowly and progressively, would have
departed like a cannonball and we'd have been crushed, broken..."

"No," the Eccentric relied, "you're exaggerating, Anna.
I've been imprudent, certainly, but it's Burrett who's a mollusk, a cephalopod. I'd told him to stoke it up, yes, but not to
that point. He should have known that a machine that travels a
hundred thousand a second doesn't move off like a sixty
horse-power, at top speed. That's obvious."

"So be it," the young woman went on. "At any rate, the
honest pastor didn't have the slightest idea of the formidable
implement he was handling. At Pickman's command he had
brought down the trolley and grabbed the wheel in both hands;
already he was putting all his weight on it..."

"Evidently, he was about to open the current at a stroke,
and that was catastrophe, instant death. I uttered such a scream
that the pastor stopped dead. He looked at me, saw my distraught face. 'What is it, Milady?' he asked. 'Are you ill?'

"'No…only, you're doing it wrong. This is how we need
to proceed…you see this hand that I'm lifting up; I'm going to
lower it slowly, and you have to follow the movement with the
wheel. It needs to take at least ten seconds. Do you understand?'

"'Yes, Milady.'

"'Go on, then…by the grace of God!'

"'All right!' howled the Baronet, stretching out his arm
to let go of the mage.

"We left…we left at a moderate speed at first, but which increased in a frightful fashion. We hurried down into the central compartment, and then there was the void, the starry night.

"I'd put my hands over my ears, ripped by a frightful screech, the horrible whistling that had made me shudder an hour earlier.

"It was the *Annabella*, bidding adieu to the Earth!"

Madame Myrandhal stopped, palpitating, carried away by the memory.

Her husband was breathless. "And then?" he asked. "Go on, my dear Anna…"

"And then, my dear Serge…there is no *and then*. At least, it's very confused. From the departure to the arrival, until the moment when we discovered the canals, it seems to me, as to you, that I've been living a dream.

"I can only remember one thing, about which I'd rather not think: that sinister firmament, that wan sun that seemed to be looking at us, following us in our audacious flight. What a frightful spectacle that implacable sky was…that *atheistic* sky, so to speak! I was really desperate then, and for the first time, I doubted God! I'm still shuddering over it.

"As for the rest—our arrival on Mars, our search up to the moment we found you, I've already told you about that."

"There's one thing," Pickman added then, "that Madame Myrandhal hasn't said and that I want to tell you about myself. It's her courage, her valor during the journey, and especially on arrival, when we finally saw the *Velox*. As soon as we understood that you were still alive, that you were there on the beach…

"It was a matter of getting down as quickly as possible, but where and how? On land or water? Taking a plunge into the water was the safer course, but also the longer. It would have been necessary to close up the *Annabella*, transform her…you'd have had time to die a hundred times in the interim.

"It was then that your wife had an idea of genius. Close by, on the coast, there were shifting dunes, and our captain

238

threw us at them at top speed. The *Annabella* went through the first one like a bullet, traversed the second less rapidly, and came to a stop without any fuss or damage. I wanted to say that...

"And now, my friends, it's time to sleep. It must be late, and I can see Anna's eyes fluttering. What's more, my dear Friday, you need rest, and personally, I'm exhausted. We'll resume tomorrow...you can tell us your story, which I'm dying to hear. Then we'll hold a council to decide what to do next. Now, good night; I'm falling asleep, in truth."

The three castaways immediately made their arrangements for the night. While the young woman lay down on the divan that was the vessel's only couchette, her companions, rolled in blankets, lay down side by side on the floor.

A sonorous snoring soon announced that the Eccentric had departed for the land of dreams.

Anna too, worn out by fatigue, went to sleep almost instantaneously. Then Serge became drowsy in his turn.

IV. The First Excursion

When Serge opened his eyes the next day, it was broad daylight. He propped himself up on his elbow, and almost immediately, a burst of youthful laughter resonated in his ear. It was Annabella, coming back from the kitchen, carrying three silver bowls on a tray, from which an aromatic odor was emerging.

Sitting at the table, Pickman was making sandwiches, which he was piling up methodically in front of him, building an appetizing pyramid.

The Eccentric raised his head.

"Good Morning! *Bonjour!*" he said. "Did you sleep well, sir?"

"Marvelously, thank you. But I'm truly confused. You should have woken me up."

"Why? Sleep is good and you have a right to it."

"Yes," said Anna, setting down the tray. "How is your wound?"

"Couldn't be better. I can't feel it anymore."

"To table, then! What would you prefer, husband? Coffee, chocolate, sandwiches, cold meat?"

"Your husband will take all of them," the Englishman replied. "He needs to get his strength back. Yesterday was hard work, and today will be no less so. So we have a right to double rations."

"I think you're being very prodigal," said the engineer. "It's probably the opposite that we need to be doing."

"What do you mean? Explain, my dear Friday."

"I mean, my dear Robinson, that we ought to eke out our provisions wisely. We don't know when we'll find others, in fact."

"Pshaw! Bah!" the Eccentric expostulated. "It's our first breakfast on this new world—and then, Mars is a big place;

we mustn't judge it by what we've seen so far. You seem to think that Mars is a dead, sterile world."

"I never said that. I only think that it might be best to anticipate the worst. One thing is certain, at any rate, and that is that the desert surrounding us extends for a long way. You must have seen that, as I did, when you were flying..."

"That's true," said Anna. "This is a black spot..."

"Bah!" said the Baronet. "We were too high up to judge. We need to take a look at closer range, and explore. Only then will we have an exact idea of the country and its resources. That's what we ought to do first. Do you agree?"

"Entirely."

"Furthermore, there's the sea. One can always find food on the edge of the sea. I'll get my fishing tackle out this evening. By the way, did you know that we were nearly carried away last night?"

"Carried away?" exclaimed Myrandhal. "How? By what?"

"By the sea—or rather, by the tide. We ought to have thought of that."

Serge ran to the porthole. In front of him, the beach was still occupied by the waves, which were seething as they retreated. Nevertheless, thanks to the position of the vessel, the danger identified by the Baronet had only been momentary. In fact, the border of foam and mud left by the sea as it ebbed was still three hundred meters from the submarine.

"That's bizarre!" murmured Serge.

"Isn't it?" said his wife. "I thought that on Mars, given its distance from the sun and the smallness of its moons, the tides would be much less noticeable."

"That should be the case, in fact. There must be another cause."

"What?"

"Jupiter. At least, our colossal neighbor surely has something to do with it. As you know, the enormous planet is quite near to Mars at the moment, and will still be getting closer for

241

a few days.[27] That will cause increasingly powerful tides, and perhaps other, less anodyne phenomena."

"What phenomena?"

"Earthquakes. Already, last night, in my sleep, I felt two or three shocks.

"Me too," said Madame Myrandhal, "and the last was very sensible. At the time, I attributed it to the piles of sand that we're resting in, and didn't attach any importance to it. Do you think there's any danger?"

"Danger...no...not immediately, at least. Nevertheless, it would be a reason not to linger in this locale, which has nothing delightful about it. Then, as I've told you, the volcanic nature of the region worries me. Just now, when I woke up, my first thought was to consult the seismograph, to see whether the shocks were continuing."

"And are they?" the American asked.

"Yes, in a peculiarly characteristic fashion. A series of undulations, all in the same direction."

"From which you conclude?"

"I conclude that we have beneath our feet a considerable quantity of lava, a kind of sea of fire. Take note that the influence of Jupiter will make itself felt on that sea like any other; hence the shocks, which will increase from day to day. When Jupiter reaches its greatest proximity, a formidable tidal wave will occur down there."

"Damn!" muttered the Eccentric. "In other words, we're on top of an overheated pressure-cooker, which might well boil over one of these days. You're sure about that?"

"Yes—and the more I think about it, how else can we explain the abnormal temperature we're enjoying? Given the

---

[27] There was a conjunction between Mars and Jupiter on 14 August 1908, although the tidal effects of the conjunction would not have been very great, given the distance between the two planets—more than twice as far as the distance between Mars and the sun.

season and at the latitude where we are, it ought to be frozen already."

"However," Madame Myrandhal put in, "you said just now that there's no immediate danger..."

"I still think so. The dangerous—the critical—moment will be when Jupiter arrives at its shortest distance from us, but we'll be far away by then, I hope."

"When will that eventuality occur?" asked Pickman.

"In a few days time. I don't know exactly...I'll only be able to reply in a precise fashion when I've made the necessary calculations. In any case, a wise precaution to take would be to refloat the *Annabella*."

"Already!" complained Pickman. "So you really think that we ought to leave right away—that it's urgent?"

"The sooner the better. Nevertheless, the day hasn't come yet. Personally, I have an excellent reason not to hurry."

"What reason?"

"The *Velox*."

"You hope to recover the *Velox*?"

"I want to try, at least. It's a project that I mulled over for some time yesterday, before going to sleep. I regret my valiant ship...and what it contains even more: the provisions, the food supplies."

"I understand," said the Baronet. "Still the fear of dying of hunger. What a task, though! If we only knew where it had sunk, into what depths..."

"I do know. Yesterday, on the way here, I was looking at the place. As for the bed, it ought to be quite accessible. In fact, the more I think about it, the more convinced I am that it's a rip in the keel that caused the catastrophe, so the vessel should be caught at present on reefs that aren't very deep. As she went straight down, she should still be there. In consequence, it will be easy to find her."

"I agree. But what will you do then? You don't suppose that you can refloat her?"

"Obviously not. The ship is lost, as I explained; it's the cargo I want to get, at least in part."

"Well. I understand the utility, but how are you going to do it? Do you have a means?"

"Yes. As I told you, the tides will increase in violence. It's probable that the submarine won't resist the thrusts of the sea for long. Once the hull's broken, we'll only have to pick up the flotsam."

"Yes, we'll be our own wreckers."

"That's right. If necessary, we can hurry things along."

"How? I don't see..."

"In the simplest fashion. A stick of dynamite should suffice. You have some, I suppose?"

"Yes," said Pickman. "A full case. I like your idea. One question, though: how are we going to leave here. You don't have the intention of taking the aerial route again, I same?"

"That would be difficult. We don't have what we need for that. The *Annabella* was flying for an entire day, and her psychic accumulators must be exhausted. We'll use her as a boat, therefore. The transformation has been anticipated, and will soon be carried out."

"Well, everything's ready for that. There's a gasoline engine, fuel..."

"How much?"

"A hundred gallons."

"That's about four hundred liters. It's not much, and we won't get far with that meager provision. Oh, if we could only recover the *Velox*'s fifteen hundred liters..."

"Perhaps we will recover them. Then again, we can rig up a sail if necessary."

"That's true, but I hope for better. On Mars, as on Earth—more so than on Earth, given the disposition of the oceans—there are numerous marine currents. It will doubtless be easy to discover one that heads in the direction we want to go. But we're wasting time talking. It's better to do something. We'll talk about all this again this evening, when we've explored the surroundings. Perhaps that reconnaissance will turn up something new. That's why, if Anna isn't too tired..."

"Not at all. On the contrary, I'm in haste to get going. I've just loaded my Kodak. So, whenever you wish, gentlemen, I'll be delighted to stretch my legs."

"Me too," said Pickman, "but not so fast! You're forgetting, sir, that you owe us a story, that it's your turn. We're eager, Anna and I, to know how that rascal of a Rajah caught you, in order to send you away—and then your arrival here, your shipwreck. You can tell us while emptying a glass of whisky. We'll leave afterwards."

Myrandhal complied with a good grace.

"Prodigious!" exclaimed the Englishman, when he had finished. "That Geyser-Volcano is a prodigious, astonishing thing. We heard it, but didn't see it. What a marvel, and how lucky you were. I would have liked to be in your place when you were dancing up there, at the summit. Do you think the prodigy will reappear?"

"Undoubtedly. When we were no our way here, we could see the deep-originated waves—indubitable proof that the volcano is still active."

"I don't care about the volcano—I've seen one of those. It's the geyser that interests me. It'll come back, you say—but when, do you think?"

"It's difficult to be precise. It's necessary to allow time for the reservoir that aliments it to fill up again..."

"Yes, I understand. It's doubtless a matter of the phenomenon known as 'communicating vessels'."

"Probably, although there's no proof. The propulsive force might be quite different. Nevertheless, if we assume that it's simply a matter of a difference in level..."

"Let's assume so. In that case, the reservoir, as you call it, is placed high above sea level."

"Evidently."

"In consequence, Mars isn't a flat world, as you claimed a while ago. There are mountains, and I'll have an opportunity to climb. There's one more thing that's necessary to consider before we set out. All three of us are going, you say—is that prudent? Wouldn't it be better for one of us to stay to guard the ship. I'll offer, if..."

"Guard the ship?" the engineer interjected, nonplussed. "Against whom?"

"Against thieves."

"What thieves? What do you mean, my dear Robinson? You're joking..."

"I've never been more serious. You seem to believe that we're alone here, but are you sure? Are you sure that there aren't any inhabitants in the vicinity, any Martians?"

"Martians!" exclaimed the American. "Where do you get that from? We've been here for twenty-four hours, and we haven't seen the shadow of one. Anyway, it's sufficient to look around: not the slightest trace of inhabitants or habitations."

"That's not proof."

"It seems to me that it is."

"And I say that it's not. You're reasoning as if we were on Earth, my dear Anna. Simply consider that you know nothing about the Martians, their nature, their mores. Perhaps they're nocturnal beings, some sort of vampires, which sleep underground by day, and only come out after dark. In fact, last night, I saw..."

"You saw Martians?" exclaimed the American incredulously.

"No, not exactly, but I saw signs that they made...well, signals."

"Signals!"

"Yes. I went out to answer a call of nature, and as I was coming back, I perceived a glimmer over the sea...oh, very small, like the flame of a match. It happened so quickly that I thought it was an illusion, or some kind of phosphorescent fish, as exist on Earth. I wouldn't have attached any importance to it if a similar gleam hadn't appeared at the same moment over there, on the lava. That one blinked twice, as if it were replying to the other. One might have thought it was an optical telegraph. That's proof—or a strong probability, at least. Don't you agree, sir?"

Myrandhal reflected. "No," he said, after a few seconds. "I thought the same, at first, but the hypothesis doesn't stand up to examination. In fact, why would Martians—if there are any Martians—who have any facility of communication, use that complicated means? It would be necessary to believe that they're impeded. Now, I can't see how, or by what."

"Even so," the Englishman objected, "those flames really did seem to be communicating."

"It's a coincidence. As for the flames themselves, as you thought at first, it's evidently a matter of a natural phenomenon: phosphorescence, spontaneous combustion of an inflammable gas on contact with the atmosphere—how do I know? You don't seem to be convinced."

"No. Scientists have an answer for everything, but I have my own ideas. Then again, there's Stop, who knows more than any of us, and who agrees with me."

"What makes you think that?" asked the young woman.

"Lots of things—and if you knew him as I do, you'd think the same. Stop has a way of sniffing the ground at intervals, growling, and then looking at me in a significant way. He's scented an enemy, I'd swear, and when he looks at me, do you know what I read in his eyes?"

"No."

"I read: *Beware! There's an enemy out there: Martians.*"

"That's implausible, inadmissible," replied Madame Myrandhal. "Why would they be hiding? It would be necessary to suppose that we intimidate them greatly—proof, at any rare, that they're not very redoubtable. First of all, where are they hiding? The country is as bare as my hand. Unless they live in the water like fish, or in the air like birds. But those— the flying men, that is—we'd be able to see passing overhead, soaring in the sky..."

"You're forgetting one thing: under the ground. Perhaps the Martians live underground. An English astronomer claims that on certain cold worlds, like Mars, the inhabitants live underground, like Siberian bears during the winter. Anyway, what's the point in arguing about it? The best thing is to go and see. Stop has a marvelous nose; I'll take you to where I saw the light, and get him to sniff the holes and fissures we encounter; if he doesn't find anything, I'll agree that I was wrong."

The Eccentric stood up. "And now, let's go. I'll get my equipment."

"You're going with us," observed the young woman, not without malice. "So you don't believe in Martians as much as all that?"

"Yes, by Jove. Except that, on due consideration, I don't think the thieves would take the risk in broad daylight. Besides which, the *Annabella*'s visible from a long way off; it'll be sufficient not to lose sight of her.

"At any rate, I'll bring a carbine and cartridges with explosive bullets—and you ought to do the same, my dear Friday, or at least take a hunting rifle. If any game appears within range, you'll easily be able to pot it."

"Indeed—but I doubt that I'll have that agreeable surprise. It seems to me that the region is absolutely deserted, and I'm sure in advance not only of returning empty-handed, but of not even having had an opportunity to fire a shot."

After that, the three castaways discussed the itinerary of their first excursion on Mars.

"To begin with," Pickman proposed, "we'll beat the surroundings. If we don't see anything suspect, we can chance going a little further, perhaps even not coming back until nightfall. In that case, we'll have lunch out there, when we rest. That's why I've made so many sandwiches."

Madame Myrandhal had retired momentarily to the forward compartment, in order to change her clothes.

Once they were equipped, with their knapsacks on their backs and their rifles slung over their shoulders, Serge and Pickman emerged from the submarine. The American joined them soon afterwards. With her felt hat, ornamented with a cockerel's plume, her bicycle shorts and her Kodak attached to her left hip, along with a small keg containing food-supplies, she looked both martial and mettlesome. The engineer was advancing to compliment her when she suddenly burst out laughing at the sight of her guardian, who had put on what he called "full kit": leggings, short trousers and a khaki jacket, with an enormous knapsack, to which an ice-ax and two coils of rope were attacked.

"Ropes!" she said. "What are you expecting to do with ropes and that ice-ax? One might think that you were getting ready to climb Mont Blanc."

"You're a little fool, Anna," the Englishman replied. "An ice-ax is always useful, if only to test the ground. Ditto the ropes. We might encounter crevasses, or precipices. Besides, your husband is almost as heavily laden."

"It might all prove useful," said Serge, smiling.

"As you please, after all," the young woman continued. "When you're too tired, you'll only have to put your bags down on the ground."

"Enough chat! Let's get going."

"Not before I've taken a photograph. Stand over there, both of you, under the platform. Take Stop with you. That's right. Now, don't move!"

Then the American posed in her turn.

"Those," she said, when it was done, "are photographs for which our friend and sponsor Norton Bennett will pay dear. By the way, we still haven't had a reply from the *Herald*. I fear that our dispatch hasn't reached its destination."

"That's probable," he engineer replied. "As soon as we have time, therefore, I'll try to improve our telepath."

"Let's go!" said the Eccentric, becoming impatient. "I have ants in my feet, and so has Milady."

"Milady?" queried Serge.

"Yes," said the Englishman, displaying his alpenstock. "Lady Pickman. Remember what I told you in New York. Milady is my cane. She's getting impatient too. She's fidgeting—as fretful as a sorcerer's magic wand—and that's an indication. She's sniffed something. I'm telling you the truth: there's an enemy lurking nearby."

Meanwhile, the excursionists had already set off over the plain of lava that extended behind the *Annabella*. The dog ran back and forth around them, making furious bounds.

"You see," said the American, eventually. "Stop isn't showing the slightest sign of anxiety. In consequence, there's no one here—no Martians!"

"That's not proof," Pickman replied. "I agree, however, that there's no danger for the moment. The Martians who were prowling around here yesterday must have gone. Thus, we can venture further. It remains to decide which way. I can't see any reason for turning right rather than left."

"My opinion," said the engineer, "is that we should continue westwards. The terrain slopes upwards slightly in that direction, so we're sure of not losing sight of the ship."

"All right," said the Eccentric—and the excursion continued, without incident.

Madame Myrandhal's Martian watch, set at the moment when the sun passed the meridian, marked two o'clock when the castaways stopped for lunch.

Almost without perceiving it, so gently did the terrain slope, they had reached a kind of ridge, from which the view extended a long way into the distance. For a few moments, they contemplated the immense plain of lava that extended all the way to the horizon.

"Still the same thing," Serge murmured. "The proof is there; there's nothing to be obtained from this desert, and the sooner we leave it, the better."

The Eccentric shook his head in a melancholy fashion. "Yes," he said. "I'm beginning to believe so myself—but I'm not giving up yet. We might be able to get something out of the sea. I propose that we investigate that tomorrow. I'm a great fisherman, you know, and I have everything necessary aboard: lines, nets, etc. I'll go on campaign tomorrow. If I'm lucky enough to catch a fish, that will give us some encouragement, and permit us to vary or menu."

"Oh, I doubt that there are any fish," the engineer replied. "Not here, at least. They must stay away from the shore—far from the geyser, whose hot water, saturated with more or less toxic gases, would scarcely suit them. It's necessary, in consequence, to be able to fish in the open sea, and I don't know how you're going to manage that."

"It's easy," the Baronet replied. "I've anticipated the circumstance; I think of everything. We have a rubber dinghy; it only has to be set up. I'll do that this evening."

While conversing, the excursionists had set out their meal on a block of lava. After lunch, they spent a further hour "prospecting" in the vicinity; then, as the sky was clouding over, they decided to go back.

Although the sun was low on the horizon the heat had become oppressive. Large black clouds were accumulating in the west. Gradually, the wind rose, lifting up clouds of dust and sand. From time to time there was a rumble, like that of distant thunder.

"There's no doubt about it," said the Eccentric. "It's a storm—a squall, as mariners say. What fools those astronomers are! I've heard one of them affirm that it hardly ever rains on Mars. I won't complain, though; it will settle this dust, which is rather tiresome."

The little troop contained to advance. It was about a quarter of a mile from the *Annabella* when the dog, which had been frolicking joyfully until then, suddenly changed his attitude. He went back and forth with his nose to the ground, sniffing the lava and growling dully.

At one point he stopped, uttered a brief bark and started scratching furiously. His behavior was so characteristic that Serge and his wife were impressed. As for the Eccentric, he was exultant.

"Well," he demanded, "are you convinced now? It's obvious…this is the very spot where I saw the light shining. It's impossible to doubt it: there were indigenes here last night, and they'll probably come back tonight, to spy…"

"Are you sure?" asked the American.

"Yes," said Pickman. "So sure that I'm going to stay on watch myself. There's an excellent observation post near the boat: the obelisk. I'm going to climb up it. It won't take me long to discover what these bipeds look like."

"But there's no proof that it's a matter of bipeds," Madame Myrandhal replied. "The way that Stop is scratching the soil is suggestive of something else. In my opinion, he's simply detected some bizarre animal lurking underground—a mole or a mouse..."

"A mole!" the Englishman muttered. "As if Stop doesn't know what a mole is—and as if I could make a mistake about his manner of expression! But there's no point arguing. Let's see what happens. This is no weather for talking—I have a mouth full of gravel. What a filthy country! It's definitely a storm—more than a storm, a cyclone—that's coming. What a wind! One might think it were the simoom!"

Indeed, the violence of the wind was increasing by the second. Clouds of sand and dust were swirling everywhere, making the march increasingly difficult.

The sea, which was beginning to get choppy, took on livid tints in the red light of the dusk. The storm was gathering rapidly, and the darkness was soon complete. The thunder was getting closer, but flashes of lightning were still sparse. The fuliginous darkness of the sky seemed to brighten somewhat, however, toward the pole. There, an orange gleam with red fringes was gradually growing.

"What does that presage?" the Englishman asked Myrandhal.

"I don't know. The light is reminiscent of certain magnetic phenomena. Perhaps it's simply a kind of aurora borealis."

"I thought, myself, about an earthquake."

"That was my first idea too, and anything's possible. What astonishes me is that the ground isn't even trembling. It's true that there are sometimes deceptive calms just before..."

The engineer was still speaking when the Eccentric, who was marching on the right and slightly ahead, suddenly turned round, gesticulating.

"A cyclone! Lie down..."

At the same time, an explosion resounded, illuminating the sky all the way to the zenith, and knocking the three voyagers flat on the ground.

Around them, everything shook, and there was a terrible din. One might have thought that the carcass of the planet was disintegrating.

It went on for a few seconds, and then stopped. The whirlwind had passed over.

The excursionists were already getting to their feet, astonished to have got away with a fright.

"It's over," said the engineer. "I mentioned a pressure-cooker this morning—it's just boiled over. Look..."

Ahead of them, a few miles to the north, a hill had just surged forth, surmounted by a red plume.

"A volcano!" exclaimed Madame Myrandhal. "We can see the lava flowing. As long as it doesn't get this far..."

"Don't worry," said Serge, swiftly. "Major eruptions start differently, and this one's already calmed down. Look—the plume is falling back. As for the lava, see how it's changing color and slowing down. Tomorrow, that volcano, sprouted as suddenly as a mushroom, will be cold, and we'll be able to climb up it, as one can climb Mount Vesuvius."

"By Jove!" cried Pickman, enthusiastically. "That would be a fine ascent! So you think, sir, that there's no more danger?"

"No. Fortunately, the pressure-cooker had safety-valves, and one of those that has just come into play, that's all. The danger has passed, in consequence—and for proof, look at your dog. So turbulent a little while ago, he's observed that it's calm now. Thanks to his instinct, he divined the phenomenon long before us."

"Hmm!" grunted the Eccentric. "There's something else."

"You're sticking to your Martians?"

"Yes. Stop couldn't be mistaken about that. If he barked for a man, it's because there are men here—well, Martians. Let's just wait and see!"

V. The "Red Men"

"By Jove!" said Pickman, feeling the lava. "The ground's still hot. Are you sure that there's no danger? That the volcano is really extinct? It's not for our benefit that I'm asking, but for Anna..."

"Utterly extinct," Myrandhal replied. "The fumaroles that always precede eruptions disappeared several hours ago—but that doesn't mean that there's no danger climbing up there. The ascent, over those fractured, collapsed rocks, needs to be carried out prudently."

"Good—that's familiar. I've climbed much harder. I'll get over."

The castaways, having set out at dawn, had arrived at the foot of the Norton Bennett, as they had baptized the miniature volcano that had surged forth a few hours earlier.

"Before anything else," the engineer continued, "We're going to make a tour of the cone, as much to get an idea of the whole as to identify the most accessible slope."

They set off again, and when they were on the far side of the peak Serge took advantage of the shadow projected by the volcano to measure its height.

"What is it?" demanded the Eccentric, who had taken out his notebook in order to record the altitude of the mountain on which he was about to accomplish his first Martian ascent.

"Three hundred and a few meters."

"That makes nine hundred feet in English measurements. It's a good size for a new-born mountain."

"Indeed!" exclaimed the American, laughing. "If it continues to grow at that rate, more than a hundred fathoms every twenty-four hours, it'll be a fine mountain, capable of surpassing the famous Gaurisankar. I hope, my guardian, that you're happy now and won't make any more difficulties about telling us what you saw last night. I'm eager to know what it was.

255

What little you have said has excited my curiosity to the highest degree."

The Baronet shook his head.

"There's no urgency. It would start endless arguments. Better to act. I won't talk until we've explored the volcano. I have a suspicion that we'll discover things here that will support what I say."

"Does that mean that it was on Norton Bennett that you saw Martians? For you have seen some?"

"Perhaps. I'll tell you later."

"In that case," the American said, teasingly, "these people live in fire. Who knows? Perhaps they came out of the crater. They're no longer humans but salamanders."

"Yes, salamanders," muttered the Englishman, sulkily. "Let's climb first; we'll argue later. This isn't the time for joking. Just follow me."

"I'll be quiet. But how susceptible you are this morning, my dear guardian! It's easy to see that you slept badly."

In fact, the Eccentric had slept with one eye open that night. Several times, he had got up and made a tour of the boat's surroundings, taking Stop with him. At dawn, when his companions woke up, the Baronet had already been up for two hours. His attitude was simultaneously delighted and anxious, but he refused to explain himself.

"You'll see," he contented himself with saying, "that Stop and I were right. Either I'm nothing but an old fool, or the day won't go by without our having news of the Martians."

The Englishman's confidence and his mysterious expressions intrigued Madame Myrandhal increasingly, but it was in vain that she tried to discover more.

Meanwhile, the little troop led by Pickman, after having followed the base of the volcano for about a quarter of a mile, discovered a fairly easy path. There was a heap of fallen rocks forming a kind of gigantic stairway, which they immediately set about climbing.

The Eccentric marched at the head, testing the ground with his alpenstock, sometimes turning aside to examine the rock. He seemed to be searching for something, but he did not say what. He was heard muttering from time to time, like a disappointed man.

Half an hour later the excursionists arrived, without any hitch, at the summit of Norton Bennett. It was an almost circular plateau measuring about a hundred meters in diameter and bristling with enormous blocks of quartz and granite, still warm.

In the middle was the chimney, a partly-obstructed excavation, from which a stream of lava the width of an arm was slowly trickling.

"You see," said Myrandhal. "The volcano is in the process of gently becoming extinct. All danger from that direction has vanished, for the moment."

"You don't think it will wake up again?" the Baronet asked.

"Not soon, at any rate. We have several days before us, of which we'll take advantage by going away. This new excursion confirms the opinion I'd already formed: the sooner we leave, the better."

"What about you, my guardian?" said the American. "You're not saying anything. You have a serious communication to make to us, though—remember?"

The Eccentric had lost the serene confidence he had had a little while ago. "Yes," he said, nodding his head. "But I haven't found what I was looking for—the traces…you're going to mock me again, and yet, there were people here last night."

"People!" exclaimed Serge and his wife.

"Yes. Stop saw them too. We ought to have brought him; perhaps he would have found something."

"You're the one who wanted to leave him to guard the lodgings."

"That's true," said the Eccentric, increasingly discountenanced. "You're definitely going to think that I'm going senile..."

"Not at all," the engineer replied, wanting to put the Englishman at his ease. "On the contrary, I understand your disappointment. After all, there might well be Martians in the vicinity...doubtless some nomadic family."

"Why are they hiding?" asked the American, swiftly. "That's what it's necessary to explain. Do we frighten them?"

"Perhaps," the engineer replied. "The arrival of the psychoscaphs must have struck their imagination. They might be afraid of men coming from the sky, which is easily explicable on the part of primitive, uncultured, semi-savage individuals, like the land they inhabit. They might have taken advantage of the darkness to come and take a closer look at the *Annabella*."

"In consequence," Madame Myrandhal continued, "you're admitting our friend Pickman's thesis. You believe that Martians appeared here last night? What the devil were they doing? Don't you think that it was more probably an animal of human appearance—some anthropoid?"

"No—climbing the volcano is a reasoned action. Animals guided only by their instinct would only have thought of running away."

"That's what I told myself," murmured the Englishman. "Only the thing is so extraordinary and incredible that I'm now beginning to doubt what I saw..."

"You don't say. One might think, my dear guardian, that you're taking pleasure in keeping us in suspense."

"No, believe me—but it was so improbable that I preferred to wait. I thought we were going to find Martians here, and that they'd introduce themselves. Since they haven't, and it's what you want, I'll talk...

"It happened last night, when my watch marked one o'clock. I woke up in response to a dull growl from Stop..."

"We didn't hear anything."

"It didn't last long. I was sleeping with one eye open—like a gendarme, as you put it—and as soon as he heard me move, Stop shut up. He knows his business as a guard dog, and that there are times when it's necessary not to bark—necessary not to alert the prowlers who are approaching...

"I picked up my revolver and went out. One on the walkway I looked around, and didn't see anything suspicious. The moon—the smaller of the two—was shining between the clouds, enough to see for about a hundred meters, and besides, it's difficult to hide on that bare ground.

"Stop was trying to drag me toward the obelisk. I followed him, thinking that I might find something behind it. There was nothing there, but I discovered what was troubling him. It was the volcano in the distance. When I looked in that direction, he twitched his ears in the way he has, and I understood that he was saying: *yes, that's it*—but I still couldn't see anything.

"After a few minutes though. I saw a bizarre individual emerge from behind a rock near the summit, then another, and then a third. They were little men with enormous heads and straight limbs. Thickset dwarfs of a sort: red, or, rather, the color of brick..."

"But how could you make them out at that distance?" the engineer interjected. "Were they carrying torches?"

"No," said the Eccentric. "That's where it gets complicated. It was pitch dark here, and the red men weren't carrying any kind of torches, and yet I could see them! I could see them because the dwarfs were, well, luminous...there's no other explanation! Just luminous enough to stand out against the dark background.

"Remember how a firebrand that's about to go out, still shines sufficiently for one to make it out. It was exactly like that. At first, I wondered where that fantastic light could be coming from..."

"From the volcano," said the engineer. "Doubtless the reflection of a stream of lava."

"I thought so too, at first, but no; there was no doubt about it, the little men were luminous themselves—yes, phosphorescent. Sometimes, one of them gave off a brighter gleam, a flash—something akin to what I'd seen the previous night. Meanwhile, there were now five of the red men. They seemed to be consulting one another, holding a discussion. In the end, one of them climbed on to a rock and looked in my direction, toward the sea."

"What did it look like?" asked the American, increasingly interested. "Did you see its face?"

"No. Impossible at that distance."

"Could it see you?"

"No…at least, I don't think so. Stop and I were in the shadow projected by the obelisk—but it must have seen the *Annabella*, which was fully lit by the moon at that moment. So far as I could understand by its gestures, that as what alarmed it. It soon went back to its companions, and they began to go back down. When they got half way, they stopped in front of some kind of grotto, and suddenly, I couldn't see them anymore. It was as if they'd put out their lights—switched themselves off, as it were."

"What do you think of that, my dear Friday?"

The engineer, who was afraid of offending the narrator, hesitated momentarily.

"I don't think anything yet," he said. "It's necessary to verify certain things. Can you find this grotto again?"

"I understand. You think I've gone crazy. I'd think so too, in your place. As for the grotto, yes, I made a mental note of the spot and went straight to it just now, but nothing—the cavern has vanished. That's what's fantastic. Another mystery!"

"No," said Serge. "Your imagination's panicking. Nothing extraordinary about that. A landslide, such as must be occurring all the time on this crumbling slope, might have blocked the cave. When we go down again, we'll all look for it.

The Englishman had a constrained smile. "You don't think I'm completely mad, then?" he murmured. In a louder voice, he continued: "Personally, I never doubted for a minute that they went underground, into the grotto, and I sometimes wonder whether it might have been them who blocked the opening by rolling a rock over it."

"Anything's possible."

"Yes...just s it's possible that I've been duped by an illusion, a phantasmagoria. This morning, I hoped to find traces of the red devils—that's why I preferred to wait before speaking, and now I'm hesitant...

"Last night, at the moment when they went back underground, I didn't have the slightest doubt about it. There are still moments when it all seems true. I remember the way in which Stop, moving ahead, looked through the ground, his eyes shining as if he could see men moving beneath it...

"After all, why not? Perhaps there's nothing on Mars, no race of inhabitants or civilization, because all that's in the interior. An English scientist claims that that's the case on some planets, and his opinion seems to be confirmed here. I said to myself that it must be hot there, under Norton Bennett, but that was reasoning by Earthly standards. The Martians might be a different species, different in nature from us—incombustible, something like salamanders...

"Then I recalled the theories of one of my friends, who believes in metempsychosis, the plurality of worlds and so on. According to him, humans don't invent, they remember. So, still in accordance with our philosophy, all the beings in tales and legends—genies, fairies, monsters—existed on some other planet.

"In fact, my red men bear a strong resemblance to certain blacksmith-dwarfs, the gnomes and kobolds who are both the spirits of mines and the guardians of subterranean treasures. So much so that if we were to see one of those fellows emerge from the ground right now, and invite us to visit his palace, it would seem quite natural to me...

"You might think that's absurd, and so do I…perhaps I saw all that in a dream. That's possible too.

"After that, once the dwarfs had disappeared, as I didn't want to go back to sleep, I sat down on the bridge, with the dog beside me, and I dozed off momentarily…let's say that I was dreaming…and yet…but it's better to talk about something else. That's what I'm beginning to think. It's suggestion, in fact! There's only one means of fighting it, and that's to think about other things, and there's no lack of those at present.

"Now I think about it, I remember that I was going to inflate the dinghy and take a trip. It's necessary, then, not to waste any more time. I think we'd better go."

Pickman, who had never made such a long speech, ran out of breath and stopped, surprised by the attention that he was being accorded.

"Well," he added "you're not saying anything. When are we leaving?"

"Right away, if you like. Nothing is keeping us here."

"Just a minute," said Pickman, opening the knapsack he had deposited at his feet. "I have something to do first, which I never miss…" almost immediately afterwards, he added: "God damn it! I've forgotten my red pot."

"You're red pot?"

"Well, my pot of red paint—you know, the vermilion, with which to write my name and the date on the rock."

"It doesn't matter," said Anna. "You can come back later."

"No," the globetrotter grumbled, "it's not the same. The inscription needs to be made now, or never. That no longer works the charm. For want of paint—of ink, so to speak—one can try to engrave, but I don't have any tools, and this rock is as hard as metal."

While the Englishman was lamenting, Serge whispered something in his wife's ear. She smiled.

"My dear guardian," she said, "come this way. Just now I saw a soft rock that will suit your purpose perfectly."

As soon as they had gone, Serge went to the place where the stream of lava was emerging. There was a layer of clay nearby, still moist. He hollowed out grooves in it, forming crude letters. Then, with the tip of his cane, he caused lava to flow into the improvised moulds.

Shortly thereafter, the Eccentric came back, brandishing his broken ice-ax. The American was following him.

"You call that soft rock!" he complained. "You have the audacity! I broke my implement at the first stroke.

Suddenly, he stopped, amazed. At his feet, in the sand, an inscription was outlined in letters of fire:

PICKMAN
August 1908

"Prodigious!" he exclaimed. "Fantastic! Who did that?"

Madame Myrandhal was laughing covertly. "It's the red men," she replied, "the kobolds. They know your name and they've written it there, with lava."

The Eccentric's face had contracted. "You're being ridiculous," he said. "You shouldn't joke about such things. I shan't say anything from now on. I'm going back."

And the Englishman turned on his heel. He really seemed to be in a bad mood, and his ward, regretting her innocent joke, tried in vain to strike up the conversation again.

Serge, who strove to appease him, had no more success.

The descent continued in silence.

Suddenly, the engineer, who was bringing up the rear, uttered a cry of joy.

"The grotto! I've found your grotto, my dear Pickman—come and see!"

The Englishman's physiognomy was suddenly transformed. He came running. "I knew it…" he murmured.

"Well," Serge said to him, "do you recognize it? This opening corresponds quite well to the description you gave. You mentioned a narrow passage, a kind of fissure between two blocks of lava. Is this it?"

The Eccentric hesitated. "Perhaps," he said, eventually. "I don't recognize the entrance, exactly, but it was certainly hereabouts—I mean, on this slope and at this height—that the Red Men suddenly disappeared."

"That's sufficient," said Serge. "On this shifting ground everything is modified from one minute to the next. Then again, the tunnel might have several exits. We're going in—I've got a candle."

"A candle!" said the Eccentric, disdainfully. "I've got something better than that." He had already unbuckled his knapsack and taken out a small acetylene lamp, which he lit immediately. "In addition," he went on, "I have magnesium wire in my pocket, and you know how brightly that burns. One can take photographs with it. You can get your apparatus ready, my dear Anna. You'll have pictures to take—beautiful pictures—for the *Herald*."

The Englishman was visibly delighted by the turn that events had taken, no longer giving any thought to the young woman's mockery. Before going into the grotto, he turned to the engineer.

"Let's understand one another," he said. "I'll go first. You take care of your wife. You have your revolver—keep it in your hand."

"Why?" asked Serge, surprised. "Against whom? You're still thinking about last night's Martians, the Red Men?"

"About them—but there are other perils to anticipate: gulfs, shafts opening unexpectedly, labyrinths where there's a risk of getting lost..." The Eccentric lowered his voice. "As for the red devils, listen, sir...either I'm an old fool, or they really exist, and if they do, I have to find them...even if I have to go looking for them in the depths of Hell!"

Pickman's eyes were shining with fever. "One more recommendation," he whispered. "If, by chance, I get too far ahead and you don't see me reappear, don't wait for me. Leave—that would be better. I'll make my own way back, if I come back at all...now, let's go."

The grotto into which our heroes slid was a tunnel offering a complicated series of chambers of various sizes, with galleries and corridors intersecting it from every direction.

"It's a veritable labyrinth," said the Baronet. "A warren for elephants."

They spent nearly an hour exploring the principal ramifications. After that lapse of time, the engineer proposed that they go back.

"You can see," he said to the Baronet, "That the cave has nothing special to offer, and it's beginning to get terribly hot under these low vaults. We could do with a change of air."

"Go," said the Eccentric. "Me, I'm staying. There's obviously another exit; I want to find it. I've just discovered a new corridor that extends for a long way. I want to know where it leads, and I shall, God damn it!"

"Be careful," Myrandhal replied. "You could easily go astray in this maze."

"I'm used to it," retorted the globetrotter. "It's not the first cave I've visited. And the danger isn't what you think—so let me go, and go back. I'll come back in my own time."

"You know very well that we won't go back without you."

"You'll have to—you don't have any more candles."

"So we'll wait for you at the entrance."

"That's all right—go and breathe. I won't be long. One last corridor to explore, and I'll rejoin you."

Serge ad his wife did as they were advised, and were soon outside.

"You see," said the American. "It's an obsession, a mania. My guardian doesn't dare talk about the Red Men any more, but he's thinking about them more than ever. It's them that he's searching for. What do you think of it all?"

The engineer made an evasive gesture. "What do you expect me to think? Your guardian was probably dreaming, but let's allow him to pursue his investigation. It's the best way of convincing him—him and us..."

A quarter of an hour went by. From time to time, Myrandhal or his wife called out to Pickman, who replied, from a distance "I'm coming—just a minute!" His voice, however, seemed to be drawing further away, going further underground—to such an extent that the young couple began to get seriously worried.

They still had a few magnesium filaments, which Pickman given to Anna in order that she could take photographs. They lit one, and went into the tunnel again.

They had gone through the first chambers and were about to venture further when a man appeared from a corridor, taking long strides. It was Pickman; his hair was standing on end, his cheeks were paler and his eyes were haggard.

The sight of his companions pulled him round. He blushed deeply, and in a surly voice, like a man furious to be caught running away, he complained: "What are you doing here? Where are you going?"

"We're looking for you," Serge replied.

"You're hurt!" the young woman cried. She had just noticed a trickle of blood running down her guardian's head.

The Eccentric shrugged his shoulders. "It's nothing," he said. "A graze, sustained when I fell."

"You fell?"

"Yes. I tripped. But my lantern went out, and I was suddenly frightened. Suggestion again...

"It seemed to me that someone was moving around me, whispering. I even felt something soft and sticky slide between my legs, but it was only mud. I saw that when I relit my lantern.

"Then, as I'd lost my matches in the tumble and my reflector wasn't working very well—it had got damaged when I fell—I came back...that's all." He forced a laugh. "Nothing serious, as you can see. What upsets me is that I became as nervous as an old woman. It's ridiculous...if you want to please me, you won't mention this ridiculous incident again—it's stupid, in truth."

The young people thought, rightly or wrongly, that Pickman was hiding something, but they feared offending him by probing, so they set off for home.

Throughout the journey, the Eccentric scarcely unclenched his teeth. He was furious about the frustration of his search, and especially a having been seen in a sorry state, seemingly running away, by those to whom he had boasted that he would go into the depths of Hell.

He remained taciturn all day, and busied himself preparing the dinghy and the fishing-tackle that he intended to try out the following morning.

A surprise awaited the castaways that day, however.

It was about ten o'clock. Serge and Pickman were smoking in the central compartment, while talking about the projected fishing trip.

"A little while longer," aid the engineer, "and as soon as the tide has gone out, we'll embark. You must have noticed that the tide, as I predicted, is getting higher every day. This morning the waves were less than two hundred meters from the submarine. A few more days and the *Annabella* will be refloated; we'll only have to raise anchor, and set off on a tour of Mars."

"With pleasure," murmured the Baronet. "This country pleases me less and less, to be sure.

At that moment, Madame Myrandhal, who was going past one of the portholes, uttered an exclamation of surprise, almost of fright.

She ran to the porthole, opened it briskly and pointed toward the retreating sea. "Oh!" she cried. "A monster! A shark!"

"Where?" demanded her companions, immediately rushing to join her.

"There...look! It's coming up again. There it is!"

"Yes!" Pickman howled. "I see it! It's a whale! It's going to run aground."

In the distance, a spindle-shaped mass, white with foam, was moving back and forth amid the waves. Suddenly, a hump appeared, with a hatch standing up like an open valve...

"A conning-tower!" cried Serge. "It's the *Velox*! The sea's returning her!"

Mad with joy, he launched himself toward the wreck.

VI. The Wreck

Anna and Pickman followed the engineer.

While they were crossing the distance separating them from the wreck, still running, the tide completed its retreat. When they arrived, the *Velox* was lying on her keel, buried about a foot deep in the wet sand.

Serge launched himself on to the walkway and tried to open the door.

"Blocked!" he shouted. "The submarine is full of water. We need to empty it first. That's the most urgent thing."

He got down, and the three of them discussed means of emptying the hull.

"I have a pump," the Eccentric began. "We can get it out..."

"It would take too long," Annabella interjected. "It would be much simpler to tip the *Velox* over, and let it empty by itself through the conning-tower..."

"Quite a task!" said Pickman. "Turning the *Velox* upside-down...we'd need fifty horses to haul her. There's a quicker way, and that's simply to bleed the *Velox*. I have the necessary tools; I'll drill a hole through the sheet metal, low down, and it'll run out of its own accord..."

"You've got it!" cried the engineer. "That's it!"

"You approve?"

"Entirely. Except that there's no need to inflict a new wound on my poor *Velox*. She has one already."

"I can't see it."

"That's because the boat's upright. The compressed sand is forming a plug and blocking the water's path. Hang on...can you see those trickles of water, there, toward the middle of the keel. That's the breach. I assume that it's the issue of the ballast-tank that gave way. A few blows of a pick-ax, and it will come flooding out..."

"All right!" cried Pickman. "I have the tools we need back home. Follow me!"

Then minutes later, the friends came back, each carrying a different implement. Serge was dragging a jack, and Pickman had a ditch-digger's complete outfit—picks, levers, spades etc. As for Anna, who fully intended to pitch in, she was pushing a small folding wheelbarrow made of sheet aluminum, in order to transport sand if the need arose.

"Before we do anything else," Serge said, "it's necessary to stabilize the boat. The *Velox* is leaning toward the sea, and the emptying will unbalance her. This isn't the time to let her fall over..."

The jack was set in place and the two men began digging the vessel out. Working in the loose ground, it only took ten minutes to expose a gash beneath the keel. Already, the water filtering through the sand was beginning to flow more abundantly. The stream was visibly increasing.

"Look out!" cried Serge, leaping out of the trench.

Pickman had followed his example. "What is it?" he asked. "The vessel hasn't budged. I thought..."

"No—but the *Velox* might empty in a sudden rush. I don't want to be underneath that shower."

"My dear Friday," the Englishman jeered, "I can see that you're afraid of getting wet."

"It's not a matter of getting wet. We have nearly fifty tons of water overhead. If that liquid mass came down on your head, it would be very inconvenient, Better to wait. The operation will proceed on its own. In the meantime, I'll go fetch a lantern; we'll need one to go into the hold."

Serge went back to the *Annabella*, but he was only twiddling his thumbs when the Eccentric leapt into the ditch and disappeared under the hull.

"Be careful!" shouted Anna. "Watch out for the shower!"

"You're a chicken," the Englishman replied, jovially. "A damp chicken, like that froggy." And he continued to dig.

The stream became a torrent. Suddenly, a cataract sprang from the breached hull, hollowing out the sand, at the Eccentric was swept away, dragged ten feet by the surge.

Frightened, Madame Myrandhal ran forward, shouting: "Help!"

Already, though, the flood was spreading out, and Pickman stood up in the middle of a pool, thoroughly soaked, yellow with mud and streaming like a triton.

"Shut up, little girl," he said. "It's nothing. A bath, that's all. A muddy bath, but bah! I've had many others."

His appearance was so piteous that he young woman burst out laughing; her guardian joined in with a good grace. "What a little fool you are!" he muttered.

Myrandhal was laughing too. "As you see, my dear Robinson," he said, "my advice was sound."

"That's true," the Eccentric admitted. "I'm a trout. But I was in a hurry. This way, we can go inside straight away."

"We'll go inside," said Serge, who was no less impatient. "But first let me examine the leak, I want to determine the gravity of the wound as soon as possible."

He disappeared beneath the hull in his turn. He soon reemerged, his face radiant.

"It's all right," she said. The wound isn't dangerous, and our dear *Velox* will recover from it. It's the bolt of the ballast tank that gave way. The seal is slightly damaged, but it will be easy to repair, so the disease is curable. I even have a portable forge in the *Velox*; unfortunately, it's combustible material—coal—that we lack."

"Coal," exclaimed the Eccentric. "We might find some, if we search..."

"I doubt it."

"We might be able to make some fuel," the American put in.

"How, little girl?"

"With wood."

"Where shall we find it? This satanic country is flat, and as bald as an egg."

"That's true. Anyway, my dear guardian, go and change. You might catch cold."

"No need. I'm used to it. Anyway, the sun's going down. I'll be dry in half an hour."

"No!" the young woman persisted. "Go and change." She pointed at the *Velox*. "Dou you think that I'm going to let you into my home, my drawing room, covered in mud as you are.

"Pooh!" murmured the Eccentric. "The *Velox* must be just as dirty." Nevertheless, he did as he was told.

While he went back to the *Annabella*, Serge and his wife went through the valve-door in to the *Velox*. The engineer's first concern was to move back the shutters protecting the portholes, and the light came flooding in.

"What luck!" he exclaimed. "The glass resisted. That would have been more difficult to replace.

They ran to the front, and then came back to the central compartment.

"It's bizarre," said Myrandhal, sounding the floor. "I can't find any crack. Something must have given way, though, in order for the water to rise up into the living quarters."

"Let's look under the furniture."

The advice was sound, and less than a minute later, they had found the fissure. It was under Serge's bed. He was content to replace the planks displaced by the pressure of the sea-water.

"That should suffice for the moment," he said.

They began a more careful inspection of the *Velox*, examining everything in detail and exchanging their increasingly favorable impressions.

"We're in luck," said Serge, delightedly. "The *Velox* could have been broken up, but apart from the luminous coating on the walls, which has gone, and the staircase, which it's necessary to consolidate, I can't see that she's suffered overmuch. That's lucky, especially after the fall from the summit of the geyser. The leak only occurred afterwards. The *Velox* was snagged by a reef; fortunately, we were in calm water at that moment, not far from a sand-bank—the same one that forms the shore—and the ship ran aground not far from the coast without too violent a shock."

"Hello! Good morning!" shouted Pickman, who came in at that moment. "Well, how's the *Velox?*"

"Not bad, as you can see. Well, her hull's solid—not even a dent—but it's the rest, the machines. As far as I can tell, they're in good condition. A few gears jammed by sand, no doubt."

"What about the food-supplies?"

"The food-supplies are my concern," Anna replied. "Everything in sealed vessels—tins, bottles and jars—is safe. The rest—biscuits, flour, dried vegetables, etc.—is lost, only good for throwing away or boiling broth for Stop."

"No!" the Baronet protested, sharply. "Don't throw anything away. You're a wastrel. We can dry it out, and I'll show you how. This isn't the first time I've been shipwrecked."

While laughing, Anna went in search of a bottle of old whisky. She uncorked it and held out a glass to the Baronet. "Your health, my dear sir!" she said, cheerfully. "Drink that. It'll finish off drying you out."

"Famous!" Pickman declared, clicking his tongue. "These three days at sea have aged me two years." He took another gulp. "Now it's a matter of getting down to work. I can see that my ward is in a hurry to take up residence. Where to begin? The first step, obviously, is to block the leak. If not, the incoming tide will invade her again. That's the danger..."

"Yes," said the engineer, but there's another matter more serious than that one, which is that when the sea retreats tomorrow, it will take the *Velox* with it."

"We could moor her solidly."

"That's difficult on this loose ground. Then again, a cable might break and the *Velox* might escape. On the other hand, blocking the leak isn't a sufficient guarantee. Better to carry out a complete repair. That operation, cleaning the machines, the furniture and everything else, the verification of the submarine from top to bottom, will take several days. Thus, we're going to move the *Velox* and put her in dry dock, so to speak, beside the *Annabella*. Once she's there, we can work at our ease."

"Move the *Velox!*" protested the Eccentric. "What Roman toil! We'd need rails, a locomotive..."

"We'll have to get by without. It'll be hard, but we'll get there in the end. Unfortunately, we only have one day to do it. At all costs, even if we have to work all night, the *Velox* has to be sheltered, out of reach of the waves, before the next high tide."

"And what if the tide gains ground, as it has already begun to do? We'd have done it all for nothing."

"We'll see about that tomorrow. I hope, however, that we'll have time to repair the ballast-tanks, at least, before the tide reaches us. I can only see one way to haul the ship out. I'll submit it to your competence; I believe you told me that you were once in the British Navy?"

"Yes, but it was a long time ago."

"Well, to begin with," Myrandhal continued, "We're going to unload the *Velox*, relieving her of all her contents: cargo, machinery, etc. The hull itself only weighs a few tons."

"Good! You don't imagine we can haul it manually, though. At the very least we'd need a capstan..."

"There's one in the *Velox*: a small version made of reinforced steel tubing, which, like everything else, can be dismantled. An apparatus I recommend to you, powerful but light. On the other hand, we have cables, pulleys, several gasoline engines and a solid fulcrum—the *Annabella*, which, full as she is, weighs twice as much as the empty *Velox*. With all that, I think we can bring the operation to a successful conclusion."

"Perhaps," murmured the Baronet.

"That said, the most urgent thing is the unloading. I'll take care of the machines, which I'll have to check and whose every component I'll have to grease. As everything can be dismantled, I'll be sufficient for that job, and will even be able to give you a hand with the rest, which I leave to you."

"All right," said Pickman. "On with the job, children!"

They set to work immediately."

In two hours the removal was complete, and the castaways had built up a formidable appetite by the time they sat down to lunch. What remained to be done was less difficult but more delicate.

It took more than four hours to extend the cables between the two ships, and then to fix the capstan solidly in the ground, along with the internal combustion engine that was to drive it. The sun had set some time before when the engine was started up, but the heavy work was done.

Less than three quarters of an hour later, the *Velox* was in place beside the *Annabella*, and our heroes uttered a cry of triumph.

"Hurrah!" proclaimed the Eccentric. "Tomorrow evening, it will all be finished. Everyone will have a cabin."

That night, again, they slept fully-dressed in the *Annabella*'s central cabin, and the following morning, at dawn, they were at work. The entire day was devoted to washing the *Velox* with clean water and re-equipping her. In order to do it more rapidly, part of the cargo—everything that could remain outdoors—was left on the sand, covered by a tarpaulin, forming one of those piles that are sometimes seen on the docks of ports.

When dusk fell, the installation was complete.

"Finally, it's done!" exclaimed Pickman. "Not without difficulty, by Jove! Everyone can be at home, in his own bed. How glad I'll be to slip in between the sheets. I suppose that you, too..." He suddenly interrupted himself, on seeing his ward blush deeply. "What a brute," he murmured. "I'm an old brute! It's true so many things have happened since, that it seemed to me that they were already an old married couple, whereas..."

A few hours later, by the light of the two Martian moons, Deimos and Phobos, Serge and Anna were wandering along the beach.

The Eccentric, offering the excuse of a sudden headache, had gone to bed, and they were alone for the first time since they had been in the gardens of Almowrat, when the pastor had drawn away after having blessed them.

They were walking in silence, savoring the unique hour. Soon, Anna raised her eyes toward the firmament. On high, Jupiter, the monarch of the heavens, was advancing at the head of his brilliant cortege of stars.

"How he shines," she murmured, very quietly. "One might think that he's calling us, as he did back there in the convent garden—do you remember? And that star on the horizon is Earth, isn't it?"

The young woman had shivered as she pronounced that name, and Serge was already anxious. "Yes," he murmured. "Earth, to which we'll return, if..."

"Why say that?"

"I thought you were seized by regret."

"No," the American declared, distinctly. "Arrange for me to have news of my friends, and I'll follow you anywhere, everywhere, ever further and ever higher. *Excelsior!* That's our motto."

"How glad you make me!" Serge sighed, delightedly. "I was remorseful already—so it's really true? You have no regrets?"

"No," the young woman murmured, in a voice that sang delightfully in Serge's heart. "No, my dear friend, I have no regrets. I'm with you. I'm happy."

VII. A Departure...

The newlyweds' honeymoon did not last long. Circumstances scarcely lent themselves to the idle strolls and sentimental promenades that are fashionable in such cases. They set to work again the following day.

The necessity was imperious. Since he had recovered his vessel, Serge Myrandhal had only had one thought in his head: to conclude the repairs to the *Velox* as quickly as possible and to reach a more hospitable region than a coast that was simultaneously icy and volcanic.

The engineer, who carefully monitored the indications of the thermometer every day, observed that the temperature was gradually declining—slowly, to be sure, but regularly and continuously. He pointed it out to the young woman and the Eccentric.

"It's one more proof," he said, "of the theory I explained the other day. The heat that renders the atmosphere bearable is emanating from the ground. The birth of the volcano, which we witnessed, demonstrates that in this region, the geological crust of the Martian soil is very thin—a thinness that would scarcely be reassuring for us, if we were obliged to remain here for long..."

"In other words," said Pickman, "if it weren't for that subterranean pressure-cooker, that gigantic hot water bottle, this would be a true Siberia."

"Fortunately, "Annabella put in, "we're not going to stay her for long—at least I certainly hope so."

"Even if we wanted to," the engineer added, "it would be impossible. I anticipate a date in the not-too-distant future when the cold will triumph over this artificial heat. The season is moving on rapidly. In a few weeks, perhaps sooner, we'd be icebound. We'd share the fate of the first polar explorers."

"God damn it!" muttered the Eccentric. "After the obstacles we've already overcome, that would be a bad way to end up. It wouldn't have been worth deserting our old terrestrial planet."

The young couple smiled at that remark.

"Don't worry," said the engineer. "We won't arrive at such an extremity. We've solved more difficult problems." In a more serious tone, he added: "We don't have a minute to lose, however. It's absolutely necessary that, a week from now at the most, the *Velox* is repaired and ready to put to sea..."

Pickman started in surprise. "By Jove! Seven days isn't much. You don't like it at all here, then? Personally, I don't mind it. Although arid, I find the region very interesting. There are studies to carry out, research..."

The engineer, who had quite forgotten the Red Men, in whom he had almost believed momentarily, wondered what the Eccentric was getting at.

Anna smiled. "I can guess what's keeping you, my dear guardian. It's your kobolds, the spirits of the caves..."

Since his adventure, the word "caves" rang badly in the Englishman's ears.

"Let's leave the kobolds out of it," he said, in a surly tone. "If there are inhabitants here, as I persist in believing, they'll show themselves eventually, but that's not what I mean. I simply mean that the cold doesn't seem so..."

"It's not just a matter of the cold," Myrandhal put in. "I have more urgent reasons for diligence: among others, the fact that since we've been here the tides have been visibly increasing in intensity. The distance that originally separated the *Velox* from the waves at high tide has diminished by a good third. In addition, the high tides are getting earlier by about an hour a day."

"With the result," said Annabella, "that as well as being frozen, we're running the risk of being inundated."

"A danger that would become immediate if the tide were assisted by the wind. The waves, driven by aerial current blowing with gale force, could surpass their usual limit by several meters. We've had no reason to fear that thus far, but we can't rely on it. It would only require an abrupt change in the weather, and I'm too much of a novice in Martian meteorology to anticipate that in advance."

With a gesture, the engineer indicated the pale line of the slowly-ebbing waves.

"That's different," said the Eccentric. "It's a matter of preventing the sea from invading the *Velox*—of restoring her seaworthiness. We'll see after that whether there's a reason to leave right away. In that regard, I'm in complete agreement with you, and ready to set to work right away. I also think that we should start right away—which is to say, tomorrow."

"Or even sooner," said the engineer.

This conversation had taken place a few yards from the *Velox*, after a breakfast comprising tea and condensed milk taken from the ship's reserves.

It was decided that an excursion to the interior planned by Pickman should be pitilessly erased from the program and that they would get to work immediately improvising the forge necessary to repairing the *Velox*. The Eccentric yielded to the necessity, but was secretly discontented. Although he no longer talked about them, he had not given up on finding the fantastic Red Men. He dreamed about them every night. He told himself, not without reason, that the first thing to do, if they wanted a forge, was to set out in search of the indispensable fuel. Nevertheless, he set to work without complaining too much, and, once warmed up, did his best to assist the engineer.

They began by erecting a tent and placing the tools they needed inside it. Then they dug a trench under the *Velox*, unscrewed the heavy door of the ballast tank and carried it to the tent—not without difficulty.

When these preparations were complete, the Eccentric said, sarcastically: "That's all well and good; all that our factory lacks now is coal—black diamonds, as we say in England. We need to go in search of some—perhaps we should have started with that..."

"What's the point?" replied the engineer. "There's no coal here, I'm sure of that..."

"All right…but we can make fuel, as Anna proposed. We've only explored the immediate vicinity; further away, beyond the desert, there are certainly forests."

"Undoubtedly," said the engineer, slightly impatiently. "But we might have to travel hundred of kilometers to reach them. Between now and then, the *Velox* would have had time to be carried away by the waves. Given what I've observed since our arrival, I have every reason to believe that this desert region is no richer in vegetation than Spitzbergen or Iceland, to which it bears a considerable resemblance."

"Why not replace coal with the gasoline that we have in reserve for our engines?" asked Madame Myrandhal.

"I've thought of that, but I'd require special apparatus for that, which we don't have, and without which we'd squander a considerable quantity of precious liquid fuel without obtaining the high temperatures required to melt large pieces of metal."

"I've got another idea," said Pickman, gravely.

"Let's hear it," said the engineer, politely, but without any great confidence in the Eccentric's imagination.

"This is it: around the orifice of the volcano, I noticed some superb sulfur crystals. Nothing burns better. What prevents you from forging with sulfur instead of carbon?"

"A simply law of chemical affinity," the engineer replied, smiling. "My iron or steel would be transformed into iron sulfide. You must remember that the property in question was used on our old terrestrial world for sealing iron fittings in stone. That's another means we'll have to abandon."

"Too bad!" said Pickman, ill-temperedly. "Install your forge directly above or around the volcano itself, then. You won't be able to complain that the temperature isn't high enough. It would be very economical!"

That humorous sally had the response it merited—which is to say that it was welcomed with general laughter—and the discussion continued. Of all the methods proposed, however, none were veritably practical.

"There's only one means," the engineer concluded, finally. "I've been thinking about it for some time. We're going to install an electric forge."

"How are you going to do that?" Pickman asked, incredulously. "That seems scarcely more realizable than my volcanic forge."

"On the contrary, Mr. Pickman, it's quite simple. We have engines and gasoline, so we can produce electricity. With a sufficiently powerful current, nothing is easier than softening, or even melting, the metallic components in question. The only real inconvenience is the considerable diminution of our fuel reserves—but we don't have any choice."

This time, the stubborn Pickman gave in.

The rest of the day was employed in setting up engines, dynamos and accumulators; by the time dusk fell, the "factory," as Pickman called it, was ready to function. That evening, Monsieur and Madame Myrandhal retired early. They were exhausted by fatigue, and the next day promised to be just as laborious as the preceding one.

Pickman did not feel weary. When he went to his cabin he refrained from getting undressed. While whistling a vague tune between his teeth he waited until the darkness and silence were complete inside the hull of the *Velox*.

When he was quite certain that the young couple were asleep, he slipped a revolver into his pocket and went out, carefully closing the door behind him. A few moments later he set off on foot across the sand and plunged boldly into the darkness.

Still haunted by the obsession of finding the Red Men, the Eccentric was setting off on a mission of discovery. He had been careful not to let his companions suspect what he was planning. He feared their mockery, and wanted to have some conclusive evidence to invoke.

However, he came back three hours later, frozen, exhausted and covered from head to toe in red-tinted mud, without having glimpsed any of the mysterious Martian kobolds.

281

The next day was entirely taken up by charging the accumulators. Everything went well. Before the day's end, the engineer had the satisfaction of seeing a steel bar brought to red heat by the electric current.

That evening, the stubborn Pickman went out again—and came back as he had departed, without having discovered anything.

The following day, the repair of the *Velox* commenced, and was carried forward with great activity. The waves of the high tide were now beating the shore a few meters from the ship. They all understood that the minutes were precious, and worked with a veritable fever.

Finally, thanks to Myrandhal's ingenuity, the task was completed in time. The *Velox* was repaired, and ready to put to sea. It was just in time. The cold was still getting worse, and the tide was following the same progression. Every night, now, the waves came to beat the keels of the submarines. In another day or two, they would be afloat.

Serge resolved to profit from that interval to give satisfaction to his wife, who was pressing him to put the telepath in a state to communicate with the Earth.

"Remember," she repeated, "that my father is waiting for news of me. And there's the *Herald*..."

There, however, Myrandhal was less fortunate; all his attempts to improve the apparatus and enter into communication with the neighboring planet failed.

"Which is bizarre," he said. "Theoretically, the problem seemed to be solved, and that wasn't easy, given that there's a station—the one in New York—that I can't improve. I thought I'd overcome the difficulty by augmenting the force of the radiation emitted and the sensitivity of our receiver, but there's nothing! I've called in vain; the *Herald* continues to remain deaf. There must be another cause..."

"What cause?" Pickman asked.

"I can only think of one," Myrandhal replied. "According to certain observations, I have every reason to believe that we're very close to the Martian magnetic pole here. Its influence must be deflecting the waves."

"In that case," said Anna, "if we move away—if we go closer to the equator—we'll be able to enter into communication?"

"I hope so."

"What joy!" exclaimed the young woman, clapping her hands. "All the more reason for leaving as quickly as possible."

"You're in a great hurry," Pickman could not help saying.

Serge, however, had not yet despaired of attaining his objective. He had installed two posts on the coast some ten miles apart, with which he continued his experiments.

As often happens, he made a discovery quite different from the one of which he was in search. One morning, when he was corresponding with Pickman, who was at the other post, he was astounded to hear the Eccentric's customary oaths resounding in his ears.

The entirely fortuitous phenomenon ceased almost immediately, but the engineer soon succeeded in reproducing it in a constant fashion. It was an agreeable surprise for all of them, particularly for Pickman, who casually attributed a share in the invention to himself.

"We've found a wireless telephone!" he proclaimed, "and a long-distance telephone loudspeaker, if you please— which could be very useful to us, if ever we're separated."

"Are you thinking of leaving us, then?" asked Madame Myrandhal.

"Who said anything about that?" the Eccentric murmured, a trifle embarrassed. "What makes you think that, Miss Anna?" His attitude passed unnoticed in the midst of the work and preoccupations of the moment.

In fact, the departure was imminent. It was to take place the following evening, between ten and ten-thirty, to be precise.

That day—the penultimate one—was devoted to stowing aboard the submarines everything they had removed from them: items of furniture, scientific instruments, tools and machines of all kinds. It only remained to fit the vessels with the propellers and rudders that would enable them to navigate, an operation that did not present any difficulty. It was the same for the two inflatable rubber dinghies that were go back and forth between the two vessels.

When that was done, the two submarines were linked by a solid steel cable. It had been agreed, in fact—to Pickman's great displeasure—that in order to simplify the maneuvers and, more importantly, to save fluid, they would only employ one engine, that of the *Velox*, which as the more powerful and efficient of the two.

When all the preparations were terminated, it was nearly ten o'clock in the evening, and Serge uttered a sigh of relief. "Finally!" he exclaimed. "That's that! In twenty-four hours, we'll depart."

"Finally," his wife repeated, alluding to the promise made by the engineer, "we'll have news of the Earth. I can't wait to get to the equator and pick up the dispatches that are waiting for us there, at the post office!"

The Eccentric did not share in the general enthusiasm.

"What's the matter with you?" his ward demanded, as they sat down at table. "One would think that you'll miss this vile place..."

"Me—no, by Jove."

"Yes, yes, that's it. You'll miss your kobolds, the goblins of the mountain. You've been searching for them every night. Do you think we didn't see you coming back the other morning, covered in dirt?"

"You're a little pest," muttered Pickman.

"I saw you," the young woman continued, teasingly. "You might well look embarrassed. One could tell by your expression that you'd drawn a blank. No trace of Martians— vanished, melted away..."

"Hmm!" said the Englishman, sullenly. "Don't crow so loudly, my dear ward. It's not yet proven that I'm mistaken on that account. The Martians are hiding, it's true, but there's no proof that they'll let us depart in peace. I have a suspicion, myself, that we haven't heard the last of them..."

VIII. Footprints in the Sand

Serge and his wife had only smiled at that vague threat, in which they saw nothing but a further manifestation of the Baronet's obstinacy.

He's stubborn, they thought. *He'll never concede that he got it wrong, and that there are no Martians here.*

The following day modified their opinion on this point.

That morning, shortly after dawn, Serge was woken up by a handful of sand thrown at the porthole of his cabin. He immediately leapt out of bed and saw Pickman, armed from head to toe, who was gesticulating with his alpenstock, bidding him to get dressed as quickly as possible.

"I'm coming," he said, in a low voice, so as not to wake his wife, who was asleep in the next room. And he set about dressing in a hurry.

As on as he was ready he slipped a small revolver into his pocket and left the *Velox* without making any noise.

"Well?" he said as he joined the Baronet. "What's happened?"

"What's happened," replied the Englishman, swelling with pride "is that I was right. Remember what I said yesterday?"

"You've seen the Martians again?" exclaimed the engineer, incredulously. "The kobolds—the famous Red Men?"

"Yes," the Eccentric replied, arrogantly. "Or at least, something closely resembling them. But let's leave it at that, sir; we can chat later, if you please. But know this: what's happened is grave; it's no time for joking, by Jove!"

"I swear to you, my dear Baronet, that not for a moment have I..."

"Well, let's pass on. While we're arguing, they're taking action. A little longer and, they'd have been inside."

"Who the devil are *they*?"

"The Martians. Another minute, and I'd have been well and truly burgled."

The engineer's expression was so bewildered that the Englishman, content with his success, smiled self-importantly, fully confident in himself. "You still doubt me. Come and see the traces of their tools. They're burglars, as I said."

Pickman led the engineer to the rear of the Annabella and pointed at the hull. "Look!"

Serge frowned. "That's a bit much!" he muttered, between his teeth.

There was a groove in the metal fifteen centimeters long, which looked as if it had been made by a metal saw.

"Well!" said Pickman, triumphantly. "There's the proof. You know as well as I do that it would need a well-tempered implement to dig into that hull. You know better than anyone how hard it is."

"Yes, but how is it that you didn't hear anything. It must have grated?"

"Yes—except that I wasn't here. At least, I suppose so."

"What about the dog—Stop?"

"Him neither; we went out on patrol, and they chose exactly the right moment. They're cunning..."

"Indeed. But what surprises me is that neither you nor Stop heard or saw anything. You must have been a long way off."

"Fairly—more than half a mile."

"How long did this patrol last?"

"At least twenty minutes. I don't know exactly."

"That's not long. Are you sure that this attempt took place during your absence?"

"As I said, I assume so. I can't be certain. It might also have happened afterwards, while I was asleep, because I ought to mention that I went to sleep afterwards."

"But the dog?"

"That's true, I forget to say: the dog has disappeared."

"Why didn't you say so sooner. They've killed him, then?"

"I'm beginning to believe so. At first I thought he'd gone of his own accord. As you know, Stop has a habit, once his guard duty is over, of going to take a bath in the sea. That's why I wasn't worried when I didn't see him when I woke up..."

"You're admirable! But my dear Robinson, that was a clue—perhaps the most important..."

"Pardon me, Mr. Friday, but no—at that time, I hadn't yet seen this scratch. When I discovered it, my one thought was to come and tell you."

"I understand. In any case, we'd better go look for Stop right away."

"There's no point...at least, it's not urgent. I know my dog. If he hasn't come to bid me good morning, it's because he's a prisoner, or dead. It might also be that he's found a trail and let himself get carried away momentarily, but if that's the case, he won't be long. Let's wait..."

"If you wish," the engineer replied, distractedly. He had bent down and was examining the confused imprints left in the sand by the feet of their aggressors.

"You're trying to read the tracks," said the Eccentric. "I tried too, but they're too blurred. All one can say for sure is that they weren't very numerous—two, or three at the most."

"Let's follow them," Myrandhal replied. "Perhaps we'll find something further away. Look—as they get closer to the shore, the imprints become clearer."

Suddenly, Myrandhal stopped, his eyes widening.

In front of him, profoundly imprinted in the damp sand, he had just perceived the form of a foot of frightful proportions. That mold—a signature of sorts—left by the mysterious visitor, was very impressive. The enormous heel, and the large and separate big toe, were suggestive of a formidable bone-structure.

The engineer's intention had become intense. "That's precise," he murmured. "The man—or, rather, the anthropoid—who stopped here...for he must have stopped, and put his whole weight on one leg momentarily, for his foot to have

288

made that characteristic print…is some kind of giant. Our cave-dwelling ancestor, the terrible hunter who confronted the mammoth and broke its skull with a blow of is club, must have left such large, forceful footprints. This certainly isn't a spoor that one could attribute to the homunculi you claim to have seen on the Norton Bennett."

"Why not?" said the Eccentric.

"You're sticking to your dwarfs, then?"

"Yes I am. That mark isn't contrary evidence. Dwarfs often have very big extremities—the hands and feet of giants."

"That might be one explanation, obviously—but there's another objection to your thesis. All these tracks, as you can see, are heading, not toward the volcano, but toward the sea. It's from the sea that our aggressors have come…from which they emerged, one could say."

"Hold on—we haven't seen the beginning. It's necessary to follow the tracks all the way. I'm ready to wager that…" The Englishman interrupted himself, extending his finger. "There! Blood! God damn it!"

He was pointing to a flat rock in which there was a large red pool, seemingly still fresh.

The two men went pale. For a long minute, they remained silent.

"I understand now," murmured the engineer, eventually. "The attempt on the submarine happened this morning, while you were asleep. Stop had detected the enemy. He went forward, and battle was engaged at this very spot. That deep mark might allow us to reconstruct the scene. The valiant animal leapt at the Martian's throat, but the latter's arms closed in a terrible grip. Stop was choked, crushed, before he was able to utter a howl. After that rapid drama, the unknown individual and his companions headed for the *Annabella*."

"Poor Stop!" said Pickman. "The brave beast…"

They were so absorbed that, when they suddenly heard the sand creak close at hand, they shivered and reached for their revolvers, as if they expected to see the terrible Martian surge forth.

"Good morning, my friends!" cried Madame Myrandhal, joyfully. "What are you doing here? You look as if you're acting a scene from Conan Doyle or Fenimore Cooper: the subtle hunter on the trail of the elk..."

"That's right," said Serge, "but this time it's serious—grave, even. I would have preferred not to tell you immediately, but it's probably better not to hide anything from you."

"Yes, speak. I'm not a little girl."

Once she had been brought up to date, she murmured: "All this is, indeed, grave. It's evidently a matter of human beings...gigantic human beings. But where did these giants come from? Did they emerge from the heavens, the earth or the water? And poor Stop—do you think they've killed him?"

"It's very probable," Myrandhal replied. "Let's go on. We might end up finding something more definite, if only the place where they disembarked."

"You're assuming they came by sea, then?" said the American.

"I can't see any other explanation."

Pickman muttered a few unintelligible words, while the young woman continued: "By boat or swimming?"

"They came on foot," muttered Pickman, increasingly furious. "They crossed the sea with dry feet, like the Hebrews." And so saying he turned on his heel and departed, taking long strides.

Ten paces away, he stopped and started gesticulating. "Hip, hip, hurrah!" he proclaimed, in a sudden fit of joy. "Come and see, sir!"

Serge ran to join him, and understood the cause of his sudden enthusiasm at a glance.

In front of them, the tracks abruptly changed direction, heading back inland.

"Well!" cried the Englishman. "Who's right? Do you still claim that the Martians came out of the sea? They came from the interior, by Jove! Probably from the volcano...we'll soon find out."

The castaways moved forward, crossed the beach at the double and reached the plain of lava that followed. There the tracks stopped, and they were forced to pause. The Eccentric, so full of ardor a few moments before, made a gesture of discouragement.

"Nothing more," he murmured. "That was to be expected."

His ardor soon returned, however. "In any case," he went on, "the Martians aren't far away. They passed this way less than an hour ago. We'll surely end up finding them. Forward ho!"

The engineer was thoughtful, his brow furrowed, but when he saw the Eccentric set off, revolver in hand, he grabbed him by the arm almost rudely. "Look out!" he said, curtly.

"What is it? What's the matter with you, sir?" the Englishman stammered, more surprised than irritated by that violent gesture on the part of a man as calm as Myrandhal.

"I'm trying to prevent you from doing something foolish."

There was such authority in Serge's voice that the Englishman, who had been on the brink of becoming angry, changed his attitude.

"Something foolish, you say? Explain yourself. I don't understand."

"You will, my dear Robinson, and unless you're determined to get us killed, you'll moderate that juvenile ardor. Until now, I believed, wrongly, that the Martians were far away, and that we could risk operating in the open. Now, the situation has changed suddenly, and we're obliged to change tactics. I agree with you that the Martians are nearby, on the prowl. In consequence, we have numerous and redoubtable enemies around us and before us. We can't see them yet, but they can undoubtedly see us. They're cunning individuals, as they've just proved. Undoubtedly, they're watching us at this moment, lying in wait for us, ready to surround us, only waiting for an opportunity to take us by surprise—and we're going to fall into the trap head first."

"You think that they're as malevolent and as terrible as that?" the Eccentric relied. "Why are they so quick to run away, then?"

"I've told you," said the engineer. "We intimidate them, and that's fortunate—otherwise we'd doubtless have been massacred a long time ago. They have force of numbers in their favor, we have the prestige of superior beings, demigods descended from the Empyrean—and it's that prestige, our best safeguard, that it's necessary to safeguard, without risking it lightly in certain encounters...

"I desire as much as you do to make the acquaintance of our mysterious neighbors, and if they continue to hide, we'll go in search of them and fight them...but before then, we ought to take measures to equalize the terms of the conflict."

"What do you mean, my dear Friday?"

"I'll explain shortly. Let's go back to the *Velox* first. There, we can confer..."

"All right," the Eccentric ended up saying. "You're talking sense—and there's Anna, whom we oughtn't to expose to danger. Go on ahead—I'll bring up the rear, making sure of the retreat. Forward ho!"

The little troop set forth immediately. The Eccentric, conscious and proud of his role as rearguard, turned round from time to time, but did not have to take action; the enemy did not put in an appearance.

"What did I say?" Pickman muttered between his teeth. "They're afraid, but it's us who are running away. That's utterly ridiculous."

In the meantime, Anna, increasingly intrigued, interrogated her husband, by whose side she was walking.

"Well, my dear Serge, what do you think of all this? Do you believe in the Red Men too?"

"No...and yet, I daren't deny it. One thing is certain: we have a mysterious, invisible enemy prowling around, spying on us, against whom we can't take too many precautions."

"Yes," the American murmured, in a low voice." Don't you think that this mystery surrounding us—gripping us, as it were—is disturbing, maddening? Do these Martians, like certain fabulous heroes, have the ability to make themselves invisible?"

"I don't think so," said Serge, smiling.

"Me neither—but then, where do they come from, and where are they hiding? The country is bare for ten leagues around..."

"How do they vanish without leaving any traces? One might think—it comes back to this—that they've descended from the clouds and departed by the same route. Without those enormous feet, which are scarcely those of flying creatures, I'd be inclined to admit the existence on Mars of winged monsters, flying sphinxes..."

Myrandhal shivered slightly. He had just remembered the fantastic apparition he had experienced on the morning of his arrival on Mars, but he hastened to chase the image away. "No," he said, with a smile, "Let's not let our imagination off the bridle. The truth, such as it appears, is already sufficient cause for anxiety. Anyway, we'll try to get ourselves out of trouble. We'll carry out a disciplined search, which will allow us to locate the Martians...unless they really can fly."

"You said a little while ago that they were there, in front of us."

"They might well have been. It was necessary to prevent your guardian from throwing himself head first into a possible ambush—probable, even."

They reached the vessels.

"Well," said the Eccentric, "you can see that we were wrong to be frightened. The Martians aren't as brave as us; they've stayed in their holes. I hope we can go after them soon. You have a plan, my dear Friday: tell us what it is. I'm eager to know whether these damnable devils, who are so handy with a file, have skins impermeable to bullets."

"Listen," said the engineer. "If the Martians are still out there, which isn't certain..."

293

"It's certain," Pickman protested. "I'm certain of it, personally. They're waiting for us, by Jove."

"So be it. It's a matter, as I told you, of equalizing the chances between us. We have just the war machine required for that, a rolling fortress that will permit us to approach the enemy without exposing ourselves. You can guess what I'm talking about..."

"Yes," said Annabella. "The automobile."

"Exactly. I'm reluctant, of course, to upset our packing, which is all ready for the departure this evening, but since it's necessary. Besides which, the damage will be quickly repaired. The auto can be set up in forty minutes, so we can be out on campaign in three quarters of an hour."

"All right!" roared Pickman, enthusiastically. "Excellent idea, my dear Friday. Why didn't we think of it sooner? As for me, aboard the *Annabella* I have a Maxim machine gun that fires twelve hundred bullets a minute. With that toy, one can scythe down a regiment at two thousand meters. I'll let you have it..."

"Thanks, but I have what I need: two machine guns improved and adapted by me for their future usage. You can judge for yourself; we'll start assembling the auto right away. The engine is ready, and greased. It's only a matter of getting out the various pieces of the chassis and fitting them together, which won't take long, the machine having been designed for it."

Indeed, half an hour later, the auto was full assembled and ready to roll. It was a sixteen horsepower, small but robust, equipped with solid pneumatic tires with metallic hubs. It had three seats-two in front and one behind—sheltered by a system of chromium steel shields that could be lowered over the wheels like mudguards. In case of danger, it was sufficient to lift up the plates and fix them in place by means of a bolt.

Two machine guns mounted on pivots, one forwards, on the hood, and one aft, on the trunk made the vehicle into a veritable mobile fortress, as the engineer had said.

Enthused by these bellicose preparations, the Eccentric congratulated the constructor warmly.

"It's admirable," he said. "Simple, light and solid, capable of going anywhere. With a machine like this one, one could make a tour of Mars in thirty days without a breakdown. Now, the Big-Feet can come; we're ready for them; they'll get a warm welcome."

The American was no less enthusiastic. "It's a marvel," she said. "A jewel of precision."

"Oh," said Serge, looking at his wife tenderly, "the jewel's a trifle primitive, and only reminds me distantly of the luxurious coupé that stopped one evening at the gate of Norton Cottage.

"Nevertheless, such as it is, our sixteen-horsepower will be very useful to us. I anticipate, for example, that you'll be jolted somewhat; I've only retained the indispensable components. It's a somewhat crude war machine. Anyway, you can judge for yourself. I'll start the engine. I'm eager to see what the Martians will do at the sight of this new monster racing toward them. I'm sure they'll turn on their heel at the first gunshot. If you'd care to get in..."

"Forward ho!" cried the American, leaping into the driver's seat. "I'll take the wheel to begin with."

"Bravo!" cried the Eccentric, taking the back seat. "That's mettlesome. You can step on the gas, you know— there aren't any policemen on Mars to tick you off, and you have the right to run over anyone who gets in your way..."

The three were full of confidence and impatience, and had almost forgotten the alarm they had experiences a short while before.

"Which way shall we go?" asked the American, pressing on the accelerator.

"As you please," replied the engineer. "Don't go too far to begin with, though. It's not probable that the Martians will come back to attack the ships, but we ought to be ready for anything."

The American looked at her guardian. "Suppose we head for Norton Bennett?"

The Eccentric made a gesture of indifference. "If you like. I can't see any reason for choosing that direction rather than another. Just try to run into the bandits—I'm avid to avenge my poor Stop."

"Let's start with the volcano," Madame Myrandhal decided.

In a matter of minutes, the distance was crossed. The excursionists made a circuit of the hill at high speed, and then headed back toward he submarines at the same pace. After having observed that nothing abnormal had occurred, they set out in another direction.

For three hours the auto wandered back and forth over the lava, enlarging its circle of investigation every time, but without success. Several times, the motorists, reassured by the solitude that reigned around them, got out in order to look for tracks on the ground, but found nothing suspicious. Every time the Eccentric got back aboard more disappointed and more furious. The check was all the more sensible because, thus far, events had seemed to have proved that he was right.

"God damn it!" he muttered, once or twice. "I thought we were going to confront these damned red devils, but now they've escaped, and everything's confused again. It will all clear up. We have to be patient—wait until the end. He who laughs last, laughs longest."

"If you wish," Myrandhal offered, "We can get out and climb Norton Bennett. Your kobolds will have to show themselves in the end. In my opinion, that further excursion doesn't present any great danger—but I'm hesitant, because of Anna."

The Englishman reflected momentarily, but ended up saying, with a discouraged expression: "No, it's pointless; we won't find anything today. The red devils have gone back to their underground holes. They only come out by night—but I'll be waiting for them. I'll have my revenge, God damn it!"

The Englishman was somber and preoccupied; he only replied in monosyllables to the questions that were put to him thereafter.

His companions thought that he was ruminating, and left him to his mutism.

As midday was approaching, however, Serge judged that the experiment had lasted long enough. "I think that we can go home for lunch," he said. "Our first impression was doubtless correct: the Martians arrived and departed by sea, and they're far away by now. Don't you think so, my dear Pickman?"

"Yes," replied the other, curtly.

"However," said Anna, rallying to her guardian's defense, desirous of shoring up his self-respect, "those tracks on the lava, the Martians' detour toward the volcano..."

"A ruse, quite simply. They wanted to put us off their track. Believe me, my dear friends, the more time passes, the more convinced I am that the Martians came by sea and left the same way. They're essentially maritime beings, and I doubt that they often go past the dunes where they land."

"What about those my guardian saw on Norton Bennett?" countered the American.

At that objection the eccentric uttered a grunt whose meaning it was impossible to determine.

Wanting to save their companion's pride himself, the engineer replied: "Oh, I'm talking about the mass, the majority of Martians. It's quite possible that some, the leaders, venture further on, even that they scaled the volcano."

"Why?"

"We can only make hypotheses: to examine our position, perhaps to make sure, before attacking us, that we really were alone."

"That puts your two theses in accord," said Anna. "I imagine, my dear guardian, that you approve..."

"Yes," growled the Eccentric, increasingly sullen—and from that moment on it was impossible to get another word out of him.

Serge and his wife had abandoned the Eccentric to his reflections, and started taking about the departure, still fixed for the next high tide, when—to their great surprise—the Baronet emerged from his obstinate mutism and exclaimed: "So you're leaving? You're going anyway?"

"Yes, my dear Robinson. Do you have any objection?"

"None," the Englishman replied, in a slightly sarcastic tone. "Go, if you want to, as quickly as you like. Everyone's free, God damn it. Personally, I'm staying."

IX. Port Burrett

"You're staying!" Annabella exclaimed, falling from the clouds.

"I'm staying," the Eccentric repeated, categorically. "I swore that I'd go in search of the Martians in the depths of their lair, and I'll go, God damn it. Otherwise, I'd no longer be Pickman..."

That was said in such a tone that Serge understood that there was no point in arguing for the time being, and that it was better to indulge the obstinate gentleman's new whim.

"So be it," he replied. "As we don't want to abandon you, we'll wait for you. We'll stay, even though the delay worries me. The cold is beginning to make itself felt, and I don't want to winter here."

"It's not a matter of wintering—just a few days."

"All right. It's a settled matter, to which we won't return. It's still necessary to make arrangements for those few days, and that presents a difficulty, which you must have envisaged. Soon, the submarines being afloat, it will be a matter of finding a haven for them, of sheltering the delicate machines from the hazards of the sea. Obviously, we could ride out big waves in the open sea, but our motive force is too strictly measured for us to waste it. We'll therefore be constrained to run aground again, unless we have the good fortune to find a bay of calm water, a kind of natural harbor..."

"The port is already found!" exclaimed the Eccentric, joyfully. "I've been looking for it for several days."

"You've been looking for it? So you knew that we'd need it?"

"I suspected as much. Your plan to raise anchor right away didn't meet with my full approval, and I promised myself that if there was anything new, if the Martians put in an appearance, to stay a few more days in order to see what they had under their skin. I would have let you leave."

"What!" cried Madame Myrandhal, indignantly. "You consented to be separated from us! You think that we're not sufficiently alone on this desert world?"

"Oh," the Baronet relied, "it would only have been for a few days. And we'd have stayed in communication, thanks to the telephone. So I looked around for a shelter for the *Annabell*a, and the other evening I discovered not far from here, a kind of port that will suit our purpose very well. It's a very small haven, but marvelously sheltered by a line of breakers forming a dyke. The swell and the tide are scarcely sensible there. One might think that everything had been provided by nature with us in mind.

"Nothing is lacking there—not even the mooring-dock. A rock will serve that purpose very well; it's right on the coast, so that at low tide one can disembark with dry feet. At high tide we'd have a hundred meters to travel by dinghy. Our friend Burrett would say that Providence had hollowed out that basin expressly for us; that's why I gave it its name. And now, if you wish, we can go and visit Port Burrett!"

"Right away," replied Serge, getting to his feet. "I'm in haste to obtain information on this important point. Come on, Anna…is it far?"

"Two miles to the north. We could walk there."

"No, better take the automobile. It's more prudent..."

Half an hour later, the castaways arrived at Port Burrett, which conformed in every respect to the description given by its discoverer.

Serge congratulated Pickman. "It's a real find," he said. "Our submarines will be perfectly sheltered here, and I won't hide it from you that it was the matter that worried me most..."

"I know," the Eccentric replied. "I'm English, a former mariner. I thought of that too, right away."

"I only ask one thing, my dear Robinson, and that's that our sojourn here shouldn't be prolonged too long. Do you know why?"

"I know—but don't worry. Just give me time to get my hands on one of those damned Martians, who seem to be playing hide and seek, and I'll go with you. Agree, my dear chap, that it would have been ridiculous to come so far to see the inhabitants of Mars and then turn your back on them just at the moment..."

"But we aren't turning our back on them," said the engineer. "On the contrary, we're getting ready to chase them over the sea, their own element."

The Eccentric could not suppress a grimace of ill humor. "Listen, sir," he said. "Let's leave that. What point is there is starting that argument again. We'll never be able to convince one another. You think the Martians are far away, out at sea; I'm sure that there here, close by, gone to earth like field-mice. I've seen them with my own eyes, damn it, and I wasn't seeing things.

"Anyway, to reassure you, I promise that I'll leave with you in three days' time, come what may. As for the Red Devils, I'm so sure of my fact that I'll make you a proposition. In Paris, at the Dunkan & Co. Bank, I have a deposit of ten thousand pounds. If I'm mistaken, and I don't bring you the proof of what I'm saying within the next three days, that money belongs to you.

"And now, instead of arguing any longer, let's occupy ourselves with the departure—by which I mean the reflotation."

That was what they did. Having returned to the submarines, the castaways proceeded with the final preparations. The auto was dismantled and the pieces stowed in the hold again. An electric reflector was set on the prow of the *Velox*, which would serve as a searchlight.

These various operations and the dinner that followed went on rather late into the night.

It was ten o'clock when the high ride began to moisten the sand round the explorers.

Pickman made a final visit to the *Annabella*, carefully closed the hatch on her conning-tower, and came back to join his companions in the central compartment of the *Velox*.

Already the waves were beating he hull of the submarine, which oscillated occasionally. Installed at his captain's post with his head protruding from the conning tower, Serge checked the functioning of the machines one last time. "All's well," he announced. "A few more minutes and we'll be off."

As the mist increased, he switched on the electric beacon fixed to the prow. At that moment, the vessel suddenly tilted backwards, and that abrupt pitch sent Pickman sprawling at the far end of the compartment. He got to his feet, rather sheepishly.

"What was that?" he asked, feeling his sides. "We're not afloat yet?"

"No," said the captain. "It's our supportive bed of sand disintegrating, but it won't be long now; the *Annabella*'s already afloat."

There was a further shock, which righted the *Velox*.

"Pay attention!" cried Myrandhal. "This time, we're going. Forward ho!"

They heard the propeller start to spin, and the *Velox* moved off, towing the *Annabella*, which was dancing madly. The inshore waves were negotiated with ease, and not long afterwards, the two boats were moored in the bay so opportunely discovered by Pickman, who applauded himself once again for his find.

"The water's perfectly calm here, as you see. We're scarcely moving. Just enough to lull us to sleep. We'll never have slept better!"

He was still taking when a vague rumor became audible in the distance, on the coast; there were confused shouts and seemingly-stifled barking, in which Serge thought he recognized Stop's voice.

Intrigued, Serge and his wife pricked up their ears, and then looked at Pickman. To heir great surprise, the latter, either because he had not heard or for some other reason, remained perfectly calm.

"What's that?" Serge asked. "Can't you hear it?"

"Yes, vaguely," the Eccentric replied, quite phlegmatically. "What do you think it is? The noise of the sea—the tide, I mean."

"Yes, perhaps," Serge replied. "Personally, I thought about Martians."

"That's possible too." In a slightly sarcastic voice, the Baronet went on: "It is, in fact, their time. Deimos is rising, and it's time for the kobolds to dance in the moonlight..."

"I admire your phlegm. You're joking."

"No, by Jove! Why should I be astonished? The Martians are on the prowl, you say—personally, I never doubted it. So what? As for being anxious, there's no reason. The submarines, once on the water, in their element, have nothing to fear."

"I agree. That doesn't mean if I weren't fearful of a trap, I'd go as far as to hop over there, to watch, as you put it, the kobolds dancing in the moonlight..."

"It would be a waste of effort," the Englishman replied. "The devils are as cunning as you are, and it's necessary to play them at their own game, coolly. That's why I'm not getting excited. What's the point? I'm sure of what I'm doing, sure of winning the bet I mentioned a while ago.

"It's tomorrow that I intend to take possession of one of those goblins, which are permitting themselves to disturb our sleep. I've just discovered a means for which I've been searching for some time—oh, a very simple means, a sort of bait. We'll both lie in ambush on the beach with a lasso, like cowboys.

"That requires some preparation, however; that's why we're waiting until tomorrow. After a day of excitement and fatigue, we're all worn out. Personally, I'm falling asleep, so I'm going to take the dinghy and go home, back to the *Annabella*."

"To the *Annabella*!" said Anna, nonplussed. "I thought you were going to stay here. You'd be just as comfortable."

"Not on your life," said the Eccentric. "I'd embarrass you and you'd embarrass me. I'd rather be on my own at home. An old bachelor's habit..."

All insistence was futile. Pickman climbed out of the conning tower, took one of the dinghies moored there and headed for the *Annabella*.

As soon as they were alone, Serge turned to his wife. "What does that mean?" he asked. "Your guardian was in a hurry to leave. Evidently, he's got an idea in the back of his head."

"All the more so as he'd tacitly accepted that he was sleeping here. He's planning something. You noticed that he assured us that all danger was past and that we could sleep easy. He surely wants to profit from our sleep to go ashore and hunt for Martians."

"We've both had the same thought—and that's what we must prevent, at all costs. Trouble arrives quickly. I intended to stay on watch during this first evening—this is another reason..."

"Is that absolutely necessary?" Anna asked. "You're worn out too, and need sleep. Do you want us to take shifts mounting guard?"

"Not on your life. I feel perfectly fit. Go to your room, my dear Anna. I'll have a two-hour siesta tomorrow, and that will take care of it. As for your guardian, I'll keep an eye on him. Woe betide him if he tries of go out: he'll be punished like a conscript who goes absent without leave.

"There he is now, switching off the electric light. It's a feint. Just wait—we'll see who tires first. Now, my dear Anna, *bonsoir*—until tomorrow. Sleep tranquil: I'll keep watch."

Myrandhal escorted his wife to the door of her cabin; then he came back, picked up a book and started reading.

From time to time, in order to combat the drowsiness that was invading him, he took a few strides around the cabin.

At about five o'clock, it seemed to him that the mooring-rope was grating more loudly and that the *Velox* was dancing.

He went to the porthole, wondering whether the Eccentric was playing some prank.

He opened it, saw nothing, and was about to close it again when he perceived a bizarre noise close at hand, twice over: a kind of whistling similar to that of certain snakes. He tried to pierce the darkness, to discover the animal making the strange sounds, but could not do it.

"It must be some sort of fish," he murmured. "There are eels that whistle like that, I think..."

His watch concluded without any further incident.

As dawn began to break, Serge stretched himself out in an armchair. *Now*, he thought, *I can doze a little. Our man won't go out now. Anyway, I won't go to sleep—I'll be on my feet at the slightest noise.*

He had overestimated his strength. When he woke up an hour later, pale daylight was whitening the windows.

"What's happening?" he murmured. "I thought a heard the sound of oars. Is it Pickman?"

Serge ran to a porthole.

"Exactly!" he exclaimed. "His dinghy is no longer there. Our man has escaped, but he can't have got far. It was only a few minutes ago that I heard the oars—that's what woke me up. It's a matter over catching up with him."

During the monologue, Serge had taken his place in the second dinghy. He extended the oars, and rowed vigorously toward the coast, which he soon reached. As he landed he perceived Pickman's boat, which the latter had taken the precaution of mooring on land.

Close at hand, he heard the whistling sound that he had heard before rise up again, and could not help feeling a vague apprehension.

"There's my fish again," he murmured, trying to make a joke of it. "It's hissing to the left. Is that a bad omen on Mars too?"

Without hesitating for a second, however, he launched himself along the trail of footprints that Pickman had left in the sand.

He soon reached the lava plain. There the tracks ended. Serge looked round, and did not see anything hopeful.

Before continuing his search, he scanned the entire region with his eyes. He was on a vast rocky plain that rose up at a gentle slope to the horizon.

In front of him, less than fifty meters away, a line of rocks extended from left to right—blocks of all sizes, as if polished by the weather. One might have thought it the moraine of some vanished glacier.

Myrandhal continued searching for Pickman with his eyes. *Where the devil can he be?* He wondered. *A man can see for two leagues in this desert. He must be hiding behind those boulders over here, in order to lie in ambush, as he put it. I'll take a look.*

He was moving forward when a puff of white smoke rose up from among the rocks in question. At the same time, the sound of a gunshot drilled into his eardrums.

Serge set off like lightning. "It's him," he murmured, his heart gripped by anguish. "It's Pickman—he's been attacked."

He had covered the distance in a few bounds and ran through the rocks. Fifty meters further on, he stopped, his legs buckling, mute with horror.

Lying on the ground, which had been trampled by a violent struggle, were two objects: Pickman's helmet and his revolver, still smoking.

Of the Eccentric, there was no trace; he had disappeared, as if through a trap-door.

"That's fantastic," Serge murmured, his hair bristling fearfully. "One might think that the ground had opened up and swallowed him. What has happened here confounds the imagination. There's something here—some form of life—with an occult, mysterious power, which surpasses all our earthly conceptions."

Forgetful of the danger he was running himself, if the kidnappers were still there, he wandered around for some time, making a tour of the moraine.

In the end, he scaled one of the blocks of stone and looked into the distance, seeing nothing but the bleak and empty plain.

He turned round hen, and saw his dinghy dancing on the water. Suddenly, he shivered, and a cold sweat inundated his temples. He had just thought, not about his own danger, but that which an individual dear to him might be in.

"Anna!" he stammered. "I forgot about Anna, to whom I owe...what a horrible situation for her, if I were abducted in my turn, or if she were!"

His teeth chattering with horror, he leapt down and ran toward the beach like a madman.

X. *"Hello! Hello!"*

The days that followed were lugubrious for those who remained. Never had the desert world seemed so sinister to them.

All their searches had been fruitless. Having carried out their coup, the Martians had disappeared like enchanted beings. The lava kept its secret.

Anna was still hopeful, however, contrary to all appearances.

"No," she often repeated, "I can't believe that my dear guardian is dead. It seems to me that I would have known, that his soul would have come to bid me adieu. The incomprehensible beings that have abducted him, those mysterious spirits of some kind, can't be as ferocious as that. They spared Stop."

"Is that certain?" Serge objected.

"Yes, it was definitely his voice that we heard the other evening, a few hours before the misfortune. I recognized it, and poor Pickman did too, of course. Do you remember his strange attitude? And besides, remember, there was no trace of blood where the latest drama occurred. Everything suggests that the Martians had set an ambush to capture our friend alive. Why would they have killed him afterwards?"

"Let's hope so," Serge replied, not daring to voice the abominable thought that had been haunting him for some time: that it might perhaps be better if he were dead...

The days went by, and Madame Myrandhal also began to despair. At first she had imagined that the Eccentric would find the means to escape, that he would come back unexpectedly, at the moment when he was least expected. Then it was from the Martians themselves that she expected his liberation. She persisted in believing that the kidnapers would reappear sooner or later, that, having a hostage—which seemed to have been their objective—they would attempt to open negotiations; but nothing of that kind happened, and her last illusions flew away, one after another...

It was necessary to look reality in the face, to think about the salvation of the survivors, of their future on this baneful planet—all the more so because the abnormal temperature, from which they had benefited thus far, was lowering in an increasingly disquieting fashion. In ten days the thermometer had fallen fifteen degrees, to the vicinity of zero. Winter was approaching, with its cortege of frosts and privations.

One morning—it was the fourteenth day after Pickman's disappearance—when the young couple woke up, they saw that the coast was white with snow. Ice-floes were drifting on the sea, doubtless detached from some distant ice-sheet.

Anna was depressed by the sight of that polar landscape, and Serge took advantage of that impression to put the question of an immediate departure back on the table.

"This time," he said, "there's no more room for hesitation. Only pray to God that we haven't waited too long and that the heat and power we have at our disposal—our reserves of electricity and gasoline—are sufficient to take us to a more hospitable shore. We need to leave today. Who can tell whether, at the pace things are going, we might not be blocked in by ice tomorrow?"

"You're right," Anna replied, "and I won't resist any more. I can no longer hope to see my guardian again. We can leave whenever you wish. I only ask one thing, and that's to go over there to the moraine one last time, as one visits a grave. We'll build one of those monuments that polar explorers build, a cairn. We can even leave some food underneath it, and a letter for our guardian, indicating the direction we've taken. I doubt that he'll ever receive it..."

Madame Myrandhal could not finish. Tears were steaming from her eyes. Her husband, equally emotional, strode back and forth in the compartment, searching for words of consolation that he could not find.

They had been silent for a few moments when, before their startled eyes, the bell of the telephone vibrated, and a joyful voice resounded, bursting in their ears like the sound of thunder.

"Hello! Hello! Are you there, Anna? And you, my dear Friday? Good morning! Well, say something then, damn it!"

Serge and his wife looked at one another, mute with amazement, not daring to believe the evidence of their senses.

Finally, the American precipitated herself toward the apparatus and said, in a crazed voice: "Is that you, my guardian, is that you?"

"Not so loud!" howled a furious voice. "Not so loud, by Jove! You'll give the game away...I'm not alone, God damn it! Not alone, you understand..."

Madame Myrandhal only understood one thing, which was that the Eccentric was alive, really alive. Her joy and stupor were such that she felt her legs giving way underneath her. She tottered, and Serge came forward to support her.

She shoved him away, and in a lower voice, trembling with emotion, she said: "Hello! So, my dear guardian, it's you, it's you! I'm mad with joy, but how can it be? Explain yourself. Where are you? How can you talk? You have a telephone, then?"

"Of course—I've got mine: the one from the *Annabella*. I brought it with me in my knapsack. Didn't you notice that?"

"No, no, we'd lost our heads..."

"It's necessary to keep one's head—one's brain...I always keep mine. Where would I be without it? It's like my knapsack, you see. You mock when I fill it with all sorts of things...but I was right, God damn it! The other day, in particular, I stuffed it—three days' food supplies, ropes, crampons to explore the fissures, machines of every sort. But you were asking me where I am..."

"Yes—you're killing me. Speak! Where are you, then?"

"Where I am...where the Martians live, by Jove."

"Where the Martian live?"

"Yes, among the kobolds, the red devils—although they aren't as red as all that. Does that surprise you?"

"Oh! Yes..."

310

"I swore to get here; I did it. What I say, I always do. What do you think of this reportage, eh, Anna? This is an interview that that old buffalo Norton Bennett would pay dearly for, isn't it? Answer me..."

"Yes, undoubtedly, but I beg you, my dear guardian, don't joke any more...you're keeping us on tenterhooks. Talk about yourself, only yourself. We thought you were dead, and here you are, resuscitated all of a sudden. You seem joyful, quite well...

"I've never been better. What next?"

"Next...but you haven't told us anything yet. Where are you? I mean, in what part, what region of Mars, in the air, under the sea or underground?"

"Underground, God damn it! What a thick head you have. Underground, by all the devils! I knew that there were inhabitants under the lava, that we had a subterranean world under our feet, a city—in a word, a Martian city. It only remained to discover it. That's done!"

"And is it far away, this city—far from us?"

"I can't measure it. Between twenty and fifty miles."

"And Stop!" exclaimed the young woman, seized by a sudden thought. "Poor Stop..."

"Stop's here, and says hello."

"Is he well too?"

"Very well—a trifle melancholy. Evidently, living like a mole doesn't suit him."

"And the Martians?" Madame Myrandhal went on. "You haven't said anything about the Martians. What kind of people...?"

"Good people," Pickman interjected. "A trifle coarse, but that would take too long—later..."

"One more word," said the American, breathlessly, her thoughts pressing in a crowd. "You're not unhappy? They're not maltreating you?"

"No—what a ridiculous idea!"

"Then why haven't you called before?"

"You're asking too much, damn it. I'd have liked to do so..."

"But you couldn't. You're a prisoner?"

"Not exactly—merely kept under surveillance. But the damnable rascals stole my bag, all my resources. I had to use cunning to get it back. Someone helped me: Tao."

"Tao? Who's that? A Martian?"

"Yes—my guard. I must admit that we didn't get on to begin with. He wanted to put one over on me, but I got the better of him. I'll tell you later. Now, he's my houseboy—he polishes my boots. He's the one who's watching me at the moment, while I chat He's just told me that the Martians are prowling around. That's enough for now, Anna. Pass the apparatus to that fellow Myrandhal, so I can hear his voice."

Serge did not make him repeat the request. "Hello!" he said, immediately. "Bonjour, my dear Robinson. Are you well?"

"Entirely," the Eccentric replied. "Bonjour." In a triumphant voice he added: "Well, what do you say, Monsieur Frenchman, Monsieur Scientist? You've lost the bet. I was right."

"I agree, humbly."

"Enough," said Pickman. "Time's pressing. Oh, you can boast of having exasperated me, you. I was enraged, God damn it! I wanted to crush you with my victory, but here are more important things to do. We'll chat soon. I've promised myself to get out of here, and I'll get out."

"You're planning to escape?"

"Yes. Tao's on board, so it'll go quickly, God willing."

"Can we help? Speak, command..."

"Look after yourselves. Don't budge—you'd spoil everything. Don't do anything until I tell you. Until then, play dead. I'll explain everything. Before then, have you anything important to ask?"

"Masses, but this isn't the time...I understand."

"No."

"There is one thing that troubles me more than the rest, though."

"What?"

"How did you disappear like that the other morning? I arrived almost immediately…and nothing! Are there trap-doors in the lava, then, and secret passages?"

"I think so, but it's impossible to say. I received a blow that knocked me out, and when I came to, I was far underground. Obviously, there are passages…"

"Good—that must indeed be the case. One more word about the Martians—what kind of beings are they?"

"I told you—dwarfs…a trifle baroque, of course. They're furry, like bears, and their fur has a reddish tint at times, although that gleam comes, not from them, but from the ambient atmosphere. Since I've been underground, I shoot off sparks from my own hair. There's a lot of electricity here.

"I should tell you that I haven't been able to investigate much. I'm not free, and I've used the time making myself comprehensible to my boy. Then again, they only talk about certain things. These people don't have brains conformed like ours, as regards ideas…as for words, their language, it's something unimaginable, that I don't expect ever to master. The Martians don't talk, they sing—or rather hum…"

"Don't they whistle?"

"Yes, when they're angry, or to call out. As for the words, they're cries, onomatopoeias. All vowels—I can scarcely recognize two or three consonants: a language fit for monkeys or parrots. And yet, these little monsters have a soul, or something similar. They know things, it seems to me, that still escape us no doubt…

"But I'm talking too much, and there are more urgent matters…let's talk about my escape. It will be soon…"

"We can't do anything to help you, you say?"

"No, nothing. Stay silent. I can do it alone."

The Eccentric's voice was suddenly cut off, and there was a sequence of little inarticulate squeaks, a kind of mewling modulated in three different tones.

313

Serge and his wife listened in anguish, fearful of some surprise. Unable to contain herself any longer, Madame Myrandhal leapt to the apparatus.

"Hello!" she called.

"Not so loud!" complained a furious voice. "Quietly, by Jove! What a piercing voice you have, Anna. God, damn it, you nearly..."

There was another interruption, during which the young couple could hear their own hearts pounding. Then the Eccentric called again: "Hello! Are you there, Myrandhal?"

"Yes, but what a panic! What's happening? Those shrill cries..."

"That was Tao, my boy. He was warning me that the Martians are coming. And here's one coming now... Shh! I'll call you soon..."

XI. The Anthropoid

It was almost midday when that conversation came to an end, and from that moment on the Eccentric gave no further sign of life.

As the hours went by, Ana felt the immense joy that had invaded her at first give way to a vague anxiety...

"What do you expect?" she replied to her husband, who tried to reason with her. "It's too much for me. I can't believe in so much happiness—and then, there are many things that are obscure. My guardian, although he didn't admit it, is purely and simply a prisoner. Who knows what might happen before his escape? To think that at this moment, while we're chatting tranquilly, a drama is unfolding down there. Don't you find the situation horrible...atrocious?"

"You're being unreasonable," the engineer replied. "Yesterday, we would have given half our blood just to know that Pickman is alive. Now we know much more than that. We've heard his voice; we're going to see him soon, I'm sure of it! You ought to be delighted—instead of which, you're tormenting yourself..."

"What do you expect? One isn't in control of these things. Until the last minute, until my guardian is here in our arms, I'll be in doubt!"

The evening passed in this state of apprehension. Darkness fell...

Even Serge could not help looking at the telephone bell continually.

Finally, the frail hammer began to vibrate. Anna stood up, breathless.

"Hello!" shouted the jovial voice of the Baronet. "Are you there? Good—I can only give you a minute. This is to tell you not to be impatient—there's a delay. The escape's been put off until tomorrow..."

"A delay?" said Anna, in an anguished tone. "What delay?"

"How do I know?" Pickman exclaimed. "I don't know everything, damn it! Tao tells me that there's a delay. I thought I ought to do the same, by Jove. That's women all over—curiosity! That's the way the Devil always gets hold of them. With that, good night—I'm sleepy. Good night, Milady…good night!"

Anna tried to call her guardian back, but he did not deign to respond.

As for the engineer, entirely reassured by that further communication, he smiled.

"You see," he said to his wife, "you were wrong to be anxious. The Baronet is still as cheerful and as jovial—that's a good sign. He's taking a malign pleasure in astonishing us. Who knows—perhaps he has a surprise in store for us?"

"The best surprise would be his unexpected arrival."

"That's more difficult. It's already a lot to know that soon—perhaps tomorrow—he'll be here, with us."

Myrandhal suddenly shivered. A whistling sound had just become audible in the darkness: the sinister whistling that he had heard before.

Water was splashing close by.

At the same time, violent blows struck the hull. Precipitate footsteps ran over the deck…

"Martians!" shouted the young man. He was launching himself toward the conning tower to close the hatch when a laughing face appeared in the opening.

"My guardian!" stammered the American.

"In person. What's astonishing about that? Hello, Anna; hello Mr. Friday."

The Eccentric had stepped into the conning-tower and was coming down the small spiral staircase, as calmly as if he were just coming back from smoking a cigar on the deck.

"What's astonishing," he said, "is that you're looking at me with such wide eyes. One would think that you'd never seen me before."

Already recovered from her stupefaction, however, Anna threw herself into her guardian's arms. Serge did likewise; and then there was a volley of questions, which overlapped chaotically.

The Eccentric, once his effect had been produced, emerged from his forced phlegmaticism. He gesticulated and uttered guttural exclamations.

"Hip, hip, hurrah!" he shouted. "What a joke! I didn't think it would succeed so well. So you didn't suspect?"

"Not at all, my dear Robinson. You saw our amazement..."

"Well, you had pale faces and utterly blank expressions..."

"But what's going on?" Anna demanded. "How did you get away? Have you been on your way for a long time?"

"Apparently. In brief, this is it: this morning, when I called the first time, I wanted to tell you about the projected escape, but I was disturbed."

"By whom?" Anna interjected. "The Martians?"

"Who do you think? Only, if you interrupt all the time, we won't accomplish anything. Let me talk first; you can question me later.

"So, I wanted to tell you about the projected escape, when there was a change of circumstances. Tao had just told me that the passage was free—a subterranean passage that we'd been keeping an eye on for some time—and we set of, Stop and I."

"Stop's here! Where?"

"On the shore, with Tao."

"Tao too!"

"Yes, he's keeping him quiet—had to be done, or the beast would have barked and it would have gone awry..."

"But that whistling?" asked Serge, in his turn. "Who was whistling?"

"Me, of course!" said the Eccentric, laughing. "I speak Martian...where was I? The escape...so, I was saying, all three of us decamped and went like rabbits in their burrow...eight

317

miles at least, we covered at a trot. I scarcely thought of tele-phoning, as you can imagine."

"You were pursued?" asked the young woman.

"No, but we could have been. Then, when I thought of you, I said to myself: *I'll give them a surprise.* We'd just come out on to the lava. For three more hours we marched at the double, and then Stop started gamboling. He'd caught your scent..."

"Brave Stop!"

We approached the boats, and, as I feared that the dog might give the game away, I gave him to Tao to hold. As I still had my apparatus, that suggested the idea of doing better still, so I telephoned as if I were still back there, in a pickle—and there you go! As jokes go, it was a good one, by Jove!"

And the Eccentric laughed, slapping his thigh. His listen-ers were no less delighted to see him, so cheerful and looking so well, in all respects.

"You've never looked better," said Anna, ecstatically. "My word, you've put on weight...I imagine you were going to come back thin, dying of hunger, but you don't seem to have suffered at all You've been well cared for, then, and well nourished?"

"What did you eat, then?" Serge asked, his scientific cu-riosity resurfacing.

"Fish, uniquely—fresh or conserved. The Martians are ichthyophages. And mollusks. There are grottoes down there in which they're abundant."

While speaking, the eccentric was looking round.

"What are you looking for?" Myrandhal asked.

"The radiator. Turn it up, then. Brrr...it's not warm here."

"Not warm?" said Serge, astonished. "But it's over twelve degrees."

"Seriously, you're cold?" asked Anna, prompt to take alarm and running to the storage-locker. "I'll make you a hot toddy."

"No, don't make so much fuss. Just a glass of whisky. It's the reaction, and the change of environment. Oh, it's horribly hot down there, in their molehill. That's the only thing I suffered from—God damn it, it was hard, especially at the beginning. Except that the proof is made, and you've lost again, Mr. Frenchman. Oh, you made fun of my dwarfs, my Red Men. Well, I've brought one of them. That's proof, that is, by Jove!

"Oh, you claimed that in volcanic terrain there couldn't be inhabitants underground, that no one could live there…well, I've lived there, me, who wasn't used to it. Yes, I acclimatized—and that's one in the eye for you, eh?

"I was hot, of course. I was sweating like a sponge. Oh, I'll remember it, by Jove—my sojourn next to the Central Fire!"

Serge Myrandhal wondered whether the Eccentric was talking seriously. "Come on, my dear Baronet, don't abuse your advantage. There's no need to exaggerate. Your adventure is astonishing enough already. Was it really as hot as all that down there? What was the temperature, approximately?"

"I didn't have a thermometer, but believe me, it was forty or fifty centigrade at least. What's more, I'm talking about the place where I was, a kind of cool cave. Elsewhere, it was much worse."

"And the Red Men can live in that furnace!" Anna exclaimed. "What are these Martians, exactly?"

"Strange beings quite fantastic—some kind of subterranean spirits, kobolds, who live in fire, close to fire, as fish live in the water."

"Come on, my guardian," Ana murmured. "Enough joking. You're not going to make us believe in salamander-men…"

"I'm not joking—or only a little. What's astonishing about it, after all? Habit is second nature, and for them, undoubtedly, it's nature itself. After all, there are people of almost similar kinds on Earth—puddlers, glassworkers—who live naked in their furnaces."

"That's true," said the engineer. "All in all, there's nothing scientifically impossible about it. The human body has marvelous faculties of adaptation. Among others, one can cite the case of a baker who, for a bet, went through a hot oven where anyone else would have fallen down dead. There's also the classic example of the founder plunging his hand into a vast of boiling lead. Those phenomena of exceptional calefaction are the rule on Mars, that's all."

"Nothing simpler," said the Eccentric sarcastically, in his ward's ear. "Scientists can explain everything...afterwards! As for divining it, or going to see it, that's another matter. Now me, I've seen it. While you argue, I go in search of proofs, and bring them back...there! Are you convinced now?"

"Yes," said Madame Myrandhal.

Pickman swallowed a final gulp of whisky and clicked his tongue. "All the same," he said, "the goblins, the kobolds, extraordinary as they are, don't seem so to themselves... Now, let's go fetch Tao."

"That's true!" exclaimed Madame Myrandhal. "And Stop! In our joy, we'd quite forgotten them. Where are they?"

"Close by, in the dinghy."

"What dinghy?" asked the engineer. "You have a dinghy?"

"Yes—I didn't swim out here, by Jove! I had a dinghy—mine, which was still on the beach."

"That's true. The sight of it made Anna feel ill, and I left it over there...until further instructions."

A minute later, Stop, mad with joy, hurtled into the compartment.

"Here's Tao, now," Pickman announced—and Serge and his wife saw a grotesque dwarf appear, with an enormous head and feet: a kind of anthropoid covered in russet frizzy fur, wearing as a kind of fish-skin loincloth, still fresh and bloody.

The Martian looked around wildly and fearfully, uttering little plaintive squeals from time to time.

The Englishman had seized one of his hands and was encouraging him in a low voice.

Extremely interested, Serge watched. One thing that struck him right away about the anthropoid was the eyes: cerulean, translucent eyes in which the fear agitating there cast violet shadows; child-like eyes, which contrasted strangely with the bestial face. One might have thought that all the intelligence, all the soul, of that bizarre being had take refuge therein, beneath the bushy eyelashes.

Gripped by an imprecise repugnance, Anna recoiled behind her husband. Her guardian called her to order.

"What are you doing?" he said. "Don't worry, Tao isn't malign. Are you scared?"

"No."

"Come forward, then," said the Englishman, as if he were introducing a clever ape. Tao will greet you first; he knows about gallantry. Come on, Tao, say hello..."

Tao was not listening. At the sight of Anna, suddenly moving forward, he had been immobilized, his eyes wide, ecstatic. Evidently, that brutal creature, that soul still wrapped in the swaddling-clothes of animality, had a sense and understanding of beauty.

Then his eyes moistened. He began to tremble, while a hoarse gasp was exhaled from his vast bosom.

Without knowing exactly why, the two men had launched themselves forward, but Tao's attitude had already changed. He recoiled, clicking his teeth, raising his hairy hands, as if to protect his dazzled eyes and beg for mercy. He was uttering moans, in the midst of which two inarticulate syllables recurred incessantly: *Zoa*.

He went to take refuge in a corner, near Stop, whom he took in his arms and began to caress, lamenting softly.

Gripped by a strange emotion, the castaways looked at one another, interrogating one another with their gaze.

"What does that signify?" asked the engineer, finally. "Do you know what it means, Pickman?"

321

"Hmm! Not really…and that annoys me, by Jove! You're forgetting that Tao and I only possess a hundred words in common, at the most, and that if we understand one another, it's mostly by means of sign language."

"But you must have some idea—a hypothesis. What does that word *Zoa* mean, which he's repeating incessantly? Where has that sudden terror come from?"

"I don't know. We're touching on a mystery there—the great mystery of Mars, the one whose knowledge would probably reveal to us the whole history of the planet, but which we don't yet have. Then again, remember what I said: the Martians don't talk, they sing. Every word changes its meaning according to the intonation, and the gesture that accompanies it."

"Yes, but in this case the gesture is particularly significant. Anna and I, who are seeing Tao for the first time, understood immediately."

"What have you understood? You speak first, Anna."

"I understood, or rather I supposed, that *Zoa* designated superior beings, spirits of some kind, of whom the dwarfs have a superstitious terror."

"That's right. I admire your perspicacity."

"It remains to be determined," Myrandhal added, "exactly what these *Zoa* are. Do you have any idea about that?"

"Yes," said Pickman, "but don't ask me for proof here. It's an impression I've derived from a heap of things, impossible to analyze. When you've been in Tao's company for a few weeks, and you've succeeded in exchanging a few impressions with him, I think you'll agree with me.

"Like you, the first time I heard the word *Zoa* I was struck by it, all the more so because I'd just had a nasty moment. By Jove, just thinking about it makes me hot under the collar…"

"What moment? Explain yourself, my guardian."

"Later. Let's not quarrel, by all the devils! So, that was how I began my investigation, and I suddenly saw things magnify, embrace the whole of the planet. That's how I formed an idea—a theory—about Mars and its inhabitants; a theory which, if it isn't true, isn't as far away from the truth as all that.

"That posited, I'll start with Mars, and say: Mars, as our astronomers have divined, is an empty, desert world—a dying world, as you declared right away, my dear Friday. The seas are gradually disappearing, filled in by the lava that's emerging all over, because although Mars is a moribund world, its central fire is by no means extinct.

"Nevertheless, the lava hasn't yet covered it entirely, fortunately for us. In the tropics, there are vast regions covered with splendid vegetation, immense oases of a sort. That's all that I was able to get out of Tao concerning his planet.

"Let's come to the inhabitants now, the Martians, who are getting rarer and rare, for the planet is becoming terribly depopulated. But it hasn't always been like that. Once—which is to say, a few thousand centuries ago—Mars possessed two kinds of inhabitants, two great rival races: the *Zoa* and the dwarfs, the *Houâ*, as they call themselves in their own language.

"If I've understood correctly, in the beginning, the superior race, the *Zoa*, were winged beings. That doesn't seem too absurd to you?"

"Not at all. It's entirely concordant with the feeble intensity of gravity here," the engineer approved. "Flying humans, if there ever were any, must have arisen naturally on Mars."

"Well," the Eccentric continued, "after terrible wars—Tao still shivers when he talks about them, either with rage or fear; one never knows with him—the dwarfs were vanquished, reduced to slavery, driven underground…they were sent into the Martian excavations as we send convicts to the mines. Once there, as the ground lent itself to it—Mars, from what I've seen, is hollow; by which I mean pierced, riddled with holes like a gruyere cheese—the dwarfs adapted to it and multiplied! Thus, with time, this bastard subterranean race was born, these mole-people, the *Houâ*…"

"What about the others?" asked Myrandhal. "The *Zoa*—where do they live? Will we have a chance of meeting them?"

"Too late—we've arrived too late. The *Zoa* have disappeared from the surface of the world. According to Tao, though, two *Zoa* still exist: a man and a woman, the last couple of the superior race. They're two very beautiful, very knowledgeable beings, but sterile, angels of a sort, like seraphim, in whom the spirit has worn away the matter, the envelope, the sheath. They know everything, they've conquered disease and old age, and have succeeded in prolonging their lives in a marvelous fashion. There's only one thing they haven't been able to conquer: Death! And at the present moment, they're dying, going out like a lamp running out of oil."

"Where are they?" exclaimed Madame Myrandhal. "Where do these strange beings live?"

The Eccentric made a vague gesture. "Somewhere far away, to the south. Doubtless in one of the oases I mentioned just now."

"We have to go there, as quickly as possible."

"That's my intention, but I doubt that we'll succeed in reaching them. The *Zoa*, who are all-powerful beings, don't allow themselves to be approached just like that. Besides which, their empire, like Armida's garden,[28] is guarded by monsters, dragons, flame-throwers..."

"You're exaggerating again."

---

[28] Armida is a character in Torquato Tasso's epic poem *Gerusalemme liberate* (1581), whose French translation was long used as a standard text in French schools. She is a Saracen enchantress opposed to the invading crusaders, who becomes infatuated by the Christian knight Rinaldo and creates a magic garden where she holds him captive in a deluded state, but he is eventually recalled to his supposed Christian duties. The episode became a popular theme for operas, including examples by Handel, Vivaldi, Gluck, Haydn, Rossini and Dvořák.

"Not at all. At least, I'm only repeating what Tao has told me. You can interrogate him yourself. It's possible, though, that he exaggerates slightly. One thing that's certain is that the gnome has a holy terror of the *Zoa*. According to him, they're magicians of a sort, masters of water, earth and fire: the Great Fire that burns at the heart of the world, which they sometimes cause to spring forth through the burst crust. Their power isn't limited to that; it extends to the neighboring planets. It was them, still according to Tao, who made us come here, drawing us from the Earth—which singularly diminishes your glory and your invention, my dear Friday: the invention of which you were so proud…" The Eccentric concluded on a sarcastic note.

"Fortunately," Anna replied, "those are merely the dreams of a savage."

"But Tao didn't tell you the names of these seraphic beings?" said the engineer. "Their personal names…?"

"No. Tao thinks that if he pronounced their names, he'd be struck dead immediately."

Serge was pensive. "Are you sure that you've understood correctly?" he asked, eventually. "Perhaps Tao meant that the name meant 'thunderbolt'…"

"It's possible," said Pickman. "Yes, perhaps. Oh, the *Houâ* language is rather ambiguous…as for English, I've tried, but nothing doing. The palate, and the deformed vocal organ of one of these little monsters, will never be able to articulate a word of English, which is a superior language: the language of spirits and gods, by Jove!"

Having pronounced the final phrase in a resounding voice, the Eccentric stopped, as if to draw breath "Oof!" he said. "That's two hours I've been talking. I've never said as much, by Jove. So my throat's dry…another glass of whisky, my dear Anna…thank you! To your health, my dear Friday!"

"To yours, my dear Pickman, to your fortunate return, to the glory of the first man who penetrated the Martian realm. That's a record that no one can take away from you! So, I raise my glass and I drink to your health, my dear friend. To the glory of Sir Washington Pickman!"

"No!" cried the Eccentric, gripped by a sudden enthusiasm. "To the glory of England alone—all for old England! England forever! And now, let's eat. I'm devilishly hungry. I still have a couple of bottles of Cliquot in my own reserves. Now or never is the time to pop their corks, God damn it!"

XII. Southward Bound

Joyfully, they sat down at table, and the conversation continued while Tao and Stop shared the scraps of the feast fraternally.

"There's one thing that bothers me," said Myrandhal, "which is the sudden, inexplicable disappearance of the Martians after you were kidnapped. I arrived almost at the same moment...your revolver was still smoking, but I didn't see anything—nothing at all...

"They must, as we were saying just now, have secret passages through the lava, known only to them."

"Evidently," said the Baronet, "but I wasn't able to take account of them. I was unconscious; I only know what the worthy Tao has told me, which is rather confused. If I've understood correctly, the passage is hidden under the moraine itself. That's why the dwarfs lured me in that direction. There must be a block that pivots..."

Serge slapped his forehead. "Of course!" he exclaimed. "I should have thought of that sooner. I remember that while I was searching for you, I felt one of the rocks oscillate under my hand. One push, and I could have come to your aid..."

"Thanks for the intention," the Eccentric replied, "but I'm glad, by Jove that you stayed here. You'd only have succeeded is getting yourself caught, and Anna would have been alone—a fine thing you'd have achieved!"

"That's true," Serge murmured. "It's better that I didn't find the issue."

The young people talked further about the dwarfs, the world they inhabited, their civilization, their mores, asking many questions—but Pickman had recounted almost everything he knew.

"What do you expect me to say?" he replied. "I emptied my knapsack in one go. You're forgetting that I wasn't free down there, and that I only saw what they wanted me or allowed me to see. My principal source of information—I could say the only one—is Tao, and you'll see, when you've had a little more practice, that the damnable fellow isn't easy to decipher at all. What a hard head, God damn it! It's more than patience that's needed, or stubbornness. You can't imagine..."

"Yes, my dear Robinson, I understand the difficulty perfectly—so well that I'm astonished that you've been able to take the deciphering so far in a matter of days. It's a veritable feat, which does as much honor to your sagacity as to your perseverance."

"It's necessary to say," replied Pickman, flattered, "that I had a capital interest; it was a matter of my head...well, of my liberty, at least. Then again, I had nothing else to do. I was like Pellisson with his spider[29]...and one always ends up reaching an understanding.

"That doesn't affect the fact that it was a great step forward. We've ended up getting our hands on a Martian, one of those mysterious goblins that were playing tricks on us. What a pity that we can't inform our friends in New York of that."

"Patience—that will come."

"And what a success when we go back," the Eccentric continued. "For we will go back..."

"I'm counting on it."

"Me too, if only to show Tao to the populations of the old world. I can already see myself strolling through the

---

[29] Paul Pellisson was a supporter of the French statesman Nicolas Fouquet; he was imprisoned in the Bastille when Fouquet fell from grace in 1661, during the reign of Louis XIV. The story was subsequently put around—popularized, but not originated by Alexandre Dumas—that while he was there he tamed a spider, teaching it to eat out of his hand when he summoned it by playing the flute. Allegedly, the skeptical governor of the prison, M. de Baisemeaux, demanded a demonstration of the feat, and promptly crushed the spider underfoot.

streets of London with my phenomenon on my arm—what a triumph!"

The three castaways burst out laughing.

"One more thing," the engineer resumed. "You told us just now, my dear Robinson, that the Martians were, in your opinion, semi-savage, only possessing a rudimentary industry. But they have weapons, and fishing tackle?"

"Well, they have weapons—axes, knives, clubs, harpoons—but crudely fashioned. For the rest—household utensils and so on—they seem to be more backward than negroes. No trace among them of any mechanical artistry whatsoever."

"Are you quite sure?" Myrandhal objected. "They must possess tools, and even quite well-tempered tools. Have you forgotten the groove made in the hull of the Annabella?"

"No."

"Then how do you explain it? You said yourself that only a file could have produced such a deep gash."

"I thought so then, but I've changed my mind. It wasn't a file that scored our hull but a stone, a kind of exceedingly hard agate, which the Martians have succeeded in working—I don't know how. They're still in the Age of Polished Stone, you see. However, I believe that the *Houâ* were once more civilized, and that some still exist, elsewhere on the plant, who are less backward than the ones I've had dealings with. The future will tell..."

After this brief digression, the Eccentric told the story of his captivity, which Anna was demanding clamorously.

"I can do so quickly, having not much more to add. As I've told you, when I recovered consciousness I was in an immense underworld—catacombs of a sort extending in all directions—being carried by four dwarfs, russet gnomes of some sort, who were holding me securely. Like gorillas, which they resemble, the *Houâ* are endowed with a prodigious strength.

"Anyway, I wasn't thinking about escaping. On the contrary, I was delighted with the adventure. Finally, I had found the Martians. I'd be able to study them, to interrogate them—

329

and what a sensational interview that would be, as they say! Why the devil hadn't I thought of it sooner? I'd have got myself captured deliberately; it was the best means—the only one.

"The dwarfs weren't numerous: a dozen in all. Behind me came four individuals carrying my things. The first had my rifle, the second my alpenstock, the third my knapsack, and the fourth wasn't carrying anything, as in the song..."

"Pardon me," said Serge, smiling. "So there was light down there?"

"It wasn't bright, no, but it wasn't pitch dark either. Once the eyes got accustomed to it, one could make things out well enough. Imagine a very diffuse gray light. Where it comes from I don't know. In my opinion, it's the subsoil itself, the rock, that's luminous—radiant. Who knows? Perhaps I've discovered a radium mine. At ten thousand francs a centigram, the latest price in London, you can see what that represents. Anyway, rare metals and precious stones are abundant down there, particularly diamonds. Look, my dear ward, here are some I brought for you."

With a negligent gesture, the Englishman threw a handful of diamonds as large as pigeon's eggs on to the tablecloth.

"I found these stones on the ground. The *Houâ* make use of them to play knucklebones." Without taking any notice of his listeners' admiring exclamations, the Eccentric continued: "To think, my dear Anna, that back there, in the Far West, your father, old Allan, is breaking his back looking for nuggets, when we can get them here simply by bending down.

"With that, I'll continue my story. I mentioned the heat that reigns down there. It's something you really can't understand unless you've experienced it. As for me, I was melting, literally streaming. I even think, by Jove, that I fainted a time or two, like some little miss.

"The Martians, who didn't want me dead—I'd observed that right away, and this was one more proof of it—must have been worried that I might die in their hands. They carried me to the far end of the underworld, into a cooler grotto...less fiery, I mean, for I sweated there afterwards, but at first, I experienced a veritable wellbeing, an immense relief—that's the right word.

"There, the Martians set about examining me, feeling me all over. Evidently, I astonished them. It was my shoulders that intrigued them most, especially my shoulder-blades. I thought that, having seen us fall from the sky, they'd imagined that I was hiding wings under my jacket, and wanted to make sure of it. Perhaps, too—although the idea didn't occur to me until later—they took me for a cousin of one of the *Zoa* they fear so much.

"Then the other Houâ left and I remained alone with Tao, who was in charge of guarding me, I immediately started trying to enter into communication with my jailer, but he didn't want to hear anything. The understanding didn't make any progress that day.

"In the evening, Tao brought me a fish cooked under ashes, a sort of haddock, but much larger, and a gourd full of water. The gourd—made, so far as I could judge, from the swim-bladder of a fish—didn't seem appetizing, but the water was fresh and I was dying of thirst in that sweat-room. There was no cutlery either, but I scarcely gave that a thought. I was hungry and thirsty. I swallowed it all and became drowsy afterwards, like a boa digesting its meal.

"I was woken up some time later by Stop licking my face. Tao had gone to find him while I was asleep. That was a good sign. I thought that my jailer was softening, and I immediately began making signs to him, a host of gestures. A waste of effort; it was as if I were singing. The gnome remained as deaf and dumb as a corner-stone. I was seething with rage, God damn it.

"Finally, I lost patience, and headed for the exit as if I were going to leave. Then Tao, previously impassive, suddenly woke up. He threw himself in front of me and we stood there, looking at each other, ready to strike. It was a terrible moment. I could see everything going awry...

"Tao—who would believe it, to look at him now?—was bristling, hissing like an angry viper. Then, suddenly, he beat a retreat, as he did just now, before Anna. It was then that I heard the word *Zoa* for the first time. Tao was trembling, avoiding my gaze.

"Then I understood that there's something in our eyes— in the human gaze—that intimidates these brutes and tames them. From then on, the game was won. It was no longer a jailer that I had but a domestic, a houseboy.

"Immediately, I tried to strike up a conversation with him, but it still didn't work, in spite of Tao's willingness, and the days went by...

"Since my arrival down there I'd only had one idea: to get back, if not my weapons, my knapsack, and my telephone, which would permit me to reassure you. But Tao didn't understand, or perhaps didn't want to understand. He was afraid of the other Martians, and doubtless afraid of me too.

"He understood perfectly well that I wanted to escape, but the revolver shot I'd fired on the moraine had struck his imagination. He must have figured that if I had possession of my knapsack I'd open fire again, out of malice, killing him and the others, exterminating them all.

"It was necessary to put his mind at rest, to win him over with kind treatment and caresses. Finally, this morning, he gave in. Since then, everything has gone like clockwork. Tao, who was in fear of the consequences of his action, was even keener to get away than I was, and watched for an opportunity.

"Soon—it was exactly one-thirty by my watch—he came to me joyfully to say that the dwarfs, who had been prowling around when we were on the telephone, had just left. The way was free and we left at the double.

"After having run for a long time, I saw a red light in the distance, at the end of a sort of tunnel—it was the setting sun. I hadn't seen it for two weeks, and it had quite an effect on me, God damn it. I launched forward. Finally, as night was falling, we came out on to the lava through a natural fissure.

"Three hours later, I was here."

"Do you think that the Martians are pursuing you?" asked the engineer.

"No—but we'd do well not to wait for them. If you want my advice, we should lift anchor at daybreak."

"I'd like nothing better," said Myrandhal. "What surprises me is that you're in such a hurry. Is there a danger, perhaps? Do you think that the Martians might launch a direct attack?"

"I doubt it—but Tao seems much less confident. He's convinced that his brethren will try to get him back. Better not to run the risk, and to set sail for other climes. We have no more to do here, in any case. We know what we wanted to know; we have an interpreter and a guide who will be useful in going elsewhere. Don't you think so, Monsieur Myrandhal?"

"Yes, I always have. One thing astonishes me, though, and that's your haste to raise anchor. This might be the moment, it seems to me, to study these Martian a little—these *Houâ*, whom we've had so much difficulty discovering..."

"We'll find Martians elsewhere," the Eccentric interjected, "and more civilized ones. Those hereabouts are brutes, from which we won't get anything more. In sum, I'm in haste to go elsewhere to see what happens. Ever since Tao told me about these marvelous *Zoa*, I've been dreaming about them night and day. I've sworn to discover them, if any remain, to take one of those strange beings, who have wings on their backs such as one sees in paintings, back to London—and I've just proved that I keep my word! It's a matter of arriving in time; so, let's go, let's flee—the sooner the better, as you repeated yourself not long ago. Don't you agree, my dear Anna?"

"Entirely. I only want one thing: to get away from this place."

So, a few hours later, at dawn, the *Velox*, followed by the *Annabella*, emerged from Port Burrett and set a course southwards.

In the open sea the wind was blowing from the east, throwing the waves against the *Velox*'s flank and causing her to pitch and roll terribly.

The first hour of navigation in the small vessels were difficult, but towards evening the swell eased, and the passengers could get their breath back. The wind had dropped, and the voyage seemed to offer fortunate auspices.

XIII. Diving

From then on, the navigation continued without incident. The sea was as calm as a mirror.

While her husband and her guardian took turns on the captain's bridge, Madame Myrandhal, in order to occupy her leisure, tried to educate Tao, who still remained a trifle unsociable.

Renouncing any attempt to master the inextricable *Houâ* language, she set out to teach him English, by means of a new and eminently practical method invented by an American pedagogue, and, in spite of Pickman's contrary prognostication, the Martian made evident progress.

After a few days, Tao possessed a hundred words, and was beginning to make himself understood—although his brain, of course, remained refractory to certain abstract ideas.

Meanwhile, the temperature became rapidly milder. They sensed that they were arriving in a kinder climate, in a warm, animated region. As early as the second evening, the Eccentric claimed to have seen a seagull, or something very similar. At any rate, fish were beginning to show themselves, and were not very shy. They danced in the submarines' wakes. Tao caught several in his hands, which he ate raw.

Armed only with his cap, the Eccentric fished out a dozen of them, which were fried, but the dish was not a success. The flesh was tough, the odor nauseating, and Pickman was the only one who ate them.

Myrandhal had announced that at her average speed, the *Velox* would take five days to cover the distance of approximately three thousand kilometers separating the polar circle from the tropic of Aquarius, but he soon observed a significant acceleration.

"We must have encountered a current," he said. "At the moment we're making more than thirty kilometers and hour, which is half a Martian degree. You know that the Martian degree measures scarcely sixty kilometers."

In fact, on the evening of the fourth day, the engineer, having calculated their position, announced that they had crossed the tropic.

"All right!" said Pickman. "If we continue at this rate, we'll have passed the equator in a week and we'll be at the south pole by the end of the month. Except that there's no rush. First, I'd like to take a look at one of the lands of Cockayne that exist in these parts, according to Tao."

"Yes," said Serge, "but it's a matter of finding them, and our maps leave a great deal to be desired. Nevertheless, we have land to the east, which can't be anything except Copernicus, the largest continent on Mars. I'll take us closer to it."

From that moment on, the captain of the *Velox* redoubled his attention. Constant vigilance was necessary in those unknown seas, the reefs of which had never been identified by any geographer or pilot. However, the Eccentric lent Serge his devoted collaboration, and alternated shifts of that tedious sentry duty with him.

The engineer was carrying out a minor repair in the engine room when he heard Pickman's voice ring out from the central porthole, where he was on watch. The engineer ran to him.

"Land! Land!" cried the Eccentric, brandishing the marine telescope with which he was equipped in broad gestures.

Annabella had also come running, and even Tao, who remained timidly behind her.

The three explorers observed, with an indescribable emotion, the presence of a long somber strip above the horizon.

"It can only be the continent of Copernicus," said the engineer solemnly. We're finally going to see the habitable region of the planet. We've finished with the icy deserts of the polar region, and arrived at the magnificence of the tropics.

Their impatience was so great that Serge Myrandhal, ordinarily so economical with his motive force, could not resist the temptation to increase their speed.

Hour by hour, as they drew nearer, the details of the continent emerged more clearly. The marine telescope was passed from hand to hand, and already, thick masses of vegetation could be made out, which had to be forests of gigantic plants. They were ornamented, to the extent that the distance permitted assessment, by the richest colors of yellow, orange and red, as certain terrestrial forests are in autumn.

"It seems to me," said the Eccentric, "that I saw a flock of white birds rise up just now."

Serge Myrandhal and Annabella, looked in the same direction, but could not see anything. As usual, the eccentric's imagination was slightly in advance of events.

The aspect of the ocean had modified along with that of the horizon. The waters were encumbered by an inextricable tangle of marine plants analogous, or very nearly so, to *Fucus natans*, which sometimes grows to several hundred meters in length, to the "tropical grape" and other gigantic wracks of the terrestrial oceans.

All of these algae, some of which produced enormous corollas or fruits disposed in yellow or violet clusters, were iridescent with all the colors of the spectrum. Some of them were indented like acanthias, dark red in color with pink veins; others, similar to clumps of rhubarb or broad-leafed bananas, were bright yellow or pale green. Yet others, blue-black with silvery-white veins, displayed the complicated and fantastic indentations of certain German illuminated manuscripts of the Middle Ages.

Annabella never tired of admiring them. She would certainly have started a herbal, and regretted that the time was lacking to complete a collection of them.

That submarine forest had, in places, the emerald green color of spring forests, and little golden fish were wriggling there in millions. Nor was that the only manifestation of animal life. Crustaceans, blue or pink, were crawling under the foliage and using their pincers to crush small oval mollusks attached in clusters to the fucus stalks. There were other mol-

337

lusks, and vast jellyfish with transparent gelatinous bodies, whose bells were dappled with the colors of the spectrum.

"In sum," the engineer explained, "this garden of enormous wracks offers many analogies with the Sargasso Sea, well known to all mariners who have crossed the Atlantic. In the same way, it's a dead area, a lake of tranquil water in the midst of currents. There, all the wrecks, all the alluvia and all the debris carried by the waves comes together and piles up, thus favoring this opulent submarine vegetation, which doubtless reserves for out descendants, when the oil wells have run dry, incalculable stocks of carbon, and also of soda, phosphate and iodine."

"Where does the name Sargasso Sea come from?" asked the Eccentric.

"It comes from a Spanish word meaning *floating seaweed*. It's the name that the companions of Christopher Columbus gave it, who spent three long weeks traversing those floating prairies. I can easily form an idea of the difficulties they must have encountered. Since we came into this marine marsh of sorts, I've been obliged to take a host of precautions In spite of the impatience that I'm in, as you are, to reach the shore, I'll certainly be obliged to reduce speed to a minimum..."

Annabella interrupted abruptly. "Look there!" she murmured, with a fearful gesture.

Serge Myrandhal and the Eccentric looked in the direction indicated, and perceived a hideous animal moving placidly, just under the surface, among the stems of wrack. Yellowish in color, it was almost entirely composed of an enormous mouth, which opened and closed continuously, in an almost automatic fashion. The body was non-existent, so to speak; the caudal fin commenced almost immediately after the jaw, which was surmounted by two white eyes, protruding and globular.

"What is that monster?" asked the young woman, trembling. "No creature as frightful exists on Earth."

"You're mistaken," said the engineer, smiling. "That fish, which is certain far from being beautiful, possesses certain structural details analogous to an Earthly relative, *Eurypharynx*, recently discovered—in the Sargasso Sea—by the scientific expedition of the *Talisman*.[30] It's inoffensive, however, feeding exclusively on mollusks."

"I'm reassured. What if we tried to catch it…?"

As if it understood the danger it was in, however, the eurypharynx had just dived down to the sea-bed.

They continued to advance at a prudent pace. The marine fauna revealed an extraordinary richness, offering species that only presented a distant analogy with Earthly species. Serge Myrandhal noticed, in passing, spiny fish furnished with fantastic fins, which left the inventions of Japanese artists, although fecund, far behind. There were fish reminiscent of blackfish, seahorses and moonfish, turtles with large fins and thin necks, like those of snakes. Thus far, however, apart from two bizarre varieties of sharks with red-striped black bodies, the travelers had not seen any animal capable of doing them serious harm.

It was only toward evening that Pickman, who was on watch, witnessed a submarine drama that gave him cause to reflect. He first perceived, lying on the giant wracks, a crustacean of considerable dimensions. With its spiny triangular carapace and its enormous legs, it was reminiscent of the sea-spider, but it measured at least one and a half meters over the broadest part of its carapace, and was a dark pink color. The animal, however redoubtable it appeared, seemed to be trembling, frightened and ill.

Pickman obtained an explanation of that attitude when he saw the debris of a mollusk shell floating some distance away. He was not unaware that the majority of crustaceans change

---

[30] *Eurypharynx pelicanoides*, the "pelican eel", was discovered in 1882 by the zoologist Léon Vaillant, who undertook four scientific expeditions in the *Talisman* between 1880 and 1883.

their shell once a year, not unlike certain reptiles. The former armor is detached of its own accord, and until the new vestment has had the time to harden and become saturated with calcareous molecules, the animal is exhausted by fatigue, ill and at the mercy of its enemies. Such was certainly the state of the giant crab sprawled amid the wrack.

Suddenly, Pickman saw the animal shiver and attempt to flee. It did not have time. A kind of fleshy arm emerged from beneath the foliage and circled around the crab with the flexibility of a snake. A second, and then a third arm succeeded in immobilizing it. The animal was shaken by a convulsion of agony and disappeared, dragged away by the trunks that had enlaced it.

The Eccentric did not say anything about what he had seen to his ward, but he thought it as well to inform the engineer.

"The crustacean whose tragic end you have just witnessed," Serge explained, "was the victim of an animal of the cephalopod tribe, to which the squid and octopus belong. But if it has attained the dimensions that its suckers indicate, it must be a prodigious monster, a Martian realization of the kraken of the Middle Ages, which, according to legend, seized sizeable vessels with its tentacles and dragged them down to the bottom of the sea."

"It wouldn't be pleasant to have to deal with such a creature..."

"I don't know whether a cephalopod could cause us serious damage, but this unknown ocean might contain other monsters, more redoubtable from our viewpoint. A swordfish, for example, armed with a solid ivory spike, which might take it into its head to pierce our hull. You're not unaware that examples of that circumstance have been cited."

"It would require one of considerable dimensions."

"Undoubtedly but I intend to be ready for anything. These depths might enclose other apocalyptic fish. I shall, at any rate, set up my torpedo-launcher. A place to install it has been reserved for it in the engine-room. I only have a few plates and bolts to screw in."

Pickman approved of the engineer's prudent resolution, and the latter immediately set to work. Before darkness fell, the torpedo tube was in place and ready for use.

The night passed without the slightest incident.

The temperature was admirably mild; the breeze brought perfumed effluvia from the distant shore of the mysterious continent, and the eccentric claimed that he could already discern the odor of magnolias and orange-trees.

The next day they resumed their progress through the submarine flower-bed, which continued to deploy all the splendors of its iridescent multicolored flowers like a magical robe.

Toward mid-morning, Pickman, who had completed his watch, came down to eat breakfast, and was replaced by the engineer, who had preceded him at the table.

Serge Myrandhal had only been at his post for a few minutes when he uttered an exclamation of annoyance. It seemed to him that the submarine was no longer moving forward.

He was not mistaken; the *Velox* was now still, completely immobilized amid the fantastic vegetation.

The engineer ran to the engine-room. The propeller, trapped in an inextricable tangle of wrack and other algae, was no longer rotating. Serge tried putting the engine in reverse, but only tightened the knots that were paralyzing the locomotive apparatus of the submarine. The stout plants, as elastic as rubber and as viscous as glue, offered an extraordinary resistance.

It was necessary to find a means of obviating the situation, which might lead to dire consequences,

Serge went to warn Pickman and Annabella, but neither of them could think of an expedient right away.

"We can't stay here, though," the Eccentric repeated, impatiently. "We have to find a way."

"I can only see one," said Serge, having reflected for some time, "and I'm not absolutely certain that it will be effective. I can make a kind of scythe, with the aid of a long bamboo pole and a sharpened saber. Then I can climb into one of the dinghies and scythe the marine weeds all around the propeller."

Annabella clapped her hands and looked at her husband admiringly. "I wouldn't have thought of that," she murmured, "but you're never confounded!"

The engineer's idea was, moreover, a complete success. The improvised scythe worked marvelously, and after an hour's work, the propeller began to rotate again.

Unfortunately, in that impenetrable thicket, it was to be feared that the same accident might recur frequently.

Serge decided not to leave the engine room for the rest of the day, but it was written that a series of natural events would occur that would defeat all his anticipations.

Scarcely an hour had passed since the propeller had been freed than the vessel ran into a veritable submarine jungle. Algae as stout as tree-trunks formed a dense thicket, rendered more impenetrable by the vast sticky foliage; one might as well have tried to traverse a rampart formed of rubber balls.

It was then that Serge congratulated himself on having brought a provision of powerful explosives. With the aid of a large cartridge of dynamite, he would try to blast a way through. If the submarine forest did not extend too far, he had a good change of opening a passage; otherwise, it would be necessary to go backwards and delay the time of landing even further.

The dispositions were rapidly made; after a few maneuvers, the *Velox* was positioned at the place where the algae seemed least dense. Serge Myrandhal then launched the cartridge, equipped with a special detonator.

The explosion was due to take place after a lapse of seven minutes. The engineer hastened to put that interval to good use, moving the vessel backwards and sheltering her as much as possible from the blast.

With one hand on the tiller, he held his chronometer in the other. Annabella and the Eccentric watched through one of the portholes.

At the precise moment when the chronometer ticked the sixtieth second of the seventh minute, a muffled detonation was heard; the *Velox* was shaken violently, and a long jet of water and foam shot up above the algal forest.

The sea was covered with the debris of crushed, torn and shredded plants, alongside which myriads of fish killed by the explosion were floating belly-up.

The passage was clear; a broad channel, cleared of all gigantic vegetation, extended ahead of the submarine.

"Hurrah!" cried the Eccentric.

"Hurrah!" repeated the young woman—and launched herself toward the stairway to the conning-tower, followed by Tao, who never left her.

Scarcely had they reached it, however, than a frightful roar was heard, comparable to the sound of a steam siren.

The little Martian came back down to the compartment precipitately, and hid under the table, uttering inarticulate cries.

Serge Myrandhal had launched himself toward the conning-tower in his turn. "What is it?" he asked Annabella.

Slightly pale, the young woman showed him, a few cables from the submarine, a deformed head with a blood-red crest, emerging from a monstrous body.

"I don't know what that frightful beast is," he murmured, "but go back down quickly. We need to get way, to dive."

The young woman obeyed, and Serge hastened to seal the hatch with a feverish hand.

As he came back down in his turn he bumped into the Eccentric, who was running in a panic, furious at not having seen anything. They both went back into the compartment.

"No more frightful vision was ever offered to me," the engineer murmured. "It's possible that we're in the presence of a relative of the ichthyosaur, some giant animal of prehistoric times."

"What are we going to do?" asked Pickman.

"Dive first. I hope that we can get away from it, thanks to the marine plants..."

The engineer had run toward the engine room.

"Undoubtedly," the young woman explained, still very emotional, while the submarine was slowly immersed, "the leviathan was frightened by the explosion of the dynamite."

"With all that, I haven't seen it," grumbled Pickman. "I'm decidedly out of luck!"

"As long you don't see it at closer range than you'd like," said the engineer, coming out of the engine room. "I couldn't see anything through the porthole. In a little while, we'll go back up; it would be the greatest imprudence to go down to extreme depths. We'd run the risk of getting entangled in the algae without ever being able to get free..."

The engineer had already gone back to his machines. A few minutes later, the *Velox* resurfaced. At the same time, taking advantage of the channel that had opened before her, the submarine speeded up.

"This time," I think," the Eccentric said, "the monster has lost track of us."

Serge Myrandhal shook his head. "No," he said. "I'm almost certain that it's following us. Can't you hear something like the sound of flippers, like a loud splashing?"

All three hastened to the aft portholes.

Serge had guessed correctly. The monster was there; its hideous red-crested head, about the size of a elephant's, was looming up a short distance from the *Annabella*, above a sinuous neck as thick as a ship's mast. More than fifteen meters away, a scaly tail was thrashing the waves noisily.

"But that's a sea-serpent!" exclaimed Serge. "Our lives are at the mercy of that monster..."

The engineer fell silent. All three waited, their hearts gripped by a horrible anguish.

Serge thought then of diving gain. But what was the point? A battle with the leviathan in the submarine depths would be even more terrible than on the surface.

At that moment, the monster's crest dipped; it rushed furiously at the hull of the *Annabella*. There was a metallic shriek, as the teeth of the sea-serpent tried in vain to bite through the polished surface.

Then, all of a sudden, the same roar was heard. The towrope that attached the *Annabella* to the *Velox* broke like a thread of cotton, and the smaller submarine, launched into the air, fell back, broken, an enormous distance away.

The *Velox* was rudely shaken by the reaction to the breaking of the cable.

"The torpedo!" cried Serge, who had lost his balance because of the shock. "It's our only hope! It'll come after us now."

The engineer had hurled himself toward the engine-room. The *Velox* swerved sideways in order to present the mouth of the torpedo-tube to the enemy...

But it was too late.

With lightning rapidity, the sea serpent stretched its long sinuous body like a bowstring, and coiled around the submarine.

"We're doomed!" cried the engineer.

Already, the monster was diving with its prey. Dragged down into the depths, the *Velox* plunged. The passengers saw the light dwindling rapidly. Through the upper porthole, the sun could still be seen for some time, like a red patch, but then it was extinguished.

There was darkness...

XIV. The Leviathan's Cavern

The passengers had the frightful sensation akin to that of a lamb carried away in a vulture's claws in order to be devoured at leisure.

For a second, Serge had a vision of some submarine gulf pullulating with similar monsters, in which the *Velox* would be crushed like a nut against the rocks.

In the darkness he felt Annabella's hand squeezing his own.

"Most of all," said the eccentric, whose calm voice sounded lugubrious in the darkness, "we need light."

"Yes," stammered the engineer. "Let's all go into the central compartment. There, we'll see."

Serge Myrandhal's voice was strangled by a profound emotion—not that he feared for himself, but the idea of the superhuman danger to which his beloved wife was exposed was unbearable.

It was not without difficulty that they were able to reach the compartment; the *Velox* was still being jolted by the somersaults performed by the monster as it dragged them away in a frenetic rage; they were obliged to crawl, supporting themselves on the furniture and the walls.

Serge succeeded in reaching the commutator. "Finally, we'll be able to see," he murmured.

There was a momentary silence.

"Well?" demanded the young woman, in anguish.

Serge Myrandhal made no reply.

"Light, in the name of Heaven!" shouted the Eccentric.

"The commutator is no longer working," the engineer finally replied, in a somber tone.

No one responded to that despairing statement. In the silence, heavy with anguish, they could distinctly hear the monster's tail thrashing the waves, and the friction of its scales against the metal of the hull, around which it was wound in a spiral and which it was continuing to drag at vertiginous speed.

The Eccentric struck a match.

For a few seconds, its light illuminated the pale and consternated faces of the three explorers. Suddenly, however, the flaming wax escaped Pickman's trembling fingers, and he uttered an exclamation of amazement.

Abruptly, without transition, the entire compartment had just lit up with a soft pale green phosphorescent glow. One might have thought that all the walls and all the furniture were coated with phosphorus, illuminated by thousands of glow-worms.

They all turned toward the crystal of the porthole, from which that fantastic illumination was coming.

A unanimous cry of surprise and fear emerged from their mouths.

It was the sea-serpent, the hideous face of which was stuck to the glass, that was emitting the macabre light. It was the globes of its eyes, twelve centimeters in diameter, like two balls of fire, that were radiating the luminous effluvia.

The profound holes of its nostrils gave it the appearance of a death's-head, and the gaping mouth, garnished with conical teeth, was hideously agape.

The monster stared at the three motionless friends, paralyzed by a supernatural terror.

At that moment, its jagged crest was swollen with blood, and a kind of uninterrupted whistle was escaping from its immeasurable throat.

Annabella looked away; she sensed that contemplating that horrible vision even for a few seconds might drive her insane and strike her dead with horror.

Serge Myrandhal wondered, with terror, whether the crystal of the porthole had the strength to resist that terrible pressure.

Crystal, it is true, is an exceedingly resistant substance; in recent experiments in fishing by means of electric light carried out in the North Sea, plates of that material only seven millimeters thick were seen to resist a pressure of more than fifteen atmospheres, although they allowed the passage of powerful calorific rays. Now, the portholes of the *Velox*, solidly embedded in their metallic armatures, were twenty times as thick. Serge Myrandhal knew that, but he was not unaware that crystal, so resistant to pressure, is also extremely brittle. An abrupt flick of the serpent's jaw, the impact of a single one of those conical teeth, might shatter the porthole to smithereens.

Fortunately, that mode of attack did not enter into the monster's plans—for the moment, at least. It stared.

It seemed to have been calmed temporarily by the expenditure of nervous fluid required by the emission of luminous rays from its pupils, from which two broad beams of that strange pale green light continued to emerge, as if projected by powerful reflectors.

Once he had overcome his initial and perfectly comprehensible terror, the Eccentric looked at the enemy with veritable admiration; he searched within himself for some means of attacking it, of becoming the chevalier Gozon relative to this other dragon.[31]

All these sentiments had succeeded one another in the souls of the three explorers with lightning rapidity. Meanwhile, the submarine's jolts had ceased. Still surrounded by the serpent, now calm, the vessel shot through the darkness like an arrow, drawn by a rapid current.

Suddenly, however, the fulgurant pupils were extinguished; the *Velox* oscillated momentarily, and then became motionless. The bellowing of the monster resounded, more

---

[31] Dieudonné de Gozon was the Grand Master of the Knights of Rhodes in the mid-14th century. He was credited by legend (long after his death) with having killed a dragon that emerged repeatedly from a swamp to prey on the livestock of the island's farmers. The story was repopularized in the modern Romantic era by a ballad by Schiller.

terribly than ever and more sonorous, as if reverberated by an echo.

"One might think that it were fleeing..." stammered Serge Myrandhal, bewildered.

The engineer did not finish the thought; the electric light bulbs had lit up again, simultaneously, and everyone uttered a sigh of relief.

"I knew that my apparatus couldn't have failed like that—instantaneously, so to speak—without a reason," murmured the engineer. "How was it that the presence of the monster as sufficient to disturb the mechanism of the sources of electric energy so profoundly? That's a phenomenon I can't explain." He reflected momentarily, and added: "Unless the leviathan is organized in the fashion of certain electric fish, like the electric eel. I need to found out..."

Evidently, in the midst of the most redoubtable peril, the engineer was still haunted by the spirit of scientific research, the noble ambition of discovering the truth. Almost immediately, however, other preoccupations reclaimed him.

"We're floating!" exclaimed the American. "One might think that we were floating!"

"That doesn't surprise me," the Eccentric replied. "I took account of the fact that, after being taken down to a great depth, we progressed almost in a straight line, horizontally, to rise up again afterwards in a very evident perpendicular fashion. The schema of our trajectory could be represented diagrammatically by a capital letter U. At any rate, we're floating."

"That's impossible," said the engineer. "It was broad daylight when the monster dragged us down to the sea-bed, scarcely a quarter of an hour ago. It's still dark."

"Perhaps we're in cavern," Pickman replied. While speaking, he ran toward the conning-tower, soon followed by Serge and Annabella.

"That's it," Pickman went on. "We're in a submarine cavern where the *Velox* is floating in calm water...but what a cavern!"

Serge and Anna looked, and were overwhelmed by admiration.

Above dark waters an immense vault was rounded out, supported at intervals by natural columns, so high that its summit was lost in the darkness. From that summit, masses of stalactites descended, of a boldness and lightness to discourage the most audacious of Gothic architects. There were arcades, pendants and roseate stone flower-formations that sometimes launched forth from a stem that seemed as thin as a thread to blossom into a cluster of arabesques. And the entirety of that décor, worthy of a genies' palace, carved in an unknown crystal and brightly lit by the *Velox*'s electric searchlights, was sparkling with all the colors of the spectrum.

It was a petrified firework display, an indescribable wizardry of color and light. No spectacle more marvelous had ever struck an explorer's gaze.

In the somber mirror of the waters, the colonnades, domes and frontons were reflected infinitely with fantastic clarity. The *Velox*, suspended, as it were, between heaven and earth, seemed to occupy the center of a gigantic luminous fountain, a Niagara of flamboyant gemstones falling silently from unknown heavens.

After the first moment devoted to admiration, Serge Myrandhal found his voice. "Evidently," he said, "it's by means of a subterranean—or, rather, submarine—channel that the serpent dragged us into this splendid grotto, which is its lair."

"Are you sure of that?" asked the Eccentric.

"Look!" With his hand, the engineer pointed at a mass of gigantic bones in a cleft in the gloom.

"But in that case, I can't explain why it has disappeared."

"We'll explain it later," said Serge, curtly. "We need to begin by putting ourselves out of its reach. Look at that pale patch in the depths of that long dark corridor: that way lies salvation. That patch is distant daylight, shining at the entrance of the cavern.

"Let's not wait for the horrible beast to come back. I'm going to check the condition of the engines and the propeller right away."

The engineer ran to the engine room. A moment later, the dynamos purred, and the *Velox* moved slowly beneath the sparkling vaults, leaving a wake behind her dusted with diamonds and shimmering nacre.

As the submarine moved forward, the distant patch of external light became clearer and brighter, eventually causing the electric lights to pale.

Suddenly, however, Annabella screamed. "There it is!" she stammered, mad with terror. "It hasn't gone. It's blocking the passage...we're doomed!"

A cable away from the *Velox*, the sea serpent raised its neck once again, curved like that of a swan. They were able to make out the gills to the right and left of the head, which formed a sort of hideous bloody collar.

The engineer went pale. "It's playing with us like a cat with a mouse," he murmured. "It thinks it has us, but this time, we have its measure..."

The sea-serpent was no more than half a cable away. The coils of its vast body were writhing in the water.

Serge Myrandhal had seized the handle of the commutator controlling the torpedo-tube. He took careful aim at the monster's head. His heart was beating forcefully, but his hand did not tremble while he gradually adjusted the apparatus.

The engineer summoned up all his composure and all his energy. He knew that a single instant, a single gesture of distraction or weakness, would mean the most horrible of deaths for himself and those he loved.

Chilled by fear, Pickman and Anna remained motionless, not daring even to look up at Serge Myrandhal, dreading that they might distract him.

The sea-serpent was still advancing. One might have thought that it was sure of its victory, so prudent were its slow movements. Its behavior contrasted completely with the abruptness of its initial attack. They sensed that here, in the cavern, it believed that it was at home; doubtless none of the prey that it had succeeded in dragging in here had ever got out again. Thus, it was putting leisure and reflection, so to speak, into its fashion of approaching the *Velox*.

Now, it was no more than ten meters away.

His forehead bathed by cold sweat, Serge Myrandhal took account of the fact that he was doomed if, for some reason, the torpedo did not fire, or if it slid obliquely along the scaly armor. He had to strike it full on. The engineer had only waited so long in order to be sure of his aim.

Ten seconds—ten centuries—went by.

The leviathan, raising itself out of the water, was almost touching the hull of the *Velox*. Its vile mouth descended slowly toward the *Velox*'s searchlight, which it doubtless mistook for its enemy's eye, and with whose glare it seemed to want to match with the phosphorescence of its own eyes.

Serge pressed downwards.

The shot departed, causing a column of water to spring up, unleashing a rumble of thunder beneath the vaults. A big wave threw the *Velox* backwards with an irresistible violence.

Serge, Anna and Pickman remained inert, white with terror.

The engineer was the first to stiffen himself against the fear and look out. Through the smoke and water vapor that was slowly dissipating, the shattered and still phosphorescent head of the leviathan appeared, floating a few meters away from the *Velox*. Further away, the body extended, thrashing the waves and the walls of rock in a supreme convulsion.

XV. Eden

The sea-serpent, so fortunately exterminated, might not have been alone. Contrary to the opinion of the Eccentric, who would have liked to study the debris and bring back at least a fragment of its epidermis, covered with overlapping scales and coated with calcareous concretions, Serge Myrandhal increased the speed of the propeller.

Traveling rapidly through the blood-stained water, the *Velox* soon went though the rocky portico that gave access to the open sea.

Warm sunlight was playing on the clear water, which was no longer obstructed by the clustered vegetation of arborescent algae.

Only then were the explorers able to take account of the configuration of the cavern from which they had emerged.

Externally, it offered the aspect of a massive block composed of a brilliantly reflective quartz-like rock, extending for no less than a kilometer in its greatest width. The monster had chosen its lair admirable in that hollowed-out reef, whose two exits gave it complete security.

"It was a veritable stroke of luck that we were able to escape that ferocious specimen of the Martian fauna," the Eccentric murmured.

"That luck was due in large part to the cool head of our captain," said Ana, looking at her husband tenderly.

Serge's only reply was to hug his young wife to his heart, emotionally.

Pickman had taken hold of the marine telescope and as exploring the horizon, where land appeared in the form of a long violet strip, strewn at intervals with large patches of a dazzling whiteness.

It was toward the most apparent—and consequently the closest—of those patches that Serge Myrandhal steered the *Velox*.

As in certain regions of the tropics—in the gulf of Mexico, for example, where the sea-bed is clearly visible in spite of fifty meters of water—the sea was admirably limpid, and its surface was as flat as that of a lake of oil.

On the emerald green velvety carpet of the submarine meadows, giant turtles with shiny carapaces were moving tranquilly among shoals of pink fish with silvery undersides.

"In a few hours," said the engineer, who was more emotional than he wanted to appear, we'll finally make the acquaintance of the living regions of Mars, the palpitating heart of the planet...

"Are we going to land in an Australia or a Florida, a land still virgin of the scars and devastations of human labor? Are we, on the contrary, going to find the ruins of giant cities like London and Paris, the vestiges of an unknown civilization?"

"Perhaps we'll find nothing at all," murmured the Eccentric, always prompt in contradiction. "And in truth, I wouldn't be sorry."

"I'd like to settle the matter as soon as possible," said Annabella, looking at her husband.

Serge Myrandhal was smiling. "Which means, my dear Anna," he replied, "that the *Velox* isn't traveling fast enough for your liking, and that I'm invited to accelerate her speed?"

Annabella nodded her head affirmatively.

Serge, who now knew that, once ashore, he was almost certain of being able to renew his supplies of electrical energy easily, complied with his young wife's desire. The metallic spindle of the submarine hastened at redoubled velocity toward the anticipated continent.

The contours of the still-distant landscape became more distinct. The white area toward with the engineer had orientated his rudder was magnified, seemingly advancing to meet the *Velox*.

Soon, the explorers made out a majestic promontory, beyond which a bay of grandiose aspect curved. The entire landscape seemed to be tinted with the pastel shades of watercolors; pale pink, bright yellow and pale blue were dominant there. The chalky cliff that formed the cape was crowned by a ruined construction entirely built in large blocks of white marble. Like the ancient tower erected at the entrance to the port of Alexandria, it was formed of several open stages surrounded by balustrades, retreating from one another.

Red mosses and golden creepers, however, covered the crumbling edifice with a sumptuous mantle.

"We're doubtless in the presence of a lighthouse that became useless and was abandoned," the engineer conjectured. "It's evident proof of a Martian civilization. A modern architect wouldn't have chosen to build a 'fire-tower' in any other location than the cape that dominates the extent of the gulf, which is visible at a great distance..."

Leaving the ruins of the lighthouse to the left, the *Velox*, once she had doubled the promontory, went into the bay, the profound concavity of which formed a near-perfect ellipse. For some time she moved parallel to a low-lying strand where clumps of ruddy thistles grew capriciously among heaps of azure seashells.

The shore was covered with majestic forests surpassing in sumptuousness the most beautiful terrestrial bays—Naples, Rio de Janeiro and various Oceanian bays. Trees of unknown species allowed their lower branches, heavy with flowers and fruits, to hang down all the way to the blue water. Others expanded in vast foliage that left far behind, in terms of dimension, than banana-trees, the talipot palms and the aquatic *Victoria regina* of Australia, whose leaves are several meters in breadth.[32]

Very few of the opulent vegetables, however, were green in color. Their leaves passed through the entire chromatic scale, from the crimson of autumnal cherries to straw and lemon-yellow. Annabella even noticed several clumps of a

---

[32] The *Victoria regina*, as it was then called, was actually native to South America, and is a species of water lily. It is now classified as *Victoria amazonica*.

kind of poplar whose foliage, agitated by a perpetual tremor, was white with a reflective sheen like silk.

Flowering lianas extended between the branches made the forest into an inextricable thicket, which served as a retreat for thousands of radiant birds, like living gems, of all the colors of the rainbow. They showed no fear at the sight of the *Velox*. They watched the submarine pass by a few meters from the shore without quitting the flexible creepers that served them as perches, where they were swinging in hundreds.

Annabella watched this marvelous décor unfold delightedly. "But it's a true terrestrial paradise!" she exclaimed. "It's the Martian Eden. I've never breathed in perfumes sweeter and more intoxicating than those that the breeze is bringing us. And the birdsong! It's truly a divine music! Thus far, I have heard a single one of those disagreeable and unharmonious cries from which the most brilliant terrestrial birds, peacocks and parrots, are not exempt.

"I'm eager to land, in order to pick those flowers."

"A little patience," Serge murmured. "We'll have plenty of time to visit this country at our leisure, which is certainly admirable, but I want to reach the depths of this beautiful gulf, to kind a safe haven for the *Velox*. If we're going to find a port, it's there that Martian logic will have excavated it..."

The *Velox* navigated thus for two hours along the enchanted shore.

Serge Myrandhal was not mistaken in his conjectures. When they rounded a clump of large trees with heart-shaped leaves, constellated with a profusion of white lilies, the shore abruptly curved inwards. The mouth of a vast canal appeared, bordered with white marble quays. It was about thirty meters wide, and it waters were covered with a carpet of aquatic flowers with blue corollas and fleshy leaves of a beautiful bright copper hue.

To the right and the left, tall pylons of the same white marble as the quays and the ruins of the lighthouse supported statues of animals made of an unknown metal, as pale as silver but with a slightly roseate tint.

In spite of the yellow and brown mosses that covered them, and the parasitic plants, it as easy to recognize that the statues in question represented the same leviathan or marine dragon that had attacked the *Velox* a few hours earlier.

"It has the same bizarrely jagged crest," observed Annabella, "the same globular eyes…and the gills displayed in the firm of ruffs, and the hideous mouth paved with conical teeth."

"Perhaps it's the Martians' god?" Pickman joked, laughing.

"I don't think so," said the engineer. "A god would be installed in a temple. These statues seem to me to have been placed there with a simple decorative intention."

"Perhaps," the young woman murmured, pensively, "the monster that almost devoured us is the dragon guarding this Eden, this Garden of the Hesperides?"

"One might think," Serge added, "that we were arriving in a country abandoned centuries ago. I feel a strange emotion in the presence of these majestic ruins. Are we going to encounter the debris of some Martian Palenque or Babylon? This canal obviously connected the sea to a powerful city; it's constructed in such a manner as to admit ships of the largest tonnage…"

"To judge by those lotuses and those splendid water-lilies," said the Eccentric, "it's a long time since anyone sailed along it."

"The *Velox* will sail along it!" proclaimed the engineer, proudly. "We shall find whatever Martian capital it leads to!"

Everyone's curiosity was excited to the highest degree. As they penetrated into the mysterious region, they felt a sort of terror: the kind of sacred apprehension that must have gripped the likes of Columbus and Vasco da Gama at the moment they arrived in new worlds.

For a moment, Serge thought he could make out, lost in the underwater lianas, the profiles of gigantic hulls with elevated prows, rotting there in oblivion, and his ardent imagination evoked the disasters of a Martian armada.

But the vision had already faded.

To the right and the left, the forest continued to deploy the sumptuousness of its rubescent foliage, undulating in a light breeze. At intervals, clearings opened, revealing new perspectives, magical horizons lost in a blue-tinted mist.

"It's a true realm of enchantment," observed the Eccentric. "It seems to me that we'll never arrive anywhere, that the enchanted voyage will continue perpetually between two banks of flowers, for days on end...

"In the meantime, I'm going to go down to eat a slice of corned beef and drink a whisky and soda..."

Pickman had scarcely taken a couple of steps to put his plan into execution, however, when a cry from his ward recalled him precipitately.

"The city!" proclaimed the young woman, excitedly.

The engineer had come running too.

An abrupt bend in the canal had just unveiled a grandiose panorama.

Above the line of the forests, an accumulation of towers, domes and cupolas surmounted by tall obelisks appeared in an aureole of light.

A few towers had collapsed, a few domes were caved in, and many obelisks were broken, but the ensemble had a certain richness and a desperate beauty, and one might have thought it a city built entirely of gemstones and carbuncles.

The three explorers were mute with admiration.

"I'm afraid," said Annabella, "that those radiant cupolas might dissipate in a puff of wind, flying away like a fallacious mirage. Truly, it's too beautiful! It's not possible for it to be true."

"We'll soon find out," said the engineer.

"But what the devil can that architectural style be compared to?" muttered the Eccentric. "Nothing that I know. It's as grandiose and severe as the old palaces of the Pharaohs at Luxor, Thebes and Karnak! It's as sumptuous and florid as Hindu pagodas, as bold as the Gothic, with I don't know what

358

softness and purity in the lines, that I've never seen anywhere else. By Jove! I'm going to take photographs..."

At that moment the *Velox* was only advancing with extreme slowness. The canal suddenly seemed to be barred vertically by a high rampart of rutilant enameled bricks, similar to the *azulejos* with which some rooms of the Alhambra are lined.

"We can't go any further," said the Eccentric. The canal stops here—and in truth, I won't be sorry to set foot on land."

As they got closer, however, the explorers realized that the canal forked to the right and the left, bathing the foot of the ramparts in such a fashion as to form a vast moat round the fortifications.

A section of the waters passed through the wall, beneath a vast portico formed by a single arch, and penetrated the interior of the mysterious city.

Flowering bushes and bizarrely tangled lianas mirrored their foliage and their corollas in the water, as calm as a Venetian glass, making the gateway an admirable thing. After a few moments of reflection, Serge Myrandhal did not hesitate to take the *Velox* through it.

"Judging by everything we can see," he said, "it's evident that we're going into a city that has long been abandoned by its inhabitants."

"Mars really is a dead planet, then," concluded the young woman.

"That doesn't follow. Suppose that a Martian voyager, arriving on Earth, disembarked in the ruins of Ellora or the devastated streets of Timgad, or near the still-existent vestiges of the Inca cities of the Peruvian uplands. Should he conclude that the planet was uninhabited because he'd found a desert region to begin with?"

"Anyway," said Annabella, "there's one Martian, already!" And she pointed at Tao, who, completely recovered from his terrors, was actively occupied in polishing the Eccentric's boots.

"There must be others," murmured the engineer. "It certainly wasn't beings of such rudimentary intelligence that raised these magnificent edifices skywards..."

A quarter of an hour had not gone by when the submarine entered the waters of a vast oval basin: a true Martian Venice bordered by palaces and trees. It was there that the canal finally ended, and Serge conjectured, with some plausibility, that, judging by the luxury employed in its construction, the port must have be served for the exclusive use of royal ships and barges in times that were doubtless not so very distant.

In the center, on a sort of islet, an elegant tower—partly ruined, like everything else—recalled, by virtue of the disposition of its columnar stages, the lighthouse they had perceived on the summit of the promontory.

Obedient to her tiller, the *Velox* came alongside the steps of a jetty, which Serge recognized as being entirely constructed in a kind of lapis-lazuli, sky blue with golden veins, the rarest and most costly of all marbles, which many mineralogists classify among the precious stones.

That fact confirmed Serge in the opinion that the Martians must have found a way of reproducing minerals artificially.

The *Velox* was moored to a ring of yellow metal as shiny as gold, which had certainly been sealed in the stone for that purpose, and the impetuous Pickman was finally able to give free rein to his curiosity.

Since they had quit the leviathan's cavern, the explorers had not seen any dangerous animal. The prefect security that they saw the inoffensive birds enjoying as they swarmed in the bushes was a guarantee for them.

Serge did not think, therefore, that he was committing an imprudence by abandoning the *Velox* for a while, in order to undertake a first exploration of the palace and its grounds in the company of Annabella and Pickman.

The ruins, moreover, did not seem at all ominous. They did not present the traces of brutal devastation and stupid degradation that spoil the harmony of the noblest décor for spectators. The creepers and wild plants with which they were covered seemed to have grown there in order to put the final touches to a work of art rather than planted by the hazards of the wind and rain.

The living and perfumed corollas seemed to be the intended complement of the colonnette or the arabesque.

The explorers moved along gently sloping streets beneath the beautiful shade animated by an entire society of birds, which did not even take the trouble to move away. Evidently, they had no fear of human presence. One of those fliers, an admirable blue and green pigeon, even came to perch on Annabella's shoulder; she caressed it, smoothing the plumes of its wings with her finger, without the animal seeking to fly away.

Pickman gazed at that admirable tableau with ferocious eyes.

"Do you know," he said, "how long it is since I've eaten fresh meat?"

"What do you mean?" demanded the young woman, hugging the bird to her bosom as if to protect it against the redoubtable appetite of the Anglo-Saxon. "You wouldn't, I suppose, be so barbaric as to harm this innocent creature?"

The Eccentric sniggered. "I'm tired of eating out of tins," he said. "That pigeon would certainly be excellent, surrounded by a garnish of tinned peas. Give it to me! I can assure you that I'll put end to it quickly by wringing its neck."

"Mr. Pickman," said Anna, severely, "if you ever do any such thing, I'll never speak to you again as long as I live; I'll quarrel mortally with you. You can satisfy your taste for bloody flesh another time. This beautiful bird is under my protection, and I forbid you to trouble the confidence that these naïve creatures have in our peaceful instincts with your massacres..."

"Well," said Pickman, who would not really have wanted to disobey his dear ward for anything in the world, "we'll see about that..." And he added, in a tone of bravado that did not fool anyone: "Not today, then—I don't want to annoy you—but tomorrow, I'll organize a great hunt..."

The day was advancing, however; after casting that first rapid glance over the magnificent domain, they went back to the *Velox* and ate a rapid lunch. Then Serge Myrandhal, as he had planned for some time, resolved to enter into communication via the telepathic apparatus with his friends on Earth—but he was no more fortunate on this occasion than on previous ones. The transmitter emitted its waves in vain toward the old natal planet. To Annabella's great disappointment, the apparatus remained mute, the vibrator not emitting the slightest ring.

The young woman's beautiful face darkened. "So," she murmured, sadly, "they've already forgotten us back there—or perhaps the apparatus is no longer working. My God! As long as nothing bad has happened to my father!"

Serge Myrandhal did his best to reassure her. "I'm certain of the efficacy of my apparatus," he said, "but there's nothing surprising in the fact that our terrestrial friends are not at the appointed place to hear us. They must have corresponded several times and, seeing that we didn't reply, their patience has run out. Perhaps, too, their apparatus has been put out of order by some accident. It's up to us to put a little more perseverance into our attempts. I guarantee that we'll succeed; it's impossible for us not to succeed..."

Madame Myrandhal ended up yielding to his reasoning. An idea of the Eccentric's finished putting the smile back on her face.

"I'm tired of always sleeping in a narrow cabin where I don't even have room to turn over," Pickman declared. "Since there are palaces here—palaces that don't belong to anyone—I'm going to take advantage of the fact. No one will prevent me from setting up my camp this very evening in one of these magnificent halls. I'll be able to believe that I'm the gracious sovereign of the plant Mars, if the desire takes me."

And without waiting any longer, the Eccentric, aided by Tao, set about transporting the movable furniture from his cabin to a hall ornamented with fantastic unicorns that had struck him with wonder at first sight, doubtless because they reminded him of the arms of old England.

"Shall we do the same?" Serge Myrandhal proposed to his young wife. "After all, he's not wrong."

Annabella accepted the proposal enthusiastically. The two spouses chose a chamber paved with azure tiles and festooned with rose-bushes, jasmines and capricious lianas. Through the large bay window overlooking the grounds, a kind of citrus tree with enormous fruits was exhaling the sweet perfume of its flowers. The air was so warm, the azure of the sky so velvety, that they had no need to fear any chill.

While Serge and Annabella—to whom the Eccentric, delighted that they had adopted his idea, came to lend a hand—were busy with these preparations, night gradually fell.

Dew was pearling among the quivering herbage, the marvelous songs of the birds rose up from flowering bushes illuminated by soft nocturnal gleams, and millions of glowworms lit up on the lawns. A breeze of infinite freshness and sweetness was blowing from the forest and the sea.

Serge and Annabella went to sleep to the caressant murmur of foliage gently agitated by the breeze, lulled by the distant melody of birds perched on lianas. They had never felt as happy, as confident in the future. It was the beginning of their veritable honeymoon...

XXI. A Martian Mausoleum

Exhausted by the emotions, of every sort, that had filled the previous day, the explorers slept late. It was Pickman who woke up first, tickled by a ray of morning sunlight that made the supposedly British heraldic unicorns on the tiles glitter magnificently.

To begin with, he summoned Tao, whom he had sent to sleep under an armful of foliage in an adjacent room, and instructed the Martian to brush his clothes carefully and wax his boots.

The Eccentric had a plan. While Tao was in the process of rendering him the services of an attentive houseboy, he inspected his carbine, cleaned out the barrel and made sure that the firing-pin was working properly. Having done that, he rubbed his hands together with a silent smile. The idea of opposing his ward by means of a hecatomb on Martian birds seemed particularly enjoyable.

Then he headed toward the young couple's room in order to wake them up.

He was surprised to find then already up.

Annabella suddenly frowned. She had just perceived Pickman's hunting apparatus, openly displayed on his bed. "So you're counting on giving free rein to your bloodthirsty fury?" she demanded, half smiling and half severe.

"Of course," said the Eccentric, in a determined tone. "I can't eat out of tins for the rest of my life. No, that's out of the question; I'm firmly resolved to eat fresh meat today, and I will."

"We shall see!"

"I refrained yesterday from wringing the neck of one of those magnificent birds purely to please you. Today, it's my turn to do what I want."

"A lively discussion, in which Serge abstained from taking part, was engaged between the ward and the guardian.

As usual, the Eccentric ended up giving in to one restriction. He would abandon himself to his cynegetic instincts as much as he wished outside the grounds of the palace, but he formally promised to respect all its inhabitants and not to fire a shot within its sacred boundary.

The debate having been terminated and the peace treaty signed, the morning meal was concluded with no further incident. It had been agreed that the day would be employed in a more complete exploration.

"We'll begin with the park," said Serge. "It seems to me, if it's possible, to be even more beautiful than yesterday..."

"I'm eager, at any rate," the Eccentric murmured, "to taste the beautiful fruits of which I only caught a glimpse yesterday. If they're as good as they look, I'm sure that people in London would pay half a crown apiece for them."

"Much dearer than that," the young woman joked. "There's certainly a royal fortune to be made with the idea of a Martian fruiterer's in the vicinity of Trafalgar Square. In the meantime, be careful. Nothing is more imprudent than eating fruits that one doesn't know..."

"Don't worry about that. We'll take Tao, whose instinct reliably causes him to avoid plants that might be toxic."

A few minutes later, they all set forth along the mossy pathways.

It was now in dozens that birds of every kind of plumage came to flutter around Annabella and settle on her shoulders and Serge's—but they kept away from the Eccentric with an instinctive mistrust. One might have thought that they were aware of his mores and carnivorous tastes.

Meanwhile, the explorers continued their excursion, without losing sight of the polychromatic towers of the palace in which they had made camp.

The Eccentric was so convinced that nothing in Eden Park—as he had authoritatively baptized it—was poisonous that he bit confidently into any fruit, without even taking the trouble to have Tao taste them first.

"Very good! Exquisite! Delicious!" he repeated.

Tao had drawn a long way ahead, attracted by some trees as slender as poplars but covered from top to bottom with small fruits about the size of a strawberry.

Further on, Serge, after a moment's indecision, headed toward a palace with majestic domes that he perceived at the extremity of a long avenue. The trees composing it were prodigiously tall and were linked together in their crowns by lianas thrown like flowery rigging from branch to branch. At intervals, on pedestals of porphyry, agate and onyx, statues of giant birds with human faces were posed in attitudes full of serenity and smiling.

The explorers had not yet covered half of the avenue, however, when they saw Tao running toward them at top speed, seemingly prey to a profound terror. He came to take refuge close to Anna.

"*Zoa! Zoa!*" he repeated, trembling in every limb.

"What's up with him?" murmured the Eccentric. "What did he say? I couldn't quite hear…"

Serge Myrandhal made a gesture of nervous impatience. "Don't you understand?" he exclaimed. "*Zoa*—that's the name of the mysterious and powerful beings, before which inferior beings of Tao's race bow down!" The engineer's voice was vibrant with contained emotion. "Tao," he continued, "must have perceived one of those elite beings. We're going to encounter the creators of the marvels that surround us; human intellect is about to confront Martian intellect…"

Then he tried to interrogate the Martian, in order to discover where he had come from.

He only replied with his eternal: "*Zoa!*"—but Anna had seen him come down the steps of the temple at the end of the avenue.

They hastened their pace, dragging the consternated Tao with them.

They went through a monumental portico in which columns of a metal with shifting reflections that Serge Myrandhal recognized as iridium were combined with precious minerals to obtain a grandiose collective effect. They found themselves in a gallery with elevated vaults.

Tao's footprints were distinctly visible in the dust on the floor.

The gallery could have competed, for calm beauty and simplicity, with the sphinx-lined causeways of ancient Egypt, but the sphinxes were replaced by the birds with smiling human faces, several specimens of which Serge and his friends had already admired.

The footprints ended at the place where the gallery gave access to a profound and high-ceilinged hall. The explorers went in.

There, they came to a stop, amazed and ecstatic.

The hall, which had the dimensions of the nave of a church, seemed to be constructed in alabaster and rock crystal. It was a dream of dazzling whiteness. In the central aisle, gigantic vases formed of nacre, jade, moonstone and opal were filled with bright flowers. But that was not the most extraordinary thing. The side-walls of the basilica of sorts were lined with steps along their entire length and each fitted with a row of niches.

Anna, who was the first to approach one of these niches, uttered an exclamation of surprise, almost of fear.

Serge Myrandhal and Pickman ran forward and, like the young woman, fell prey to a boundless amazement and admiration.

Every niche contained an immense crystal egg, set of a kind of incline plane. Each egg contained the body of a human being, endowed with all the appearances of life; the cheeks were tinted with the red of blood; the eyes were clear and lucid.

They were motionless, the faces as if haloed with a smile full of serenity, but one might have thought that their hearts were about to beat, that their nostrils were about to palpitate, that they were about to come forward, smiling, having broken their immaterial prison with a gesture.

"They're alive!" exclaimed the young woman, enthusiastically.

The Eccentric, ever incredulous, ran his hand over the crystal. "It's extraordinary," he murmured. In Norway, I've seen fish and insects imprisoned thus in blocks of ice; they were just like that—one would have thought they were alive.

Serge Myrandhal reflected. "We're in the presence," he explained, "of a prodigious embalming process. How the Martians have succeeded in forming that crystal ovule around bodies previously rendered incombustible without subjecting them to any deterioration is difficult to explain..."

"In any case, it's admirable," said Pickman. "It's not a hideous black mummy wrapped in asphalt-soaked bandages— it's the freshness and brightness of life itself fixed for all eternity in the crystal. Death appears to be no more than a calm and restful sleep."

"Notice," said Anna, pensively, "the egg-like form. Isn't that a profound symbol? Death, for the Martians, is the prelude to a further existence. They repose there in their transparent ova, like a germ-cell in a shell, like an embryo in a seed. The expression of smiling serenity on their faces shows that they're waiting confidently for the moment when they will break their fragile cradle to surge forth again..."

"What a pity," Serge murmured, with regret in his voice, "that we didn't meet them when they were alive; they doubtless possess all the secrets for which we're seeking."

"Don't despair," said Pickman. "There's no reason why we shouldn't succeed in getting our hands on one of their descendants."

"There's no hope of that, unfortunately," the engineer replied. "I divine by certain signs—the enormous thickness of the lianas that have crawled so far into the hall, and the degree of erosion of some of the steps—that this hall must have been built several centuries ago. We're in the mausoleum of the last Martian pharaohs, perhaps the last Martians..."

The exploration of the funereal hall continued in silence.

The Martian mummies were slightly taller in stature than human beings. Their high an bulging foreheads, their symmetrical features, and the delicacy of their extremely long lands proved that they were a very intelligent and very refined race, long disengaged from the darkness of ancestral bestiality.

They were all wearing ample pale blue robes. No jewelry adorned them, but many had a weapon beside them made of some unknown metal, a kind of slender sword with a spiral blade.

Their beardless faces, free of wrinkles, and their hair, uniformly parted in the middle, did not permit any differentiation to be made in terms of age or sex.

From that hall the explorers passed into another. There was the same dazzling lily-whiteness, and the same floral urns, embalmed and luxurious, but Serge Myrandhal noticed certain particularities which showed that the construction, added after the preceding one, had to be considerably less ancient.

The character of the mummies in their transparent coffins was also quite different. As generations succeeded one anther the brains became larger and the bodies diminished in amplitude, the fingers becoming longer and spindlier.

"Look at those frail bodies, those thin wrists," murmured the young woman, "And those cheeks, so delicately pink. They're superhuman in their beauty; the imprint of brutality no longer exists in them."

"Then too," observed the engineer, "they no longer have swords by their side—it's now steles covered with characters that accompany them. That proves that in the epoch in which they lived, words had replaced blades, and thought brute force..."

"I hope," the Eccentric interjected, "that we can translate the characters engraved on the steles; people have succeeded in reading hieroglyphics, and these can't be more difficult. We'll try, but either I'm much mistaken or these emaciated and slender beings must have been the last of their race.

"We've come too late; we'll be lucky if, thanks to the steles, we can preserve a part of the knowledge of this extinct race..."

"I believe," Anna said, "that this gallery will be the last; the further we advance, the frailer and more diaphanous the mummies become..."

"No," said Serge, "there must be another necropolis behind that curtain of verdure."

All three of them went forward, but at the sight of the spectacle that presented itself in the final hall, they became immobile and silent, penetrated with respect. Here, there were no more niches, no more mummies fixes in their crystal matrix; but in the center of the vast hall, a majestic bed of State was supported by a dozen nacre columns.

On that bed lay two individuals clad in diaphanous robes made of an unknown fabric. Were they asleep? Were they dead? It was impossible to say, but they were lying with their heads inclined toward one another, their faces illuminated by ingenuous, almost puerile smiles. They were admirably beautiful, of a nobility of features and an ethereal attitude that was vaporous and superhuman, of which only the purest creations of Italian and Flemish masters and the pre-Raphaelites could give a distant idea.

One might have thought them veritable angels.

One of them, however, by her slightly wider hips and slightly rounded bosom, revealed that she belonged to the female sex. Were they brother and sister or husband and wife? Nothing in their chaste slumber offered any indication.

Around them, through large wide-open bays, the luxuriant vegetation of the park entered like a tide of flowers that came to die almost at the foot of the bed.

Amid the birdsong, in the bright sunlight, they lay there, smiling, so beautiful that any funereal ideas were invincibly set aside.

With an instinctive gesture, Serge Myrandhal and Pickman had bared their heads respectfully.

"There, certainly," said the engineer, in a grave voice, "are the last Martians. They had passed the *summum* of intelligence permitted to creatures; they had become as knowledgeable as gods; they no longer had any reason to exist. Having reached a certain point of perfection and beauty, nature is forced to stop."

"I can't believe that they're dead," the young woman murmured. "Their faces are still colored with a hint of red; one might think that their eyes were shining beneath their half-closed lids. Perhaps they're only dormant in some strange sleep. I need to know..."

Her heart pounding with emotion, Ana laid her hand on the forehead of one of the beautiful creatures. She recoiled with an instinctive gesture. The forehead was icy, as cold as marble; the beautiful Martians really were dead...

Throughout that scene, Tao had thrown himself on his knees, and prostrate, was striking the floor with his forehead and murmuring, wildly: "*Zoa! Zoa!*"

A few minutes later, the three explorers withdrew silently, prey to a violent emotion.

XVII. News from Earth

As the explorers drew away from the magical necropolis of the Martian pharaohs they gradually recovered from the profound and religious impression that they had experienced, but a perfume of the mysterious and the ideal lingered. The pious hermit of legend, to whom it was given, in their ecstasy, to glimpse a corner of Paradise, must have experienced something similar.

"Veritably," said Anna, pensively, "those beautiful adolescents resembled the first angels, before the terrestrial paradise and the sin of the first humans: the Elohim."[33]

"We'll call them the Elohim," said Pickman. It's the only name that can suggest such superhuman creatures."

"What a pity that we haven't found them still alive," Serge murmured, in a melancholy tone.

"Who knows?" said the young woman. "After what we've seen, nothing seems impossible to me."

They went slowly back to the palace; they all seemed preoccupied and pensive. Only the Eccentric, who had afforded such importance to the fruits, thought of taking a few of them back. As for Tao, he took a long time to recover from his fright. At any rate, it was impossible to extract the slightest useful information from him.

The rest of the day was employed in making the rooms in which the explorers had established their domicile more appo-

---

[33] Elohim is usually translated as "deity" or "god"; the word is both singular and plural, although it is, inevitably, usually construed in the singular in the Hebrew and Christian traditions. There is a famous illustration by William Blake captioned "And Elohim created Adam," and Blake developed an idiosyncratic cosmogony in which the primal deity is divided into four aspects that he calls "Zoas," but that might be pure coincidence.

site. Anna and Serge's room took on a comfortable and sumptuous appearance. Pickman, driven by his inquisitive instincts,
had found a room filled with furniture of every sort. There
were armchairs made of ivory and porcelain, bronze tables
encrusted with gems, incense-burners and fabrics with bizarre
designs that seemed to have been woven with metallic and
asbestos threads.

From among these objects Serge chose those which
might have a practical utility, leaving it until later to study the
others. At the evening meal, served on A Martian bronze table,
they naturally talked about the Elohim again.

"They're certainly the last of their race," said the engineer. "No one survived them to put them in their crystal coffins; they remained without a sepulcher."

"We could render them that supreme service!" exclaimed
his wife.

"If you wish," Serge murmured, "But we can't give them
the same brilliant sepulchers as their ancestors."

"It doesn't matter; I estimate that it's our duty."

"Are you sure? They've doubtless been lying there for a
long time, smiling and frozen." And he added, in a profoundly
thoughtful tone: "Does one bury angels? The Elohim?"

Anna did not insist, but the next day, she went to deposit
a bouquet of flowers next to the bed of the beautiful adolescents, and thereafter, she did not let a single day pass without
rendering them a pious homage.

The following week went by without further incident.
Life in the palace of Eden Park became organized more routinely from day to day.

Serge Myrandhal deployed an indefatigable ardor, working for fourteen or fifteen hours a day, sometimes seeking, by
means of a series of delicate barometric and hygrometric
measurements, to determine the reason for the exceptional
meteorology, and sometimes making a record of the specific
characteristics of the plants and animals.

Annabella seconded her husband admirably in these
tasks, and every day she showed herself more intelligent more

patient and narrower in her communion of ideas with Serge, whose vast knowledge in all the branches of science she admired.

There was only one shadow over the young woman's happiness: the daily attempts made to enter into telegraphic communication with the Earth remained without result. Anna's heart contracted, and Serge's reasoned arguments did not succeed in reassuring her.

In vain he suggested to her that the silence of the Terrans must be due to some fortuitous circumstance, and that an attempt as audacious as theirs could not have been to promptly forgotten.

"I'm certain," he said, "that at the present moment, the telescopes of all observatories are anxiously aimed at Mars, and that hundreds of newspapers and magazines are passionately discussing our fate. Be sure that someone will reply to us, my dear Anna—I'm firmly convinced of it."

But the young woman contented herself with shaking her head sadly, and her sadness became increasingly marked. It was only by means of collaborating in the engineer's work, in the fever of cerebral activity, that she succeeded in forgetting her obsessive thoughts.

Pickman did not notice. He was outside almost every day, either fishing from the bank of the canal or hunting in the forest, from which he never returned without some unprecedented game.

Tao never left his side. The Martian professed a devotion for the Eccentric comparable to that of a dog for its master. Pickman had taught him to use a fishing line and a rifle, and had cured him of his terror of the animals of the forest, and in a matter of days, Tao had begun to exhibit a remarkable skill, at hunting as well as fishing.

Things were thus when, one morning, after Pickman and Tao had left, Serge Myrandhal and Anna were savoring an excellent tea taken from the Velox's stores. The eternal preoccupation of the two young people, the absence of news from Earth, was the subject of their conversation.

"No," murmured Annabella, with profound discouragement, "I've lost all hope. If what you say were possible, they would have replied a long time ago..."

But at the precise moment when the young woman pronounced these words, as if hazard had assumed the responsibility of giving her a formal contradiction, the shrill ring of the telepath's bell resounded in the silence of the palace.

"My God!" she murmured. "Serge! Did you hear that?" All her blood had flowed back to her heart; she was as white as a corpse.

The engineer stood up, profoundly troubled.

The crystalline trill continued.

"They're replying!" he shouted. "They're calling us! Like you, my dear wife, I no longer believed..."

And the engineer grabbed the signaling key with a tremulous hand. Anna had followed him, her face radiant.

The engineer's action had stopped the bell; now, they both waited, their hearts beating anxiously.

After three seconds—three centuries—the blue paper ribbon began to unroll, with a dry *tick-tock* sound.

"My God!" the young woman sighed, drunk with joy. "They're replying!"

And, leaning over her husband's shoulder, she read the words on the narrow strip avidly.

Are you there? asked the terrestrial correspondent.

Who's speaking? Serge replied.

Me.

Who's that?

Allan Carpenter. Finally—you're safe. I was in despair. For weeks we've been ringing you in vain.

"Father!" stammered Annabella.

Communication was established; once the conversation had begun, Serge and Anna never left the apparatus. First of all, she brought the honorable Carpenter—who had not recovered from his surprise—up to date with their principal adventures. Then it was their turn to question him. The blue ribbons unfurled interminably.

But where are you, Father? asked the young woman.

In New York, in the study of your friend Justin Durand. Receiving no news, I came back from the Far West to...

Abruptly, the apparatus stopped. Once again, the waves coming from so far away had been deflected *en route.*

Anna was desolate.

"Don't worry," her husband said. "It's only a delay. I'll do my best to restore communication before this evening. Anyway, the main thing is done. Your father is reassured, and so are you..."

At that moment, the echoes of a mad gallop resounded in the corridor of the palace.

The Eccentric appeared, his eyes wide and his hair standing on end, beside himself, Tao followed him, trembling in every limb.

"What is it?" asked Serge.

"The Elohim have woken up!"

That was all he could articulate. He let himself fall into a chair.

Editor's Note

At this point, the interastral notes accumulated by the honorable Mr. Carpenter and put in order by Justin Durand come to an abrupt stop.

Since then, all the efforts made to reestablish communication with the planet Mars and its audacious explorers have been without result.

Was the awakening of the "Elohim" the signal for tragic events for Serge and his friends? Have they perished in a conflict with those all-powerful beings? Or have they fallen victim to some cataclysm? Or—although nothing could have allowed the possibility to be foreseen—have they voluntarily broken off all communication with their friends on Earth?

The mystery remains entire. The field remains open to all hypotheses.

Personally, we have the firm conviction that Serge Myrandhal is still alive, and that his silence is only due to circumstances independent of his will. We are sure that he will give us his news one day, and we shall keep the French public informed of anything that transpires in that respect.

Afterword

Before making some further observations regarding the 1908 version of the *Aventures merveilleuses de Serge Myrandhal*, it is worth describing the variations incorporated in the Cyrius *Les Robinsons de la planète Mars*, which reproduces some of the 1908 text in a piecemeal fashion, while gradually constructing a significantly different narrative around those skeletal elements.

The Cyrius novel begins with the same scene as the 1908 novel, with people queuing to get into the Athenaeum, and also retains the description of Pickman perching on the chandelier. There is, however, no mention of the Rajah Indraghava and his son, both of whom are eliminated completely from the plot, along with the romance between Serge and Annabella the novice reporter; in the Cyrius version, Annabel is already Madame Myrandhal before the story begins, and she remains in the background during the opening chapters.

There is no mention in the Cyrius version of the use of psychic power as a propellant, and no "human piles" are involved in the demonstration of the model spacecraft that collects Pickman from the chandelier. The plot then skips to the tour of the full-scale model *Velox*. As in the 1908 version, Pickman is determined to acquire one of the two full-scale models that have been constructed (the *Annabel* and the *Franklin*). In this version, the launch is to take place in the U.S.A., from "Mont-Winther," and the attempted hijacking that results in Serge being dispatched alone is the work of German agents. The space journey itself and the account of events after Serge's landing are a straightforward abridgment of the 1908 version, although the account of his discovery by Annabella, after losing consciousness, is far less melodramatic.

The events connected with Pickman's sightings of, capture by and escape from by the troglodytic Martians run parallel to those described in the 1908 version, but the Martian who helps Pickman escape is named Ta-Ho. The accounts of Martian life in general are more elaborate, and the underground civilization of the Red Men is described in more detail; the latter remain a nuisance following Pickman's escape, pursuing the humans until the melodramatic climax, when they are wiped out. Although Ta-Ho insists that Annabel is a Zoa, the latter remain legendary in the Cyrius version; the "Eden" described in the 1908 version does not feature in it. The Cyrius version ends once the Martians are extinct and Serge and his companions are able to set off for home.

The ending of the second volume of the *Aventures merveilleux de Serge Myrandhal*, as translated above, is far less neat, of course, and leaves numerous questions unanswered, perhaps because at least some of them were unanswerable, the author having written himself into something of a corner. The terminal note suggests that a third volume was planned but never written, perhaps because the publisher went out of business, but it is also possible that the author had run out of steam—perhaps to the extent of having someone else finish off the 1908 text as published; it undergoes a dramatic transformation of style from Chapter XIII onwards, the narrative voice taking on a much greater responsibility for description, with frequent quasi-didactic references to Earthly flora and fauna, of a kind commonplace in Vernian romances but previously absent from this particular text. The fact that none of this text is reproduced in the Cyrius version, in spite of the melodramatic value of the encounter with the sea serpent, might add further weight to the hypothesis that it is the work of a different writer.

Before commenting further on the details of the story, it is worth making some remarks about the division of the overall work into two parts, published only a month apart. The likeliest explanation for that is that the original formed one long manuscript, which the author or the publisher decided to split at the most dramatic point, but that is not the only possibility, given that the ending of the first volume, seen in isolation, does not have the appearance of a "cliff-hanger" providing a tempting lure to a continuation, but actually looks like a genuine and definitive conclusion of a markedly downbeat stripe. It is possible that the first volume was, in fact, written as a whole and coherent work, and that the sequel was a belated afterthought, perhaps added at the insistence of the publisher, who doubtless had the customary antipathy to downbeat endings.

That possibility, although purely hypothetical, raises the further question of whether volume one is a better book in isolation than it is as a prelude to volume two. Most readers, having the commonplace antipathy to downbeat endings, would presumably think not, but if one were to take the view that Serge Myrandhal really does die, and that the entire second volume is a fake, that would also open the possibility that he actually died some time before the apparent moment of his death, when the *Velox* initially blasted off (when he certainly ought to have been killed, given its phenomenal rate of acceleration) and that the entire space journey is the kind of momentary hallucination featured in the intriguing subgenre of "posthumous fantasy," whose most famous exemplar is Ambrose Bierce's "An Occurrence at Owl Creek Bridge" (1890).

Given the frank absurdity of the journey in question, as seen from the viewpoint of a modern reader who has a much clearer idea of the conditions in outer space and the efforts required to survive there than "H. Gayar" had, the latter interpretation would arguably make far more sense than taking the story literally. It would also add an interesting extra dimension to its remarkable surrealism, and the peculiar symbolism of Serge's encounter with the "*Grande Ténèbre*." Although the narrative method of the second volume—especially the section from Chapter XIII onwards—does not really lend itself to the admittedly-fanciful interpretation that it might be an extension of the posthumous fantasy, that might permit a potentially-interesting symbolic interpretation of the dreamlike development of the story and its odd quasi-religious elements.

There are, of course, other ways to account for the quasi-religious elements of the back-story, and it is possible to see *Aventures merveilleuses de Serge Myrandhal* as an extension of a long tradition of mystical interplanetary fantasies, particularly strong in France, which integrate visionary interplanetary journeys into some kind of cosmic scheme of moral evolution, usually involving some kind of "cosmic palingenesis," in which the worlds of the solar system are arranged on a scale of existential perfection, in such a way that souls reincarnated in other-worldly bodies can pursue a quest for ultimate enlightenment for which an Earthly lifespan leaves insufficient scope. That idea had been memorably incorporated into the medium of post-Voltairean *conte philosophique* by Louis-Sébastien Mercier in "Nouvelles de la lune" (1768)[34], further elaborated by Bernardin de Saint-Pierre in *Harmonies de la Nature* (1815; tr. as *The Harmonies of Nature*) and redeveloped in a more informed cosmological context, initially in *Lumen* (1866-69), by Camille Flammarion, who shared with Jules Verne the honor of being a cardinal influence on the late-19th century development of *roman scientifique*.

As a devoted spiritist and psychic researcher, Flammarion was a significant figure in the occult revival as well as the popularization of science, and it was not at all difficult to fuse his ideas about interplanetary reincarnation with such notions as the Indian mysticism developed in the triptych of 1908 novels by La Hire, Gayar and Le Rouge (Flammarion is the obvious model for a significant character in La Hire's novel). It might not be entirely coincidental that one of the few other examples of *roman scientifique* that feature the same exaggerated feelings of transcendental erotic attraction as *Aventures merveilleuses de Serge Myrandhal* is Flammarion's "Un Amour des astres" (1896; tr. as "Love Among the Stars"). There had, in addition, been previous texts linking Indian mys-

---

[34] Translated as "News from the Moon" and included in the eponymous Black Coat Press collection, ISBN 978-1-932983-89-0.

ticism with cosmic imagery, including Theodore Flournoy's best-selling *Des Indes à la planète Mars* (1900; tr. as *From India to the Planet Mars*), recounting supposed memories of previous incarnations by a medium, and, in terms of *roman scientifique*, and Louis Boussenard's Vernian adventure story *Les Secrets de Monsieur Synthèse* (1888)[35], in which the ambitious protagonist supplements his enormous scientific knowledge by means of his friendship with a teleporting yogi named Krishna.

Gayar's particular fusion of such ideas is, however, more idiosyncratic than the relatively conventional spiritist adaptations of Camille Flammarion, notably in his embryonic representation of Martian evolution—the evolution of the *Zoa*, that is—as a physical as well as a spiritual evolution toward a strangely unsustainable perfection. It is not obvious from the existing text whether the author intended to make anything significant out of the characters' decision to refer to the last Martians as Elohim, and there are very few clues as to what the consequences of their awakening might be (the tame return to Earth featured in the Cyrius text is clearly a minimal improvisation and offers no clue as to the possible development of a third volume of the 1908 text, had any been produced), but it is at least possible that an elaborate scheme of moral evolution might have been developed, transfiguring further elements of the Judeo-Christian mythos.

Perhaps the author was not capable of doing that, and was already painfully conscious of having extended his narrative reach much further than his imaginative grasp, but at least he left scope for the reader's imagination to obtain a measure of stimulus—and in that respect, the deliberately teasing ending of volume two might be reckoned preferably to the summary dismissal of the Cyrius text. There are, of course, more ways to conclude a narrative than tacking on a stock "ending," although deliberate anti-endings—such as the suspended con-

---

[35] Translated in *Monsieur Synthesis*, Black Coat Press, ISBN 978-1-61227-161-3.

clusion of Edgar Poe's *Narrative of Arthur Gordon Pym of Nantucket* (1837)—are always likely to puzzle far more readers than they please.

The author of *Serge Myrandhal* might have been doing the reader a favor by leaving the symbolism of the birds with human faces and the apparent absence of the *Zoa* previously-advertized wings from the dormant Elohim unspecified, along with numerous other teasing issues. In the same way, it might be reckoned a blessing in disguise that the reader, after finishing the extant text, has no idea whether the names of Tao and *Zoa* have any connection with any other uses of the terms in question. That way, we can at least conjecture that the answers he could have provided, given the chance and the inclination, might not have been tamely bathetic. In the same way, we remain free to wonder what Serge Myrandhal and his beloved Anna would have found when they eventually did what they were surely always destined to do, once their discoveries on Mars were in the bag, and set a course for sovereign Jupiter instead of limping home.

That, at least, is surly the direction that the non-existent third volume should have taken—and perhaps even that further adventure, had "H. Gayar" been up to the job, would only have been a prelude to further wondrous exploits, which would have revealed far more detail of the great universal scheme of cosmic palingenesis, and Elohim worth of the name.

SF & FANTASY

Adolphe Alhaiza. *Cybele*
Alphonse Allais. *The Adventures of Captain Cap*
Henri Allorge. *The Great Cataclysm*
Guy d'Armen. *Doc Ardan: The City of Gold and Lepers*
G.-J. Arnaud. *The Ice Company*
Charles Asselineau. *The Double Life*
Cyprien Bérard. *The Vampire Lord Ruthwen*
S. Henry Berthoud. *Martyrs of Science*
Aloysius Bertrand. *Gaspard de la Nuit*
Richard Bessière. *The Gardens of the Apocalypse*
Albert Bleunard. *Ever Smaller*
Félix Bodin. *The Novel of the Future*
Louis Boussenard. *Monsieur Synthesis*
Alphonse Brown. *City of Glass; The Conquest of the Air*
Emile Calvet. *In a Thousand Years*
André Caroff. *The Terror of Madame Atomos; Miss Atomos; The Return of Madame Atomos; The Mistake of Madame Atomos; The Monsters of Madame Atomos; The Revenge of Madame Atomos; The Resurrection of Madame Atomos; The Mark of Madame Atomos; The Spheres of Madame Atomos*
Félicien Champsaur. *The Human Arrow; Ouha, King of the Apes; Pharaoh's Wife*
Didier de Chousy. *Ignis*
Jules Clarétie. *Obsession*
Michel Corday. *The Eternal Flame*
Captain Danrit. *Undersea Odyssey*
C. I. Defontenay. *Star (Psi Cassiopeia)*
Charles Derennes. *The People of the Pole*
Georges Dodds (anthologist). *The Missing Link*
Harry Dickson. *The Heir of Dracula*
Jules Dornay. *Lord Ruthven Begins*
Alfred Driou. *The Adventures of a Parisian Aeronaut*
Sâr Dubnotal *vs. Jack the Ripper*
Alexandre Dumas. *The Return of Lord Ruthven*
Renée Dunan. *Baal*
J.-C. Dunyach. *The Night Orchid; The Thieves of Silence*
Henri Duvernois. *The Man Who Found Himself*
Achille Eyraud. *Voyage to Venus*

Xavier Mauméjean. *The League of Heroes*
Joseph Méry. *The Tower of Destiny*
Hippolyte Mettais. *The Year 5865*
Louise Michel. *The Human Microbes; The New World*
Tony Moilin. *Paris in the Year 2000*
José Moselli. *Illa's End*
John-Antoine Nau. *Enemy Force*
Marie Nizet. *Captain Vampire*
C. Nodier, A. Beraud & Toussaint-Merle. *Frankenstein*
Henri de Parville. *An Inhabitant of the Planet Mars*
Gaston de Pawlowski. *Journey to the Land of the 4th Dimension*
Georges Pellerin. *The World in 2000 Years*
Ernest Pérochon. *The Frenetic People*
Pierre Pelot. *The Child Who Walked on the Sky*
J. Polidori, C. Nodier, E. Scribe. *Lord Ruthven the Vampire*
P.-A. Ponson du Terrail. *The Vampire and the Devil's Son; The Immortal Woman*
Edgar Quinet. *Ahasuerus*
Henri de Régnier. *A Surfeit of Mirrors*
Maurice Renard. *The Blue Peril; Doctor Lerne; The Doctored Man; A Man Among the Microbes; The Master of Light*
Jean Richepin. *The Wing; The Crazy Corner*
Albert Robida. *The Adventures of Saturnin Farandoul; The Clock of the Centuries; Chalet in the Sky; The Electric Life*
J.-H. Rosny Aîné. *Helgvor of the Blue River; The Givreuse Enigma; The Mysterious Force; The Navigators of Space; Vamireh; The World of the Variants; The Young Vampire*
Marcel Rouff. *Journey to the Inverted World*
Han Ryner. *The Superhumans*
Angelo de Sorr. *The Vampires of London*
Brian Stableford. *The New Faust at the Tragicomique;The Empire of the Necromancers (The Shadow of Frankenstein; Frankenstein and the Vampire Countess; Frankenstein in London); Sherlock Holmes & The Vampires of Eternity; The Stones of Camelot; The Wayward Muse.* (anthologist) *News from the Moon; The Germans on Venus; The Supreme Progress; The World Above the World; Nemoville; Investigations of the Future; The Conqueror of Death*
Jacques Spitz. *The Eye of Purgatory*
Kurt Steiner. *Ortog*
Eugène Thébault. *Radio-Terror*
C.-F. Tiphaigne de La Roche. *Amilec*

Louis Ulbach. *Prince Bonifacio*

Théo Varlet. *The Golden Rock. The Xenobiotic Invasion; The Castaways of Eros; Timeslip Troopers* (w/André Blandin); *The Martian Epic* (w/Octave Joncquel)

Paul Vibert. *The Mysterious Fluid*

Villiers de l'Isle-Adam. *The Scaffold; The Vampire Soul*

Philippe Ward. *Artahe*

Philippe Ward & Sylvie Miller. *The Song of Montségur*

MYSTERIES & THRILLERS

M. Allain & P. Souvestre. *The Daughter of Fantômas*

A. Anicet-Bourgeois, Lucien Dabril. *Rocambole*

A. Bernède. *Belphegor; Judex* (w/Louis Feuillade); *The Return of Judex* (w/Louis Feuillade); *The Shadow of Judex*

A. Bisson & G. Livet. *Nick Carter vs. Fantômas*

V. Darlay & H. de Gorsse. *Arsène Lupin vs. Sherlock Holmes: The Stage Play*

Séamas Duffy. *Sherlock Holmes in Paris*

Paul Féval. *Gentlemen of the Night; John Devil; The Black Coats ('Salem Street; The Invisible Weapon; The Parisian Jungle; The Companions of the Treasure; Heart of Steel; The Cadet Gang; The Sword-Swallower)*

Emile Gaboriau. *Monsieur Lecoq*

Goron & Emile Gautier. *Spawn of the Penitentiary*

Rick Lai. *Shadows of the Opera: Retribution in Blood; Sisters of the Shadows: The Curse of Cagliostro*

Steve Leadley. *Sherlock Holmes: The Circle of Blood*

Maurice Leblanc. *Arsène Lupin vs. Countess Cagliostro; Arsène Lupin vs. Sherlock Holmes (The Blonde Phantom; The Hollow Needle); The Many Faces of Arsène Lupin*

Gaston Leroux. *Chéri-Bibi; The Phantom of the Opera; Rouletabille & the Mystery of the Yellow Room; Rouletabille at Krupp's*

Richard Marsh. *The Complete Adventures of Judith Lee*

William Patrick Maynard. *The Terror of Fu Manchu; The Destiny of Fu Manchu*

Frank J. Morlock. *Sherlock Holmes: The Grand Horizontals; Sherlock Holmes vs Jack the Ripper*

Jean Petithuguenin. *The Adventures of Ethel King*

Antonin Reschal. *The Adventures of Miss Boston*

P. de Wattyne & Y. Walter. *Sherlock Holmes vs. Fantômas*

David White. *Fantômas in America*
Pierre Yrondy. *The Adventures of Thérèse Arnaud*

SCREENPLAYS

Mike Baron. *The Iron Triangle*
Emma Bull & Will Shetterly. *Nightspeeder; War for the Oaks*
Gerry Conway & Roy Thomas. *Doc Dynamo*
Steve Englehart. *Majorca*
James Hudnall. *The Devastator*
Jean-Marc & Randy Lofficier. *Royal Flush*
J.-M. & R. Lofficier & Marc Agapit. *Despair*
J.-M. & R. Lofficier & Joël Houssin. *City*
Andrew Paquette. *Peripheral Vision*
Robert L. Robinson, Jr. *Judex*
R. Thomas, J. Hendler & L. Sprague de Camp. *Rivers of Time*

NON-FICTION

Stephen R. Bissette. *Blur 1-5. Green Mountain Cinema 1; Teen Angels*
Win Scott Eckert. *Crossovers* (2 vols.)
Jean-Marc & Randy Lofficier. *Shadowmen* (2 vols.)
Randy Lofficier. *Over Here*

ART BOOKS

Jean-Pierre Normand. *Science Fiction Illustrations*
Raven Okeefe. *Raven's L'il Critters; Rave's Faves*
Randy Lofficier & Raven Okeefe. *If Your Possum Go Daylight...*
Daniele Serra. *Illusions*

HEXAGON COMICS

Franco Frescura & Luciano Bernasconi. *Wampus*
Franco Frescura & Giorgio Trevisan. *CLASH*
L. Bernasconi, J.-M. Lofficier & Juan Roncagliolo Berger. *Phenix*
Claude Legrand, J.-M. Lofficier & L. Bernasconi. *Kabur*
Franco Oneta. *Zembla*
L. Buffolente, Lofficier & J.-J. Dzialowski. *Strangers: Homicron*

Danilo Grossi. *Strangers: Jaydee*
Claude Legrand & Luciano Bernasconi. *Strangers: Starlock*